PRAISE FOR

Rochambeau
WASHINGTON'S IDEAL LIEUTENANT

"From the very first word, to the very last, a reader will be engaged in the romance, glory, and hardships of the amazing victory of the combined French-American Continentals over England as explained in Jini Jones Vail's book, *Rochambeau: Washington's Ideal Lieutenant*. It will educate and entertain the learned reader as well as those first discovering the subject. It matters not how many other books on the subject have been read. This one is a must-read!"

— SALLIE TULLIS DE BARCZA

Chairman, Board of Directors,
Washington-Rochambeau Revolutionary Route (W3R-US)

"I like to think that history lovers of all ages and a generation of students will delight in the reading of Jini Jones Vail's book, *Rochambeau: Washington's Ideal Lieutenant*."

— JACQUES BOSSIÈRE, PH.D.

Founder and First Chair,
Washington-Rochambeau Revolutionary Route (W3R-US)

"Jini Vail's book deals with the insufficiently-known role of a remarkable hero of American independence."

— JACQUES DE TRENTINIAN

Professional Researcher on the "War for America," Vice-President-General of the National Society of the Sons of the American Revolution, Past Board Member of the Société des Cincinnati de France

---

"*Rochambeau: Washington's Ideal Lieutenant* is a fascinating, carefully researched portrait of one of the American Revolution's most influential military figures. The author has woven a colorful tapestry of biographical detail, military strategy, international relations, and human nature upon the vast canvas of events leading up to the decisive victory at Yorktown."

— WILLIAM HORTON COX

Assistant Director (retired)
Rochester, New York, Public Library

I am proud to have been asked to read this wonderful book written by one of my DAR 'sisters,' especially since one of my ancestors fought in that decisive Battle of Yorktown. For me, it was seeing the war from a different vantage point. Readers will learn so much more about General Rochambeau than they knew beforehand, and come to admire Washington's "ideal lieutenant."

—CAROL BARTO BAUBY

State Registrar, Connecticut DAR;
Regent, Trumbull-Porter Chapter, NSDAR

Rochambeau
Washington's Ideal Lieutenant

General Rochambeau at the Surrender of Cornwallis
Detail from John Trumbull's *Surrender of Lord Cornwallis*
Lithograph by D. C. Hinman (n.d.)
Anne S. K. Brown Military Collection, Brown University Library.

Rochambeau
WASHINGTON'S
IDEAL LIEUTENANT

*A French General's Role
in the American Revolution*

JINI JONES VAIL

www.jinijonesvail.com

WORD ASSOCIATION PUBLISHERS
www.wordassociation.com
1.800.827.7903

On the cover: General Rochambeau in full dress uniform wears symbols of his most prestigious honors. Across his chest is the scarlet sash of l'Ordre de Saint-Louis, while over his heart is the star of l'Ordre du Saint-Esprit. In his right hand he holds the baton of Maréchal de France, one of the last honors bestowed by King Louis XVI before his death. The last two were awarded to Rochambeau after his return to France in 1783. Not shown is his medal of the Société des Cincinnati. Artist unknown.

Anne S. K. Brown Military Collection, Brown University Library.

On the spine: Château de Rochambeau painted by Rachel LePine.

www.jinijonesvail.com

Copyright © 2011 by Jini Jones Vail
Second Print 2013

Printed in the United States of America.

ISBN: 978-1-59571-602-6

Library of Congress Control Number: 2010939745

Designed and published by

Word Association Publishers
205 Fifth Avenue
Tarentum, Pennsylvania 15084

www.wordassociation.com
1.800.827.7903

To my beloved husband, John.
And to my grandchildren—Jessie, Sam, Conor, Sophia, Jamison,
Emily, Quaid, Alden, and Cassius—to whom
I bequeath my love of history.

*"In the ever-bending road of time,
we must always remember our history."*

—JINI JONES VAIL

CONTENTS

LIST OF ILLUSTRATIONS   xiii

FOREWORD   xv

PREFACE   xix

CHAPTER ONE
From Seminarian to King's General   3

CHAPTER TWO
France to the Rescue   31

CHAPTER THREE
Hope Arrives in Newport   55

CHAPTER FOUR
Rochambeau Meets Washington   74

CHAPTER FIVE
The March to Victory Begins   102

CHAPTER SIX
Layover at New York   127

CHAPTER SEVEN
Rochambeau vis-à-vis Washington   152

CHAPTER EIGHT
The Secret March to Virginia   177

CHAPTER NINE
Admiral de Grasse
Fights Pivotal Sea Battle   207

CHAPTER TEN
The Battle of Yorktown   230

CHAPTER ELEVEN
British Surrender and Aftermath   259

CHAPTER TWELVE
Honors, Revolution, and Memorials   283

ACKNOWLEDGMENTS   302

KEY PARTICIPANTS   307

TIME LINE   324

GLOSSARY   329

NOTES   334

BIBLIOGRAPHY   364

INDEX   375

ABOUT THE AUTHOR   383

LIST OF ILLUSTRATIONS

GENERAL ROCHAMBEAU AT THE
  SURRENDER OF CORNWALLIS   FRONTISPIECE

THE FRENCH CONVOY FROM BREST TO NEWPORT   47

THE QUESTION   67

ROCHAMBEAU PLAQUE   71

THE SQUIRREL HUNT   110

THIRTY-NINE CAMPS AND MARCHES LIST   120

FRENCH UNIFORM AND EQUIPMENT LIST   136

THE ODELL HOUSE   149

GEORGE WASHINGTON   170

COMTE DE ROCHAMBEAU   175

AUGUST AND SEPTEMBER AT SEA, 1781   218

ADMIRAL COMTE DE GRASSE   223

WASHINGTON GIVES LAST ORDERS
AT THE SIEGE OF YORKTOWN   248

Independence is another word for freedom, and freedom is, for a human being, the most precious gift of all. But how many Americans in our country know their history well enough to pass it along to the next generation? Two hundred years ago America's sovereignty would have amounted to little more than the Declaration of Independence, a glorious achievement in itself but ultimately meaningless had it not been supported by a military campaign.

The British navy had conquered the seas, and the king of England, George III, was in full control of the colonies. In spite of the diplomatic skills of Benjamin Franklin while he was serving as an envoy in Paris, and the publication in Philadelphia of "Common Sense," Thomas Paine's diatribe against the despotism of King George III, the Americans who were faithful to the British tradition in America were still a majority in the thirteen states.

The 1776 Declaration of Independence, inspired mostly by Thomas Jefferson, was a powerful warning that America—at least the best minds in America—longed for freedom. Yet the road to freedom was arduous and full of ambushes. It would take five more years to start the long and exhausting march led by a combined French and American expeditionary corps to the Yorktown battlefield in Virginia.

It is that very moment in history that captured the mind of educator Jini Jones Vail. She spent years studying the fascinating life and military career of Rochambeau, going to the best sources of documentation, including Yale University's Bienecke Rare Book and Manuscript Library, and conducting interviews with Count Michel de Rochambeau and his wife, Madeleine, at their château near Vendôme, France, where the old Maréchal de Rochambeau is buried. Those interviews enabled her to explore family documents available only at the château. Jini Jones Vail's study, through a remarkable abundance of facts and anecdotes, offers new insights into the life and career of this extraordinary French general. It renews the subject and offers valuable perspective to the reader.

Rochambeau was famous for his sense of discipline. It was not easy to control the behavior of several thousand men, yet the comportment of these men was exemplary, particularly during the long months of waiting in Newport, Rhode Island. Rochambeau manifested this same sense of discipline in his personal relationship with George Washington.

Inspired by Lafayette's brilliant start under Washington at Brandywine, Pennsylvania, King Louis XVI made a decision that shocked the old courts of Europe. He placed his best general under the authority of a foreigner who had never presented his credentials to the most powerful leader in Europe—and instead relied on the recommendation of a very young Lafayette.

This extraordinary decision was an unprecedented departure from the rules concerning the command of armies in the eighteenth century, and it worked very well indeed. In the most crucial situations, when Washington and Rochambeau disagreed profoundly on essential matters relating to the conduct of battle, the French general always showed his willingness to submit to his superior's opinion.

It was the Court of Versailles, with the full support of the Court of Spain, that suggested the brilliant and final solution—to send, under Admiral De Grasse, a French fleet big enough to defeat the powerful British navy at Chesapeake Bay. The British were forced to retreat to New York City, opening the way to defeat Cornwallis in Virginia.

So went the saga of the road to American independence and the truly extraordinary victory at Yorktown, Virginia, on October 19, 1781. I like to think that history lovers of all ages and a generation of students will delight in the reading of Jini Jones Vail's account of this momentous event in history and Rochambeau's role in the American Revolution.

— Jacques Bossière, Ph.D., Founder and First Chair,
Washington-Rochambeau Revolutionary Route (WR3-US)

In 1993, in the midst of a decade of summer graduate studies at the French Universities of Touraine and of Bourgogne, I had the good fortune to receive an invitation to meet with General Rochambeau's descendants, Count Michel and Countess Madeleine de Rochambeau, at the family château near Vendôme, France. During a wonderful private tour of the home where General Rochambeau was born and raised in the 1700s, I learned of their ancestor's valuable contribution in helping to bring a triumphant end to the American Revolution. I was able to view Rochambeau's original memoirs, written in the Paris Conciergerie prison during the French Revolution, and I saw the memorabilia of his illustrious career on the battlefields of Europe and America.

At the conclusion of the tour, my son, Rusty Dyer, and I were shown a two-volume book, *The American Campaigns of Rochambeau's Army—1780, 1781, 1782, 1783*, edited by Howard C. Rice Jr. and Anne S. K. Brown. When I returned home, I knew I needed to find my own copy to learn more about Rochambeau's American campaign. A few years later, as a member of the Connecticut Governor's Advisory Commission on American and Francophone Cultural Affairs, I finally purchased the two-volume set and commenced my study. The role that France played in the American Revolution so piqued my interest that I decided to explore the possibility of writing a book on Rochambeau because surprisingly little had been written about him since the mid-1900s.

One of the major goals of the governor's commission was to promote the establishment of the Washington-Rochambeau Revolutionary Route (W3R-US), which, as of March 30, 2009, is now an official national historic trail that extends about six hundred miles from Newport, Rhode Island, to Yorktown, Virginia. To this end, I began some investigative travel and research along the route where Rochambeau and his troops had marched, still searching for other books on the subject, but finding very little that focused on Rochambeau in particular. Where I did find sources of importance, I used them to support my research. Furthermore, there are but few mentions of Rochambeau in history textbooks. I found some references limited to as little as one sentence. I then decided that the greatest contribution I could make for the W3R would be to write a book explaining in detail how important the French contribution was to the founding of America. Over the ensuing years I returned to visit the Rochambeau family and continued an extensive correspondence with Count Michel from 1993 until his death in 2007.

As I continued my research on Rochambeau's march through America, I realized that in order to paint the complete picture of this distinguished and capable military leader, I would need to cover his entire life. So, I began with his family heritage, early life, education, and European military campaigns, followed by his call to duty in America by King Louis XVI, and ending with his later years in France, all the while searching for early indications of the character qualities that made him Washington's ideal lieutenant. The deeper I delved into my study, the more I learned about the two generals, French and American. Their distinct personality traits emerged through the progression of events that played out from Rochambeau's arrival in July 1780 until his departure from America in January 1783.

In contrast to most descriptions of Rochambeau's expedition, I decided to include the transatlantic voyage of the French forces as they encountered the wonders of the sea and endured dangerous skirmishes with the enemy, cramped quarters, and disease before finding a safe port. Wherever possible in describing Rochambeau's American campaign, I allowed the voices of those who sailed, marched, and fought with Rochambeau to tell the story in their own words as it unfolded from Versailles, France, to the Battle of Yorktown. Similarly, after following Rochambeau on American soil for two and a half years, I concluded with the compelling story of Rochambeau's life after his return to France where he resumed his exemplary work of reforming the French army and suffered distress under the French Revolution and La Terreur of Robespierre. In the course of this close examination of the man and his life achievements, I found Rochambeau to have been an honest, patient man— brave, noble, focused, dependable, self-effacing, wise, loyal to his king and family; a warrior beloved by his men, a man who followed in the footsteps of his illustrious forebears.

I spent considerable time delving into the decision-making process as it evolved between Rochambeau and Washington, exploring events as they played out in the last phase of the war and the many facets of the generals' working relationship. Washington's decisions involved a complex process of methodically eliminating possibilities. With Rochambeau persistently and patiently providing his input and insight on behalf of France, Washington was ultimately successful. The long, arduous process brought out the best in Washington and Rochambeau, who had been thrown together by one king to cast out another king. They were, by necessity, forced to work together as commander in chief and lieutenant to bring independence to America and forever change the world.

The research and writing of distant history is not an exact science since the recording of historical events, even from firsthand accounts, vary. With that in mind, I chose the dates and numbers that I found most reliable. I discovered that some of the primary sources were written years after the actual events; again, I had to weigh the choices and decide which seemed most accurate—an awesome task. And I take full responsibility for any errors or inconsistencies, as I have made my best effort to represent the events contained in this book as accurately as possible.

I have provided the reader with thumbnail sketches of numerous key participants, including some who are commonly overlooked. I have also included a glossary to aid the reader in deciphering unfamiliar French, military, nautical, and medical terms.

Given that Rochambeau's name has often been omitted from history books on both sides of the Atlantic, I hope this account of his life will fill the void and be both educational and enjoyable to read. I trust that the book will also generate interest in the Washington-Rochambeau Revolutionary Route (W3R-US) and serve as a valuable resource for those who want to know more of the story behind America's victory in the War of Independence.

Rochambeau
WASHINGTON'S
IDEAL LIEUTENANT

CHAPTER ONE

From Seminarian to King's General

"To live and die as a gallant knight"
—ROCHAMBEAU FAMILY MOTTO

OFFSHORE WINDS WHIPPED THE HALYARDS, and sails were taut as the French fleet caught a steady breeze pushing them northward. It was July 11, 1780. The forward lookout warned of a fog bank dead ahead. After nearly ten long weeks at sea, a large convoy of French ships bore down on Newport, Rhode Island, where they hoped to find a safe harbor. General Jean-Baptiste-Donatien de Vimeur, Comte de Rochambeau, handpicked by the king of France to lead the *expédition particulière* to America, stood on the deck of the flagship, *Duc de Bourgogne*. "*Expédition particulière*" was the code name for the special French mission to America (literally a "special delivery" of an army and supplies). While waiting for Narragansett Bay to come into view, Rochambeau peered through his long glass, hoping that no British warships were in the vicinity. The French general, short of stature but tall in the estimation of his men, was in full military dress and eager to land in America.

Who was this remarkable French commander, sent by his country to aid the rebel Americans in their fight to win their independence? Who was this man, the king's chosen general, and how did his formative years prepare him to lead the *expédition particulière* to America? Until 1780 Rochambeau was unknown in the Western

Hemisphere and little more than a name to George Washington. He was a man born to French warriors of noble descent and learned the art of warfare on the battlegrounds of Europe. He sailed to America at a desperate point in the Revolution. Because of Rochambeau's American campaign his name will forever be linked to George Washington and to the future of the nation he helped to birth, the United States of America.

EARLY LIFE

America's new friend, General de Rochambeau, was born in the small town of Vendôme, France, on July 1, 1725, and was christened Jean-Baptiste-Donatien de Vimeur de Rochambeau.[1] The baby born on that day in the quiet Vendômois region southwest of Paris would one day, half a century later, play an important part in the shifting of the balance of power around the Atlantic. While writing his memoirs many years after the expedition to America, Rochambeau assumed that no one would be interested in the details of his personal life so he wrote mostly of the historical military events in which he played a part. His memoirs provide little in terms of his personal views of the events as they unfolded. His character traits can be gleaned from letters, from journals of men who participated alongside Rochambeau in war (even from a British general), and from his military career, more readily than from his memoirs.

As a young boy, Rochambeau grew up in Vendôme and in the nearby family home, the Château de Rochambeau. The site for the château was originally chosen because of its defensible location on a peninsula that extended into the Loir River. The Loir is a small meandering river that flows north of the more famous Loire. The river wrapped itself around the castle like a natural moat, providing a favorable defense. To add to the security of the castle were tall towers that "*baignaient dans le Loir*," meaning the towers literally stood in the Loir River.

As a youth in the valley of the Loir, Rochambeau matured with an appreciation for the beauty of his peaceful surroundings. Fishing in the river, long rides on horseback, and family gatherings gave him a sense of roots in the Vendômois. When not at school, he spent many hours in his father's extensive library, reading of the exploits of French history and the heroic deeds of his ancestors' adventures in foreign lands.

MILITARY HERITAGE:
FROM VIMEUR TO ROCHAMBEAU

Rochambeau's military heritage can be traced to the Vimeur side of his family. His earliest known progenitor, from the neighboring region of Touraine, was Jean de Vimeur, who was killed at the Battle of Mansourah in Egypt during the Seventh Crusade in 1250. Nicolas de Vimeur, another ancestor, fought bravely and died at the massacre at Naples in 1282, inspiring the Duke of Anjou, an early landowner in the Vendômois, to present an official coat of arms to Nicholas's descendants. The family motto on the coat of arms, "*Vivre en preux, y mourir*," translates as "To live valiantly and to die thus" or, in another translation, as "To live and die as a gallant knight."[2] The crest consists of a navy-blue escutcheon as the shield bearing the emblem of a golden chevron and three yellow mullets (heraldic stars) of the same color, surmounted by a golden crown.

The nobility of the Rochambeau family finds its origins in 1481 with Macé de Vimeur. As befitting a titled nobleman under the feudal system, his family was not taxed until the French Revolution, which began officially on July 14, 1789.[3] So, for a period of about three hundred years, the Vimeurs neither owed nor paid taxes per se, but as feudal lords they had the responsibility of protecting and meting out justice for those who lived on their fiefs.

Rochambeau's ancestors, though living in Vendômois and Touraine, did not live in the ancient château itself until the sixteenth century. In 1512, Christine de Belon married Mathurin de Vimeur, turning over to him the Château de Rochambeau as her dowry.

Mathurin de Vimeur took the name of his wife's estate as his own, making him the first man to carry the name of Rochambeau. His family moved into the Château de Rochambeau in 1515.[4] Thus, the name Rochambeau became a family name. The Vimeur family adopted the Rochambeau crest as their own. House, name, and family crest were united as one.

Since the château was constructed from the large limestone ledge found at the site of the home, it is possible that the name Rochambeau is inspired by its surroundings: *rocher* (rock) over-looking the *champs* (fields) that are found all around the site and *beau* (beautiful), which refers to both the fields and the stone ledge. Therefore, the name *Roch/cham/beau* may have been constructed from common usage describing an everyday observation of the site.

After 1512, the Vimeur side of the family adopted the name of Rochambeau. René de Vimeur de Rochambeau, son of Christine and Mathurin, was captain of a company of archers who were at the side of French King Henry III when he was assassinated in 1588.[5] René's grandson and namesake was a member of the second company of musketeers. He was promoted to sergeant by King Louis XIV, who reigned from 1643-1715. René's grandson later went to the West Indies where he was wounded in a skirmish with the Dutch.

IMMEDIATE FAMILY

Rochambeau's father, Joseph-Charles de Vimeur, Marquis de Rochambeau, was a prominent landowner who was known by many titles: Chevalier of the Royal Military Orders of Saint Louis and of Notre Dame-du-Mont Carmel; Seigneur de La Royauté de Rennes; and of course, Marquis de Rochambeau. The marquis also held many less significant titles. He may have earned these titles through owner-ship of various properties or feudal estates. In addition, he held the position of counselor of the king and Juge du Point d'Honneur in the province.[6]

The marquis was crippled from birth, and therefore unfit for military service. Despite his physical disability, he was made a Knight of the Order of the Holy Sepulcher of Jerusalem, presented with the Order of Saint-Lazare, and appointed Governor of the Castle of Vendôme and bailiff of the Duchy of Vendômois. Because of his varied duties and political appointments, Rochambeau's father was obliged to keep a second house in the town of Vendôme on Rue Poterie. He and his family occupied their townhouse mostly in the winter and spent their summers in the country at the family Château de Rochambeau just three miles west of town. It was here that, at great expense, the marquis happily spent many hours laying out the broad terraces and lovely gardens that graced the grounds along the River Loir. He planted the long *allée*, a pathway under a double line of linden trees, which extends one and a half miles from the château to the property line.[7]

Rochambeau's father, although titled but not wealthy by eighteenth-century standards, was known in Vendômois to be a generous, congenial, and hospitable landowner with doors always open to visitors and those in need. He was approachable and unaffected by his high station in life. The Rochambeau dinner table was rarely set for fewer than twenty family members and guests combined.[8] French Revolution writer DuChêne commented, "He was more of a good-hearted daddy *(papa gâteau)* than he was a Grand Bailiff of the Sword…. He practiced a very simple Christianity and was constantly giving thanks to God for 'the benefits bestowed on himself and his family.'"[9]

As for Rochambeau's mother, the marquise, Marie-Claire-Thérèse Bégon, she was the daughter of Jean-Baptiste Bégon, a tax collector in Vendôme, and Jeanne-Claire.[10] As secretary to the king, Rochambeau's maternal grandfather was a titled nobleman, and his maternal grandmother, Jeanne-Claire, was a capable woman of her time, intelligent and well educated. She had a talent for organization and did much to increase the family holdings.[11] The marquise followed in her mother's footsteps to become an excellent royal governess.

Rochambeau's only sister, Philippine-Elizabeth, married well to "a gentleman from Lorraine," a former colonel in the regiment of Saintonge.[12] Rochambeau also had two brothers: Gabriel-Césaire-Joseph, who was baptized on April 13, 1724, and his younger brother, Louis-Hector, who died as an infant.[13] Rochambeau, the middle son, was born on July 1, 1725, at the Château de Rochambeau and baptized by the priest Louis Bégon in the church of Sainte-Madeleine de Vendôme. As a youth, Rochambeau was sickly and frail, and no one would have expected him to become a valiant military strategist and commander.[14]

Since it did not fall on the youngest son to carry on the family tradition in the military, Rochambeau was first sent, at the age of five, to the College of the Oratorian Fathers in Vendôme. The writer Honoré de Balzac attended this school some years later and described it as "a spiritual prison house."[15] Nonetheless, Rochambeau thrived there, winning prizes in history and Latin. Guided by the Bishop of Blois, the marquis eventually removed his son from this school, claiming it had Jansenist tendencies (denying free will, saying that all men are corrupt and that Christ died only for the elect few), and enrolled him at a school in nearby Blois to become a Jesuit priest. There, because of his obvious dedication, Rochambeau became a favorite of the Bishop and the Abbé de Beaumont.[16]

FATE TURNS ROCHAMBEAU FROM THE PRIESTHOOD TO THE MILITARY

Nevertheless, a life dedicated to the priesthood was not to be for the young Rochambeau. The course of his life changed drastically when his elder brother, Césaire, died suddenly. This unexpected turn of events left the fifteen-year-old Rochambeau, as sole male heir, to carry on the family tradition as a soldier in the king's army.

Although Rochambeau did not say much in his memoirs about this radical turnabout in his life, he did mention that the bishop summoned him to tell him the news of his brother's death. He "bade him forget all that he had said to him up to that time, that he had suddenly become the only son, and that henceforth he must serve his country with the same zeal he would have devoted to God."[17] Within hours, Rochambeau had packed his small bag and stepped into a carriage bound for home. Thus, he turned his back on the priesthood and returned to "the heretical Collège de Vendôme,"[18] where he was referred to thereafter as the Chevalier de Saint-Georges, a title taken from one of his father's estates. From that time on, he began to read military history and "to follow in the footsteps of his war-loving forefathers."[19]

Rochambeau's home, the Château de Rochambeau, was filled with portraits of his ancestors as well as those of kings of France and Admiral de Coligny, the great Huguenot leader, who was one of the many victims of the murders of St. Bartholomew's Eve in Paris.[20] Coligny was assassinated in 1572 as a leader of the Protestant movement under King Charles IX. There was also a life-size painting of the Duc d'Orléans, the prince in whose household the Marquise de Rochambeau served as lady-in-waiting. In a word, the young Rochambeau was surrounded by history and military achievement. "History," he learned from the Oratorians, "is the foundation of learning; it is the theater where all men are spectators."[21]

Rochambeau is descended from a long line of soldiers who passed on to him the characteristics of leadership. It is apparent that his qualities of greatness were inherited as a blend from both sides of his family. From his mother's side, he inherited the elegance and refinement of her noble family and high position at the Court of Versailles. From his father's family, he donned the mantle of the gallant knight always at the ready to follow the king's command. Jean-Nicholas Durfort, Comte de Cheverny, stated in his memoirs that "the taker of Yorktown was completely the democrat" in the eighteenth-century sense of the word. To be a "democrat" in those days was to be a man of the people, not holding oneself aloof but respecting the needs of one's fellow man.

Not long after his brother's sudden demise, the young Rochambeau completed his schooling in Vendôme and with his father's blessing was sent to Paris to attend the famous military preparatory academy, the Ecole Royale Militaire. He settled into officers' training there. While studying in Paris, he spent any free time he had at the Tuileries Castle to hear King Louis XV's musicians. Nevertheless, always the serious student, he studied his horsemanship and fencing first.

Within months of his arrival at military school came the outbreak of the war between Austria and Prussia. Rochambeau joined the French army, thereby commencing a fifty-five-year military career. He embarked on a journey that would lead him as a soldier of the crown to the rivers Rhine and Danube, and the Mediterranean, across the Atlantic to Narragansett Bay in Rhode Island, to the Hudson River in New York, the York River in Virginia, and back home by the age of fifty-seven. Like some of his forefathers, he would be wounded, but unlike others, he would survive to write his memoirs and to return to the château and estates he loved.

As a young standard-bearer or "cornet of the horse" in the Saint-Simon regiment of which his uncle, Louis Bégon, was a captain, Rochambeau, at fifteen, prepared to enter the War of Austrian Succession with the high hopes of a young soldier in his first campaign. In late 1740 Rochambeau returned home from military school to Vendôme to say his goodbyes at Christmastime. After a family gathering, he returned to duty in a heavy rainstorm, making his way over muddy roads and flooding rivers to Paris to meet his destiny as a soldier. From Paris he rode to Strasbourg and then on to Nuremberg to join his regiment. There he learned that Frederick II of Prussia, previously on good terms with the young archduchess Maria Teresa, broke his promise to support her. Frederick's friendly correspondence with her proved false when he invaded Silesia on December 16, 1740. Frederick backed off after conquering Silesia, abandoning the French, who had come to his aid, leaving the French deep in enemy territory, facing the opposing army of Maria Teresa.

For the French it was a disappointing loss of face. Rochambeau, disillusioned in his first march into battle, was caught up in the resulting retreat in unrelenting cold winter weather with an army in disarray. He was one of the only standard-bearers left after many desertions. Although the debutant soldier performed well, his initiation into the army was christened with a defeat.

In the midst of retreat, Rochambeau became seriously ill with a fever and was relegated to a cart for a week's march. As he began his long road to recuperation, he could not help noticing the mismanagement and fruitless bickering among the French generals. He vowed that he would never let this happen if he were in charge. By the time they reached the Rhine, virtually half of the French army was decimated. Subsequently, Rochambeau did sentry duty on the Rhine for two years. His attention to duty and detail earned him a promotion to captain just following his eighteenth birthday in 1743.[22]

It took an extended period for the ailing young soldier to return to good health after his severe fever on the retreat. So he requested leave to recuperate at home. However, he was not home long before accompanying his mother to the Court of Versailles where she was employed as governess to the children of the Duchesse d'Orléans. The young chevalier preferred to be in the country rather than languish at court. When he was called back to duty, it was to defend the Port of Gibraltar. British ships had managed to slip through the French blockade, and someone had to pay for the bungle. Rochambeau, who may have had nothing to do with the failure, was dismissed. At this point, the Marquise de Rochambeau used her position to come to the aid of her son. Through her influence, he was appointed as an aide to the royal prince Duc d'Orléans, for which both mother and son were grateful.[23]

By 1746, Rochambeau was on his way with the Duc d'Orléans, King Louis XV, his son, the Dauphin, and the royal mistress to Flanders where the famous French Marshal Maurice de Saxe was winning battle after battle. When the royal entourage returned to Versailles, Rochambeau remained with the army as an aide to the

Duc de Clermont, who was preparing to lay siege to the city of Namur. Clermont planned to capture the impregnable citadel at Namur, a Belgian stronghold overlooking the fork of the Sambre and the Meuse Rivers near the French border. It was held by the Austrians but controlled by their ally, the Dutch. "Here at last was the opportunity for which Rochambeau had been waiting…he was now to be given a chance to prove himself."[24]

Wryly in his memoirs Rochambeau tells of his mission to scout out the strengths and weaknesses of the citadel. He climbed the imposing walls and precipitous rocks that surrounded the fortress, misjudged a foothold near the top but gained the summit all the same, and unexpectedly stumbled upon two guards who let him take stock of the fortifications without restraining him.[25]

This mission would become much more dangerous before he was finished at Namur. Using the intelligence gathered by Rochambeau, Clermont attacked the citadel, which resulted in the eventual surrender of the city. At the end of the siege the citadel itself was still afire, with flames centered in the highly combustible magazine, the storage place for ammunition. To extinguish the fire meant getting rid of the barrels of gunpowder before they exploded, placing both the French and the Dutch in great danger. Rochambeau saved the day for his commanding officer by racing into the burning castle and tossing out the smoking barrels before they could cause further damage.[26] Clermont was impressed. He saw in the young Rochambeau a man who could react quickly in the face of danger, put aside fear, and make sound decisions.

Realizing that Rochambeau was a man of great promise, Clermont wanted to promote him by helping him to purchase his own regiment. In those days, it was customary for a nobleman to buy a regiment and offer his services to the king. Rochambeau, although of noble standing, was not from a wealthy family and therefore could not easily afford this expense. But he could apply for assistance during the *ancien régime* under King Louis XV. The process involved writing a formal letter of request to the king's titled mistress, Madame la

Marquise de Pompadour, who handled such business quite adeptly. This was one of the prescribed routes of advancement through the military ranks in eighteenth-century France; it would be regarded as highly unorthodox in the twenty-first century.

In his memoirs Rochambeau explains that, in effect, Madame de Pompadour assumed the role of prime minister in such affairs. Court-savvy, she single-handedly managed most of the internal affairs for the king. The letter in support of Rochambeau never reached her, and was, in fact, returned to Clermont for unknown reasons. Nonetheless, the Marquis de Rochambeau managed to pay the substantial sum necessary for his son's regiment. Without help from his parents, his chances for advancement would have been nearly impossible. So, at the age of twenty-one, Rochambeau attained the rank of Colonel of the Régiment de la Marche.[27]

By this time the War of Austrian Succession was well underway across Europe. Under the direction of the illustrious Marshal de Saxe, the French won several key battles. They had marched through Belgium, dominated the Austrian Netherlands, and were on their way to the Dutch Republic, all the while re-establishing French dominance on the continent.[28]

At the battle of Laufeldt, fought July 12, 1747, in the Netherlands, the French under the ailing Marshal de Saxe, won over the British, Hanoverians, Austrians, and Dutch, leading to the end of the War of Austrian Succession. All of this transpired in spite of the fact that Saxe suffered from a severe case of dropsy and had to be tied onto his horse in battle. It was a costly triumph, for the French suffered great losses, with fourteen thousand dead and wounded, far more than any other country involved.[29]

As for the French, Saxe proved himself heroic once again, while Rochambeau conducted himself with fearless tenacity and honor. Unfortunately, Colonel Rochambeau, while leading his men in battle, received two balls of grapeshot, one coming very close to his eye, the other catching him in the thigh. The second was a more serious wound from which he suffered his entire life. The lump of iron that entered his leg was as large as a pigeon egg and exited without breaking a bone. In the aftermath he suffered a high fever and was bled at least eighteen times. The seriousness of his wounds resulted in a long recovery. Rochambeau's mother, usually in contact with her son while on the battlefield, knew of his injuries but had to wait a long time for him to be strong enough to put pen to paper with the details.[30]

It was advantageous for Rochambeau's military career that King Louis XV had been present at the Battle of Laufeldt, because the king recognized Rochambeau's gallantry and worthiness as a soldier and invited him to join the select group of men whom he permitted to ride with him in his carriage during military ceremonies and to dine with him privately at the Court of Versailles.[31] However, he did not seem to enjoy the royal attention, writing, "It would be difficult to give any adequate reason for this elaborate etiquette" at the Court of Versailles.[32] As a result of Rochambeau's injury while serving his county, the king ordered for him a pension of two thousand livres from the royal treasury.[33]

Although Rochambeau had dined with the king at least once, he refused as many invitations to return to court as he politely could. He preferred his work in the field or being at home with his family whenever possible.[34] It was widely known that loose morals were the norm at court and that faithfulness to one's spouse was not expected. As was made clear early in his career, Rochambeau remained diffident to the politics of court life. This characteristic proved more of a plus than a minus.

The king's presence at the Battle of Laufeldt is preserved in a painting by Pierre L'Enfant. In the painting, King Louis XV, mounted high on his fine bay horse, is dressed in red, his jacket embroidered in heavy gold thread. With his right arm, he is pointing in the direction of the line of French soldiers who are winning the battle. L'Enfant's son, Pierre-Charles, came to America in 1777 and eventually laid out plans for the building of the capital city of Washington.[35]

The War of Austrian Succession ended with the signing of the Treaty of Aix-la-Chapelle on October 18, 1748, at Aachen, Holy Roman Empire. In the final agreement there was no clear victor—the French returned the Austrian Netherlands and the Dutch barrier towns to their owners, and Madras, India, was ceded back to the British. In exchange, Louisburg, Nova Scotia, was restored to the French. At Laufeldt the young Rochambeau had observed British Generals Cumberland and Ligonier stagnated by petty jealousies and mismanagement. Nonetheless Rochambeau had proven himself worthy of the king's commendation and was gaining valuable military experience. The young French colonel had played a valuable role in restoring peace to France.

With the war over, Rochambeau had the opportunity to turn his thoughts to the lighter side of life. In the next year, his parents arranged for him to wed. The first two times they tried to make the match failed for reasons unknown, but the third young woman was a match made in heaven. In the eighteenth century, if the intended wife did not live in the nearby vicinity, it was not uncommon for a messenger to bring a likeness of her, painted perhaps in the form of a miniature on porcelain (or if the intended was royal, an oil painting), to show the prospective husband and his family. If the artist was good, and the likeness was true to reality, one could make a reasonable choice based on appearance. However, of course, the personality could only be described in words, usually exaggerated in favor of the girl's best characteristics. It was a little like a blind date, with truth often clouded by the size of the prospective wife's dowry.

In the case of Rochambeau and his fiancée, the choosing and the meeting must have gone well, for their marriage lasted almost sixty years. At the appropriate time, Rochambeau met the young woman who was to become the love of his life, and they began an abbreviated courtship. In his memoirs Rochambeau says, "My star gave me a wife who was all I could wish for…but especially a personality and an education which was most highly praised by all my friends. She brought me happiness all my life. I hope for my part, to have made her happy by the tenderest affection, which has never wavered for a single moment for nearly sixty years. When I was first wounded I was nearly bled white, and my health was very bad—frequent hemorrhages and fevers made it necessary for me to pass a quiet time at home under a strict regime. My wife, who was always with me, took smallpox and we nursed each other."[36]

Her name was Jeanne-Thérèse, Telles d'Acosta. She was the daughter of a wealthy Portuguese wholesale merchant in foodstuffs. The Paris notary Maître Leverrier recorded the arrangements of the marriage. Her father provided a sizeable "dowry of 316,443 livres of which about 220,000 shall be paid at once and the remainder one year after the marriage and further, to include the bride's diamonds and handmade laces valued at 20,000 livres."[37]

The bride's dowry added considerably to the pension of 2,000 livres Rochambeau received from the king. In addition, Rochambeau's belongings, which included "his furnishings, clothes, linens, personal effects, jewels, arms, horses, carriages, pension arrears, allowance and cash which he brought to the marriage, were valued at a total of 17,000 livres."[38] Since he was not a wealthy man, the Marquis de Rochambeau gave his son one of the family estates, the land of Saint-Georges du Rosay, from which he merited his first title of chevalier. The marquis also presented to his son, as a wedding gift, 25,000 pounds of silver plate, but nothing in the way of a regular allowance.[39] On December 22, 1749, Rochambeau, at the age of 24, married Jeanne-Thérèse, who was 19. Their vows were exchanged in Paris, and the wedding was announced in the Paris newspaper, the *Mercure de France.*[40]

The young bride of the up-and-coming hero of Namur and Laufeldt, by dint of her husband's recognition by the king two years prior, would be presented at court as a matter of course. On March 1, 1750, Jeanne-Thérèse, the daughter of Emmanuel d'Acosta, walked proudly into the king's presence escorted by her mother-in-law, the Marquise de Rochambeau and Marie Eléonore de Maillé de Carman, Comtesse de Sade, daughter of Rochambeau's godfather. It was *de rigueur* for the three women to make three graceful curtsies to the king. Then Louise-Elizabeth, Princesse de Conti, stepped in to personally present Jeanne-Thérèse to His Majesty King Louis XV, who spoke a few words to her. After meeting the king she turned to the queen, to her ladies-in-waiting, and then finally to the dauphin, curtsying to each before exiting the room.[41] Following court tradition, the three ladies in their sumptuous gowns, while continuing to face the king and queen, walked backwards curtsying all the way to the door.

A further note on the Comtesse de Sade who was a friend of the Rochambeau family through her father: she was the daughter of Donatien de Maillé, Marquis de Carman, Rochambeau's godfather at his baptism. The two families shared the first names of Donatien over several generations and used the name of Jean-Baptiste over and over. The Comtesse was the mother of the infamous Marquis de Sade.

Since Rochambeau did not elaborate on his private life in his writings, few facts remain about their daily life together as man and wife. During their first year of wedded life, while Rochambeau was still recuperating from his wounds, they lived in Vendôme with the marquis. The marquise, who spent a great deal of time at court working for the family of the Duc d'Orléans, was not often at home. It was a traumatic year for the Rochambeaus, for his young wife not only caught smallpox, but they also lost their first child. As a result, they waited a few years for Jeanne-Thérèse to fully recuperate before having more children.

Their first son, Donatien-Marie-Joseph de Vimeur, was born in 1755.[42] Their second son, Philippe, was born sometime thereafter. Donatien served as their father's aide-de-camp on the American campaign.

Upon their marriage or shortly thereafter, Jean-Baptiste and Jeanne-Thérèse took over the family Château de Rochambeau only minutes from the center of Vendôme. When they first moved in, the house consisted of one section to which Rochambeau added two more matching *pavilions*, one on each side of the original structure, thus tripling the overall size of their home. He then raised the center roof to coincide with the new ones, all in the manner of the architect Mansard, giving the modified château a unified appearance. He enlarged the windows and improved the grounds to include formal gardens and parterres.

The château today is virtually the same as when Rochambeau and his family lived there. The dwelling is generous in size with fourteen floor-to-ceiling French windows on each of two floors facing the Loir River. The general's formal bedroom is upstairs overlooking the peaceful Loir and the fields beyond. The château has both a basement and a fourth floor with smaller windows and several tall chimneys corresponding to the many fireplaces throughout the home. On the front of the house facing the river is a formal, curved, two-sided principal stairway, which leads up to the main entrance, reminiscent of one of similar design at Fontainebleau.

Swans still swim in the slow-moving Loir just outside the formal front door of the Rochambeau château. Across from the house, heading away from the river, is a long rock ridge with troglodyte hollows large enough to use as rooms or storage areas, and on one occasion, it accommodated 150 of Rochambeau's soldiers *en bivouac*, a temporary military encampment. The driveway, which leads to the house off the road to Vendôme, is one-and-a-half miles long, flat, and lined with the double *allée* of linden trees planted by Rochambeau and his father. When a tree dies, it is replaced even to this day in order to retain a sense of symmetry as one approaches the château. One can easily imagine Rochambeau galloping down this long driveway on his horse after an extended military campaign in a foreign country, or the family returning from Paris in a fine carriage, sending up dust clouds that signaled their arrival to the servants, or Rochambeau returning with his regiment to begin an encampment in the hollowed-out caves across from the château.

Judging by the portrait of Jeanne-Thérèse, which hangs in the portrait gallery of the château, she was a rare beauty. This fine portrait of Madame La Comtesse de Rochambeau is attributed to the famous portrait painter Maurice-Quentin de La Tour. Jeanne-Thérèse had dark hair, fine, noble features, and skin the color of fresh cream. Maurice-Quentin de La Tour, celebrated and prolific *pastélliste* (his medium was pastels), enjoyed a long career spanning the French Rococo period and lived eighty-four years (1704–1788). To preserve his works created from vulnerable pastels, he used a fixative, prepared with a closely guarded recipe, which allowed them to retain their original colors.[43] His subjects were some of the most famous people in eighteenth-century France.

Little is known of the countess's interests or of her struggles caring for their growing family during her husband's extended absences on campaign in Europe and later in America. Records show that both she and her husband were involved with the Masonic Order and that she was a member of the Ladies' Masonic Auxiliary in Paris.

Seven Years' War

Even though he was not completely healed from his wounds, Rochambeau returned to his Régiment de la Marche. Despite a period of peace in Europe, he showed intense dedication to the training of his troops. About the same time, in 1750, the French monarchy was saddened by the death of their greatest general, Maurice de Saxe.

Stirrings of the Seven Years' War signaled the end to a peaceful period in Europe. Frederick the Great moved again, this time to attack Saxony as he had done earlier with Silesia. Austria sided with France, Spain, and the German states to declare war on England, Portugal, and Prussia. There was palpable fear in England that France might launch an attack on her shores. France purposely kept them in the dark, delaying the final decision as long as possible.[44]

Rochambeau, stationed in Besançon, France, wanted desperately to join his mentor, Marshal de Belle-Isle, commander of the French troops in the north. If there was to be an attack on England, he wanted to be a part of it. Instead, he was sent to the Mediterranean with the Duc de Richelieu, nephew of the cardinal of the same name.

As it turned out, Colonel Rochambeau was fortunate to have gone south to the Mediterranean, as his involvement there proved to be a boon to his career.[45]

By early April 1756, Colonel Rochambeau set sail from Toulon with Richelieu and with the Marquis de La Galissonière, former governor of Canada. They were bound for Minorca, where they planned an assault on the island. Foul weather and rough seas brought on seasickness and caused a recurrence of Rochambeau's blood vomiting, which had plagued him periodically since Laufeldt. The sea air proved more beneficial to him than not, for this was his last bout with vomiting until many years later near the end of his life.[46]

Rochambeau noted before the taking of Minorca that the island was known for its bounty of cheap wine. He also realized how important the morale of the troops was in taking an objective and that drunkenness defeated their purpose. So he issued an order that no soldier who had been drunk the previous day would be permitted to take part in an assault. This proved to be very effective, for "the disgrace of not being allowed to risk one's life with one's comrades was something that a private in Rochambeau's regiment did not care to face."[47]

Control of Minorca meant virtual control of the Mediterranean; therefore, the French wanted to gain advantage over the British by taking over this tiny but important island. The French assault on the island of Minorca caught the British unaware.[48] When they arrived in port, the British governor of Minorca retreated to the far side of the island, leaving only the natives, who welcomed the French. Rochambeau described the arrival: "The women and the children were all Catholics and did not like the English [Protestants]; they kissed the soiled hands of a shabby Reformed Franciscan friar that I had taken on at Toulon as a chaplain, and the women kneeled to receive the blessings which he gave them unsparingly."[49]

Richelieu took the island's major cities—Ciudadella, Mercadal, and Mahon—in three days. The conquerors were treated with all manner of feasts featuring local wine and fowl: "Richelieu's chef conceived the idea of dressing of fowls with a surprising mixture of yellow of eggs and oil, which the banqueters christened mahonnaise sauce."[50]

Colonel Rochambeau's job was to see that two-thirds of the munitions and heavy artillery were transported one mile from their landing point to Fort Mahon. The Duc de Richelieu expected it would take a few days since the route started over water and continued up steep terrain over land. Rochambeau, not one to waste time, quickly set out with a fleet of small boats and effectively organized the transfer of the heavy equipment to land. On May 14, 1756, he swiftly accomplished the movement of the full lot of armaments, guns, bombs, gabion, "cannons, 15 mortars and their proportionate equipment."[51] Rochambeau's efficiency in transporting the artillery greatly influenced the outcome of the siege in favor of the French.[52]

Four days later, a sea battle began between La Galissonière and the British Admiral Byng who had finally decided to resist the French efforts to take Minorca. Rochambeau and Richelieu watched through "very good telescopes" from the hills of Minorca.[53] In quick order, the sea battle was won when Byng suddenly backed off, leaving the fort to defend itself, and thus the seemingly impregnable Fort Mahon fell to the French.[54] Colonel Jeffries, right-hand man of the British governor, was captured, and later that same day, the governor himself surrendered.[55] Minorca would be a strong bartering tool at the peace table.

In Paris, the good news about the victory at Minorca spread quickly. In the presence of Rochambeau's regiment, the *Te Deum* (Thanks be to God) was played. In the gardens at Compiègne, Madame de Pompadour passed out bonnets to the ladies and Mahon tassels to the men. When Rochambeau's regiment returned to the mainland of southwest France, they made a stop at Montpellier in the province of Languedoc. There Rochambeau and the Duc de Richelieu, who was the king's governor of the province, were fêted at a homecoming celebration. A committee presented Rochambeau with a wreath of laurels, which he immediately stripped, giving the individual leaves to his officers in order to share the honor with them.[56]

On July 23, 1756, after distinguishing himself at the liberation of Minorca, Rochambeau was admitted to the Ordre de Saint-Louis and received the rank of brigadier general. In France, the rank of brigadier was an intermediary position between colonel and general officer. Clearly, Rochambeau was growing in military skill, tact, and experience. In retrospect, he realized that the fortress at Port Mahon might never have fallen if the French had known how strong it was and that the British might never have lost it had they not relied so heavily on the strength of its fortifications.[57]

The maturing Rochambeau surmised that the Seven Years' War began because of mismanagement by Madame la Marquise de Pompadour. She was responsible for choosing the generals and sending the French army to invade Germany. King Louis XV, although mildly interested in governing, preferred to remain aloof from the politics of war. The king was relieved that he did not have to carry the entire burden of such decisions on his shoulders. It was, therefore, Madame la Marquise de Pompadour who influenced the king to choose Marshal d'Estrées to lead the forces against England, Portugal, and Prussia.

The Duc d'Orléans, Rochambeau's erstwhile protector, participated in the invasion as well. Rochambeau was pleased to renew his friendship with the Duc D'Orléans. Together they crossed the Rhine in April 1757, near Wesel where they found the Duke of Cumberland leading the British, Hanoverian, Hessian, and Prussian armies. Both the king of France and the king of Prussia were disappointed in their commanders, who seemed reluctant to enter battle.[58] In fact, the commanders were both plagued by petty jealousies and fears that held them back from performing their duties.

Estrées was soon replaced by Richelieu, who, in turn, was compelled to install a senior officer in place of Rochambeau, therefore demoting him and sending him back to his Régiment de la Marche. Rochambeau did not mind returning to his regiment, but he did mind the docking of his pay. He had just incurred large expenditures, which necessitated tapping into funds from his wife's estate to furnish his home in the style to which he had become accustomed following his promotion by the king.

In the ensuing months, the French paid dearly for the rash decisions taken on the part of Madame de Pompadour, such as "who should command the armies and where the war was to be fought." Rochambeau called it the "*malheureuse guerre*" (war of misfortune).[59] In the months and years that followed, Rochambeau would observe and learn from the bickering and jealousies of his commanders.

Before being replaced, Rochambeau had made successful inroads into Germany. At the fortress of Regenstein he misled the defenders into believing that he was backed up by a much larger French army, and they capitulated. Rochambeau gave all of the credit to his superior officer, the Duc de Noailles.

On March 31, 1759, Rochambeau was given command of one of the best regiments in the French army, the Auvergne infantry regiment, to which he formed a fond attachment. Later, a portion of his old Auvergne regiment would be reorganized and named the Gatinais. They would eventually travel with Admiral François-Joseph-Paul Comte de Grasse under the command of the Marquis de Saint-Simon to join the allies at the Battle of Yorktown in 1781. Rochambeau organized a company of *chasseurs* (a body of cavalry or infantry troops equipped and trained for rapid movement) and one with *grenadiers* (soldiers specially trained and equipped to throw grenades) to work with each battalion in the Auvergne.[60] The chasseurs were used as a screen for the other battalions in the regiment, a strategy later adopted by Napoleon. "By the formation of these companies Rochambeau accomplished two objectives. He built up an esprit de corps among the recruits of smaller stature and at the same time took advantage of their quickness and agility, qualities the grenadier under heavy marching orders too often lacked."[61]

Of the generals with whom Rochambeau interacted during the Seven Years' War, one stands out: the Duc de Broglie. He was a fearless and competent leader who had the full confidence of the troops. He was also known to disagree with the king and to find himself out of favor for long periods.[62] On July 10, 1760, the Duc de Broglie led an attack on Prince Ferdinand of Brunswick on the plains of the German state of Korbach. During the fighting, Broglie took some time out to sit near the Auvergne regiment, which had encamped by a store of ammunitions. He was "overcome by thirst and exhaustion"[63] and was enjoying a respite with a glass of wine and some bread when an enemy shell landed near him and exploded fourteen cases of cartridges.[64]

When the smoke dissipated, Rochambeau was relieved to see that neither the soldiers nor Broglie had budged. "I am greatly inspired," he said to Broglie, "to see you with your glass in your hand, without having been disturbed in your meal by that infernal accident." "Monsieur," replied Broglie, "I am much more inspired to see a regiment, after such an explosion, come back to a shelled position with such order and such coolness."[65]

By October of that year, the French were installed near the Abbey of Clostercamp. Prince Ferdinand planned to attack the French as they slept. "The French General, who suspected the prince's plan, made his army sleep fully armed: he sent Monsieur d'Assas, captain of the Auvergne regiment, scouting."[66] Assas had only gone a short distance when he was captured by the enemy at bayonet point. They warned him not to make a sound, or they would kill him. The brave Auvergne captain took a deep breath, and yelled at the top of his voice: "'Help, Auvergne—the enemy!' He fell at once, pierced with cuts."[67] He gave his life to save Rochambeau and the Auvergne regiment.

Leaping into action, Rochambeau called his regiment to follow in the attack and "above all to die at their posts rather than to abandon it."[68] By morning, his superior officer, Marquis de Castries, commended him in his report to the king: "Monsieur le Comte de Rochambeau acquitted himself in that command with a swiftness and an intelligence to which were due the first difficulties that the enemy encountered."[69] Rochambeau again took a bullet in his thigh, this time at the Battle of Clostercamp. His wound did not deter him from giving direction and inspiration to his favored Auvergne until the battle was won.[70] The bloody day ended in a costly victory with 3,000 French, including 60 officers and 800 Auvergne infantrymen, dead.[71] The Duc de Broglie admired Rochambeau's fine military abilities, especially at Clostercamp.[72]

After his success in 1760 at the Battle of Clostercamp, Rochambeau was granted a long-held wish when he was promoted to *maréchal de camp,* on February 20, 1761. Immediately thereafter, on March 7, 1761 he was named inspector of the infantry. In his new position he was given the opportunity to work directly with Choiseul, newly appointed secretary of war. Sharing common goals for the military, they worked well together.[73]

A letter from Rochambeau's father, written to a friend after Clostercamp, reveals the aging father's pride and his devotion to his son:

Vendôme, December 27, 1762

A great load has been taken off my shoulders—since I am free from the horrors of war which have threatened my son…. I have never ceased to fear the hazards of war and sickness for one who was born very frail but who has nevertheless borne up like a hero. I have given thanks to God who had not placed me in the situation of those who weep and are inconsolable. The news of peace fairly suffocates me with joy, especially since it seemed a long way off. At first I was so overcome that I could neither speak nor move, but as soon as I recovered myself, I fell on my knees and recited the *Te Deum* crying all the while with joy.[74]

The early gains made by the French soon melted into losses as the Seven Years' War dragged on. The downward spiral was beginning for France. They were being squeezed by their neighbors on the continent of Europe while losing control of their colonies and all-important trading partners across the Atlantic and in India.

A fair and principled general, Rochambeau was revered by his soldiers as well as by his counterparts in battle. After a skirmish on St. John's Day, 1762, during which many English officers were taken prisoner, Rochambeau, as usual, treated them in a humane manner. Shortly thereafter, he received a most unusual letter from Lord Granby, a British commander. It came after a battle in which Rochambeau was forced to retreat from the British. Granby wrote to congratulate him on "the brilliant manner in which he had extricated his army from the encircling German and British troops."[75] Beyond that he wished to thank Rochambeau for the excellent care he had taken of his British prisoners and to let him know how the French prisoners were faring in British hands. Granby added, "The bravery of your troops has not surprised me, since learning from your officers of the great respect every one in the corps has for their general, and for the confidence they so rightly place in his judgment."[76]

REORGANIZATION OF THE FRENCH ARMY

Gilbert Chinard of Johns Hopkins University observes in his preface to Jean-Edmond Weelen's book, *Rochambeau Father and Son*, that when the peace was signed in 1763 after the Seven Years' War, Rochambeau could have easily retired to his estates to live the quiet, rural life. Instead, he chose to stay on in the service of his country for more than seventeen years, and working under French Minister of War Choiseul, he took on the task of reorganizing the army. Rochambeau continued his work with the help of three other inspectors after his return from America with the French Revolution at his heels. His accomplishments reflected his deep understanding of how warfare was changing in his century.[77]

During his service in the War of Austrian Succession and the Seven Years' War, Rochambeau had had ample occasion to observe firsthand the lack of organization and discipline, poor preparation, and missed military opportunities due to infighting and petty jealousies among officers. If the royal army of King Louis XVI was to be successful against a world power such as Britain, there was much overhauling to be done. Eventually, in 1761, he published his *Mémoire sur l'infanterie*, and *Mémoires sur recrues et la desertion*. Rochambeau pointed out that in the business of war prompt obedience was expected. He also wrote that an infantry commander should exact fair, but rigorous discipline on his troops. To mete out this discipline he plainly preferred a strong vocal reprimand rather than corporal punishment.[78]

Rochambeau's penchant for strict discipline would put him in excellent stead while marching through America years later. He also advocated for equitable and reasonable pay for his men. At the same time he complained that foreign mercenaries were overcompensated. Rochambeau went on to set detailed quality standards for *casques* (hats) and uniforms, including how long they should be worn before being issued new ones.[79]

Emphasizing reverence for God, which he believed would prevent his men from straying from the straight and narrow path, Rochambeau posited, "Above all other, a soldier must be inspired by his respect for God and his religion."[80] In other words, a godly man is much less likely to disobey orders or to desert. To desert was one of the most dishonorable ways to disobey military orders. Further, Rochambeau wrote that he believed it was the duty of the officer to see that his men attend church every Sunday.[81]

Likewise, George Washington sent directives to his troops in a similar vein: "We can have little hope of the blessing of Heaven on our army if we insult it by our impiety and folly.... Let vice and immorality of every kind be discouraged, as much as possible in your brigade; and as a chaplain is allowed to each regiment, see that the men regularly attend divine worship."[82] Beginning with his service in the Virginia militia, Washington recommended to his soldiers that they "pray, fast, and worship and observe days of thanksgiving."[83]

During his tenure as inspecteur d'infanterie, Rochambeau worked easily under the amenable Duc de Choiseul. Choiseul had expanded and improved the French navy following the devastating Treaty of Paris in 1763. This enabled France to gain the power she needed to compete with the British navy. With Rochambeau at his side, Choiseul planned to do the same with the French army.

As a result of his close attention to the details of making war and to the needs of an unbeatable military machine, Rochambeau began to emerge as a seasoned, perceptive, and creative tactician. In peacetime, he "organized training camps, instituted a series of tactical exercises and maneuvers, studied the lessons of the last war, advocated extended field formations to minimize [the] growing effectiveness of field artillery[,] and instituted as standard companies of chasseurs in each line infantry battalion."[84]

Rochambeau observed that the age of spectacular battles and military displays had passed. He learned through close observation and study on the battlefields of Europe "that war was no longer the sport of kings, but that even military genius of the highest order would be of no avail if the commander had not at his disposal well-trained and well-disciplined troops, and that victory was the reward of long efforts and careful preparations."[85] This was the key to Rochambeau's success in the American Revolution.

Until reforms were instituted, it would be increasingly difficult for France to win a battle, if not a war, due to poor organization within her ranks and especially due to ineptness at the top. Clearly neither the king nor Madame de Pompadour (nor her replacement, Madame du Barry) was qualified to manage the country's politics of war. Further, the country as a whole was not behind the army in the Seven Years' War. The officers sensed this and so missed many occasions to pursue victory.

Rochambeau was interested in every aspect of the military, and he did not limit himself to the obvious when it came to finding ways to improve the fighting arm of his king. He examined and pondered all angles extensively. Rochambeau was fortunate in implementing some reforms since he was in a position to have the ear of the right people, namely, the king and his secretary of war, Duc de Choiseul.

In 1771 Rochambeau received La Grande-Croix de l'Ordre de St-Louis. Louis XIV created this order in 1693 to be awarded to officers for exemplary military merit. Although details are scant during this period of Rochambeau's life (1766–1776), it appears that he found it convenient to have a *pied-à-terre*, a dwelling for temporary use, in Paris. Rochambeau purchased a property suitable to his rising rank at 40 Rue du Cherche-Midi. In the cold, rainy Parisian winters the many fireplaces at the new family address would have been lit to warm the large, icy cold rooms and to welcome their many visitors.

Their four-story home in the capital of France was an elegant one in what is now the sixth arrondissement on the Left Bank. Each of the first three floors had high ceilings and was graced with six large double French windows overlooking the street. The fourth floor had six small windows across the front and was probably used as servants' quarters. Several chimneys reached high above the tall roof. It was only a few minutes' walk in one direction to the expansive Luxemburg gardens or a short walk in the opposite direction to the banks of the Seine.[86]

With the death of Louis XV and the advent of Louis XVI in 1774, mistresses were banished from the wings of government. No longer would the kings' mistresses be able to wield power or influence as had Madame de Pompadour or Madame du Barry. In April 1776, Rochambeau was granted the governorship of Villefranche-en-Roussillon, France, which provided his family additional annual income.[87]

In the spring of 1778 troops began maneuvering in Normandy under Broglie in preparation for a potential operation in England. Rochambeau was put in a difficult position as his commanding officer, Broglie, set out to test two new tactics of troop formation: *l'ordre mince* (thin front) and *l'ordre profund* (deep front). Rochambeau preferred l'ordre mince, which ran counter to Broglie's theory of tactics. Broglie was not pleased with Rochambeau's choice of maneuver; therefore, rather than be at odds with his commander Rochambeau deferred to him.[88]

Early in 1780, Rochambeau made plans to return to the family château to recover from a bout of rheumatism. Although he was at a pinnacle in his career, his health was precarious, and a hiatus from the battlefield would be welcome. Besides, he had asked for time to settle his father's estate. The timing was propitious since the long-planned invasion of England had been abandoned only months earlier. As the seasoned soldier prepared to leave his Paris residence in the middle of the night for the journey to Vendôme, a courier came bearing a message from King Louis XVI ordering him to report immediately to Versailles. Postponing his return home, Rochambeau redirected his horse-drawn carriage to the palace.

CHAPTER TWO

France to the Rescue

*"England will soon repent of having removed the
only check that keeps her colonies in awe."*

—Charles Gravier, Comte de Vergennes

During the twelve-mile journey from Paris to the seat
of French government, Rochambeau must have weighed the possibilities of his next assignment. Surely, the king would send him on
an important mission. Most likely, he would not be leading his regiment into battle against the British after all since the invasion had
been tabled in September 1779. But had the king changed his mind?
Was he planning to launch an invasion across the English Channel
as Rochambeau had long hoped? Indeed, something more revolutionary was about to unfold.

King Louis XVI, along with his foreign minister, Charles-
Gravier, Comte de Vergennes, and his minister of war, the Prince de
Montbarrey, had decided that the French would attack Britain not at
home, but in the heart of her American colonies where it was least
expected. Versailles posited that by aiding the American colonists in
their effort to gain their independence, the French could effectively
terminate the lucrative trade between motherland and colony. In so
doing the French would catch King George III off guard and, in the
end, strike a crushing blow to the British economy. This was a strategy
that had been considered, but the American Congress did not want

French regiments in the thirteen colonies. As late as September 1779 Benjamin Franklin had written that he had no hint that Congress contemplated such an operation.

When Rochambeau went to Versailles, he was presented with the plan for the upcoming American campaign, code name *expédition particulière*. The expedition was carefully outlined to Rochambeau by the king and his ministers. Rochambeau learned that he had been chosen to lead special forces to the New World. He was promoted to lieutenant general and ordered to go directly to the port of Brest to oversee deployment of some four to eight thousand French soldiers along with some foreign recruits. This innovative campaign would provide the vehicle for France to regain her bargaining power in the fast-growing world of international politics. General Rochambeau would be the point man upon whom the success or failure of the mission would depend.

EVENTS PRECEDING ROCHAMBEAU'S SUMMONS

It is important to understand the series of events that led to the commissioning of Rochambeau for the American campaign. Pursuant to the Treaty of Paris of 1763, which officially ended the Seven Years' War in Europe and the French and Indian War in America, France was the greatest loser, and Britain, her arch enemy, the greatest winner. France lost her territory on the North American continent east of the Mississippi River, namely New France (Canada), some of her islands in the Caribbean, and her conquests in India (since 1749), but she gained Martinique and Guadeloupe.

Giving up the sugar trade from the Caribbean islands was an enormous loss to France, whereas losing Canada's fur trade was of much less economic importance. By the same motion of a pen, Spain ceded Florida to Britain and gained western Louisiana, including New Orleans. France had no choice but to give up Louisiana in order to appease Spain. As a result France focused her energy on restoring her honor and lost revenues. Not content with Britain's superiority on land and sea after 1763, France sought a more favorable balance of power, and the Spanish did not support revolt in the British colonies in America because of the example it might set for their own colonies. France wanted to increase her portion of global trade, which would be garnered from the birth of a new trading partner, the United States of America. Ironically it was Britain herself who gave the French the opening they were seeking.

Unwittingly, King George III played right into their hands. After the two wars the British had incurred great financial losses. Naturally, Britain turned to her colonies to replenish her coffers and levied taxes on the colonies. The colonists responded by rebelling against taxation without proper representation in government. Thus, the result of the king's decision to levy outlandish taxes gave France an opportunity to help the rebels oust their common enemy from American shores.

Since virtually all American records were either lost or intentionally destroyed at the time of the revolt against their British overlords, little is known of the methods chosen by colonists to import the supplies and armaments needed to aid the organizing insurgents. France and Spain were willing to help, but covertly. Some insight can be gained from the role of Colonel Jeremiah Lee, successful shipping magnate and devoted revolutionary patriot, who is largely neglected in history books. He served for twenty-five years as a colonel in the British militia at Marblehead, Massachusetts. In 1774, in collusion with French and Spanish shippers, at great danger to himself, Colonel Lee initiated covert importation of armaments. It is unclear whether the arms originated in Holland, France, or Spain, but they were routed to Massachusetts through Lee's shipping agent, Joseph Gardoqui et Fils, in Bilbao, Spain. At the same time, Lee served as liaison between the citizens of Marblehead and the British king's agent in Boston, giving voice to the colonists' grievances.[1]

Colonel Lee was, according to the 1771 Massachusetts tax records, the wealthiest merchant in that colony during the pre-revolutionary period.[2] He was very likely America's largest colonial ship owner, holding full share in twenty-one vessels, mostly fishing and trading schooners from seventy to one hundred twenty tons each, and at least one transoceanic brig.[3]

A letter addressed to Colonel Lee dated February 15, 1775, Bilbao, Spain, and signed, Joseph Gardoqui et Fils, refers to an order being filled at Lee's request. Although the letter never reached Lee, it stands as a record of the clandestine dealings between Lee, the Dutch, and the Spanish. The Gardoqui agent writes, "We were determined at all events to assist you accordingly, we found out means to procure as many Muskets & pistols as were ready made on the parts for the Kings Army, the quantity was but small having only 300 Muskets & Bayonets, and about double the number of Pair of Pistols ready... besides which they must be got with a good deal of Caution & Ship... as to secrecy you may depend it is as much our Interest as any ones as the English...will look sharp in every port...however by having timely advise we can bring them [arms and powder] from Holland on Reasonable Terms & ship them as you desire. [You know we] long to see it settled with all our hearts, but should it be otherwise (which God forbid) command freely and you will find us at your service."[4]

Faithful to the American cause of independence, Colonel Lee met regularly with John Hancock, Samuel Adams, and other members of the secret committee in charge of supplies to plan the procurement of provisions and weapons. Each time that Lee arranged to ship supplies from Spain, Holland, and France to America he risked his business and his life, as the British had him under surveillance. Colonel Lee's last meeting was on April 18, 1775 (the day preceding the now famous Battles of Lexington and Concord), at Newell's Tavern in Menotomy (now Arlington), Massachusetts, with another scheduled for the following morning at the Black Horse Tavern where Lee and two other patriot colleagues from Marblehead were lodging overnight. The meeting scheduled for April 19 did not happen.

During the British army's pre-dawn march to Lexington to engage in the battle that officially began the war, the British raided the tavern. Lee and the others, Azro Orne and Elbridge Gerry, fled and hid in a cornfield. In the early morning hours the men suffered from exposure, and Lee contracted a fever that led to his death on May 10, 1775. Following Lee's untimely demise, Gerry continued working seamlessly with Gardoqui. Lee died an unsung hero of the revolution.[5] Fortunately the incriminating letter did not fall into British hands. It remains, however, proof that aid received from the French, Spanish, and Dutch had begun much earlier than the British suspected.

Only a few months after the untimely death of Colonel Lee in Massachusetts in August 1775, Vergennes, "acting on the advice of his ambassador in London, approved the sending of a secret messenger to the American Continental Congress."[6] Julien-Alexandre Achard de Bonvouloir was the man chosen for the job. His "mission was a major turning point in both American and French diplomacy. When he reached Philadelphia in December 1775 he found as a ready audience the newly appointed Committee of Secret Correspondence."[7] Between December 18 and December 27, Bonvouloir met three times with the committee, including Benjamin Franklin, at Carpenters' Hall.[8] The meetings went extremely well. The committee posed several leading questions to Bonvouloir, asking "if France were disposed favorably toward the Americans, if she would send them two good army engineers, and if she would sell them arms and war supplies in her ports."[9] They also expressed their need of naval support. Bonvouloir gave positive responses to all their requests. In his December 28 report to Versailles he enthusiastically wrote, "Independency is a certainty for 1776."[10] When Vergennes received news of the success of the meeting, he "proposed a major shift in French policy toward the American Revolution."[11]

On September 7, 1776, Vergennes sent a communication to Madrid suggesting that Spain and France become America's allies in the war against Great Britain. "It is certain," he declared, "that if His Majesty seizes this unique opportunity, which perhaps the ages will never present again, we can deal England a blow that would abate her pride and place her power within just bounds, and he would have the glory so dear to his heart of being the benefactor not only of his own people, but of all nations."[12]

It should be noted that France and Spain shared a common familial bond: their two kings, France's Louis XVI and Spain's Carlos III, were of the Catholic Bourbon line and had much to gain by working in concert. It was very risky for America's founding fathers to consider doing anything that would cut off their primary trading partner, Britain, without a contingency plan already in place, so the secret trading with France and Spain enabled them to take the necessary steps to stabilize their precarious economic position as they prepared to sever the cord to Britain.

In the months prior to the signing of the Declaration of Independence, France began using covert means to ship war materiel and supplies to America without detection. To accomplish this end, the French court secretly funded a private company known as Rodrigue Hortalez. Under a pseudonym, noted playwright and diplomat Pierre-Augustin-Caron Beaumarchais owned and directed the new trading company. On April 26, 1776 Vergennes informed Beaumarchais of the king's decision to upgrade the French navy and to support the American insurgents. By May 2 the king decided to release one million livres earmarked for arms to be sent to America under the guise of Hortalez. Spain secretly made an equal contribution of one million livres following that of France. Each supported the cause for their own reasons.[13]

The trading business provided a front that allowed the French to supply Americans with "200 hundred brass cannon, 200,000 pounds of cannon powder, 20,000 fusils [muskets] and quantities of brass mortars, bombs, cannon balls, bayonets, platines [throat plates], clothes, linens, and lead for musket balls."[14] In order to maintain secrecy, Beaumarchais set up a triangular trade route between France, the West Indies, and America. All supplies and munitions were to be bought from France and shipped from France. When Hortalez was dissolved in 1783 it had conducted business in favor of the American Revolution amounting to 42 million livres.[15] In the process of aiding America, Beaumarchais had lost four million livres of his personal fortune.[16] Although he was a well-known figure in France, known primarily for writing plays such as *The Barber of Seville* and *The Marriage of Figaro,* Beaumarchais was one of the earliest, most committed, and persistent French citizens to come to the aid of the American cause.

There was growing excitement in France for the sake of American liberty. In response to the request of the Continental Congress to Bonvouloir, volunteers were encouraged to serve in America, and many answered the call. Beaumarchais also was responsible for recruiting some of the earliest volunteers to join Washington's retinue. High on the list were military engineers who would be employed in the Continental army by George Washington. These included General Louis Le Bègue de Presle Duportail, French chief engineer, and Pierre-Charles L'Enfant, captain of engineers. Both served with Washington for the duration of the Revolutionary War. Likewise, there were officers like the young Marie-Joseph-Paul-Yves-Roch-Gilbert du Motier, Marquis de Lafayette, and his mentor, Johann, Baron de Kalb. De Kalb, a Bavarian by birth, had served in the French Royal Army and came to America in 1777 to join the uprising. Lafayette was an enthusiastic early supporter of the American cause for independence, coming to America by his own means and eventually working under the command of Washington. He would serve as an important, though sometimes impulsive, assistant to Washington. Those who returned to France brought tales of the beauty of the country and of the riches to be gained. Paris was abuzz.

With the creation of the American Congress, emissaries were sent to Europe to help raise funds for the emerging nation. John Adams, in his role as American diplomat, travelled to the Netherlands in search of monetary support for the United States. At first Adams was unsuccessful until the American victory at Saratoga in October 1777. It was only then that the Dutch felt assured that the states had the possibility of winning, and they were ready to support the colonists overtly.[17] Underscoring the differences in perspective, Jonathan R. Dull in his *Diplomatic History of the American Revolution* states that two "major causes of the French entering into the war in 1778 seem to have been the completion of their [naval] rearmament and the deterioration of their relations with Britain rather than the sudden news of Saratoga."[18]

FRANCE OPENLY ALLIES WITH AMERICA

On February 6, 1778, a Treaty of Alliance between France and the United States was signed in the Paris apartment of Silas Deane, Agent of the Colonies. The French signatory, Conrad Alexandre Gérard, held the titles of Syndic of the City of Strasbourg and Secretary of His Majesty's Council of State. The three American signatories were: Benjamin Franklin, deputy to the United States Congress from Pennsylvania; Silas Deane, deputy from Connecticut; and Arthur Lee, counselor at law. All three American diplomats were instrumental in securing this prestigious agreement.[19]

The Treaty of Alliance was a treaty of friendship that made France the first nation to officially recognize the newly formed United States as an independent entity. It stipulated that neither France nor America would agree to a separate peace with Great Britain and that American independence would be a condition of any future peace agreement. Another treaty signed on the same day, named the Treaty of Amity and Commerce, "promot[ed] trade and commercial ties between the two countries."[20] In addition, there was a secret clause of this alliance allowing for Spain and other European powers to sign on at a future date.[21] On May 4, 1778, the Treaty of Alliance was ratified by the United States Congress.[22] France would now openly help America overthrow British rule by sending troops and funds.

George Washington received this good news at Valley Forge, Pennsylvania. The Marquis de Lafayette, just twenty-one at the time, had ridden "down Berwyn Road to headquarters, burst into the General's presence and with tears of joy threw his arms about the somewhat startled Anglo-Saxon, and planted two kisses, one on each cheek of His Excellency."[23] Washington expressed uncharacteristic glee and thankfulness. "It having pleased the Almighty Ruler of the Universe to defend the cause of the United States, and finally to raise up a powerful friend among the princes of the earth, to establish our liberty and independency upon a lasting foundation; it becomes us to set apart a day for gratefully acknowledging the divine goodness, and celebrating the important event, which we owe to his divine interposition."[24] In accordance with Washington's wishes, the next day there were great festivities, beginning with religious services and a military parade and ending with an elegant outdoor feast for fifteen hundred guests. The king of France was toasted with gusto!

Unless France could be assured of the aid of the Spanish navy, France's role in the American Revolution would be limited. The price for Spain's help was going to be high, for the bottom line was that Spain had little interest in the independence of America or even in reversing the balance of power. Spain had her own objectives to consider: 1) regain Gibraltar and Minorca; 2) protect her colonies in America from British incursion; 3) recapture Florida, most importantly the port of Pensacola; and 4) regain Jamaica, then in British hands. Spain vowed to attain her goals any way possible. If she could not succeed by bargaining with the British, then joining with France would be a possibility.[25]

Spain offered to mediate between France and England. In so doing, she learned what each country wanted most and by the same token what each was least willing to concede. Britain wanted Spain to remain neutral in the coming conflict. Spain did not. Britain could have offered the return of Gibraltar and Minorca to mollify her; she did not offer it.

Spain vacillated between supporting the American rebels or England. If she supported the former, she might ignite a similar uprising in her own country and risk the overthrow of her king. If she supported England, she would be going against her bloodline and her religious ties with France. Count d'Aranda, Spanish ambassador to the French court, believed that an independent United States would pose less of a threat to Spanish interests than a united British Empire.[26]

Finally, Spain was ready to enter into an agreement with France and the United States against their common foe. At Spain's request, the Bourbon cousins agreed to launch a joint invasion of Britain since Spain believed that the direct attack would be a quick one and that she would not suffer severe financial losses at home or in her colonies. Spain reiterated her above-stated objectives, and the two countries signed the Franco-Spanish Alliance (also called the Treaty of Aranjuez) on April 12, 1779.[27] Spain declared war on England. The one hundred twenty-one French and Spanish ships of the line sent in preparation for an invasion into British coastal waters greatly outnumbered the ninety British ships.[28]

Meanwhile, in the lower Mississippi valley, "the Spanish governor of Louisiana, Bernardo de Gálvez (1746–86; the city of Galveston is named after him) proved to be one of the war's most successful generals. In a series of brilliant campaigns from 1779 to 1781, he cleared the lower Mississippi valley and gulf coast of British troops, winning his greatest victory at the siege of Pensacola."[29] These heroic efforts by the Spanish forces were crucial to the success of the American insurgents, although they did not take place along the Atlantic seaboard. Much of Spain's contribution was, therefore, of an indirect nature but, nonetheless, important.

France and Spain wanted to divert British military resources from their colonies to England's coast while the intended invasion was considered. Skirmishes followed, but the invasion of Britain was abandoned in September 1779. Gálvez had done his part by diverting British resources to Louisiana and Florida in order to achieve Spain's goals. In all, it had taken three years to convince Spain to enter the fight for American independence.

One of the results of the expert diplomacy conducted by Vergennes, sometimes in concert with other European courts, prior to sending Rochambeau to America, was the diversion of a portion of British military resources away from the waterways and battle-fields of America. One such diversion was the planned joint invasion of France and Spain on England. When the attack was called off in September 1779, King George III retained some resources until the danger had passed. In so doing, his forces were diminished in America, leaving him to protect two fronts on the Atlantic (i.e., England and the east coast of America) plus the areas of Gálvez's actions in the Mississippi valley and Florida. And also, there was the ever-present threat of danger to the control of trade in the West Indies. All countries with colonies had to be on guard. The British were forced to maintain adequate numbers of ships of the line in European, Caribbean, and Mississippi area waters. The consequential division of their military assets facilitated the American cause enormously by preparing the way for Vergennes to send Rochambeau to America.

ROCHAMBEAU PREPARES FOR THE EXPEDITION

France would need to choose carefully who would lead their forces to America. General Rochambeau was particularly well suited for the assignment. At fifty-five he was a seasoned officer and had taken part in numerous sieges over his thirty-seven years in the service of his country. He was also endowed with the patient endurance he would need to accomplish France's mission. Family members accompanying him included his son Donatien, Vicomte de Rochambeau, and his nephew, Comte Luis-François de Lauberdière. Both served as his aides-de-camp. Lauberdière expressed his feelings about participating in the expedition: "France was looking to take revenge for the Peace of 1763."[30] Simultaneously, the French cabinet appointed Chevalier Charles-Louis de Ternay as admiral of the fleet that would transport the troops to America.

One question loomed large within the gilded walls of Versailles: Did France really have the resources to carry out her ambitious plans to help the colonists? King Louis XVI was told they had the hard currency necessary to launch the fleet and to aid General Washington's struggling army. In reality Jacques Necker, the minister of finance, had overstated France's financial stability in his account to the king. There was, however, no question that France had the military means to carry out the mission in early 1780. In fact, the French army was well trained and poised for action, thanks to the efforts of Rochambeau as inspector of the army and to many others. The improvements in the organization of the French army and the increases in her navy would be put to use in Rochambeau's American expedition.

During the eighteenth century there was a movement in Europe toward the rights of man as inspired by Enlightenment philosophers such as Montesquieu, Voltaire, and Rousseau. Even though His Most Royal Christian Majesty King Louis XVI of France had levied inordinate taxes on his subjects, the twenty-six-year-old monarch nevertheless concerned himself with the ordinary people. He improved conditions in the navy by insisting on proper hygiene, began an overhaul of the army, and had taken the risk of supporting the newborn American democracy overtly since 1778.[31] It is ironic that for all his good intentions and benevolent deeds, the path King Louis XVI chose would eventually lead him and his wife, Marie Antoinette, to the guillotine.

On December 9, 1779, Admiral de Ternay was officially appointed chief of a naval squadron at the seaport of Brest, and he would command the fleet of the *expédition particulière* to America. He arrived at Brest on the Brittany shore to view his convoy on March 1, 1780. Before leaving Versailles, Rochambeau requested an increase in the king's promised number of soldiers from six thousand to eight thousand. He arrived at Brest a few weeks after Ternay only to discover that many of the expected transports were not in port. Only seven ships of the line were in the harbor since another fleet had recently been dispatched to the West Indies, thereby reducing the number he had envisioned. Rochambeau, Ternay, and Hector, governor of Brest harbor, quickly sent for more transports from the ports of Bordeaux and St. Malo. Thankfully, some arrived, but far too few. Despite their disappointment, the two officers complied with the king's order to load as many men as possible in the vessels at hand and to depart straightaway.

Consequently, Rochambeau and Ternay were forced to make sacrifices by sailing with a smaller-than-planned squadron. Four regiments, the Bourbonnais, Royal Deux-Ponts, Soissonnais, Saintonge, and a partial regiment of artillery, the Auxonne, along with part of the Duc de Lauzun's Legion (altogether 5,500 troops) were crowded into the available transports.[32]

Rochambeau's priorities were evident as preparations were made for the journey. The general made sure that the most qualified men were chosen, that there was space for the essential heavy siege artillery, and that he had the resources to pay for his needs as well as to aid the allies. Rochambeau wrote: "We will pay our allies for everything, even the straw for the soldier."[33] All the horses were left behind in Brest, even Rochambeau's own favorite steeds. "I have to part company with two battle-horses that I can never replace," he lamented. "I do so with the greatest sorrow, but I do not want to have to reproach myself with their having taken up the room of twenty men."[34] With the next convoy, the king promised to send a second division with two additional regiments, the Neustrie and the Anhalt, plus one-third of the artillery, as well as the remaining one-third of the Lauzun Legion.[35]

While these preparations were going on in Brest, a British fleet was also organizing to carry critical re-stocking supplies to their troops in America. The admiral and the general at Brest seaport were well aware of this plan and were eager to reach America ahead of the English for tactical reasons. Furthermore, they didn't want to risk crossing paths with the enemy in mid Atlantic.

When all was in readiness, the weather refused to cooperate, leading to a delay of over two weeks. The French fleet was forced to wait for the wind to shift, to assure them a swift departure and send them safely beyond the known shoals and rocky peninsula, Pointe du

Raz, the westernmost land's end along the Finistère coast of Brittany. Of course, the British were also delayed by the same weather patterns, storms, and unfavorable winds.

FRENCH FLEET SAILS FOR AMERICA

Finally, on May 2, 1780, with winds out of the favorable quarter, the French fleet set sail with the outgoing tide, ahead of the enemy. With a little luck, they would reach their destination before the British. Morale was running high. Officers and men alike had their hearts set on this great adventure to aid the American cause for freedom from the hated British.

Two adventurous young military men, Alexandre Berthier and his brother, Charles-Louis, had heard of the campaign to free America and were desperate to join Rochambeau.[36] Alexandre was trained as a military engineer and had a considerable aptitude in the art of mapmaking. He and his brother, who had similar skills, hastily sent a letter of request that they ship out with Rochambeau. They were told that the letter would not reach the general in time, and they would need to find another ship to take them to America. Months later the Berthier brothers caught up with the French expedition in Rhode Island, and both served with great distinction throughout the entire campaign. Alexandre, like many of the other men with the expedition, kept a meticulous journal, which survived, in addition to his beautifully detailed maps that were used to guide the army through many difficult and perilous routes. The Berthier maps have been an invaluable resource for the study of Rochambeau's campaign in America.

Before sailing, General Rochambeau had been given a sealed envelope containing further details of instructions from the king. It was dated March 1, 1780, penned from Versailles. The general was not to open it until he had been at sea for ten days. The king's instructions outlined General Rochambeau's duty and discipline in great detail.

The letter was written in the third person and began with an overview of the purpose of the trip, naming the leaders, Rochambeau and Ternay. It stated: "The intentions of His Majesty are...," followed by eight articles of instructions, beginning with the first and most important one: "That the general to whom His Majesty entrusts the command of his troops should always, and in all cases, be under the command of General Washington." The document was signed simply: "Prince de Montbarrey" (minister of war).[37]

The ships were sluggish due to their substantial loads of crew, military men, heavy artillery, and supplies. Not only were they carrying twelve thousand soldiers and sailors (the sailors actually outnumbered the troops), but also about five hundred servants, thirty women, and four children.[38] The women were wives of officers and troops and most served as cooks during the land portion of the expedition. Rochambeau himself had embarked with three servants.

Baron Ludwig von Closen, captain of the Royal Deux-Ponts, sailed aboard the *Comtesse de Noailles,* a typical troopship. In his journal, the baron gave his impressions of the ship and the conditions during the journey. He described the *Comtesse* as a thirty-ton ship about ninety-five feet long with a beam of thirty feet. For nearly seventy days, she was home to twelve naval and ten army officers, their domestics, a crew of forty-five, and 350 enlisted men of the Royal Deux-Ponts regiment.[39] The ship was so crowded that even the officers had to sleep ten to a cabin. At mealtime, twenty-two people at a time were squeezed into a mess hall just fifteen feet long, twelve feet wide, and only four and one-half feet high.[40] Closen wrote of his happy surprise at being appointed aide-de-camp to Rochambeau at their arrival in America.[41]

As the days passed, the stench from the men grew in intensity, and the unpleasant odors from the cows, sheep, and chickens that were aboard were nauseating. Edible livestock were a necessary part of the food supply for the long journey, so their presence was a mixed blessing.

Aboard the flagship *Duc de Bourgogne,* quarters were somewhat more spacious but still cramped. The *Duc de Bourgogne,* a ship of the line, was 190 feet long with a forty-six-foot beam and had a crew of 940 men. Large numbers of men were needed to operate the ship's eighty cannon. To fire just one of the thirty largest guns—the 36-pounders—required a crew of fifteen. Hundreds more were needed to operate the fifty other cannon on board—the 18- and 8-pounders.[42]

The *Duc de Bourgogne* also carried the treasure in her hold. This hard currency was brought to support the campaign and to provide funds for Washington's ragtag army. The lack of funds to pay, clothe, and properly outfit soldiers of the Continental army had led to the serious problem of desertions; thus, monetary help from the French was critical to the success of the campaign.

General Rochambeau had fought hard to sail with a full complement of soldiers. Even though he had been able to muster enough ships to carry 5,500 soldiers, Rochambeau felt the headcount was woefully inadequate according to his original plan. In his memoirs, he disparaged his ministers, saying that their choice to send fewer men and fewer ships was not judicious and undercut his chances for success. Rochambeau knew the urgency of his voyage and the importance of his mission to come to the aid of the American colonists as quickly and as fully as possible. He had had no choice but to sail with the compromised assets the king and his ministers had provided in the short time before embarking.

Rochambeau had hoped that the French fleet would clear land before the British left England bound for America with reinforcements. He knew that his fleet with its large convoy of troops and supplies was more heavily laden than the British fleet. As a result, the French fleet moved more slowly, was less maneuverable, and was easier to spot on the high seas. The following was the composition of the French convoy according to the diary of eighteen-year-old Jean-Baptiste-Antoine de Verger, a sublieutenant in the Royal Deux-Ponts regiment:

THE FRENCH CONVOY

Warships [Ships of the Line]:[43]
Duc de Bourgogne, 80 guns, flagship,
Admiral M. [le Chevalier] de Ternay, *squadron commander*
Flag Captain, M. [le Comte] de Médine
Neptune, 74 guns, Captain M. Destouches
Conquérant, 74 guns, Captain M. de La Grandière
Eveillé, 64 guns, Captain M. Le Gardeur de Tilly
Provence, 64 guns, Captain M. de Lombard
Jason, 64 guns, Captain M. de La Clocheterie
Ardent, 64 guns, Captain M. [le Chevalier] de Marigny
Frigates:
Surveillante, 32 guns, Captain M. [le Chevalier] de Cillart [de Villeneuve]
Amazone, 32 guns, Captain M. [le Comte] de La Pérouse
Cutters, Troop and Cargo Transports:
Guêpe, 16 guns, Captain M. de Maulevrier
Fantasque, partially armored supply ship outfitted as a hospital
Plus 32 other transports

The Army of the French Expedition
Regiments:
First Brigade:
Bourbonnais: Colonel Marquis de Laval
Royal Deux-Ponts: Colonel Comte [Christian] de Deux-Ponts
Second Brigade:
Soissonnais: Colonel Comte de Saint-Maîme
Saintonge: Colonel Comte de Custine
Artillery:
First Battalion: Auxonne regiment, Colonel M. d'Aboville
Mixed Cavalry and Infantry:
Legion of Lauzun: Colonel Duc de Lauzun
Army Staff:
Comte de Rochambeau,
*Grand Cross of the Royal and Military Order of Saint Louis, lieutenant general
of the King's armies and commander in chief*
Baron de Vioménil, *commander of the Order of Saint-Louis, major general*
Chevalier de Chastellux, *major general and chief of staff*
Comte de Vioménil, *major general*
M. de Béville, *brigadier and quartermaster general*
M. de Tarlé, *intendant*[44]
Others included chaplains, physicians, and surgeons,
the king's solicitor, and a recorder.

When the French convoy was barely out of port ten hours, fair winds were exchanged for a mighty storm, severely damaging some ships. Although a few naval officers suggested that the badly damaged ships return to port for repairs, Chevalier de Ternay was reluctant to have vessels leave the convoy for any reason. Fortunately, the crews were able to make repairs while at sea and averted further delay.[45]

According to Verger's journal, two foreign ships crossed their path when the fleet sailed off the coast of Spain and Portugal. Upon close inspection, one turned out to be Swedish and posed no threat. The other was indeed a foe, but just before the British ship seemed about to attack the French frigate *Surveillante,* the enemy commander called it off and sailed away.[46]

After the near-engagement with the British warship off the Iberian Peninsula, most of the ensuing days of the Atlantic crossing were peaceful. When the French fleet approached the American coastline, Admiral de Ternay followed the southern route to take advantage of the trade winds. As a result, the voyage was longer, but there was less chance of encountering Admiral Graves's British fleet.

For many days during the voyage the convoy did not sight any ships, and the weather was fair. The travelers had time to marvel at sea life during the days and the spectacle of the phosphorescent seas at night. Many whales, dolphins, and birds followed the ships. The men seemed to especially enjoy watching the antics of flying fish, many of which they caught and fried in butter for a delicious repast.[47] They also caught other fish, including large tuna, all of which were a welcome addition to their diet as food stores diminished.[48]

On June 11, the monotony of the voyage was interrupted when a British vessel was sighted on a quiet sea, causing the crew to race to their posts and prepare to meet the enemy. As the vessel approached, they could see the sloop, a single-masted, fore-and-aft-rigged boat riding low in the water with a cargo of fish. The *Surveillante* and the *Amazone* gave chase. After eight hours, the British surrendered to the French who commandeered the enemy's hold, which was full of cod and herring, for their own benefit.[49]

LOOKING FOR A SAFE HARBOR

What conditions would await General Rochambeau and Admiral de Ternay when they finally made port? Had the British been successful in the North as well as in the South? Sailing for many weeks without word of events that might have transpired since their departure from France, anything could have happened and not necessarily in their favor. Most likely Rochambeau and Ternay had been advised of their probable destination before leaving France, but the crew had no such knowledge. New England was the best choice, Newport being the first choice and Boston the second. Would either of the ports in New England receive the "special delivery" of French troops?

Unsure of where they would find a friendly harbor, the convoy followed the trades on a heading for the Antilles, a chain of islands in the West Indies, before heading north. They were almost into the tropics when a British cutter crossed their path, only one week after they had overcome the fish-laden sloop. The cutter, similar to a sloop, but with the mast set a bit farther astern, was captured by the *Surveillante* while heading under full sail toward the islands from Charleston, South Carolina, on an important mission. The French obtained startling information from the foreign crew and from the secret papers they found on board.[50.]

According to Admiral de Ternay's account, the cutter bore the message of the British capture of Charleston with details that the Americans, under the command of General Benjamin Lincoln, "had surrendered to British General [Henry] Clinton on May 12 after a five weeks' siege." Ternay added that "there were five English officers aboard; and [that] he placed an auxiliary officer from the *Surveillante* in command of the captured ship."[51] This stunning news changed the plans and course of the French fleet. That same day, Admiral de Ternay called a meeting of the captains of his squadron during which they agreed to take a northerly course along the east coast of America. Had they arrived at Charleston earlier, they would have lent assistance to the besieged Americans. Instead, they bypassed Charleston and sailed toward Chesapeake Bay.

Nearing Bermuda on June 20, the French fleet sighted five enemy ships led by a frigate. The frigate was within firing range and caught between the French lead ship and the rest of the fleet. As she headed out to rejoin the safety of her convoy, the enemy frigate had to first pass by the entire French line. Admiral de Ternay ordered his ships to open fire. Soon the two lines faced each other and exchanged cannonade. Both lines received broadside damage, but nothing of major consequence. By six o'clock that evening the battle lines drew off in opposite directions. Ternay decided not to give chase. By first light in the morning, the British were nowhere in sight.[52]

Later, Ternay was severely criticized for not being more aggressive in this battle.[53] He had held two distinct advantages: more ships and better positioning. In choosing not to pursue the British ships, Ternay gave up his advantage and neither captured an enemy ship nor inflicted significant damage. Nonetheless, Rochambeau commended Admiral de Ternay for his action and favorable outcome in this encounter.

Ternay probably selected the wiser course by not escalating the battle, as his greater goal was to deliver his precious cargo of troops and treasure safely to an American harbor. Besides, it was their fifty-first day at sea and many of the sailors and troops were suffering from the poor living conditions. A long protracted battle would have been difficult to sustain under these circumstances. So the fleet sailed northward.

Ternay's biographer, Maurice Linÿer de la Barbée, in his book *Le Chevalier de Ternay,* writes that during or just after the June 20 combat with British ships two French transports, *Aimable Marie and Ile de France,* were lost in the ensuing fog. The two ships were most likely cut off from their convoy in the confusion of battle and because of the fog were unable to find their sister ships.

Shortly thereafter, Ternay convened a council of war to assess past and future strategy, including the probability of landing at

Newport. Although many deterrents could prevent the convoy from anchoring safely at Newport, it was still their first choice. The variables included weather, enemy ships, and all matter of unexpected events that could alter the course of ships sailing in enemy waters.

On July 4, near twilight, the French expedition reached the mouth of the Chesapeake where they began to set anchor. Suddenly, alerts were signaled and anchors were quickly weighed. Eleven large enemy ships approached, and as darkness descended two unidentified frigates sailed in amongst the French fleet.[54] During the remainder of the night the ships cautiously tacked in and out, not knowing exactly with whom they were dealing, but certain they were not friendly ships. Lights were doused and some shots fired. Sailing ships do not fight well at night. There is too much risk of firing on one's own vessels.

When the sun finally rose, they saw that the ships were indeed British, and the French pursued them northward, but lost them in the fog. The French later learned that the ships they were chasing were bearing 2,800 British troops back to New York after the surrender of Charleston.

Once again, Ternay's fleet had failed to hurt the enemy, but the French expeditionary force was safe. Regarding Admiral de Ternay's actions in this incident at the mouth of the Chesapeake, Rochambeau wrote in his memoirs: "He preferred the preservation of his convoy to the personal glory of having captured a hostile vessel."[55]

The French flotilla sailed north once again. On July 7 the council of war held on board the *Duc de Bourgogne* confirmed the decision to head for Newport. Newport had been the first choice from the start. It was hoped that Newport would welcome the fleet. They seized one more British prize off the Virginia coast. No harm was done; only a few shots across the bow were necessary to halt the enemy. They captured the crew and garnered valuable news that General Clinton had indeed returned to New York after the British victory in Charleston.[56] Little by little Rochambeau and Ternay gathered fragments of information regarding battles won and lost and the rebels' progress from the ships they encountered. The French continued to chart a northerly bearing toward Newport. Boston had been considered but deemed far too risky.

The relative inactivity and long journey of almost seventy days at sea had taken its toll on these soldiers of action. With food stocks dwindling, time was running out for the French expeditionary force. Many of the sailors and seafaring soldiers needed urgent medical attention. Heatstroke and sunburn were rampant. Conditions were especially bad on the overcrowded troopships. Nearing the end of the voyage, they had sparse rations and little water to drink. It was like being in a prison cell shared with hundreds of inmates. Their health suffered from their meager diet, which was deficient in vitamins and minerals.[57] Inevitably, many on the ships died of scurvy, malnutrition, or dysentery before they could set foot in America.

According to the firsthand account of an enlisted soldier, Georg Daniel Flohr, who shipped over with the Deux-Ponts regiment, the conditions on board his ship, the *Comtesse de Noailles,* were deplorable. Flohr was the son of a German butcher from the Duchy of Zweibrücken and was just shy of his twenty-fourth birthday as his ship sailed into port in Rhode Island. The Atlantic crossing was the most miserable time he had spent in the service of the king of France.[58]

Most likely Flohr shared his simple linen hammock with another soldier. Either they stuffed themselves into it together or they took turns, with the other one sleeping on the deck; or if their watch duty did not coincide, one slept in the hammock by night and the other used it by day. Flohr was quoted as saying: "He who wanted to lie well had better stayed home."[59] Flohr witnessed "daily our fellow brothers thrown into the depths of the ocean."[60] The dead were disposed of at night so as not to demoralize the others. "No one was surprised, though, since all our foodstuffs were rough and bad enough to destroy us."[61]

Flohr's journal, a valuable resource for understanding the conditions encountered on the journey, lay untouched in a library for one hundred years. Its discovery in the 1970s shed new light on the expedition from the vantage point of a German-born French soldier in Rochambeau's army.[62]

The French were praying for a warm welcome in Newport, and let it be soon! It was another hot and steamy day. As the mercury rose, the winds died down and the fog moved in, slowing their entrance into Narragansett Bay and Newport Harbor. As a precaution, Ternay ordered the ships to three knots and drums beat at prescribed intervals to identify their location and avoid collision.[63]

Later on, as the fog began to lift, Ternay found that the two errant French transports, *Aimable Marie* and *Ile de France*, had not managed to rejoin the convoy. As soon as possible after landing, as stated by biographer Barbée, Ternay sent the frigate *Hermione* in search of them, to no avail. Some accounts say that eventually *Aimable Marie* found her way to Newport and that the *Ile de France* sailed into Boston harbor, tardy but safe.[64]

WELCOME BY FRENCH LILIES

As the ships rounded Port Judith, the lookouts finally got a view of coastal Rhode Island through the lifting fog. They immediately recognized the two white flags flying on either side of the entrance to Narragansett Bay. The flags were emblazoned with the fleurs-de-lis, the unblemished lilies of France, and served as signals that were agreed upon several months ago with the Marquis de Lafayette when he was last in France.[65] After his departure from France in March, Lafayette sent word to Newport to set out the flags, indicating a safe port for the French convoy. Since it was not known when or even if the French army might actually arrive, the all-important signal flags had been set out daily for weeks when conditions were safe.

At last, the forward lookout shouted to confirm that the bay was clear of enemy ships and that the American pilot boat was approaching to guide the ships into their moorings.

General Rochambeau, at 5'6", was short and stocky with the ruddy complexion of a soldier who had weathered the elements through many campaigns. In spite of his diminutive stature, he was respected, even beloved by his officers, as he stood on the tender, eager to set foot on American soil. However, his polished appearance belied the wretched circumstances of his troops who had suffered from their long confinement in miserable conditions.

The Newporters were dubious about the arrival of this great flotilla of French ships. After all, they were recovering from three years of occupation by British forces and were not sure of the intent of the latest arrival of foreign troops. It would take a few days before the colonists fully realized that the French had come to assist them in their great cause without seeking any material or territorial gains for themselves.

The American Revolution, already underway for six years, was losing momentum with a lack of funds compounded by the recent crushing defeats at Savannah and Charleston. However, with the French convoy came the experience of officers and troops who had proven themselves on the battlefields of Europe. In addition, hidden in the bowels of the flagship was the hard currency so much needed by General Washington's army.

As Rochambeau, commander of the *expédition particulière*, prepared to go ashore, he and his troops sensed that with them came the winds of enormous change in the balance of power in the New World and beyond.

The great Roman military strategist, Julius Caesar, said in 49 BC, *"Alea iacta est"* (The die is cast). In America, the wheels were in motion; there was no turning back. Thanks to General Rochambeau and his men, the war for American independence was about to take a positive turn toward freedom for the colonists.

CHAPTER THREE

Hope Arrives in Newport

*"There is little doubt that our not being able to crush this
reinforcement immediately upon its arrival gave additional
ammunition to the spirit of rebellion, whose almost expiring embers
began to blaze up afresh upon its appearance."*

—GENERAL HENRY CLINTON

AS ROCHAMBEAU AND HIS TROOPS prepared to disembark
after their long voyage, they were hoping for a pleasant welcome at
Newport. The American cause was badly in need of a jumpstart in
terms of morale, funds, and troop numbers. Rochambeau was aware
that Washington and the Continental army were at a low ebb following
one of the hardest winters on record at their Morristown, New Jersey,
winter encampment from which they were still recuperating. The
winter of 1779–1780 was the worst in memory with twenty-eight
separate snowstorms at Jockey Hollow just outside Morristown where
the Continentals had made their camp. They used the log huts the
army had built for an earlier encampment. Twelve men shared a hut
with only threadbare blankets between them and the freezing temper-
atures. The soldiers were inadequately dressed; some had no shoes.
Comfort was but a memory in the plummeting cold that accompanied the deepening snow. The snow had built up until it stood four
to six feet deep. The pathways and what resembled a road were lined
with banks of snow twelve feet high. Food was in short supply. There

was a little bread and not much else. Joseph Plumb Martin, an enlisted man from Milford, Connecticut, wrote of the severity of the conditions there, saying that he was literally starving. He had no food for four days and four nights. One man in his company fell to roasting his shoe leather and chewing on it. It was impossible to make one's way to the commissary to fetch supplies in the deep snow. New York Harbor was frozen beneath eight feet of ice.[1]

Anchoring the *Duc de Bourgogne* well offshore, Rochambeau and his immediate staff transferred to the *Amazone,* which was piloted by an American familiar with navigating the harbor. Rochambeau, in full military dress, probably stood at attention on the foredeck of the *Amazone* as they sailed quietly into Newport Harbor amidst the receding fog. Gold braid trimmed the edge of his hat and uniform, and showing beneath his navy-blue jacket was a red vest and matching breeches. He wore his above-the-knee black leather boots and the requisite spotless white gloves. Each officer carried at least two uniforms, one for standard military use and the other for ceremonial occasions such as this.

In spite of the trials of the journey, Rochambeau's officers and enlisted men were fully clad in uniform as well, crowding the rails to see what the New World promised them. They had endured the deprivations and dangers of the high seas at wartime to find this port. Claude Blanchard, chief commissary of the French expeditionary force, recounted the hours just prior to landing: "This was a great joy; our sick people came out of their beds, and this sight seemed to restore them to health. I am writing in the first moment of excitement; one should have been at sea, in the midst of the sick and dying, to feel it thoroughly."[2] Everyone was thankful that no British ships were sighted as they sailed into the harbor.

The town of Newport appeared quiet, as if asleep, although it was still daylight. The shutters and doors were firmly fastened. Georg Daniel Flohr described the first encounter between the French ships and the Newporters. He saw some small sloops approaching, and as they drew closer, he could see that the boats were manned by blacks, whom Flohr called Moors. The greeters offered apples and cherries for sale and did not seem to fear the French. The French had not expected this type of reception but rather thought they might see some dignitaries coming out to welcome their benefactors on this auspicious occasion.[3]

When Rochambeau and his staff went ashore to talk with the Newport residents, they assured the latter they were not invaders, but instead had come to assist them in the battle against the British. General Rochambeau made it clear that he would pay in silver coin for anything he and his army needed, not in the valueless Continental currency. They would not commandeer or demand, as the British had done in the recent past. The Newporters began to relax, but were still wary. The advance party spent their first night on dry land.

It had been a long time of difficult trials for the Rhode Island locals. It was no wonder they were skittish when they saw a huge fleet anchor offshore. They had been occupied and ill treated by the British from 1776–1779. The British had burned some of their homes, cut down their trees for firewood, and greatly depleted local supplies. It was no wonder the Newporters did not rush out to meet the French. They were not sure the flotilla was a friendly one.

Colonel de Deux-Ponts, commander of the Deux-Ponts regiment, related in his journal: "We did not meet with that reception on landing which we expected and ought to have had. A coldness and a reserve appeared to me to be characteristic of the American race. They appear to have little of that enthusiasm one would suppose to belong to a people fighting for its liberties."[4] In the 1921 article entitled "A Few French Officers To Whom We Owe Much," Miss M. E. Powel cited several accounts of the disappointment felt by the French on landing that afternoon. But what they interpreted as the lack of enthusiasm among the few remaining inhabitants of Newport was not coldness. It was more the apathy of suffering and exhaustion after a long period of stress and deprivation.[5]

The Newport Tories, loyalists who supported the British and King George III, had been undermining French aid since August

1778 when French Admiral D'Estaing briefly landed four thousand French troops in Rhode Island, preparing to fight the British who occupied Newport. The Loyalists insisted that the French intended to take control of their land, when in truth, the latter been sent by the king of France to help the Americans. When British Admiral Howe appeared offshore, D'Estaing quickly withdrew his troops. Amidst miscommunication about an incoming British fleet and a bad storm off the coast that left his ships in disarray, D'Estaing abandoned Newport. The French admiral had disappointed the colonists, and the Tories took advantage of the confusion, placing the blame on the French. D'Estaing's second unsuccessful attempt to aid the Americans was in Savannah, Georgia, in 1779.

Following the landing of Rochambeau, the Tories hounded their neighbors by starting rumors and even publishing false accounts in the newspapers to the effect that the French were here to claim land in the name of their king. They spread alarm by declaring that the French would impose cruel laws and disagreeable customs on the local people. Since the end of the French and Indian War in 1763, during which the British and their Indian allies fought against the French and their Indian allies, the British had propagated prejudice against the French among the colonists. They fostered anti-French, anti-Catholic sentiment for seventeen years, depicting the French as unreliable.

On the other hand, the Comte de Clermont-Crèvecoeur, artillery lieutenant and diarist in the French expedition, blamed the British, writing, "They had made the French seem so odious to the Americans…saying that we were dwarfs, pale, ugly specimens who lived exclusively on frogs and snails."[6]

SOUR WELCOME TURNS SWEET

Because of this negative sentiment toward the French, Rochambeau needed to actively prove to the people of Rhode Island that the French were sincere and did not intend to take their land or their liberty. Mathieu Dumas, one of Rochambeau's aides-de-camp, who arrived with the expedition, gave a more positive report. He said, "We were welcomed with the acclamations of a small number of patriots that remained on this island (of Rhode Island) lately occupied by the English, who had been forced to abandon it. Scarcely had the arrival of the French squadron been signaled, when the authorities and the principal inhabitants of the neighboring towns hastened to welcome us."[7]

The newcomers soon earned goodwill by their friendly and honorable interactions with the New Englanders. It did not take long for the Americans to befriend the French and cast off their misconceptions. The shutters were gradually opened and doors unlocked. American General William Heath, who commanded the Rhode Island militia, arrived just in time on the night of July 11 to receive General Rochambeau and Admiral de Ternay as his honored guests.[8] The following day, in fact, much was righted. The Newport town fathers, knowing that the people had little money to spend, distributed boxes of candles to those who wanted them. The town was systematically illuminated on July 13 and 14 as a celebration of the French arrival.

Fireworks and rockets were fired off in front of the State House. "A few days later the bell rang till after midnight…. The Whigs put thirteen lights in the window, the Tories, or doubtfuls, 4 or 6. The Quakers did not chuse their lights shd. shine before men, and their windows were broken."[9] According to the journal of Crèvecoeur, who was still on board his ship in the harbor during the illumination, "The effect was beautiful from the middle of the harbor. The next morning we saluted them with 13 guns."[10] A parade was assembled, and the town rejoiced that help had arrived. Hope for their cause was restored.

Soon after their arrival in Newport, and before landing his troops en masse, Rochambeau ordered that his men add black to the white cockade adorning their hats, as a symbol of the French-American Alliance. And in a spirit of collaboration, upon receiving news that the French fleet had arrived, Washington issued an order to his army officers to alter the colors of their plain black cockades on their tricorn hats from all black to "black as the ground and white as the relief." That is to say, the "ruched" circle of pleated heavy ribbon on the front of the official American headgear was arranged in two layers, with the black (used in America at the time) underneath and the white (symbol of French royalty) on top. It was another outward sign of cooperation between the two countries.[11]

An eyewitness described the appearance of the French troops at Newport: "The uniform of the Deux-Ponts was white; Saintonge, white and green; Bourbonnais, black and red. The regiment of the Soissonnais was particularly picturesque, with rose colored facings to their coats, and grenadier caps adorned with white and rose colored plumes. All wore cocked hats and their hair was carefully done up in pigtails."[12] Not mentioned by the witness was the Auxonne regiment, part of the Royal Corps Artillery, the second battalion of which also accompanied Rochambeau to America. The artillerymen wore dark blue coats and breeches with red turnbacks. Present, too, was Lauzun's Legion of light infantry and cavalry in brilliant dress uniforms.[13]

As quickly as the French and American soldiers' colors came to symbolize their alliance, Rochambeau let the Americans know that he placed himself under the command of General Washington for the campaign they were about to undertake. To quote Rochambeau's words from a letter written to the American general upon his arrival: "We are now, sir, under your command…and I hope that in a month we shall be ready to act under Your Excellency's orders.… It is hardly necessary for me to tell Your Excellency that I bring sufficient funds to pay in cash for whatever is needed by the King's army, and that we shall maintain as strict discipline as if we were under the walls of Paris."[14] His actions were as good as his promise.

The diarist Crèvecoeur, then on shore, observed that Newport must have been a true haven before the British laid waste to it: "We saw everywhere the pathetic remains of what nature had once produced in abundance for the use and pleasure of the inhabitants."[15]

Rochambeau set about to lease land, rent and rebuild lodgings, and buy all his supplies. The town benefited from the business he brought to the local tradesmen. Later, as winter approached, he was eager to move as many of his men as possible into better shelter. The French commander came up with a reasonable scheme, which would be to the benefit of both his men and the townspeople. Upon seeing the severely damaged homes in Newport, as well as the houses left vacant by fleeing Tories, the general and his *intendant* (quartermaster) in charge of logistics, Benoit-Joseph de Tarlé, assessed the situation. Rochambeau offered to rebuild these homes if, in return, he and his men could use them during their stay. The construction would be done at no charge to the locals and when they left, the structures would be reverted to their original owners free of charge. In the end, the housing plan was profitable for the French, for the rebuilding turned out to be less expensive than building new barracks, and the local tradesmen benefited from the employment. In this way, Rochambeau housed all his men, and the Americans welcomed the idea.

Another high priority for Rochambeau and Ternay was to care for the sick soldiers and seamen. Many were incapacitated with scurvy. As many as eleven hundred of the land forces were sick, and many of the sailors arriving in Newport needed immediate medical care. Colonel Ethis de Corny, with the help of Lafayette, had been sent to Rhode Island well in advance of the landing of Rochambeau and his expedition in anticipation of the need for hospitals when the ships arrived from France. So, as noted in Blanchard's diary, Corny arranged for physicians and caretakers to receive the sick. He secured 280 beds twelve miles from Newport on the mainland in the small town of Papisquash, Rhode Island, as well as some four hundred beds in Newport itself. Many of the sick were placed in old, unused buildings, while some were put into makeshift beds in the old State House and the Congregational Church.[16] The seamen were cared for in separate hospitals in Boston, Providence, and Newport.[17] Fortunately, most of the sick soldiers and sailors soon recovered their health. To bolster the forces, Washington sent General Heath with five thousand militiamen from Boston to Rhode Island. Further, the *Ile de France* sent her men overland from Boston to rejoin the main expedition.

At the same time, as the flurry of excitement and activity continued in Newport, Rochambeau and Ternay were well aware that their convoy might be attacked at any time by the British. The anchored fleet and landed troops needed to be protected. They knew that General Clinton controlled a superior force with many more ships and men than they could muster in Rhode Island. As stated in his memoirs, General Rochambeau conferred with Admiral de Ternay about a possible attack on New York, since they knew that was what Washington wanted, but Rochambeau decided against it. They would hold off until the second division of troops was sent from the king of France and until the English deployed more troops and ships to the south, which in turn would weaken New York City defenses.

Next, Rochambeau and Ternay worked on setting up defenses at Newport as swiftly as possible. They searched the environs for the remains of enemy fortifications and found many earthworks, which they would modify for their own defense. The healthy portion of Rochambeau's army had little more than two days' rest before they were called to begin digging trenches and fortifying locations where the enemy might attack.

The soldiers who had remained on the ships were then called ashore. It took several days to offload all the men and their equipment. Then they began to set up their tents in the middle of an apple orchard across from what is now Bellevue Avenue at the corner of Narragansett.[18] It is said that the French troops were so polite and respectful of the Americans and their property that not one soldier plucked an apple from the trees under which he slept.[19] They camped there for three months.

As for the four main regiments—Bourbonnais, Deux-Ponts, Soissonnais, and Saintonge—they camped in one line across the narrow portion of "the Island of Rhode Island" ending at the northern section now known as the Cliff Walk.[20] Altogether they spanned the "Island of Rhode Island" from Newport Harbor on the west side to the Sakonet River on the east side, in order to be able to thwart an attack from either direction. Fort Brenton (at the entrance to the bay), Goat Island (opposite the town of Newport), and Rose Island (a little to the north in the bay) were taken over and armed with substantial artillery.[21]

The Legion of Lauzun settled on a peninsula at the "Neck" to have a superior first view of any unwanted comers. Some Soissonnais were sent to the "Island of Conanicut," which lay between Rhode Island and the mainland in the southern end of Narragansett Bay.[22] They set up camp there to be a first line of defense against any enemy vessels entering the harbor.

The artillery was placed advantageously around Newport and on nearby strategic islands. Crèvecoeur's journal records that it consisted of "twelve 24-pounders, eight 16-pounders, eight 12-pounders, sixteen 4-pounders, two 8-inch howitzers, eight 6-inch howitzers, six 12-inch mortars and four 8-inch mortars."[23] Only after all the men and artillery were in place did Rochambeau and Ternay feel confident in their position at Newport.

At the same time as defenses were being secured, an official welcoming ceremony was planned by the Committee of the General Assembly of Rhode Island and of the Providence Plantations. On July 21, the Americans officially welcomed Rochambeau, Ternay, and the French forces. The French general responded in kind with good wishes from his king and promised that "the French troops...will live with the Americans as their brethren and nothing will afford me greater happiness than contribution to their success."[24]

Washington's troops, stationed in the Hudson Highlands above New York, were in a deplorable state when the French fleet arrived. Their numbers had been fluctuating downward from fifteen thousand to a low of three thousand. Rochambeau observed in early skirmishes that the American army fought valiantly when their hearth and home were threatened, but when the danger was past, "the army melted away."[25] In short, they returned to their farms. Since the British had taken Savannah and then Charleston, they had literally been marching up the Atlantic coast acquiring territory as they went. By contrast, Washington talked of "the totally deranged situation of our affairs" and "of the utter impracticability of availing ourselves of the generous aid [i.e., Rochambeau's army] unless the States would rouse from the torpor that had seized them."[26]

ROCHAMBEAU RECEIVES LAFAYETTE

On July 24 Rochambeau received a messenger, the Marquis de Lafayette, who arrived from General Washington's camp with "full powers from him."[27] He brought good news to reassure the Rhode Islanders that Rochambeau's arrival was expected and that all was going according to plan. Rochambeau would have preferred to see Washington in person, but that was not possible at the time.

Lafayette's presence was beneficial in that the young visitor could relay to the newly arrived Rochambeau in his native language the current state of affairs. Lafayette took the opportunity to stress that this was the time to attack New York while the British were in disarray and confusion concerning the arrival of the French army, but Rochambeau and Ternay knew that they were a long way from being battle-ready for an offensive against New York. Due to the severe depletion of resources by the British in the Newport area, it might take months before the French had all the horses, oxen, and wagons they needed. After a visit of several days, Lafayette returned to Washington with a message from Rochambeau requesting an interview as soon as possible to decide on strategies against their common enemy.

Later, on his own volition, Lafayette wrote to the French general asking him to prepare for an immediate attack on New York. In his youth, inexperience, and exuberance for action since his countrymen had arrived in full force, the young lieutenant general overstepped his chain of command and nearly created trouble for himself and Rochambeau. However, Rochambeau, old enough to be Lafayette's father, answered his bold, outrageous request with diplomacy and stern wisdom: "Permit me, my dear Marquis, an old father to reply to you, as to a tender son whom he loves and esteems highly."[28] Rochambeau went on to admonish the lieutenant general by return courier, reminding Lafayette that the allies were greatly outnumbered. Rochambeau estimated that there must have been at least fourteen thousand regular British troops plus the militia in the New York area alone, and beyond that, the British were forming a blockade of the French flotilla at Newport. Furthermore, it would not be wise or even possible to depart Rhode Island at this time, leaving the French ships with little or no land protection.[29] It is fair to say that Lafayette's high rank of lieutenant general, given him by Washington, did not match his military experience. On the other hand, his enthusiasm and total devotion to the American cause were exemplary.

The Marquis de Lafayette apologized profusely to both Washington and Rochambeau. From then on, General Rochambeau resumed his correspondence directly with Washington to avoid misunderstandings, each time requesting a face-to-face meeting. He often wrote his letters in English with the help of translators as he realized the advantage of learning the language of his host country. The Vicomte de Rochambeau, the general's son, took another of these messages to Washington.

BRITISH FLEET HARASSES FRENCH FLEET AT NEWPORT

Wasting no time, the British threatened the French fleet at anchor in Newport Harbor. They moved in with four, then eleven, and then nineteen ships, nine of these being battle-ready warships. Ternay called their bluff and held his line between Rhode Island and Goat Island. The British sent messages back and forth within their command regarding a possible combined land and sea attack on the French at Newport. When Washington heard of this possibility, he quickly prepared to defend Rochambeau and readied his men to march. The local militias answered the call and hurried to Rhode Island to form a much larger force than British Commander in Chief General Henry Clinton cared to encounter. Clinton, being a man of hesitation and unclear decisions, took too long to make up his mind to send in troops. Fortunately for the allies, he backed off on August 1 after giving up the idea. Little did he know at the time that he had missed his best opportunity to wipe out the friendly French.

General Rochambeau wrote to General Washington on August 22, 1780, to inform him that the British had the French port of Brest under heavy blockade. This was disheartening for the French expedition in Rhode Island who waited for a second division, promised by Montbarrey, to bolster their numbers.

INDIAN EMISSARIES VISIT ROCHAMBEAU

At about the same time, a delegation of approximately eighteen to twenty Indians from different nations, mostly Oneidas and Tuscaroras, arrived in Newport to meet with General Rochambeau and to set eyes on the French army. In his journal, Verger reported the visit of "deputies of the Four Nations who had come to make sure of our arrival and to offer us their alliance."[30] By tradition the Iroquois Nation, to which these Indian tribes belonged, favored the British during the Revolution. However, many of them had fought on the side of the French nearly three decades earlier in the French and Indian War. The Iroquois Confederacy was composed of six nations: the Seneca, Cayuga, Mohawk, Onondaga, Oneida, and Tuscarora. These tribes formed an alliance for military and political reasons, with the Oneida and Tuscarora openly siding with the British.

By the time Rochambeau arrived in Newport in mid-1780, the Oneida and Tuscarora, breaking tradition, were eager to meet with the French general to determine where his interest stood and to confirm their allegiance to King Louis XVI. The general received them with pomp and circumstance. Apparently, he was prepared for their visit because he offered them gifts with which they were well pleased. He regaled them with a military and then a naval drill, which they enjoyed by all accounts.[31]

The Question

Rochambeau receives Oneida and Tuscarora Indian delegation at
Newport. August, 1780. Artist: David R. Wagner.

During the visit, one of the Indian chiefs posed a rhetorical question to General Rochambeau: "My father," he said, "I wonder that the King of France, our father, should send his troops to protect the Americans in an insurrection against the King of England, their father."

"Your father, the King of France," Rochambeau replied, "protects the natural liberty which God has given to man. The Americans were no longer able to bear the burdens with which they were loaded, and he listened to their just complaints; we shall always be the friends of their friends and the enemies of their enemies: but I must urge you to preserve the strictest neutrality in all these quarrels."[32] Rochambeau assured them he was their friend, while diplomatically urging them to remain neutral. According to his memoirs, Rochambeau believed that he had indeed placated the Indians with gifts and hospitality, which he lavishly bestowed on them. After the departure of the Indian delegation Rochambeau stated that the Native Americans, as a result of his generosity towards them, posed no further threat during his

American campaign.[33] History tells us, however, this scenario did not last. By the time of the Treaty of Paris 1783, egged on by the British, the Indians made many raids from Canada attacking Americans.

Returning to the pressing matter of meeting the needs of his army, Rochambeau estimated that he would require a minimum of 375,000 livres a month to maintain his men while in America.[34] Colonel Jeremiah Wadsworth of Connecticut, commissary general of the Continental army, was named purchasing agent in charge of gathering supplies for the French army. He had already begun to scout the adjoining colonies and Pennsylvania with an impressive list of needed supplies that he had received on July 15, 1780. It read as follows: "two hundred cattle that will average 400 lbs...and 200 sheep" per week, not counting the "extra 200 head in reserve."[35] While looking over his orders for the coming January for the French troops, Wadsworth had "an order for 3,000 barrels of flour, 300 barrels of salt pork, 15,000 gallons of cider, 1,000 cwts (hundredweight, approximately 112 pounds) of peas, 3,600 gallons of vinegar, and 300 cheeses."[36] He had two months to gather this order together and deliver it.[37] By mid-May of the coming year he would also have to purchase "1,500 horses and close to 1,000 oxen" to make the expected march to meet with General Washington on the Hudson River.[38] Wadsworth worked hand in hand with the French chief commissary, Claude Blanchard. Once begun, the demands of the job were enormous in an already war-torn country.

Blanchard, taking his orders from Rochambeau, worked closely with the French general for the entire expedition. They did not always see eye to eye, but Blanchard got the job done. In his diary he admitted that his general "...has good qualities and that he is wise, that he desires what is good.... He has served well in America."[39] According to Blanchard's account, he found abundant supplies in Providence. This being the case, he found a suitable house that was "formerly occupied as a college" in which he established a makeshift hospital. The buildings he referred to are now part of Brown University.[40] He visited there often to see to the needs of the hundreds of French soldiers and sailors still recuperating from the sea voyage.[41]

The French, thorough in their preparations for the *expédition particulière,* brought a printing press to publish a newspaper in their native language. This helped to keep everyone informed and gave the men something to read in a foreign land. It was, in fact, the first French language newspaper published in America by an expeditionary force.[42] The press, which some called the propaganda machine, printed the *Gazette Française.* The Redwood Library of Newport stated that this French-language newspaper was the ancestor of *Stars and Stripes,* the newspaper of the American armed forces during the two world wars. There is a plaque to commemorate this endeavor on the garden wall at the Hunter House in Newport.

WINTER QUARTERS ESTABLISHED IN RHODE ISLAND

Preparing winter quarters for the officers and enlisted men remained a critical issue, perhaps one of the most daunting items to be resolved by the French in their new surroundings. No one knew how long they would be staying in Newport—six months, a year, maybe longer? Before the end of summer, the houses for which Rochambeau negotiated were rebuilt in preparation for cold winter weather. These were mostly for the enlisted men. Rochambeau happily paid twenty thousand *écus* for the repair of the houses.

Before work began, all plans had to be approved by General George Washington. Ultimately, Rhode Island Governor Greene, the Rhode Island Assembly, and the new American quartermaster general, Timothy Pickering, who took over in August 1780, all needed to review and agree to the strategy.

Thanks to a French billeting list, first published in 1879, it is known how the housing dilemma was ultimately solved. The Newport list is unique among the many towns (except Providence) where the French camped during their two and one-half years in America. Much of the planning was carried out by Newport barrack master Jabez Champlin, and assistant quartermaster Robert Cooke, in conjunction with French quartermaster Pierre François de Béville.[43]

The number of homes in Newport had been about eleven hundred before the British laid waste to nearly four hundred of them. After a three-year occupation, the British vacated Newport in November 1779, leaving the town in shambles. The French assigned numbers to about seven hundred of the remaining homes, beginning at the southern end of town and working their way northward until the job was finished. Number one was George Washington's and number two was Rochambeau's. Although the complete list does not exist, it appears that every possible shelter, store, outhouse, and still were utilized. The officers were lodged in private homes with many of the owners present, while the soldiers took up residence in the newly renovated houses left empty by the Tories. The existing "V.I.P. list of officers" billeted includes only 91 names and locations, less than half of the complete list of French officers actually lodged in Newport. The moving-in date was November 1, 1780.[44]

Since many of the street names have been changed over the years, a "glossary" of old and new names has since been created so visitors can locate the houses. Rochambeau and his son Donatien were taken in by the Vernon family at 302 New Lane (on the corner of Clarke and Mary Streets today). The house has a low-hipped roof with a flat deck surrounded by a balustrade. The exterior is made of blocks of rusticated wood that resemble stone. The house was built around 1700 as a four-room home, and by 1760, it became a two-story mansion. Samuel Vernon, in the absence of his father, William, proved a gracious host to the general and his son.[45] William Vernon was at the time president of the Eastern Naval Board in Boston, and as such was the first secretary of the navy.[46] By July 14 Rochambeau and "his whole family of aides" were installed on Clarke and Spring Streets.[47]

Rochambeau Plaque

Bronze bust of Rochambeau affixed to the house he used as his
headquarters in Newport at 46 Clark Street; Artist and date unknown.
Vernon House, property of Newport Restoration Foundation.
Photo: Jini Jones Vail.

To provide his officers with some entertainment aimed at maintaining morale during the long winter to come, Rochambeau built
a pavilion with a dance floor behind the Vernon House. It became
known as the "French Hall." Rochambeau said that since his men

could not march due to the heavy snow, they might as well dance. The young ladies of Newport and surrounding towns were most agreeable to the plan.[48]

Admiral de Ternay was housed at the Hunter House (now 54 Washington Street).[49] The house was built in 1748 as a two-and-one-half-story, balustraded Georgian colonial for Deputy Royal Governor Jonathan Nichols Jr. In 1756 it was sold to Colonel Joseph Wanton Jr. and then in 1780 to William Hunter, a U. S. senator. It was purchased in 1945, leading to the formation of the Preservation Society of Newport County.

Before leaving for winter quarters in Lebanon, Connecticut, with part of his legion, the Duc de Lauzun was lodged at another Hunter house, 264 Thames Street. The owner, widow Deborah Hunter, was in residence with her two daughters.

Brothers Antoine and Charles Vioménil, both generals serving under Rochambeau as first- and second-in-command, respectively, led a modest existence at the home of Joseph Wanton (Wanton House) at 274 Thames Street.[50]

Major General Chastellux, Rochambeau's chief of staff, stayed at the Maudsley House at 91 Spring Street. Chastellux often invited friends to his new home, and his soirées are still the object of conversation in Newport.[51]

The Vicomte de Noailles was happily housed with the Quaker family of Thomas Robinson at 614 Water Street.[52] A long-term friendship began here for Noailles and the Robinson family, particularly with Molly Robinson. Many of their personal letters still exist as examples of the flowery gratitude of the French soldier to his host family.

On Church Street there was another ballroom owned by Mrs. Cowley. George Washington danced there with the famous Miss Margaret Champlain on the occasion of his formal visit to Rochambeau in March 1781. The general was asked by the musicians to choose a tune for their dance. He turned to Miss Champlain to ask her for her favorite song, to which she replied, "A Successful

Campaign." At that, Rochambeau and his aides picked up the instruments themselves and played the popular tune. Her choice of a tune turned out to be a portent of events to come.[53]

While waiting for winter quarters, the French soldiers lived in a tent colony patrolled by sentries, and there was no going out or coming in without advance permission. In other words, mingling was not allowed. The reason was to prevent any troublesome situations that might arise between the enlisted French and the American locals. The rules were strictly enforced. On the subject of rules, Rochambeau wrote, "Not a man has left his camp, not a cabbage has been stolen, not a complaint has been heard." Peace was maintained in Newport.

The Newporters, at first fearful of the arrival of the French fleet, were, by the end of summer, reassured of their noble mission in coming to America. More hopeful than they had been in years, the people of Rhode Island welcomed General Rochambeau and his army with open arms. Purposeful now, after suffering under British occupation, the locals willingly supported their new allies for the coming battle against their common enemy.

CHAPTER FOUR

Rochambeau Meets Washington

"The Comte de Rochambeau...gained...glory...for his vigilant concern to maintain strict discipline in his army, for his care to avoid any incidents, and for winning the friendship of the Americans, who were not naturally drawn toward our nation."

—JEAN-FRANÇOIS LOUIS COMTE DE CLERMONT-CRÈVECOEUR

IMMEDIATELY AFTER HIS ARRIVAL in America, General Rochambeau wrote to George Washington. First, he offered his services and his allegiance to their common cause, putting himself and his army under the command of the American leader. This was the express wish of King Louis XVI. Next, he requested a face-to-face meeting with his commander in chief. Washington, camped north of New York, could not leave immediately for an initial meeting with Rochambeau due to other pressing matters, including the return of General Clinton to New York and the fear of a possible attack on West Point.[1] The timing of the arrival of the French troops could not have been better; Washington's army was in desperate need of assistance. The Continental troops were dangerously low in number as it was nearly harvest time and many had taken leave to return to their farms to bring in the crops.

In the course of six years of constant struggle to subdue and expel the British, General George Washington formulated a strategy with regard to the ongoing fight for freedom. Joseph J. Ellis, in his book, *Founding Brothers,* observes that over time, as Washington gained maturity as a military leader it was not necessarily the winning of battles or the taking of ground that mattered. Washington found that if he persisted in keeping the Continental army together over the long run, they would continue to be a threat. So, in the face of low-to-zero funding and seasonal dwindling of numbers, he managed to sustain the Continental army as a continuing presence. And, as Ellis notes, "Space and time were on his side."[2] With the arrival of Rochambeau and his French army in Newport, Washington's mission would be easier.

Before riding to meet with Rochambeau, Washington decided to give the French time to get established in Newport and to begin to learn their way around in this new country. Language would be an obstacle, but not impossible to overcome. Washington knew no French, but Rochambeau was already learning English. Both sides would send emissaries to keep up the communication until a suitable time and place could be agreed upon for their first meeting.

Rochambeau, who had been working to reform the French army, was ready to put much of what he had learned into use. He would implement some of the very techniques he had studied and advocated at home. As a result of his role as inspector general in the French army and his involvement in two wars in Europe, he had formulated four rules:

1) Generals and admirals of the same country should cooperate and wholeheartedly assist one another to carry out national plans;

2) Allies should cooperate, should make joint plans, and should faithfully carry them out;

3) In war a nation should have clear goals and should have well developed plans to achieve them; and

4) Troops should be carefully trained for the tasks to be assigned them and should be well equipped, not

only with appropriate weapons, but also with things conducive to their comfort (good clothes, blankets, tents).[3]

As obvious as these rules were, it was amazing how frequently they were disregarded. Often, allied commanders were at odds with each other and failed to succeed as a result. As Rochambeau later observed, this was the case with the British generals in the American War of Independence. When Rochambeau detected a rift between General Clinton and General Cornwallis, he acted decisively to take advantage of division and hesitation on their part as it occurred; it made all the difference.

Under optimal conditions, allies worked together to plan and coordinate their offense and defense to prevent the enemy from finding an opening that would set them against each other. Rochambeau had to be prepared to avoid such shortcomings to be successful in his goal to aid America. He had to be ready to take advantage of any weaknesses seen in the enemy camp. Rochambeau knew the importance of solid, thorough training for the real tasks ahead. And not only did he know the rules of pre-engagement planning, he put them into practice.[4] With the importance of these principles at the center of his thinking, and armed with his many years of practical application on the battlefields of Europe, Rochambeau was eager to confer with Washington. He hoped that they would find common ground upon which to plan, but what type of rapport would it take to lead to a successful outcome?

THE HARTFORD CONFERENCE

On September 8, 1780, Washington sent a courier letter to Rochambeau: "I have the honor to propose the 20th instant for an interview in Hartford where I hope we shall be able to combine some plan of future operations, which events will enable us to execute."[5] Hartford, Connecticut, was chosen as the meeting place to initiate their working relationship, and the date was set for

September 20. Hartford was nearly equidistant between the Rhode Island and New York camps. It was also the home of Jeremiah Wadsworth, the commissary general of the Continental and French armies. In the advance planning for the conference, Washington engaged Wadsworth's aid in making all the necessary arrangements in Hartford.[6] The dignitaries would be housed at Wadsworth's home, and the meetings would take place there as well. A copy of George Washington's September 13 letter to Elihu Hubbard Smith reads: "You will be pleased to provide the best quarters which the town affords…. I shall have an escort of twelve to fifteen dragoons. The French General will probably have a like number."[7]

Leaving from Newport on September 18 were Rochambeau, and three of his aides-de-camp, Donatien de Rochambeau, Axel von Fersen, and Mathieu Dumas. Also accompanying him were Admiral de Ternay, who was not feeling well, and the French chief engineer, Colonel Jean-Nicolas Desandrouins. One account includes the Duc de Lauzun in the traveling party to Hartford, but he is not mentioned in the notes of Count von Fersen, a Swedish officer in the French army.Fersen was known as a favorite of Queen Marie Antoinette. All of the above kept diaries of the conference.[8]

Donatien's journal reported that they spent the first night in Providence before continuing on via "Sutuate (Scituate), Coventry, Voluntown, Canterbury, Scotland, Windham, Bolton, East Hartford."[9] In his memoirs, Rochambeau described the trip to Hartford as being hard; he also related that Ternay "was very infirm," a continuation of his ongoing illness, perhaps gout, from which he suffered during the sea voyage.[10] Ternay, in turn, wrote that the roads were filled with rocks, and it was difficult for four-wheeled vehicles. Because of his weakness, Ternay rode in a carriage with the French general.

The conveyance in which both the general and the admiral rode broke down near Scotland, Connecticut. Rochambeau sent Fersen to find a wheelwright about a mile away. Fersen returned, saying that the man was too ill with ague to help anyone. In fact, even for "his hat full of guineas he would do no work at night."[11] At that, both the

French general and the admiral went to reason with the man, saying that if they did not get on their way, they would miss an important meeting with George Washington the next day. The man replied, "You are no liars, at any rate, for I have read in the Connecticut paper that Washington was to be there to confer with you; as it is for the public service, I will take care that your carriage shall be ready for you at six in the morning."[12] Rochambeau thought this was "an anecdote which is strikingly characteristic of the manners of the good republicans of Connecticut."[13]

That evening, September 19, they most likely dined and spent the night in Andover at Daniel White's Tavern, located on Hutchinson Road at the sign of the Black Horse.[14] The next morning they made good time to the Connecticut River ferry crossing in East Hartford, where four ferries waited.[15] There were two large ferries for carriages and two smaller ones, mostly for horses. The river was deep and generally fast moving at East Hartford, but they had no difficulty in crossing.

Washington, then forty-seven years old, received a hearty send-off from his camp in New York, though he and his army were "ragged of body and sore of heart."[16] Their expectations were not very high. His entourage included "five Aide-de-camps. In order of their rank, the personnel were as follows: General Knox, Chief of the Artillery, aged 30. Lieutenant Colonel de Gouvion, Chief of Engineers, aged 32. The Marquis de Lafayette and Alexander Hamilton, of one age, 23."[17]

En route to meet the French in Hartford, the American *cortège* stopped in Litchfield, Connecticut, where they encountered Elihu Hubbard Smith, who said this of Washington: "I remember the air with which he mounted his horse, a fine bay, the furniture without fine lace or other ornament; & the saddle covered by a black bearskin. Characteristic simplicity!"[18] Regarding Lafayette, he said: "But his person, his horse, his rich trappings with which he was decorated, still possess a place in my memory."[19]

Despite bad roads and accidents, all parties arrived in Hartford around noon on September 20. The American delegation was the first to arrive. Colonel Jeremiah Wadsworth, one of Connecticut's wealthiest merchants, and other distinguished persons welcomed them. The Governor's Guard presented America's commander in chief with a thirteen-gun salute.[20] The excitement was building among the Hartford onlookers.

Soon after, the French cortège arrived at City Landing and was greeted by another thirteen-gun salute. From there, Rochambeau's suite marched to the Old State House where they were officially met by Washington and his military entourage "in State House Square in front of the old Court House."[21] A large crowd of onlookers was gathered to observe the first meeting of the two great generals and to witness the moment when France and America shook hands. "There were the noble-looking Frenchmen, gaily dressed, and sparkling with jeweled insignia. There was Washington—erect, tall, commanding— in his buff vest, buff breeches buckled at the knee, long-spurred boots, white neckcloth, and blue, buff-lined coat, that shone with a pair of rich, massive epaulettes."[22]

After the formal welcome, "the two leaders and their entourages then walked a few blocks south to the home of Jeremiah Wadsworth for a reception. Wadsworth's home, where the Wadsworth Atheneum now stands at 600 Main Street, was also their conference site."[23] All that is left of the Wadsworth house is a panel taken from the southwest chamber of the second floor where the historic conference took place. It is preserved in the Wadsworth Atheneum where it stands testament to the first meeting of Washington and Rochambeau.[24]

The generals stabled their horses at the Wadsworth Stable across the street from the family's stately home in the center of Hartford. The stable, built in 1730, was destroyed by fire in the early 1800s. It was rebuilt in 1820, and by 1954 was scheduled for demolition but fortunately was saved, moved, and restored as an excellent example of classic Palladian style architecture. The Connecticut Society of the Daughters of the American Revolution offered a site for the stable on the grounds of the Governor Jonathan Trumbull House in Lebanon, Connecticut, where it now stands as a museum.[25]

The other officers and accompanying soldiers were provided lodging throughout the center of the capital city at taverns such as the Collier-Ripley Coffee House (demolished in 1826) near the present junction of State and Main Streets. Others stayed at David Bull's Tavern just across from the Old State House, which stood at 800 Main Street. The Tavern was known as "The Bunch of Grapes."[26] The owner was suspected to be a Loyalist.[27]

Governor Jonathan Trumbull was summoned from Lebanon by Washington to join them as soon as he was able. He arrived after the meetings ended, but in time to greet everyone before their departure. Washington was relieved to discover that the governor had arranged for the state of Connecticut to foot the bill for the entire conference.[28] September 21 had been spent behind closed doors with both the French and Americans huddled over a large table in serious conference. Security had been meticulously planned. Lafayette and Hamilton had used their facility in both French and English to translate, interpret, and record the dialogue between the two parties as they worked on a Franco-American strategy.

According to a letter sent by Count von Fersen to his father in Sweden, "Washington had brought an 8-page outline for an operation against New York, drafted by Alexander Hamilton, with him, in the hope that he would be able to convince Rochambeau and Ternay to stage such an attack before the onset of winter. Rochambeau and Ternay would not be rushed. Once the meeting had started, they methodically wrote their ideas and requests in column form on the left-hand side of a sheet of paper. Once they had been discussed among the Americans, Lafayette would write Washington's answers in a column on the right-hand side of the page. This was a slow process, but it forced both sides to put their needs and wishes in writing."[29]

The American general did not have much to offer at this time, hoping it would be primarily a French initiative, which he would support as best he could. His army was practically nonexistent. Rochambeau's hands were tied without the expected additional troops and ships promised by the king. Rochambeau did, however, suggest this premise, which Washington accepted: "No major enterprise could be undertaken unless there was at least temporary command of the sea along that part of the coast closest to the proposed action. The agreement on this principle was to have a major influence in later campaigns in America. It also made Washington more dependent on the French since only they could establish control of the sea."[30]

Toward the end of the day, September 21, a message was received in Hartford that Admiral Rodney had arrived at New York with a fleet that tripled the size of the British presence already stationed there. The meeting was cut short. Not wanting to risk an amphibious attack while away from their respective armies, both generals prepared to depart as soon as possible.

On Friday September 22, Rochambeau and Washington signed a joint memorandum, stating agreement on four major points:

1) New York would be the chief object of their operations.

2) More men would be required than they currently had—at least 24,000 and possibly 30,000.

3) Both parties would seek reinforcements. Ternay would seek more ships, and Rochambeau would request 10,000 more men.

4) Until reinforced, the French would remain on the defensive.[31]

Following the Hartford meetings Washington recorded ten points, the first of which was that "There can be no decisive enterprise against the Maritime establishments of the English in this country, without consistent naval superiority."[32]

That same day, the French delegation left for their return trip and were again accompanied by the Governor's Guard to the ferry and sent off by another thirteen-gun salute. The next morning, after thanking Wadsworth and Trumbull for their fine hospitality, the

Governor's Guard also escorted Washington and his men out of Hartford.

Incredibly, on the return trip, Rochambeau's carriage broke down again near the same spot in Scotland, Connecticut, and he and his entourage were forced to engage the assistance of the same wheelwright. This time the unnamed, kindly wheelwright could not hold back a question: "But, tell me, before I do the work, although I do not wish to inquire into your secrets, how did you like Washington, and how did he like you?" to which Rochambeau replied, "We assured him we had been delighted with him; his patriotism was satisfied, and he kept his word. I do not mean to compare all good Americans to this good man, but almost all inland cultivators and all landowners of Connecticut are animated with that patriotic spirit which many other people would do well to imitate."[33]

Admiral de Ternay, who had suffered ill health during the entire trip to Hartford and back, was undoubtedly relieved to exchange the bumping and jerking of the carriage over the terribly uneven roads for a quiet bed in Newport.

Of the first conference Dumas wrote, "George Washington and General Rochambeau decided on passing the whole winter in passive observation, always holding themselves ready to profit by the most favorable circumstances which might present themselves."[34] On October 4, 1780, Washington wrote to Silas Deane to report that "the interview at Hartford produced nothing conclusive because neither side knew with certainty what was to be expected. We could only combine possible plans on the supposition of possible events and engage mutually to do everything in our powers again against the next campaign."[35]

There were many positive outcomes recorded, however, regarding the first face-to-face meeting of Washington and Rochambeau. Two of Rochambeau's aides-de-camp made the following observations upon meeting General Washington. Dumas said, "We had been impatient to see the hero of liberty. His dignified address, his simplicity of manners and mild gravity, surpassed our expectation and won every heart."[36] Fersen, somewhat more reserved, found the American general "illustrious, if not unique in our century. His handsome and majestic, while at the same time mild and open countenance perfectly reflects his moral qualities, he looks the hero; he is very cold, speaks little, but is courteous and frank. A shade of sadness overshadows his countenance, which is not unbecoming, and gives him an interesting air."[37] The two generals made an instantaneous good impression on each other, so much so that they continued to correspond until Washington's death on December 14, 1799.

On his way back to New York, Washington stopped in Litchfield, Connecticut, to stay "at the hospitable mansion of General Oliver Wolcott" who would later become the governor of the state of Connecticut.[38] En route to his encampment on the Hudson, Washington met with M. de La Luzerne, French minister to the United States, at Fishkill, New York.

WASHINGTON DISCOVERS PERFIDY OF BENEDICT ARNOLD

On September 23 Washington then set out to meet with his friend and general, Benedict Arnold, at the Robinson house on the Hudson River where Arnold and his wife, Peggy Shippen Arnold, were staying. On the way, Washington heard some startling news. An aide to General Clinton, Major John André, had just been taken into custody. Apparently, André had been discovered in Continental dress behind American lines. He was searched by local militia and in his sock were papers incriminating himself and General Arnold. The papers included a letter to General Clinton from Arnold along with detailed maps of West Point, the fort under the jurisdiction of, and protected by none other than, the same General Arnold. In return for his treasonous act, the British offered Arnold a Royal Commission in the British army and 10,000 pounds. The plot was foiled just in time.

Taking advantage of Washington's out-of-state meeting with Rochambeau, Arnold had met with André just before midnight on

September 22, the day Washington departed from Hartford. Arnold met with him expressly to hand over the West Point plans. André then prepared to find his way to the British ship, the *Vulture*, which had brought him to the rendezvous, and return to Clinton with the booty in his sock. Unable to find the ship, which by that time had anchored farther downstream, André put on a disguise and headed out in the middle of the night to escape on land.

When Washington arrived at Arnold's home, Arnold had just narrowly escaped, while his wife, Peggy, feigned innocence of the entire treasonous affair. It was later discovered that Arnold had gotten away by rowing a small boat out to the *Vulture*, which carried him to safety. Arnold defected to the British, taking the *Vulture* back to Clinton's camp at New York. On September 25, 1780 in a letter to Colonel Wade at West Point, Washington expressed his thoughts in a simple sentence: "General Arnold is gone to the enemy."[39] He was never captured nor tried for his crime.

André, on the other hand, paid for his crime immediately. Washington convened a board of officers which called for André's execution. Joseph Plumb Martin, American diarist, remembers what he saw of the incident. He wrote, "Soon after our arrival here [on the Hudson near Arnold's residence], a British brig [the *Vulture*] passed up the river, the same that had conveyed the unfortunate Major André to his bane. Poor man! [H]e had better have staid where he was better acquainted."[40] Not long after, Martin saw the *Vulture* again. This time, recorded the soldier, the brig "came down the river with her precious charge—Arnold—on board. There were several shots discharged at her as she passed the block house, but she went by without paying us much attention."[41]

Apparently, like Martin, even some American soldiers felt pity for the "poor André," carrier of the message of betrayal who met a swift end as a result. Earlier, Martin had observed some odd behavior on Arnold's part. He had seen the general reconnoitering, or "taking observations" as Martin put it, of the pathways in the woods, which, at the time, raised questions in Martin's mind as to the reason a general would be doing such a strange thing alone.[42] Arnold may have been plotting his exit strategy that day in the woods.

Arnold had been a hero in the earlier days at Quebec, at Lake Champlain, and at Saratoga, but never received the honors he felt he deserved. He lost his seniority despite the fact that his friend, Washington, backed him. Acting against orders in the Battle of Saratoga, he charged heroically into the fray, which contributed to the backing down of General John Burgoyne. In the course of the siege, Arnold's horse was shot out from under him and fell on his leg (which had already been injured at Quebec), causing him to be crippled for life. Congress finally did restore his seniority, but it was too late for Arnold. He never did forgive the Congress for past slights and perceived injustices.[43]

Benedict Arnold spent the next winter of 1777–1778 at Valley Forge and, in May of that year, signed the Oath of Allegiance to his country, witnessed by Henry Knox. General Washington then appointed him commandant of Philadelphia where Arnold met his future wife, Peggy. Soon they were outspending his pay, and he was using government supplies for his personal lifestyle. He was court-martialed and found guilty.[44]

Washington supported his longtime friend, even offering him the position of commander of the left wing of the army. Arnold might have coveted the position as a younger man, but he used his injured leg as an excuse for turning down the offer. He said he preferred the post at West Point. Washington gave it to him and played right into Arnold's traitorous scheme as Arnold was already plotting with the British. West Point would be his bargaining tool with the enemy. Washington considered "West Point as the linchpin of the Hudson corridor and therefore the most strategic location in the entire northern theater."[45] When he learned of Arnold's betrayal and of Major André's complicity, he "was not in a sentimental or generous mood," and had André hanged as a spy.[46] Rochambeau noted in his memoirs, "All the world is acquainted with the tragical end of the ill-fated André, whom everybody pitied, even his judges."[47]

ERRAND TO FRANCE

Rochambeau judged that it was important to inform King Louis XVI of the results of the Hartford Conference, to seek additional funds for the campaign, and to determine when the promised reinforcements would be sent. Therefore, he dispatched his son and aide-de-camp, the Vicomte de Rochambeau, from Newport on October 28, 1780, to return to France. Rochambeau's confidence in his son's appropriateness for this mission is evident in his memoirs: "My son had committed to memory the whole of my dispatches, so as to be able to render a full verbal account of them to the ministers lest he should have the misfortune to fall into the hands of the enemy."[48]

The Vicomte and his entourage set sail with Captain La Pérouse on the *Amazone,* accompanied for the first day until she reached high seas by the *Surveillante* and the *Hermione.*[49] As expected, British vessels were blockading Newport Harbor and Narragansett Bay to keep the French ships in check. La Pérouse, however, one of the most able of France's naval officers, took advantage of a "sudden violent blow which had scattered the English Squadron" and made their getaway undetected.[50] The *Amazone* arrived at the port of Lorient on the Atlantic coast of Brittany on November 15, an unusually quick passage navigated and sailed expertly by La Pérouse. The speed of this crossing set a record that stood for decades. In fact, it was another sixty years before any ship surpassed the time of the *Amazone,* and that took a totally new type of ocean-going vessel—a steamship.[51]

La Pérouse returned at the end of February, but the Vicomte de Rochambeau remained at Versailles, waiting in limbo for the answer from the king regarding the funds and sending of the second division. Meanwhile, La Pérouse did bring some good news in the form of 1,053,000 livres, which were desperately needed to feed and house the French army during the rest of the winter.[52]

The Americans also sent one of their own on an errand to France. On February 11, 1781, Congress sent Colonel John Laurens to France on the American frigate *Alliance* to seek additional funds.

He arrived at Lorient on March 9, 1781. Laurens, born in Charleston and trained as a lawyer in London, was fluent in French. He was the son of Henry Laurens, former president of the Continental Congress, who was at that time a prisoner of the British in the Tower of London.[53] Washington told the younger Laurens to relay the following message to Vergennes: "Without a foreign loan our present force which is but the remnant of an army cannot be kept together for this campaign, much less will it be increased and in readiness for another."[54] In Rochambeau's words, "This officer received orders to represent to the Court of France, in the clearest light, the state of distress of his country."[55] Laurens was successful and returned to Boston on August 25, 1781 with funds and promise of more.

ADMIRAL DE TERNAY SUCCUMBS TO ILLNESS

Admiral de Ternay remained ill after returning from the Hartford Conference, but Rochambeau did not notice that he was any worse and was not alarmed when, in December, Ternay was confined by a fever. Washington received "the afflicting intelligence of the death of the Chevalier de Ternay. The French corps will do him the justice to say that it was impossible to conduct a convoy to its destination with greater skill and vigilance than he did the one confided to his charge."[56]

French Commissary Claude Blanchard commented, "On the 14th [of December 1780], [t]he cold was very severe. M. the Chevalier de Ternay...had been sick for several days and had just been taken on shore. M. Corte, our chief physician, had been sent for, who told us that he found him very ill."[57] He fell victim to his disease; they said it was a putrid fever. He died December 15, 1780, at the Hunter House, 54 Washington Street in Newport, and was buried the next day in the Trinity churchyard "on the 16th in fine weather with great pomp. All the land forces were under arms."[58]

There is only one surviving American account of the Ternay funeral, that of a Mr. Hornsby:

The catafalque was erected in the Wanton House on Washington Street. It was draped in black crepe and covered with the national flag upon which were placed the hat, the epaulettes, and the many insignia of the distinguished orders that the admiral had worn in life. The room where he lay was shrouded in black but lighted by very many wax candles. From here he was carried to Trinity churchyard by the sailors of the flagship. All the distinguished officers of the fleet and the army followed on foot and then came the troops. Such an assemblage of soldiers and sailors with well-appointed arms and accoutrements had never been seen in Newport before this day. The interment was at twilight, and the coffin was preceded by twelve priests, each with a lighted taper in his hand…. The troops then gave the last salute to their brave commander and left him to sleep in American soil under the protection of the American flag.[59]

King Louis XVI ordered a monument to be erected on Ternay's grave. A history of praise is inscribed on his tombstone, written in Latin by Rochambeau: "His greatest enemies can never deny that he had great probity and that he was a very skillful navigator. The French Corps rendered him the justice to say that it was impossible to conduct a convoy with greater vigilance and skill than he displayed in bringing it to its destination."[60]

This stone tablet was later removed and affixed permanently to the wall of the tower room inside the church for safekeeping. According to the Newport Historical Society, Admiral de Ternay was Catholic, but since there was no Catholic church in Newport, he was laid to rest in the Anglican Trinity churchyard with last rites pronounced by a Catholic priest. Many of Ternay's French comrades spoke or wrote in his favor. Lafayette, in a letter to his wife, Adrienne, said this: "The French Squadron has remained blockaded in Rhode

Island and I imagine the Chevalier de Ternay died of grief in consequence of this event. However this may be, he is positively dead. He was a very rough and obstinate man, but firm and clear in all his views, and, taking all things into consideration, we have sustained a great loss."[61]

Captain Chevalier Destouches was appointed to temporary charge of the fleet, which the enemy continued to blockade at Newport by forces of superior numbers. In May 1781, Admiral Barras, who served with Admiral D'Estaing in earlier campaigns off the American coast, arrived and took over the command of the French fleet.

NEWPORT CONFERENCE

That Washington had not hastened to visit Rochambeau to review his troops and give him encouragement was becoming a sore point for the French in Newport; then again, Washington was dealing with mutinies in Pennsylvania. British General Clinton tried unsuccessfully to hire the mutineers, but ultimately, the soldiers professed their patriotism and returned to the Continental army.

The winter drew on with no campaign plan in place. Then Rochambeau penned an ice-breaking note to Washington in February on the occasion of the latter's birthday. "Yesterday was Your Excellency's birthday. We have put off celebrating that holiday until today by reason of the Lord's day, and we will celebrate it with the sole regret that Your Excellency is not a witness to the gladness of our hearts."[62] The response was immediate. Washington was so moved by the unexpected warmth of Rochambeau's note that he wrote back saying that he would come to visit soon.

Rochambeau immediately sent Baron von Closen to escort the American commander "from the Hudson to the sea."[63] Shortly after his arrival at Washington's headquarters, Closen received an answer "under the seal of secrecy that he [Washington] would accompany me the day after tomorrow to Newport."[64]

On the way to visit Rochambeau in Newport, Washington lunched in Bolton, Connecticut, trotted through Andover with his twenty-man guard of dragoons, reviewed Lauzun's Cavalry Legion, and slept in Governor Trumbull's house in Lebanon.[65]

The American contingent arrived on March 6 at Jamestown, Rhode Island, where they were met by a barge that rowed them out to the *Duc de Bourgogne*. Rochambeau, along with all the ranking officers of the French fleet and army, received them on board. After a short sail they arrived at Long Wharf where a welcoming volley was fired as they were accompanied to headquarters with "all the pomp and ceremony accorded to a marshal of France or a prince of the blood."[66]

This second meeting between Rochambeau and Washington included private talks and gala events. As reported by an eyewitness, Mr. Updyke, the door was guarded by a "major-domo who presided over the festivities… He wore a short, close jacket; a rich, silver-fringed coat; pink shoes; a hat emblazoned with armorial bearings; and a cane with an enormous head after the fashion of the heraldic tabard of the feudal age."[67]

The dinner that evening was elaborate and in the French style. M. de La Luzerne served a similar, even more ostentatious dinner to Washington in northern Westchester at a later date. It was said that "there was a wagonload of silver for the service."[68] It appears that the French hardly traveled light in those trend-setting days of extravagant lifestyle dictated by the court of Louis XVI. The era of ultra *luxe* at the Court of Versailles was endangered, but no one saw that yet, least of all the king, whose eyes were covered by scales, a state in which one has eyes but cannot see the truth.

All this decorous celebration set forth by the French must have been impressive to the American leader whose army was bereft of even the most basic supplies, such as shoes, not to mention proper uniforms. Even the ships were hung with lanterns and the streets and houses lit with candles in honor of the great American hero.

There was a grand procession during which the French troops stood three deep to watch Washington and their leader pass by. They doffed their hats to the great men as they strode by unbonneted.[69] The brothers Vioménil, both generals, were handsome and worth more than a glance. "They were both of commanding height."[70] Rochambeau was described by Updyke as "a small, keen-looking man, but with the dignity and simplicity of the French country gentleman."[71] That night, Washington was honored at the requisite ball on the flagship.

Another event was planned for Washington's stay, a formal tea given by the widower Christopher Ellery. His daughter, Betsy, "a young woman of beauty and refinement, presided at the tea table."[72] The following is a curious, if not verifiable, account of Betsy's bad sore throat and the helpful advice given to her by the visiting general. Washington commiserated with her not being able to talk above a whisper and offered his never-fail solution. His family remedy consisted of "taking onions boiled in molasses three times a day."[73]

Evidently, Washington's remedy worked for Betsy and its use persists to this day in Newport.[74] An ironic, but unfortunate post-script to this story and the efficacy of this home remedy relates to a similar illness leading to the death of George Washington at Mount Vernon some twenty years later on December 14, 1799. He suffered from a sudden onset of quinsy, or acute laryngitis. A mixture of molasses, butter, and vinegar was offered to sooth his sore throat, but he was unable to swallow the preparation; his condition was grave, taking his life that night. If Washington had been treated with his old family remedy of onions instead of vinegar, he might have lived. Perhaps there were no onions in the Mount Vernon larder that mid-December.

Much later, reflecting on that night, Rochambeau reminded his friend George Washington of the dinner they shared that night in Newport. "Do you remember, my dear general," he wrote, "of the first repast that we have made together at R[hode] Island? I [made] you remark from the soup the difference of character of our two nations, the French in burning their throat and all the Americans waiting wisely [for] the time that it was cooled. I believe, my dear general, you have seen, since a year, that our nation has not change[d] of character. We go very fast—God will that we [reach] our aims."[75]

Although the formal ceremonies had helped to distract both delegations from their winter concerns, there was still the daunting matter of how best to proceed as allies. The officers' discussions during the March conference had to contend with the defection of Arnold, who had begun to wreak havoc in Virginia, burning, looting, killing, and freeing slaves.[76] Under British protection, Arnold continued to elude capture. The situation in Virginia worsened.

Then too, Lafayette had vied for a command of his own, which he was granted. He soon would make his way to Virginia with his one thousand light infantry, not only to reinforce the Virginia militia, but also to monitor Cornwallis who was moving north into the state. It was beginning to look like there might be a shift of concentration to the southern theater; Washington remained against it.

While the high-level meeting of Rochambeau and Washington in Newport was more a social occasion than a true military planning event, the two generals had discussed the need for Ternay's successor, Destouches, to sail to Virginia with aid and supplies. In fact, on March 6, the first day of the Newport meeting, Washington and Rochambeau watched as Destouches safely skirted the British and sailed out of Newport for Virginia. The Newport meeting lasted a week, with Washington reviewing the troops and spending time getting to know the senior French officers with whom he would be working closely over the next months. He was impressed and heartened by their order and discipline. At the same time, the French were not disappointed at what they observed in Washington, the great man of whom they had read and heard long before sailing to America.

CONFLICT AT CHESAPEAKE BAY

Rochambeau and Washington wanted to stop Benedict Arnold's rampage of destruction in Virginia by bringing aid to the Virginia militia. Destouches was, therefore, prepared to land twelve hundred troops under the command of General Antoine-Charles Vioménil in Virginia to augment existing land troops as well as to bolster Lafayette's army, which would be arriving in a matter of weeks. Destouches set out from Newport with his entire fleet, taking the long route via the open sea to avoid detection by the British, whereas British Admiral Mariot Arbuthnot, who had been guarding the French fleet from Gardiner's Bay off the eastern tip of Long Island, New York, made directly for Chesapeake Bay. Arbuthnot left Gardiner's Bay a day and a half later and arrived in the Chesapeake ahead of Destouches, positioning himself at the mouth of the bay, barring the entrance to the French.

The British ships had the advantage of being coppered, but the French ships were not, making them much slower in the water. "The squadrons were of about equal size, the slight British superiority in canon being matched by the fire power of the troops on the French ships."[77] The two squadrons engaged in battle on March 16, 1781. First the French held the advantage of the wind, then the British, with cannonading beginning in the early afternoon. Both sides took a hard battering with extensive damage to ships and men. Arbuthnot did not renew the attack, and Destouches decided he could not force his way into the bay, so he ordered his ships to head back to Newport.[78]

The French suffered more casualties than the British, with 72 killed and 112 wounded, while the British counted 30 killed and 73 wounded.[79] The results were not as the French and American commanders had hoped. No French troops were landed, but the British managed to reinforce their army in Virginia. Unfortunately, Destouches had been unable to keep the advantage he held at the start of the encounter. According to his report to Rochambeau, had all of his ships been coppered like the British, he could have won a decisive victory and gained control of the mouth of the Chesapeake. When the American public received news of the battle, even though the outcome was indecisive, they were heartened to hear of the bravery of the French, who dared to face the mighty British navy with a modicum of success. Following this first Battle off the Virginia Capes, sometimes referred to as the Battle of Cape Henry, the Royal British Navy ceased to keep permanent watch on the French fleet at Newport from Gardiner's Bay.[80]

Regarding the first Battle off the Capes, Rochambeau wrote, "Just as the Chevalier Destouches was preparing to get his ships round to re-engage, he perceived the British fleet making off to leeward, towards the entrance of Chesapeak[e]; this maneuver on their part induced him to put back to Rhode Island.... He finally returned to Newport with the Baron de Vioménil, after hard but doubtful combat, and with the bitter regret of not having accomplished his mission."[81]

FRENCH INTERCHANGE

In the meantime, events were occurring rapidly in Europe during the winter of 1780–81. Marie Antoinette's mother, Maria Theresa, Archduchess of the Holy Roman Empire and Empress of Austria, died on November 29, 1780. This event rocked the French royal family and had far-reaching effects on where France would choose to concentrate her army and how she would spend her treasure. France would have to guard her borders more heavily, since the close ties of neutrality between France and Austria had been loosened.

Faces were also changing in Louis XVI's cabinet. The Marquis de Castries became minister of the marines. The Marshal de Ségur replaced the Prince de Montbarrey as minister of war. Jacques Necker, Swiss-born Protestant, remained at his post as minister of finance, a position that he had held precariously since 1777. The powerful Vergennes remained in place as minister of foreign affairs.

On the other side of the Atlantic, Washington had early misgivings about a foreign country sending a general and large numbers of troops to help America expel the British. Having been a prisoner of the French twice in the Ohio territory during the French and Indian War, it was only natural for the American commander in chief to question the true motives for King Louis XVI's generous aid. Would the French want to stake a claim to the states, which they might conquer while aiding America? After knowing Rochambeau for only a short while, meeting with him but two times and exchanging a multitude of letters, Washington observed, reasoned, and drew his conclusion. Much to his surprise over time he found that he could trust Rochambeau.

Washington resumed his military journal on May 1, 1781. In this entry, he wrote: "Instead of having any thing in readiness to take the field, we have nothing; and instead of having the prospect of having a glorious offensive campaign before, we have a bewildered and gloomy prospect of a defensive one; unless we should receive a powerful aid of ships, troops, and money from our generous allies."[82] In so writing, there is no question the "generous allies" to whom he referred were the French, whom he hoped would reverse the "gloomy prospect."[83]

While waiting for the return of the Vicomte de Rochambeau and news of the dispatch of the second division, the Vicomte de Noailles admitted, "The gallant Frenchmen had come to America to deliver America entirely from the yoke of her tyrants, but all they seemed to be doing was waste time and money in Newport."[84] After Washington's visits the passage of time weighed heavily on the French forces as they prepared for an eventual march to meet with Washington's army at New York. They had been in Newport nine months already with no definite plan.

FRANCE RESPONDS

After four months of negotiations with the king and his ministers, the Vicomte left France on March 25, 1781. He arrived in Boston on May 6, 1781, aboard the *Concorde* and immediately traveled overland to Newport to report to his father, General Rochambeau.[85] He brought with him Admiral de Barras who was to be the permanent replacement for Admiral de Ternay as commander of the French fleet in Newport.

Two days later Rochambeau received the news he had been waiting for over seven months. The bad news was that the king would not send more troops directly from France to America. The king's new minister of war, Ségur, did not agree to send the second division of soldiers, weakly reasoning that if he did, the British would only increase their numbers and there would be no advantage in the end. In reality the Vicomte had been a poor negotiator on this point and might have achieved better results had he paid more attention to his duty rather than succumbing to the many temptations to attend balls and fancy gatherings at Versailles. He had in fact wasted precious time in France while his father and the French army waited in limbo in Newport.

The good news was that the Vicomte de Rochambeau had returned with some six million livres that were sorely needed to continue the financing of the war effort in America. That the French foreign minister was still willing to send financial support came as excellent news to Rochambeau's ears. The king had also borrowed from the Dutch another ten million livres, bringing the sum "total of advanced funds equal to twenty-four millions by Vergennes' estimate."[86] The outlay of funds to help the American cause, compared with their resources, was astronomical considering the precarious state of France's treasury in 1780. King Louis XVI was criticized for extravagant spending as was King Louis XIV, who one hundred years earlier had spent about five and a half million livres to expand Versailles from a small hunting lodge to a lavish palace.

Along with the funds sent from France came more good news. It came in the form of a promise that superior naval forces would come in the latter part of July or August via the West Indies. The coming of this "superior naval force" would fulfill the main principle that Washington and Rochambeau had agreed upon at the Hartford Conference.[87] The intervention of the French navy would be the most important tactic of their combined success.

The Marquis de Castries, minister of the Marines, included a personal letter to Rochambeau indicating that the fleet he was sending would be under the command of Admiral de Grasse and was heading for the French West Indies. It would consist of twenty ships of the line, three frigates, and 156 transports to which he would add ten ships in the islands.[88] Barras's squadron of eight from Newport would join with De Grasse when the time was right. When combined, the two fleets would pose a mighty threat to those of the British navy. Castries concluded his note with this: "I hope that for quite a long while he [De Grasse] will be master of the coasts of America and will be able to act with you if you wish to undertake some engagement."[89]

Also included in the packet, which the Vicomte delivered personally to his father from the Court of Versailles, was a letter from Jacques Necker, French finance minister. He enclosed letters of credit to be spent only on food supplies for the French army. Necker wrote, "I shall continue to furnish the effective force…and nothing will be closer to me than what is important to your army. I observe with great satisfaction the care which you give to economic matters. It is in looking after everything at once that you outstrip the ordinary man. I beg you to believe me most interested in your welfare, in yourself, in your fame."[90]

This was all very reassuring, but in a few months' time the all-powerful holder of France's purse strings, Necker, would be dismissed. After publishing his *compte rendu du roi* (the king's financial statement) in which he drew up an all-too-rosy balance sheet of France's current state of finances, he would be packing his bags for early retirement.

Despite these promises, Rochambeau was disappointed. He wanted the extra men that the king had promised and felt that seven months of work on the part of his son had brought paltry results. "My son has come back to this country quite unaccompanied; whatever may come of it, the king must be served as he wishes to be and I am going to begin this second campaign with all the zeal and, I dare to say, the love with which I am filled for himself and for his service, using as best I can the very limited means which he leaves in my power."[91]

Although there had been talk in the fall of 1780 of attacking British General Clinton's forces in New York City before the cold weather set in, it was now spring, and without the second division, an attack on New York was still far too risky. According to Bertrand Comte de Lauberdière's reports, General Washington was more than eager to attack New York, while General Rochambeau still disagreed. But in the spirit of Franco-American cooperation, which General Rochambeau more than anyone else represented, the French commander promised his full support as soon as the decision was made.

Once Washington received word of the Vicomte de Rochambeau's return with the funds, Washington decided the time was ripe for the French army to join him at Philipsburg on the Hudson.[92] There was no more time to waste. When the two armies and their leaders united, the American general would decide the best course of action to take against the British.

WETHERSFIELD CONFERENCE

Finally, a third meeting between Rochambeau and Washington was set for May 21, 1781, in Wethersfield, Connecticut. Again, Washington traveled a similar route, passing through Litchfield where, on the morning of the 19th, Elihu Hubbard Smith made an entry in his diary referring to his meeting the general. Smith had prepared a basket of apples, which he remarked was a treasure at that time of year. He planned to present it to Washington, and only

Washington. Apparently others in Washington's party, namely Knox, Hamilton, and Duportail, had fixed their eyes on the beautiful red fruit, hoping to partake of the treasure before it was bestowed on their leader. Smith wrote, "At length, the Commander in Chief came. I made known my business, & presented my fruit. With what a look did he accept my proffered present! It penetrated to my soul! It was full of kindness, full of complacency. Exalted Man! Wast thou not born to sway the minds of men with glowing, yet serene admiration?"[93] The fruit was then shared with Washington's officers.[94]

Washington was offered the Joseph Webb House on Main Street, Wethersfield, to be used for both his lodging and the meeting site. His staff was offered the Silas Deane House next door. Deane, who had been instrumental in signing the 1778 Treaty of Alliance with the French, was still in France. These two houses today make up the Webb-Deane-Stevens Museum in Old Wethersfield. They are owned and maintained by the Colonial Dames of America. Rochambeau and his staff made their headquarters nearby at the Nathaniel Stillman Tavern, which no longer stands. The allied generals were joined by Governor Trumbull and Jeremiah Wadsworth. On the evening of May 21 the American and French dignitaries were feted by a concert at the Wethersfield Congregational Church and dinner the next night at Stillman's Tavern.[95]

On May 22, Rochambeau and his entourage, with Trumbull and probably Wadsworth, left for Wethersfield via Hartford, where the French contingent was again entertained at a sizeable reception including the Matrosses artillery followed by dinner at Collier's, according to Herbert J. Stoeckel's *Washington Visited Here...He sure did!*[96] The title intimates that the dinner party was costly to the state of Connecticut's taxpayers. The wine flowed most of the night. The drinks alone numbered: 80 bowls of punch, 81 bottles of Madeira wine, 26 bowls of toddy, 32 bottles of port wine and 50 bowls of grog, as quoted in the *Courant Magazine,* February 20, 1966.[97] Evidently, the Governor's Foot Guard not only escorted the visitors but also celebrated with them that late night in Hartford. The French continued on the next day and arrived in Newport on May 26.

The important result of the Wethersfield Conference was that "the deadlock was broken when Rochambeau agreed to move his troops overland to link up with Washington outside New York."[98] He did not agree to attack New York, only to go there with his troops. They would hold off on a strategy agreement until they gathered on the North River (the Hudson). Washington still pinned his hopes on his primary objective, the siege of New York. For him, the march south would be a secondary objective at best. Lauberdière saw that Washington was not considering the southern theater as a possibility.

There has been a great deal of discussion and divergence of opinion over the years as to the real outcome of the Wethersfield Conference. Walter W. Woodward, Connecticut State Historian at the University of Connecticut, wrote an article in the *Cincinnati Fourteen, Journal of the Society of the Cincinnati,* Fall 2006, in which he postulated four salient points gleaned from the best documents available. They are worth considering. Keep in mind that the meetings were adjourned by May 22.

> **Point One:**
> As of May 22 1781, neither commander was in a position to fully commit to a course of action; therefore, no final campaign plan was fully committed to at Wethersfield.

> **Point Two:**
> Each commander had a preferred course of action for the summer campaign.

> **Point Three:**
> The developing situation after May 22 ultimately determined the course of the 1781 campaign.

> **Point Four:**
> The flexibility of the strategy planned at Wethersfield was what made the victory in 1781 possible.[99]

All four points are valid. Because of the open-ended plan adopted by the allies, Rochambeau and Washington were free to respond to events as they happened. Rochambeau had vowed to fully support his commanding general's final decision. In the interim, Rochambeau would prepare his army to march west to join forces with the Continental army. So, although the deadlock was broken and there would be action, it was not at all clear what track the ensuing action would ultimately take as they left Wethersfield and Hartford to go in their separate directions.

CHAPTER FIVE

The March to Victory Begins

"The Soissonais in Minorca and the Bourbonnais, les petits vieux,...at Clostercamp...were the flower of the French army."

— ARNOLD WHITRIDGE

AFTER ROCHAMBEAU RETURNED to Newport and Washington was back at his headquarters in Philipsburg, they continued their correspondence via long-distance courier. They knew that with the imminent advent of summer they would want to combine the French and American troops at Washington's camp. Preparations had begun for the march to Philipsburg in the late fall of 1780. A touring party left Newport headed by Major General Chastellux, a professional soldier who distinguished himself in the Seven Years' War. He was also a literary man of note, a member of the French Academy, a friend of the Encyclopédistes, and author of a two-volume work on public welfare, *De la Félicité Publique,* which Benjamin Franklin said "showed Chastellux to be a real friend of humanity."[1] General Rochambeau wanted Chastellux to check the routes for the army to travel and to locate campsites that would accommodate large numbers of men and their equipment. Colonel Ethis de Corny, one of the commissaries, helped to establish the winter quarters for Rochambeau's army. He had been sent as an "advance officer to America to make initial contacts about hospitals, accommodation[s] and supplies" and a year earlier may have taken many of the same routes as Chastellux.[2]

Providence, Rhode Island, was Chastellux's first stop. Then he headed into Connecticut to Voluntown (now Sterling), where he stayed the night at Dorrance's Tavern. Chastellux recalled that his cart did not arrive with the rest of the party, which prompted him to complain, "Neither my excellent supper, nor the books of Mr. Dorrance, nor even the fine eyes of Miss Pearce made my cart arrive."[3] The cart was of utmost importance to him, as it was carrying some of his fine wines that he had hoped to share with his host.[4] It was important to impress the proprietor since his relatives owned the fields most likely to be used as a campsite months later.

According to Chastellux's journal, the Americans he met along the way were extraordinarily patriotic and were involved in the war one way or another. He had "not found two who have not borne arms, heard the whistling of balls."[5] As he traveled southwest to Plainfield, Connecticut, he found this town much to his liking, and soon determined the town could provide "a camp fit for even ten thousand men!"[6] From there he went to Canterbury and Windham and described in his notes such details as the landscape, the terrain, the number of houses in each community, and the status of the country roads, town streets, and squares.[7]

In Windham Chastellux dined with the Duc de Lauzun who was en route from Newport to his winter quarters in Lebanon with about one-third of his legion. Lauzun was arguably the most colorful of Rochambeau's soldiers. Armand-Louis de Gontaut, Duc de Lauzun, later known as the Duc de Biron, was born a nobleman in Paris in 1747. His military career began at the age of fourteen in an elite regiment commanded by his uncle, the Duc de Biron. At age nineteen he was married against his will, and the marriage was impersonal and childless. Like Rochambeau, he preferred the life of armed forces to that of the court. Reportedly, he was popular with the ladies. He was more lighthearted, perhaps, than Rochambeau; nevertheless, they each had a love for the military. Lauzun's desires for such accoutrements as musicians for the voyage to America gave him a reputation for extravagance and self-indulgence. He was, no doubt, a spirited man, determined in his pursuit of military responsibility and influence.

From 1767 until Lauzun's first legions were formed, he served in a variety of ways in Europe, including: aide-de-camp to the Marquis de Chauvelin during an expedition to Corsica in 1769, colonel of the Legion Royal (1774-1776), and colonel of the cavalry regiment Dragons du Roi (1776-1778). In 1776, Russia, under Catherine the Great, recommended Lauzun to command a company of foreign hussars. However, King Louis XVI did not allow him.[8]

Lauzun earnestly continued to request military duties, and on September 1, 1778, the Voluntaires Étrangers de la Marine (Foreign Volunteers of the Navy) was created. The Duc de Lauzun was appointed to organize and command the new corps of foreign volunteers comprised of eight legions. Each legion would have eight companies, six of infantry or artillery and two squadrons of hussars, for a total of four thousand men.[9] Only three of the eight legions were established; the recruits were primarily French, but many European countries were represented among the troops.

Lauzun was dispatched to Senegal on the west coast of Africa late in 1778, and the infantry he took with him was not from his regiment, except for two or three officers. He remained nominally in charge of his three legions of Voluntaires Étrangers de la Marine while he was in Senegal. One of the legions was dispatched to the West Indies and another to the Indian Ocean. The Second Legion remained in Brittany, and when he returned to France, Lauzun obtained the legion and sought to be engaged under Rochambeau for a potential landing in England.

In early 1780 Lauzun learned that General Rochambeau had been given the command of a special expedition of troops to America. Lauzun commented, "I asked if I should be employed in that army.... Rochambeau needed light troops; those offered him did not suit him; he asked for me, he was refused at first; he insisted [on me]."[10] Lauzun accepted the position and joined the exciting campaign to the New World.

Shortly thereafter, under the *Ordonnance du Roi* of March 5, 1780, Louis XVI called for a reorganization of the Second Legion of the Voluntaires Étrangers de la Marine into an autonomous legion having its own administration under Lauzun's command. The legion would be deployed to the colonies and was named Volontaires Étrangers de Lauzun. This new legion was composed of two companies of fusiliers, a grenadier company, a company of chasseurs, and an artillery company. The cavalry component consisted of two squadrons of hussars.[11]

The term hussar was first used to describe a type of fifteenth-century Hungarian light cavalryman. The hussar officer wore a sky-blue jacket adorned with as many as one hundred buttons connected by much gold braid, a red cummerbund liberally decorated with the same braid, brilliant-red riding breeches, tall boots, white gloves, and a tall marten fur hat called a busby, worn over a white-powdered wig. He carried a long, curved sword in a golden sheath, standard issue for a legionnaire.

The Duc de Lauzun, as commander, stood out from the rest due to his oversized leopard-skin dress blanket, which covered his saddle and half of his horse's hindquarters. Lauzun's Legion was the most ornate unit to serve in the American War. The legion had fifty-six officers, mostly French. The majority of the troops were from the French provinces, with the remainder from other countries, including Hungary, Denmark, Sweden, England, Ireland, Poland, and the German states.[12]

When Lauzun's Legion was formed in 1780, it consisted of eight hundred men. However, when it was time for the newly formed legion to ship out with Rochambeau, only six hundred men departed due to a shortage of transport ships. Nearly two hundred of them were hussars, and they had to purchase horses in America since there was no room to bring their mounts with them.[13]

LAUZUN MAKES CAMP IN LEBANON, CONNECTICUT

Lauzun's Legion, reduced somewhat in size due to deaths from illness since setting sail from France, disembarked with the rest of the French forces in Newport. About two-thirds of the legion would winter there. Rochambeau, thinking that the cost of billeting all the men and horses was too exorbitant in Rhode Island, relegated the remaining third (about 225) of the legion to Lebanon, Connecticut, for the winter. For the society-loving Lauzun, this was like being banished to the hinterlands in an unfamiliar country. As Lauzun lamented in his memoirs, "I started for Lebanon on the 10th of November...Siberia alone can furnish any idea of Lebanon, which consists of a few huts scattered among vast forests."[14]

During his temporary stay in Newport, prior to moving to Lebanon, Lauzun had been billeted in the widow Hunter's house at 264 Thames Street. The Duc de Lauzun enjoyed the widow's gracious hospitality and the company of her three daughters who must have caught his fancy. Lauzun behaved himself and maintained the highest standards of dignity during his stay in Newport and throughout his tour in America. The same, however, could not be said about the behavior of his troops during the ensuing winter in Lebanon, Connecticut, when Lauzun was away on an extended trip.

Lebanon, Connecticut, often referred to as the "Heartbeat of the Revolution," was named for the stands of white cedar in Cedar Swamp, which reminded the Reverend James Fitch of the biblical white cedars of Lebanon. Although the North American white cedar is not the same species as the true cedar of Lebanon, it was not surprising that the Puritans would make the association. The legislature confirmed Fitch's choice of name for the town in 1697. It was the first town in the colony to bear a biblical name.[15]

Connecticut's indispensable participation in the Revolutionary War was directed from the town of Lebanon by its own local son, Governor Jonathan Trumbull. He was the driving force who encouraged the men of Connecticut to join the independence movement by enlisting in the Continental army and offering their resources to support the war effort.

Preparation for the move of Lauzun's Legion to Lebanon was handled by Commissary Jeremiah Wadsworth before winter set in.

As for housing for the winter season, Lauzun was offered the most beautiful and commodious house in town, that of David Trumbull, third son of the Connecticut governor, Jonathan Trumbull Sr. The Trumbull family was well known in Connecticut during the War of Independence. The governor had five children, Joseph, Faith, Jonathan Jr., David, and John. David Trumbull's house, located on the southwest end of the Green, was known as the Redwood House and became the headquarters for French officers during the winter of 1780–1781.[16] Lauzun held many strategy meetings at the nearby War Office situated on the Green. Before the war, this building was known as Governor Jonathan Trumbull's store. During the war, the governor made this humble building his headquarters. Today this building is owned by the Connecticut Society of the Sons of the American Revolution.[17]

René-Marie, Vicomte d'Arrot, Lauzun's second-in-command, made his headquarters at the home of Jonathan Trumbull Jr., second son of the governor. George Washington probably stayed in this house in March 1781 on his way to meet with Rochambeau in Newport. While in town, the American general took time to review the hussars on the Green, which provided a welcome change from their everyday routine.[18] Washington was so impressed with Jonathan Jr. that he employed him as his private secretary and aide-de-camp for the grand march to Virginia.

John Trumbull, the youngest son of Governor Jonathan Trumbull, was born in 1756 in Lebanon, and was the "Patriot Artist of the American Revolution." He drew his inspiration from English painters Benjamin West and John Singleton Copley and later from the French portrait painters of the French Revolution, such as Jacques-Louis David and Vigée-Le Brun. John Trumbull was best known for his anthology of four paintings of the American Revolution: *George Washington Resigning His Commission, The Surrender of Burgoyne, The Surrender of Cornwallis,* and *The Declaration of Independence,* all of which were commissioned for the rotunda of the United States Capitol Building.[19]

Adjacent to the famous Lebanon Green was the home of Governor Jonathan Trumbull Sr. Amelia Dyer Trumbull, widowed daughter-in-law of the governor, served as hostess to the French. Trumbull's wife, Faith Robinson Trumbull, had died before the French landed, thus explaining the need for Amelia to take on the responsibility of helping serve the French. The house is owned today by the Connecticut Daughters of the American Revolution.[20]

Colonel Robert-Guillaume Comte Dillon, Lauzun's *colonel-en-second,* was housed with William Williams, the brother of Dr. Thomas Williams, near the Redwood House. William Williams was one of the signers of the Declaration of Independence. When the legion arrived, Mr. Williams was away, leaving Mrs. Williams to accommodate the foreign visitors until his return. By March, Mr. Williams was back home long enough to become intolerant of Lauzun's Legion. He said that the people of Lebanon were promised "that the French troops were kept under the best government and discipline and that the inhabitants of Newport had not lost a pig nor a fowl by them which was a great inducement to provide them quarters here…but soon they began to pilfer and steal."[21]

During the course of the winter, the hussars were quartered in simple wooden barracks much like the ones used by George Washington's troops during the winter encampments at Valley Forge and Morristown. These simple log huts, meant to hold twelve men each, were hastily constructed in the fields along the west side of the Lebanon Green.[22] The hussars conducted daily drills and trained their horses on a regular basis on the Green. They constructed bread ovens in a bake house on the Green.[23] Unaccustomed to American bread making, apparently they had no taste for the local whole wheat and cornmeal, preferring to make their own crusty white bread.

The cost of timber to build the huts and bake house was quite high, not to mention food and drink for the workmen who set up the camp in Lebanon. Wadsworth had left David Trumbull, Assistant State Commissary, in charge of the local preparations.[24] His expenses included payment for a barrel of pork, 10 barrels of West Indies rum, 9½ tons of flour, 14,223 pounds of wheat flour, and 4,421 pounds of rye flour. His men built a slaughterhouse as well as a guard-house to protect the French currency and serve as armory and jail.[25] Trumbull ordered the required amounts of straw, hay, and oats for the 236 horses quartered in Lebanon.[26] The total supplies needed for Lauzun's army were as follows: 145 tons of hay, about 23 tons of straw, more than 1,700 bushels of corn, 800 bushels of oats, 101 cords of wood, 7,359 pounds of beef, 1,092 pounds of mutton, 28 head of cattle, and 46 sheep.[27] Naturally, local suppliers' costs escalated rapidly, and they demanded pay in silver rather than the virtually valueless Continental paper currency. Rochambeau's kegs of silver coin were put to good use in Lebanon that winter.

As the winter progressed, there were the usual duties to keep the hussars occupied. Rochambeau, well aware of the dangers posed by bored soldiers without close supervision, requested that the hussar corps "should be in the same place under the inspection of its chief who will answer of the discipline of his troops."[28] Occasionally, visitors came to Lebanon on war-planning business, as did Rochambeau in December 1780.

Wadsworth expressed in frequent letters to Rochambeau and others the complaints that came his way regarding the high cost and poor quality of hay for Lauzun's horses. Wadsworth wrote, "There is such a train of under staff officers at Lebanon and so much difficulty with them. I am going there tomorrow. We are to be the dupes of all these people." After leaving Lebanon, he added a postscript to his note: "I am tired of quartering troops. I had rather live outdoors all my life than undertake such a job again."[29]

WINTER VISITORS

1781 began on a positive note with a visit from Chastellux on New Year's Day. He and Lauzun spent the day squirrel hunting. Chastellux wrote in his journal, "These [squirrels] are larger and have more beautiful fur than those in Europe."[30]

The Squirrel Hunt

General Chastellux (L) and the Duc de Lauzun (R), after a squirrel
hunt at the Redwood House, Lebanon; New Year's Day, 1781.
Artist: David R. Wagner.

Rochambeau wrote of Lauzun in his memoirs, "I will relate
an anecdote, which will convey a just idea of his [Duc de Lauzun's]
private character. One of the good villagers asked him of what
trade his father was in France. 'My father,' replied De Lauzun, 'is not
in business; but I have an uncle, a marshal.'…'Ah, indeed!' said the
American, giving him a hearty squeeze of the hand; 'There are worse
trades than that.'" The joke was that in France, a marshal (*maréchal*
in French) was a nobleman, which was the highest military rank. In
America the word marshal was used for a farrier (a blacksmith).[31]
Lauzun never corrected the American's erroneous impression.

Before the winter was out, some of the legionnaires deserted.
The records show that more German-speaking soldiers deserted than
French-speaking. One reason is that they found it easy to assimilate
into American society because of the friendly enclaves of German-
speakers, particularly in Pennsylvania. Actually, an entire hussar
patrol disappeared in December 1780, and just prior to the final

march in June 1781, more than twenty-four hussars did not report for duty. Lauzun punished deserter Jacques Sauker, age twenty-five, of the second squadron of hussars. He was executed by firing squad in Lebanon December 26, 1780.

Of utmost importance for the entire operation in Rhode Island and Connecticut was clear communication between Washington and Rochambeau and all of their key people. For this purpose, Washington established a chain of communication with Rochambeau in the summer of 1780 through one of America's most hard-working units, Sheldon's Dragoons.

Colonel Sheldon's Dragoons, consisting of three hundred mounted men, were America's first commissioned cavalry. By June 4, 1780, George Washington had many of these dragoons guarding western Connecticut and both Westchester and Putnam Counties in New York State. Some twelve to fifteen dragoons were assigned to Washington as his personal escort. Other dragoons carried mail between the French command in Newport and Washington's camp. Still others sought information about British troop movements and relayed this knowledge back to Washington. Thus, Sheldon's Dragoons assisted in many of the same duties as Lauzun's cavalry and played an important part in the success of the Franco-American campaign.[33]

The dragoons began their express mail service shortly after Rochambeau's arrival in Newport. There was only one intercept before the close of 1780. After this incident, Sheldon made immediate changes to routes and avoided further British interception of Rochambeau and Washington's communications. "Sheldons," as they were often called, prepared and guarded routes for Washington when he left to meet with Rochambeau and other key military and civilian personnel in 1780 and 1781.

As tradition would have it in the late eighteenth century, the Sheldons might have rested in the winter, since warring factions generally retired into winter seclusion. The horses needed the winter rest as much as the men. The two worked as one, day and night, to get express messages through to their destinations. By December 8, 1780, they were finally permitted to take time off to rest and refit, but it would not be for long. Washington needed his communications with the French, so the Sheldons were soon ordered back on duty.[34]

In the spring, as scheduling for the campaign began to take shape, George Washington made constant use of the couriers for intelligence and for securing supplies.[35] By May, the Sheldons had earned high respect from all the principals involved for the superb quality of service they offered to both the Americans and French.

Advance parties continued to scout out campsites and sources of supplies along the route from Rhode Island to New York State. Connecticut, known as "the Provisions State" during the Revolution, provided most of the needed supplies for the stay in Lebanon, as well as for the eventual march. Colonel Jeremiah Wadsworth gathered the materials needed for the expected march to New York and paid for it with French currency.[36]

It was not all work for the French officers and soldiers those winter months in Rhode Island and Connecticut. On the contrary, many found time for a full schedule of parties with the Newporters and Lebanoners. In truth, when the time came to leave New England, they found it hard to say farewell to the friendly Americans who had invited them so freely into their homes. At last, however, the dancing had to be set aside for the serious business at hand, that of final preparations for the march out of Newport to Providence, and then across Connecticut and into New York. Rochambeau's plans included leaving Newport well guarded under the command of M. de Choisy. The British still posed a real threat there.[37]

On May 6, 1781, Rochambeau's son returned from France with six million livres in hard currency. Washington's decision to start the march was a *fait accompli* and milder weather permitted travel and the final gathering of provisions. There was much work to be done and plans to be finalized. By June 11, 1781, everything was at last in readiness for the monumental march to victory.

Adieu to Lebanon

Rochambeau relayed orders to Lauzun to depart from Lebanon, and thus Lauzun's Legion prepared to bid adieu to their winter hosts. During the *expédition particulière* in America, it was generally the case that, for reasons of strategy, Lauzun's Legion camped or marched separately from the main body of Rochambeau's army. They wintered in a location many miles from the main army, and when it came time to march to New York to join forces with Washington, Rochambeau assigned them a separate route to fend off Tories or guard against a possible attack from the British who held the Connecticut shoreline.[38] Great care had to be taken to pass through undisturbed. All skirmishes were to be avoided during this important movement of French forces.

Fifty hussars had been retained in Newport and were heavily used expressly as couriers chiefly between Rochambeau and Washington. Lauzun's Legion was also deployed to guide and protect shipments of specie (coined money), which arrived from France on the New England coast. Their work included guarding shipments of much-needed supplies for Rochambeau and his army.

The hussars and infantry that had wintered in Rhode Island met Lauzun and the rest of the legion at Lebanon for the march to Washington's camp. Lauzun's entire legion left Lebanon on June 20th, 1781 and headed to New York by a circuitous route. According to Closen's diary, "Lauzun's Legion was detached from our army to cover our left flank and to act separately, according to circumstances, in concert with the American army."[39] Alexander Berthier offered more detail: "This column was to march in a separate column 9 miles to the left of the army in order to cover its left flank on the march."[40]

Lauzun marched with his 600 troops including 200 cavalry and 400 infantry and artillery. Bringing up the rear were the field artillery, commissaries, and baggage train, most of which progressed at a slower pace than Rochambeau's regiments that took the right flank to their north. The field artillery company was made up of "6 officers and 65 NCOs [non-commissioned officers]. A local witness counted 810 wagons, each pulled by two yoked oxen and a lead horse."[41]

Soon after departing Lebanon, at the current junction of Connecticut Routes 207 and 16, Lauzun's Legion split into two columns, both south of Rochambeau's column.[42] One took the northern route or right flank and the other the southern route or left flank as they crossed the state from east to west. The right flank traversed Colchester and arrived in Middletown on June 22 on the west bank of the Connecticut River.[43] Then, as thanks to the French officers, a dance was held on the Philip Mortimer property.[44] On June 25 Lauzun's right flank moved on toward Wallingford, and the next day followed the Quinnipiac River to North Haven and New Haven where they joined their left flank.[45] The left flank had passed through Colchester, East Haddam, Chester, and Pettipaug, and picked up the Boston Post Road before entering New Haven to join the right flank. On June 26 the full legion, wrote the president of Yale College, Dr. Ezra Stiles, "pitched their Tents in the new Town half a mile East of the College. I paid my respects to the Duke and was received very politely at the House of the late Gen. Wooster."[46]

Rochambeau confirmed the route of Lauzun's Legion in a note to Washington on June 23, 1781: Lauzun "is marching ahead of my first division via Middletown, Wallingford, North Haven, Ripton [today's Huntington], and North Stratford [became Trumbull in 1797]."[47] The French general may have confused North Haven with New Haven, a common error in the case of either one being written as "N. Haven."[48] Rochambeau put his aide, Mathieu Dumas, in charge of "the establishment of the quarters of the legion."[49]

On June 27 Lauzun and his men marched to Derby/Oxford and camped on Sentinel Hill from which they could view Long Island Sound. Next the entourage moved into Stratford/Monroe where they rested for three days. The route that Lauzun took is difficult to authenticate, but the late author Jane de Forest Shelton, of Derby, confirmed the order of the march as follows: "Lauzun, with his legion of six hundred men, cavalry, hussars, grenadiers, and lancers, passed through New Haven June 27, camped on Sentinel Hill, in Derby, then wound down the steep roads, crossed Naugatuck and Housatonic Rivers, and took the winding way up the west bank of the latter, finding it necessary at times to improve the road with a double corduroy for the passage of the heavy wagons. Finally…it reached 'the Centre' of New Stratford, now the town of Monroe."[50] The legionnaires made their encampment on the west side of the town Green. As they were in great need of hay for the horses and oxen when they arrived at Stratford, William Scott, a local man, did the French hussars a favor by rallying friends to mow his field by the light of the moon to provide the feed.[51]

The officers settled into patriots' homes while the Duc de Lauzun was lodged in the tavern on the west side of the Green, which was owned by Nehemiah de Forest.[52] Mr. De Forest, being of French Huguenot descent, was happy to host America's French allies. He was so pleased with having the opportunity to host the Duc de Lauzun that when his wife gave birth to a son while the duke was in residence, he and his wife named their son Lauzun De Forest. It was with great pride that his name was passed down through the De Forest and Nichols families for many generations.[53]

Another French namesake became a reminder of the Lauzun visit. The duke's Irish *colonel en second*, Comte Dillon, made a generous gift of a rapier to Squire Samuel Lewis, and in return, his relatives, the Scott family, named their son Dillon.[54]

On the evening of June 30 the French military band played lively tunes for a summer ball, which was held on the second-floor ballroom of the Daniel Bassett Homestead (later Edward Coffey's home). The patriotic and polite young ladies of Monroe were enthralled to see such finely dressed Frenchmen. Lauzun and his legion wore the most extravagant uniforms in Rochambeau's expedition. "Weary as the army was with the ascent, an array of six hundred men with all the splendor of gold lace and nodding plumes, the horses bravely caparisoned…was a rare sight…to those whose knowledge of military display had been limited to the 'training' of one small company of men not even in uniform or an occasional 'trooper' as he rode to his camp."[55]

On that last night in Stratford, in the midst of a dance, Lauzun received orders from Washington to leave early the next morning to meet Rochambeau and his troops in Bedford, New York. So, at daybreak on the morning of July 1, Lauzun and his famous legion of hussars and light infantry marched out of Stratford/Monroe bound for New York. In a matter of hours they would join forces with Rochambeau and Washington in their first skirmish with the British.

ROCHAMBEAU'S MARCH
TO NEW YORK

On June 11, 1781, Rochambeau's troops readied themselves for their departure from Newport. They took their leave prior to that of Lauzun's Legion from Lebanon. However, a serious disagreement took place just before the departure of the troops from Newport. With departure time at hand for the French in Newport, Rochambeau's nephew, Lauberdière, needed to purchase some horses. Since the Marquis du Bouchet had been ordered to remain as chief of staff in Newport, Lauberdière offered to buy his horses. Apparently, the former was not content to stay behind when most of the army was departing on what purported to be one of the most glorious campaigns of the century. Du Bouchet was highly insulted at this slight and challenged the latter to a duel. "Lauberdière was 'seriously wounded' and Du Bouchet was almost killed. A second had to help pull Lauberdière's sword out of Du Bouchet's shoulder where it had lodged underneath his collar bone."[56] This incident only recently came to light when Lauberdière's journal was discovered after more than two hundred years. This long-lost journal of Rochambeau's nephew consisted of 350 pages of his hand-written notes illustrated with fourteen of his hand-drawn maps. In the introduction he cited that he kept the journal not only to provide for his own memories, but also "to recall...certain events of the most extraordinary and most glorious revolution recorded in history."[57]

General Rochambeau gave orders to move the troops and supplies from Newport to Providence, which was to be the first staging point on the cross-country trip. Most troops were ferried up the Providence River on small craft to the capital where they waited for a convoy of French ships escorted by a fifty-gun ship, the *Sagittaire,* to arrive from Boston. The ships finally arrived, bringing "two companies of artillery, some recruits, and ammunition and equipment of every kind" to join the Rochambeau entourage.[58] Once assembled, they were ready to begin their 220-mile journey to New York along roughly the same route travelled by Chastellux.

As General Rochambeau watched his army leave Newport to commence its march to New York, he experienced a moment of great pride. He was especially fond of two of his regiments; he had fought alongside the Soissonnais in Minorca and the Bourbonnais at Clostercamp.[59] As Arnold Whitridge so aptly wrote in *Rochambeau, America's Neglected Founding Father,* "They were the flower of the French infantry, and to Lieutenant-General Jean-Baptiste-Donatien de Vimeur, Comte de Rochambeau, commanding His Most Christian Majesty's forces in America, the French infantry was the most beautiful instrument in the world."[60]

Due to the great numbers involved, Rochambeau's four regiments left Providence, Rhode Island, in waves of about one thousand each day, for four consecutive days. Rochambeau departed with the first regiment, the Bourbonnais, on June 18. The next day, the Royal Deux-Ponts, under Baron de Vioménil, took their leave, followed by the Soissonnais under Comte de Vioménil, brother of the baron. Lastly, the Saintonge regiment, led by Comte de Custine, left on June 21, 1781.

Before leaving Newport, Rochambeau sent a series of dispatches to Admiral de Grasse. He included copies of the articles of the conference at Wethersfield while pointing out to him that the situation in the South was worsening, especially in Virginia, and that if Cornwallis, with his army of eight thousand, should attack Lafayette's small army of twelve hundred, things would quickly worsen. In these same dispatches, Rochambeau took it upon himself to suggest to

De Grasse that it might be advisable to attempt the long march south with the American allies. By so doing, the combined armies might engage a smaller force in Virginia than they would encounter in New York. The French general wrote, "I then suggested, as my own opinion, the propriety of attempting an expedition to Chesapeake against the army of Lord Cornwallis, and which I considered more practicable."[61] It would have the additional aspect of being unexpected by the enemy. The British would be surprised indeed, should the allies decide to march such a long distance to engage the unsuspecting Cornwallis. At this point George Washington was not aware of negotiations being made by the French to secure the much-needed naval support.

Further, as the French commander recorded in his memoirs, "I begged of him [De Grasse] to intercede with the governors of San Domingo to let us have the French brigade, under the orders of M. de Saint-Simon.... I begged him also to raise a loan of twelve hundred thousand francs [1.2 million livres] in our [Caribbean] colonies, to ensure the success of the expedition."[62] General Rochambeau eagerly awaited De Grasse's response as did French Minister Vergennes and Spanish envoy D'Aranda at Versailles, as well as La Luzerne in Philadelphia. They all counted on De Grasse to make the voyage to the Chesapeake, which would be favorable to the combined American, French, and Spanish interests. De Grasse's aid to the Americans in their plight could change the outcome of the Revolution. Remember the abiding principle on which Washington and Rochambeau had already agreed: without the support of the French fleet, the campaign would fail.

Because it was summer and the weather could be exceedingly warm in New England, Rochambeau's men were awakened at 2:00 a.m. each day and the march was underway by 4:00 a.m. This allowed the expedition to commence their twelve- to fifteen-mile march between stopovers in the cool pre-dawn hours and be at their next campsite before noon.

While tents were being set up, repairs commenced, bread was baked, and the butchering was done. Once the white canvas tents were pitched, they remained in place until the last regiment used them. The general officers were usually given quarters in a nearby tavern or in homes of the local gentry while company-grade officers slept on the ground in two-man tents.

Each regiment was led by an assistant quartermaster general and was preceded by workmen commanded by an engineer who directed the filling of potholes and the removing of obstacles. The Vicomte de Rochambeau headed the first division of Bourbonnais. Then came the officers and men, horse-drawn artillery, seven wagons of Rochambeau's baggage, and regimental wagons carrying tents and officers' luggage. Besides their muskets, the soldiers, dressed in gaiters, wigs, and tight-fitting woolen underwear, carried equipment weighing almost sixty pounds. Following closely behind were the division's hospital wagons, other wagons that carried the valuable military chests under the supervision of the chief treasurer, wagons for the butchers, wagons for bread, fodder, the "king's stock," and the brigade for wagonwrights and shoeing smiths. Livestock on the hoof brought up the rear.[63] Accompanying "Rochambeau and his fellow generals [were] eight, ten or more servants, some free, some slaves… On June 5, 1781 [Rochambeau] acquired a black slave who had been captured during Admiral Destouches's expedition to Virginia."[64]

Rochambeau and his troops made their way through Connecticut, camping at nine sites along the route: Plainfield, Windham, Bolton, East Hartford, Farmington, Southington (Marion), Middlebury, Newtown, and Ridgebury (Ridgefield).

The 39 camps used by General Rochambeau and the French army between Providence, Rhode Island, and Williamsburg, Virginia, June–September 1781, on their way to initiate the Battle of Yorktown, are listed on the following page. The origin of the main march was Newport, Rhode Island, for most of the army; Lauzun's Legion, except for the artillery, infantry and a portion of husssars who re-joined the legion in Lebanon just prior to the long march, originated in Lebanon, Connecticut, and took a different route from Rochambeau's main column.

List of marches and campsites between Newport and Williamsburg:

1. Camp à Providence, le 10 & 11 Juin.
2. Camp à Watermans Tavern le 18 Juin.
3. Camp à Plainfield, 19 Juin.
4. Camp à Windham, le 20 Juin.
5. Camp à Bolton, le 21 Juin.
6. Camp à East Hartford, le 22 Juin.
7. Camp à Farmington, le 26 Juin.
8. Camp à Barn's Tavern, le 26 Juin.
9. Camp à Break-Neck, le 27 Juin.
10. Camp à New-town, le 28 Juin.
11. Camp à Ridgebury, le 1er Juillet.
12. Camp à Bedford, le 2 Juillet.
13. Camp à North-Castle, le 3 Juillet.
14. Camp à Phillips'burg, le 5 Juillet.
15. Camp à North Castle, le 19 Aoust [sic].
16. Camp à Huntz-Tavern, le 21 Aoust.
17. Camp à King's Ferry, ou Verplanck, le 22 Aoust.
18. Camp à Hawen-Staw, le 24 Aoust.
19. Camp à Suffrantz, le 25 Aoust.
20. Camp à Pompton-Meeting-House, le 26 Aoust.
21. Camp à Wippany, le 27 Aoust.
22. Camp à Bullion's Tavern, le 29 Aoust.
23. Camp à Sommerset-Courte-House, le 30 Aoust.
24. Camp à Prince-Town, le 31 Aoust.
25. Camp à Trenton, le 1er Septembre.
26. Camp à Read-Lion's Tavern, le 2 Septembre.
27. Camp à Philadelphie, le 3 Septembre.
28. Camp à Chester, le 5 Septembre.
29. Camp à Wilmington, le 6 Septembre.
30. Camp à Head-of-Elk, le 7 Septembre.
31. Camp à Lowe[r]-Ferry, le 9 Septembre.
32. Camp à Bush-Town ou Hertford, le 10 Septembre.
33. Camp à White Marsh, le 11 Septembre.
34. Camp à Baltimore, le 12 Septembre.
35. Camp à Spurier's, le 16 Septembre.
36. Camp à Scott's House, le 17 Septembre.
37. Camp à Annapolis, le 18 Septembre.
38. Camp à Arche's Hope, le 25 Septembre.
39. Camp à William's Burg, le 26 Septembre ... Fin.[65]

Near the Bolton campsite was Daniel White's tavern known as White's Tavern at the Sign of the Black Horse, where Rochambeau stayed overnight. This seven-year-old tavern had fine accommodations for dancing. It was well known for its independently suspended dance floor, which rocked with the dancers. On the second floor, the center wall was cleverly fitted with hinges so that it could be raised and fastened to the ceiling to make space for the ballroom. Two bayonet holes were found in the ceiling of the upstairs bedroom, an example of atypical behavior by the French forces.

According to the journals of Baron von Closen and another of Rochambeau's aides-de-camp, Cromot du Bourg, although there were some women who marched with Rochambeau's army, they officially did not exist since they held no paid positions. Marriage for the enlisted men was frowned upon, but on occasion, some wives and a few children managed to tag along *à la ration*. These unofficial camp followers were obliged to sleep on their own outside the tents or barracks and were lucky to be given daily bread for sustenance.

For instance, there was an incident in Bolton, Connecticut, that involved a married couple and the property owner where the Royal Deux-Ponts regiment was encamped in June 1781. The Bolton host of the regiment was the well-to-do Reverend George Colton. He took a fancy to the four-year-old daughter of grenadier Adam Gabel and his wife who remains nameless. Colton offered to adopt the little girl for forty gold louis, a goodly sum that the reverend thought would entice the girl's parents to let her go and at the same time ease their finances for the remainder of the expedition. To the parents' credit, they would hear nothing of such an offer and turned him down. This is one of the few written accounts of Rochambeau's entourage, which involved the wife and child of one of his foreign soldiers who evidently accompanied the *expédition particulière* from start to finish. By all accounts, Gabel's wife and child walked with his regiment to Yorktown and back to Boston from which they all embarked with the Deux-Ponts, eventually returning to France. After arriving in Connecticut some fortunate women were hired as cooks, while others were assigned jobs in hospitals along the route to Yorktown. At the time of embarkation from America, the number of women and children travelling with the French army was thirty-four.[66]

Leaving Southington on June 27, they next marched through Waterbury, and the entire Bourbonnais regiment could be seen at once as it came down the hill past the intersection of Mill Street and East Main Street. It was an impressive sight. The soldiers marched two by two, and their brilliant white uniforms reflected the sun on that warm summer's day. The long narrow column of marchers stretched from one horizon to the next, as far as the eye could see. The French headed toward Middlebury, where they pitched camp number nine. Some soldiers complained that they had never seen such high hills and poor stony roads as they encountered on their way to Middlebury.

Two soldiers died from unknown causes at Beach's Tavern in Waterbury and were buried across the street in a small cemetery (now known as East Farms Cemetery). Their names and origins in France remain unknown.

The troops labored to get their artillery up to the Breakneck Hill campsite. Whether Breakneck (*casse-cou* in French) is named after the French army's difficulties in getting their tired, stubborn oxen to pull artillery up the steep approach to the camp or whether it was already called Breakneck matters not—it was an arduous task at the end of a long, hard day's march.[67] According to Crèvecoeur, "Our horses could do no more, so we had to commandeer all the oxen we passed and go far afield to find others in order to reach camp with our guns. Many of our wagons broke down. We never had a worse day considering the fatigues and misfortunes we endured."[68] Once ensconced at Breakneck, bread ovens were hastily built to make the many loaves needed to feed the men. It was reported that the thirsty soldiers and their animals drained dry all the wells in Middlebury during their stay.

Rochambeau likely dined at Josiah Bronson's Tavern and slept at Isaac Bronson's at Breakneck. There were few houses in the hamlet, and the hill was barren of trees. Josiah's home, halfway up the hill, had a fine view. Lauberdière said Josiah's daughter resembled "the queen of France."[69] Upon the departure of the army, it is said her father locked her in the house for fear that she would run off with a French soldier.[70] And so it goes throughout the trip—the French soldiers were debonair and the girls smitten!

While the main force was camped at Middlebury, one division pitched their tents along the main road in Old Woodbury. Their tents extended a distance of nearly three miles, and many of the locals wandered among them to greet the foreigners who had come so far to help them in their battle for independence.

During the evening, the French held a dance in which the Woodbury damsels joined with the polite Frenchmen dressed in their colorful uniforms. The soldiers found the local girls to be fine in looks and manners and good dancers as well. A party was held at the home of the Honorable Daniel Sherman. He served twelve bushels of apples and eight barrels of apple cider, and all had a happy time.

After leaving Woodbury, Rochambeau led his soldiers through Southbury and across the Housatonic River over a bridge "presumably built in late 1778 when 'his Excellency Gen. Washington sent a part of his army and built a bridge across this great river between... Woodbury and Newtown at Hinman's Ferry for the benefit of the army on their march.'"[71] It was known as Carleton's Bridge and "sat on piers made of framed boxes filled with pebbles."[72]

On July 1, the fifty-sixth birthday of General Rochambeau, the troops made their last camp in Connecticut at Ridgbury (Ridgefield). Of course, there was a celebratory fête that night before they moved on to meet Washington in Philipsburg.

According to Rochambeau's aide, Baron von Closen, while at Ridgebury Washington sent his new aide-de-camp, Colonel David Cobb, to attend Rochambeau's birthday party. It can be assumed that Cobb brought with him the letter his commander in chief penned to Rochambeau as follows: "Headquarters near Peekskill, June 30, 1781...There is another matter which appears to me exceedingly practicable upon the same night that we attempt the works on York Island, and which I would wish to commit to the execution of the Duke de Lauzun, provided that his Corps can be brought to a certain point in time. It is the surprise of a certain Corps of Light troops under the command of Colonel Delancey which lies at Morrisania without being covered by any works."[73] Washington was planning a first skirmish against the British with his French allies.

Before marching out of Newtown toward Ridgebury, Rochambeau had reorganized his forces from regiments into brigades. His first brigade was made up of the Bourbonnais and the Royal Deux-Ponts, and they left Ridgebury in the early morning of July 2. The second brigade, a day behind, consisted of the Soissonais and the Saintonge.[74] Washington's plan hinged on the simultaneous arrival of Rochambeau and the Duc de Lauzun at Bedford, New York, that evening. Since the British occupied the Connecticut shoreline at that time, Lauzun and his legion had taken up the left flank of the French army as they traversed the state of Connecticut. They had marched about ten miles to the south of the main army. In this way the mounted legion could fend off a possible British attack from the south.

Rochambeau's original route into Westchester County, New York, was planned to pass through Crompound to Peekskill near King's Ferry. Instead, at the last minute, due to intelligence relayed to him by Washington, Rochambeau rerouted the march to Bedford.[75] With the French ready to enter New York, Washington ordered a joint offensive against the British on the northern end of Manhattan in the form of a two-pronged surprise attack. The American leader, with new-found confidence, had decided to tweak the enemy at New York City since he would have the aid of the French.

After laying out the plan, Washington cautioned Rochambeau as to the importance of maintaining a high level of secrecy regarding this joint offensive. "One reason which makes it more than commonly necessary in the country where you are, is that the enemy will have emissaries in your camp in the garb of peasants with provisions and other matters and will be attentive to every word which they may hear drop."[76]

Colonel Cobb, who commanded at least 160 mounted dragoons (Sheldon's Dragoons), accompanied Rochambeau into New York State toward Bedford since he and the dragoons knew the area well and could act as guides for the French army. For Washington to send his highly trained dragoons as escort to welcome Rochambeau was seen as a sign of great respect for the visiting military leader.[77]

With a forced march Lauzun's Legion met up with Rochambeau's infantry and Cobb's dragoons on July 2 as planned near the burned-out village of Bedford. As reported in Crèvecoeur's journal that day, Bedford "had already suffered much damage, and, in fact, hardly any houses [were] left standing. This settlement is very small and denuded of every resource—not surprisingly, considering that this region has been a battlefield for three years."[78] They were astounded by what they saw. Over the past three years of the British occupation, the immediate area surrounding New York City had been virtually devastated. Most of the homes were burned to the ground, some just before the French arrived. For the French it was a rude awakening to see the destruction wrought by the British.[79]

While on the cross-Connecticut march, the French had mingled with the Americans and found them hospitable. They had been entertained at impromptu balls, and enjoyed lively music and dancing until late at night at camps across Connecticut. All in all the Americans had warmly welcomed their French saviors. The French troops, well-trained and well-disciplined from years of service in Europe, had generated goodwill nearly everywhere. It was no different in New York State, where a proud Lauzun declared, "The French army marched through America in perfect order and with perfect discipline, setting an example which neither the English nor the American army had ever furnished."[80]

The *Connecticut Courant,* now the *Hartford Courant,* America's oldest continuously published newspaper, had this to say about the French forces on July 3: "A finer body of men were never in arms, and no army was ever better furnished with every thing necessary for a campaign. The exact discipline of the troops, and the attention of the officers to prevent any injury to individuals, have made the march of this army through the country very agreeable to the inhabitants, and it is with pleasure we assure our readers that not a single disagreeable circumstance has taken place."[81] Presumably, the paper did not hear of the bayonet holes in the ceiling of White's Tavern and the pillaging that took place in Lebanon.

The French made their camp in Bedford, New York, on July 2. It was dangerously near the enemy. The French diarist Crèvecoeur noted that this day was the moment at which the allies marked the beginning of their combined campaign.[82]

CHAPTER SIX

Layover at New York

*"We next proceeded to reconnoiter minutely every part of the works
of New York, and the adjacent island."*

—COMTE DE ROCHAMBEAU

ONCE IN NEW YORK, all revelry ceased; Rochambeau and his
army were just minutes away from British headquarters when the grave
tactics of war commenced. Morale was high and the troops eager for
action, which would come in the form of an immediate two-pronged
attack on the enemy. Lauzun directed the French column to advance
toward Morrisania, Bronx County, New York, on the east bank of the
Harlem River. Morrisania was the former estate of Brigadier General
Lewis Morris of the New York militia and delegate to the Continental
Congress of 1775. At that time Morrisania was held by those loyal to
the crown of King George III.[1]

The American offensive, headed by General Benjamin Lincoln,
involved a detachment of one thousand men engaged in a prelimi-
nary reconnoitering excursion at the north end of Manhattan
Island to Forts Washington, Tryon, and George. Washington and his
army met the French first brigade near Kingsbridge where British
Colonel Delancey was expected to be camped. The success of this
plan depended on the element of surprise and was the first of
Washington's proposed threats against the English after the arrival of
Rochambeau and his men.[2]

Regrettably, this first combined offensive was a failure. Delancey's corps must have gotten word that Lauzun was on his way to engage them, for the British had left Morrisania and were safely away at Williamsbridge. The remainder of the allies, in lieu of surprising the enemy, were themselves surprised by nearly three thousand British who fanned out to block their assault.[3] General Lincoln decided not to attack the Manhattan forts and called off the offensive. Was there a spy in the camp who overheard the plan, as Washington feared? Thus, according to Berthier's diary, the allied action was aborted after "a brisk fire during which several Americans were killed."[4] Unfortunately, four Americans were lost and fifteen wounded; Lauzun lost none.[5] Washington was disappointed.

ROCHAMBEAU MAKES CAMP IN THE HUDSON HIGHLANDS

In his journal, Berthier recounts that on July 3, as his French regiment approached enemy territory, he was sent ahead to requisition wagons to carry the sick and exhausted. He was ordered to use any means necessary, that is, cash or force, to procure what he needed to keep the troops moving. The French were close to their destination—Philipsburg, New York. Berthier also reported that the French army camped for two nights, July 4 and 5, at North Castle, New York, during which time Rochambeau and General Washington had an opportunity to meet for the first time since the Wethersfield Conference.[6] The Chevalier de La Luzerne, French minister to Philadelphia, was on hand for the welcome as well.[7]

In his account Crèvecoeur remarks that on July 6, the combined French divisions marched south from North Castle to Philipsburg (Ardsley/Hartsdale area) onto the heights between White Plains and Dobbs Ferry to complete the last leg of their march from Rhode Island. They covered the remaining seventeen miles to reach their camp in the scorching heat; over four hundred soldiers collapsed from exhaustion. "The roads were so bad that the last division of artillery, to which I was attached," wrote Crèvecoeur, "did not arrive in camp until an hour after midnight. The troops had been on the road since three o'clock the morning before without anything to eat. They found nothing to drink on the way."[8]

"That day the army left behind more than 400 stragglers," wrote Closen, "but they all rejoined us during the night, with the exception of two men from the Bourbonnais and three from the Deux-Ponts, who decided in favor of deserting to the woods, where they found shelter. Those from the Deux-Ponts were brought back, some days later, by some Americans, good Whigs, and were flogged."[9]

At last Rochambeau's four divisions and Lauzun's Legion were safely encamped with Washington at Philipsburg. There had been no unexpected events along the route across Connecticut, and although the trek was difficult at times, it was always orderly. The French pitched their fourteenth camp (since leaving Newport) in a line on the highlands of Westchester County. They were situated near the Americans between the Bronx and Sawmill Rivers in the town of Philipsburg, merely seventeen miles from New York. The "combined French and American line extended all the way from the Hudson River at Dobbs Ferry easterly to White Plains."[10] Berthier pointed out that the French camp at Philipsburg was well placed and had three routes of approach, one along the Hudson, one into the center, and one to the left; there were also three routes of retreat, all of which were via bridges. Guards were placed at the high points and at all other strategic locations, as the French encampment was only a few leagues from the British post.[11]

Make no mistake, New York City was not chosen at random by the British as a point of importance to defend. Similarly, Washington and Rochambeau had more than one reason to want control of this strategic city. Obviously, New York was a key seaport in North America. Beyond that, it was long recognized that to control the great trading center of New York was to control the Hudson River and, thereby, the northeast coast of America as well as the interior corridor to the north and to the west. The mighty Hudson was a link in a channel north from New York through Lake Champlain into the

St. Lawrence River, north to Canada, west to the Great Lakes, and east to the Atlantic. By virtue of this extensive natural corridor, it remains today, as in the early days of the building of the new country, a strategic access route in and out of the heart of America.

On July 6, General Washington officially welcomed Rochambeau and the French forces into his camp: "The Commander in Chief with pleasure embraces the earliest public opportunity of expressing his thanks to his Excellency the Count de Rochambeau for the unremitting zeal with which he has prosecuted his March in order to form the long wished for junction between the American and French Forces…. The Regiment of Saintonge is entitled to peculiar acknowledgements [sic] for the Spirit with which they continued and Supported their March without one day's Respite."[12]

On July 8, Washington reviewed the French troops near Philipsburg as they set up camp after their strenuous march. Lauberdière remembered "our troops nevertheless appeared in the grandest parade uniform. M. de Rochambeau took his place in front of the white flag of his oldest regiment and saluted General Washington…. Our general received the greatest compliments for the beauty of his troops."[13]

The following day the French officers were invited to observe as the American army presented arms. Baron von Closen was surprised at what he saw: "I had a chance to see the American army, man for man. It was really painful to see these brave men, almost naked with only some trousers and little linen jackets, most of them without stockings, but, would you believe it? Very cheerful and healthy in appearance. A quarter of them were negroes, merry, confident, and sturdy…. Three quarters of the Rhode Island regiment consists of negroes, and that regiment is the most neatly dressed, the best under arms, and the most precise in its maneuvers."[14]

French Commissary Blanchard had gone ahead of the main army to prepare for hospitals and supply depots along the Hudson north of their proposed destination. Eventually he had the hospitals and supply depots moved to North Castle to be nearer the final encampment. He had originally arranged for bakeries at Fishkill Landing (Beacon) north of West Point and later built seven huge bread ovens near the Bates (now Odell) House where General Rochambeau was lodged. These latter ovens were "about six feet long and two and one-half feet wide, built mostly underground and made of cobblestone."[15] Sparse remnants of these can be seen today. When in Philipsburg, much of the food and supplies for man and beast were still brought in from Connecticut, as they had been when the French were in Rhode Island. All these installations were based on the army staying put for some time in New York. All the better to fool the British.[16]

In early July Commissary Blanchard had the honor of dining with George Washington. "There was a clergyman...who blessed the food and said grace after they had done eating...I was told that General Washington said grace when there was no clergyman at table, as fathers of a family do in America."[17] On July 10, Blanchard dined again with him and noticed that Washington "was rather grave; it was said that there had been a little misunderstanding between him and General Rochambeau."[18] No doubt, the two generals had been discussing the feasibility of laying siege to New York; they had yet to come to a consensus on the subject.

It must have been very stressful to coordinate supplies for the troops, especially in the heat of the summer. At one point, Blanchard, in a fit of anger at being reproached by Rochambeau over a mishandling of the bread supply, vented his frustration in his journal. He later made amends in a footnote, admitting that he wrote it in a "moment of ill-humor."[19] He concluded by praising Rochambeau's accomplishments in America but wrote that, on the other hand, "His [Rochambeau's] reception of me is usually cold."[20]

The combined armies numbered about nine thousand men, and much was needed to keep them fit. Foraging expeditions ventured out regularly to purchase the necessities for the army. These shopping expeditions ranged from "the camp and Long Island Sound extending from Rye, Mamaroneck, East Chester, and Chester to a point as close as possible to King's Bridge" where the enemy was camped.[21] The French commissaries always went out with a protective force of about 1,500 men and a detachment of hussars and were fortunate when they fell upon barns filled to the brim with the first cutting hay and other caches obviously ready for shipment to the British.[22]

On July 8, General Rochambeau had written to Admiral de Barras in Newport to advise him of his safe arrival: "We have made the most rapid march to arrive here at General Washington's request, without a single complaint and without leaving a single man behind, except for the ten love-stricken Soissonnais who returned to see their mistresses in Newport and whom I beg you to apprehend."[23] Describing the success of the march to New York, General Rochambeau also wrote to the Marquis de Ségur, minister of war at Versailles: "We have covered 220 miles in eleven days of marching. There are not four provinces in France where we could have traveled with more order and economy and without lacking anything."[24]

The British who held New York prepared their own welcome for the French forces. As Rochambeau put it, "The forced marches of the French corps had rendered their victualling very difficult, and a flotilla, which the enemy had sent up the Hudson, captured a vessel laden with four days' rations of bread intended for the French. The allowance of our soldiers was, in consequence, reduced to four ounces per diem, but they submitted to these privations cheerfully as their officers had undergone the fatigue of a tedious march performed on foot and at the head of their troops. We sent a battery of 12 pounders and mortars …to the most narrow part of the river to await the return of the British flotilla, and the latter met with such a reception that I should think it had no desire to attempt such another expedition."[25]

According to his memoirs, Rochambeau had found it necessary to leave "the whole of our heavy artillery" and munitions behind in Newport under the charge of M. de Choisy on land and under the charge of Admiral de Barras on the sea.[26] This plan had definitely lightened their load on the overland trip. The field-batteries that they brought with them on the eleven-day march, however, had already proved cumbersome to pull up and down the hills and over the rocky, unpaved roads of Connecticut. If the plan to march south was accepted, the heavy siege artillery and munitions would travel by sea to the Chesapeake. Choisy was left with a detachment of about five hundred French soldiers plus a supplement of one thousand American militia to protect their anchorage of French ships at Newport.[27]

While in New York State, Rochambeau lodged at widow Sarah Bates's home on Ridge Road in Hartsdale (town of Greenburgh) on the east side of Sprain Brook. Rochambeau's headquarters was three-quarters of a mile from Washington's headquarters. John Tompkins built the original house in 1732 with only two rooms and an attic. In 1760, Gilbert Bates bought the home and added a wing, doubling the size of the living space. Well before Rochambeau took up residence in the Bates house, Mr. Bates had been captured by the British, and like so many other American prisoners, he died in captivity. Colonel John Odell later owned the house that today is known as the Odell House and is a museum preserved as an historic site by the Sons of the American Revolution.[28]

According to the McDonald Papers, a compilation of interviews conducted by Judge James Maclean MacDonald between 1844 and 1850, Rochambeau took some time for socializing and entertaining.[29] A Mrs. Churchill, who lived near Hart's Corner, told MacDonald, "While there, General Rochambeau gave four or five large dinner parties to the French and American officers in the old barn northwest of the house which was then owned by Mr. Bates."[30] The barn is no longer standing.[31]

Washington's headquarters was established "at Joseph Appleby's, about half a mile from the Dobbs Ferry Road about the same (as much) from the Saw Mill River" on the west side of Sprain Brook.[32] All that remains of Appleby's house are stone fences and cellar holes on a wooded lot.[33] Even though Washington's headquarters was officially in Philipsburg, he preferred to say it was near Dobbs

Ferry since Philipsburg was home to British sympathizers. Major General Chastellux resided at the house of John Tompkins.[34] Lauzun was billeted at the home of Captain John Falconer on Broadway in Philipsburg.[35]

There are numerous references to the Duc de Lauzun in the McDonald papers. He was described as "very polite, had a handsome person, wore moustaches, [and] was liberal with money."[36] The existence of his facial hair was corroborated by a William Griffen of Mamaroneck in 1845 when he quoted Lauzun: "The women of this country don't like my whiskers—but I can't cut them off."[37]

Several of the officers—Alexandre Berthier, Mathieu Dumas, and Charles de Lameth—were assigned a house that was an unacceptable distance from their commanding officer, Quartermaster General de Béville. Berthier explained that because he and his fellow officers were assigned housing three miles from Béville they took it upon themselves to build their own camp "situated in a hollow at the left of the French lines."[38] They requested five soldiers' tents, which they "pitched on a knoll in the midst of a copse where there were some 30 superb trees shading a small stream."[39] He goes on to describe their self-styled camp: "To the right the brook wound its way along the foot of a great ledge, which you ascended by a steep path. Halfway up was a den in which a big English bulldog was chained to warn us of the approach of strangers."[40] It was much more convenient to the center of operations. Apparently, the three officers spent "six weeks of perfect happiness" therein, even going so far as to brag that General Washington visited them.[41]

On his first night in New York, Crèvecoeur described an unusual phenomenon he experienced as he was trying to fall asleep in a field. At first he thought it was sparks left over from such a hot day. However, upon closer inspection, he saw that the tiny glow came from small flying bugs that populated the entire field and fairly lit up the night. They reminded him of the "glowworms" he knew from home, but with wings. The English called them fireflies and the French knew them as *mouches de feu*.[42]

The French could not help noticing firsthand the wretched condition of the American soldiers, meagerly equipped and pitifully low in number; only about four thousand men currently made up the northern Continental army. Crèvecoeur wrote, "In beholding this army, I was struck, not by its smart appearance, but by its destitution: the men were without uniforms but covered with rags; most of them were barefoot. They were of all sizes, down to children, who could not have been over fourteen. There were many negroes, mulattoes, etc. Only their artillerymen were wearing uniforms. These are the élite of the country and are actually very good troops, well schooled in their profession. We had nothing but praise for them later."[43]

The Comte de Lauberdière, Rochambeau's twenty-one-year-old nephew and the youngest of his aides-de-camp, observed in his journal that the American army, in contrast to the French, lined up according to seniority, not size.[44] A tall soldier might stand between two short men and vice versa. "This method infinitely hurts the eye and the beautiful appearance of the troops."[45] It made for a very shabby-looking column, whereas the French were "well-lined up, of an equal height, well dressed."[46] On a more positive note, Lauberdière stated: "But I remember their great accomplishments and I can not say without a certain admiration that it was with these same men that General Washington has so gloriously defended his country."[47] The Americans may have appeared roughshod; nonetheless, their outlook was improving because Rochambeau had arrived to help them.

In making further notes on the appearance of the American camp, Lauberdière remarked that the French were generally over-dressed for summer compared to the Americans who wore a shirt or jacket and a pair of roomy, linen trousers and often wore no shoes or regular uniform. The American soldiers carried only a woolen blanket and a small amount of food in a haversack weighing less than forty pounds.[48]

Following is a list of the uniform and equipment carried by a French soldier in the army of General Rochambeau, 1780–83:

1 Regimental Coat.

1 Tricorn Hat with black trim and white, red, and black cockade. While it was not regulation Grenadiers wore a bearskin bonnet.

1 Fatigue hat or polakem.

1 Sleeved vest.

1 Sleeveless vest to be worn under the sleeved vest in the months of November, December, January, and February.

2 Pairs of Breeches.

3 Shirts.

2 Pairs of shoes, 1 to be new.

1 Pair white linen gaiters for parade.

1 Pair black linen gaiters for service.

1 Pair black wool gaiters for winter.

2 Pair gaiter cuffs of white linen with black buttons.

2 Handkerchiefs.

2 Pairs stockings.

2 stocks – horsehair.

2 Neck bands.

1 ribbon for queue.

1 Stock buckle.

1 Pair shoe buckles.

2 Pair garter buckles.

2 Pair breeches buckles.

2 Pair gaiter buckles.

1 Sack powder and powder puff for hair.

1 Comb for hair.

1 Comb for cleaning.

1 Clothes brush.

2 Shoe brushes.

1 Small brush for cleaning brass.

1 Paint brush to whiten buff leather straps.

For sewing, needle and thread.

1 Button hook.

1 Ball puller for musket.

1 Touch hole pick.

1 Screw driver.

Pieces of old cloth for cleaning uniform.

Pieces of linen for cleaning weapon.

Musket with sling.

Cartridge box. Fusiliers carried the Cartridge box on the right hip with a strap over the left shoulder, which also carried the bayonet. Grenadiers and Chasseurs carried the Cartridge box the same as the Fusiliers with the Bayonet and Saber on the left hip with a strap over the right shoulder.

1 Calfskin haversack.

1 Linen distribution bag for carrying bread, which was at times to be also used as a sleeping bag.

Coat, vests, and sleeveless vests to be replaced every 3 years, 1/3 each.

Foreign regiments every 2 years due to lesser quality of material – sleeveless vests every 3 years as they were only worn in the winter.

Shirts, gaiters, and gaiter cuffs to be marked with the letter of each company.

It was forbidden to use wax or grease on mustaches.[50]

Rochambeau and his army wore full uniforms, sometimes including woolens, and were obliged to carry a weighty pack of nearly sixty pounds plus a musket. Another obvious difference between the American and French soldiers was that most American soldiers were married and sporadically returned home to their families and farms to complete seasonal duties. By contrast, the French soldier was usually celibate and rarely returned home when serving in Europe. Lauberdière thought, "In general our allies are slow and they don't inconvenience themselves more than absolutely necessary."[49]

It must have been reassuring to Rochambeau when the locals began to speak favorably of the French forces. One such New Yorker named Dr. James Thatcher commented in his journal about meeting the French: "We now greet them as friends and allies, and they manifest a zealous determination to act in unison with us against a common enemy. This conduct must have a happy tendency to eradicate from the minds of the Americans their ancient prejudices against the French people. They punctually paid their expenses in hard money...[which] is to be considered as of infinite importance at the present period of our affairs."[51]

It was noted repeatedly in American journals and personal interviews that Rochambeau kept the strictest discipline in his camp. This was much appreciated by the Americans who had experienced endless looting and destruction under the British. Nevertheless, there were some exceptions to the stringent code of conduct exacted by the French. Occasionally, a few French soldiers opted to desert the ranks and disappear into the American landscape. The unlucky ones were caught and punished, an example of which was thirty-three-year-old Corporal Jean Pierre Verdier who was hanged in spite of fifteen years of service.[52]

As the layover in New York wore on, word came that three French frigates and the *Romulus* under the command of Captain de La Villebrune had sailed from Newport and attempted a surprise attack on Fort Lloyd near Huntington, Long Island. Their goal was to neutralize the British munitions stored there. It failed in much the same way that the first joint raid on Delancey had failed: poor timing foiled the surprise. The captain "found the fort more strongly held than he had expected and the enemy defenses entirely different from what he had been told."[53]

Commissary Blanchard said the news was being passed around "that the English were evacuating Virginia, which, it was said, was to be ascribed to the march of our troops [to New York]."[54] As a result, General Cornwallis would surely be sending troops north to relieve Clinton. The French officers also discussed the possibility of the arrival of De Grasse's fleet from the West Indies. Frederick Mackenzie, an Englishman, recorded in his diary on August 9, "Seven Continental deserters came in this morning.... They say the common talk in the army is that New York is to be besieged as soon as the French fleet appears, which is daily expected."[55] The logical outcome appeared to be an attack on New York, but if the rumors were true, and De Grasse and his fleet were headed north, what was their destination? New York or the Chesapeake? Meanwhile, Washington and Rochambeau had finally joined camps and were going about the business of evaluating their positions and planning their joint campaign, gathering supplies, and reconnoitering the enemy's position.

MONETARY ISSUES

Toward the end of the French stay in New York and just prior to the long march to Yorktown, their specie supply dropped very low. Indeed, it was due to run out by August 2. Rochambeau gave half of what he had to Washington, who would pay it back in October. The financing of this entire expedition had been monumental from the start; the cost to the French far exceeded the estimates made early in 1780.[56] The French ministers knew at the outset that the Americans were destitute and unable to pay their own way or help finance the French in any way once the latter arrived on American soil. The monetary issues, while substantial for the operation as whole, had a demoralizing effect on the soldiers' daily life.

To avoid misunderstandings, Rochambeau forbade fraternizing among the enlisted men of the two allied camps. There was the obvious language barrier, but more importantly, there was tension about the fact that the American army had not been paid in years except in rare cases, and their currency was virtually worthless. The French army was much better paid and supplied. Now and then, a Frenchman would enter the American camp and try to sell them a loaf of bread. Naturally, some of the Continentals took offense and in return began to "abuse the French, and say that they who have never done any service to the Country are well paid, fed, and clothed while themselves, who have been fighting for the country, are almost destitute of everything."[57] The last reason to restrict fraternizing between the armies was based on unkind stories that tended to circulate about the French as a nationality, mostly manufactured from biased Tories and others who favored the British in the war.

McDonald Papers interviewees recalled that "the presence of the French was synonymous with money."[58] On the subject of funds, a letter from Joseph Rouse, a Connecticut soldier, was published in *Rivington's Loyaliste Gazette* on August 14, 1781. In the letter Rouse expressed the feelings of the enlisted men as well as the officers: "They [the French] look much better than our lousey army who have Neither money nor close. God Bless the State of Connecticut...you noes what I mean."[59]

Soon after the French joined ranks with the Continentals, Washington responded to the need for the soldiers of both armies to purchase necessary items by making provisions for two markets in Philipsburg, one for the Americans and one for the French. "Provided they [the vendors] had a certificate 'signed by two civil Magistrates' showing 'their attachment to the American Cause and Interest,' they could sell their wares 'without Molestation or Imposition.'"[60] However, there was a problem in that the Americans had almost valueless paper money, and the French had hard-to-value gold coins.

It was a challenge to figure out how to purchase goods and establish an exchange system that would be beneficial to either the

French or Americans. Author Lee Kennett summarizes the predicament this way: "Since the Americans had only paper with which to buy army supplies, the French would have an undue advantage if they offered gold. This would depreciate the paper further and make amicable relations difficult. If the expedition made its purchases with paper, there would be no such problem and probably some advantages. If the French acquired large quantities, the paper dollars might well appreciate to the betterment of the American economy and also to the King's profit."[61]

Since Spanish currency was in use in America at the time, Rochambeau had converted 2.65 million livres into Spanish currency (piastres).[62] Upon arrival in America, Rochambeau and Ternay found that French coin was also acceptable. The Court of Versailles soon determined that it was risky to send specie via ship when there was the chance that the vessels carrying the treasure could be captured or lost at sea. They did not want to hazard sending precious metals out of the country any more often than was necessary. "The coin was carefully packed in barrels, with buoys and lines attached in case they had to be jettisoned. In all, there were nine 'runs' to North America with specie, eight of them by frigate. Several had close calls, two were wrecked on arrival, but in only one case was there a loss."[63]

RECONNOITERING BEGINS

It took some time to get the French established in the camp before going out on the *Grande Reconnaissance*, a grand name for a fact-finding mission to gather information on enemy fortifications. Setting up camp so close to the British put everyone in great danger. Both Crèvecoeur and Closen recount the following incident. The night of July 17–18, an officer of Lauzun's Legion, Sous-lieutenant Jacques Hartman, was killed by Delancey's British dragoons while on patrol. The enemy disappeared into the woods and was not found. After the legion officer died, his horse could not be caught and fled back toward the safety of his enclosure. The watchman heard the horse gallop up in the dark and asked, *"Qui vive?"* (Who goes there?). Since there was no rider to respond, the guard shot blindly into the night and killed the horse only minutes after his master had died.[64] Hartman and his horse were the first combat losses for the French on land, whereas the French had already experienced loss of lives at the first Battle off the Capes in March.

On July 18, a party of French and American officers, including Rochambeau and Washington, went out to observe the British encampments on the north end of Manhattan Island, only ten miles away from Philipsburg. Rochambeau took Colonel Desandrouins, chief engineer, and General Béville, quartermaster general. General Duportail, chief engineer, and an escort of 150 of the Jersey Troops accompanied Washington. Their mission was to get a good look from both sides of the Hudson in preparation for the Grande Reconnaissance.

The following day, July 19, pursuant to a pattern used at the Connecticut conferences, Rochambeau put a few written questions before his commander, George Washington. When he asked whether preparations for a march southward should be made, Washington responded that unless certain conditions were met, "the enterprise against New York and its environs has to be our principal object."[65] From his fortified position in New York, Clinton found himself in a hot spot of enemy activity without knowing whether an attack was imminent or not. As a result of Washington's position, Clinton kept his army and some ships alert to the allies' activities on shore. His ships followed the allies daily as they continued their reconnoitering operation, constantly firing volleys upon them, but not initiating a full-out battle.

General Clinton had already missed opportunities to attack the French force, beginning with their first few days in Newport while the newcomers were getting settled, dealing with illness, and learning the terrain. He then missed a second opportunity to attack Newport after the major force left on the march to New York in mid-June 1781. The French had left the port guarded only by a small contingent of soldiers and ships. Clinton showed signs of ineffective leadership and indecision, and he waffled between taking the initiative to attack the French/American encampment or simply continuing to annoy them while waiting for reinforcements from the south.

On the night of July 21, Rochambeau's first brigade plus the grenadiers and chasseurs of the second brigade (about 2,200 men plus their 175 officers) set out for the high ground above King's Bridge, overlooking New York City. Also heading out were Washington and about 2,000 American troops led by Generals Lincoln and Parsons and 25 of Sheldon's Dragoons.[66] The aforementioned made up the right column of the march. Chastellux and Lauzun commanded the left column. They brought along two twelve-pounders, two four-pounders, and two howitzers. During the night's march the twelve-pounders fell down a forty-foot ravine, and it took hours to retrieve them. [67]

The next morning Clinton was shocked to see five thousand Americans and French camped above him. He wrote, "Nothing, certainly, could have been more alarming as well as mortifying than my situation at the present...the enemy's parading on the heights on my front for two days, and no possibility of my stirring against it."[68] Still there was no attack from the allies, only continued threatening activities meant to keep the British on edge and in the dark. The allied officers inspected the enemy camps and positions for two days under sporadic cannon fire from land and from frigates anchored in the North River. One American lost a leg; M. de Dumas, aide-de-camp of Rochambeau, had his horse shot out from under him.[69]

In their journals, Berthier and Closen gave full accounts of the three-day Grande Reconnaissance across the Harlem River onto the northern end of Manhattan to Forts Washington, Tryon, and George. These three forts formed an impressive triangle against invaders, with Fort Washington being dominant and situated at the highest point of the three. Upon close observation it appeared that if Fort Washington fell, the other two would fall as well. The three forts were perched on three tall hills and were connected by lines of circumvallation that extended from one side of the island to the other. Behind this line of protection lay the British camp.[70]

Later, on July 22, the allies ran across a group of Loyalists who challenged them with vigorous fire. Some of the latter took refuge in a house, were quickly surrounded, and then at last forced out in the open. When the surrounded Loyalists saw that about two hundred of their men who had come to support them were still shooting at Dumas, Vauban, Closen, Lauberdière, and Berthier, the previously surrounded Loyalists began to shoot at the French, too. The French forces found themselves caught in the crossfire. "One of them," wrote Berthier, "approached me shouting, 'Prisoner!,' as he drew a brace of pistols from under his coat and fired on me at 5 paces, grazing my ear, and crying, 'Die, you dog of a Frenchman!' He was about to fire the other one when I got ahead of him by putting a ball through his chest, which killed him on the spot."[71] Eventually, the allies prevailed and captured the British prisoners, some of whom threw themselves in the river and drowned.[72] This skirmish was a very serious one for the French allies who were very nearly overcome by deadly enemy fire.

While still on reconnaissance on July 23, Rochambeau wrote of an event that happened while he, Washington, and their engineers were inspecting the British defenses. This time they set out to calculate the distance across an inlet on Long Island. After fording waterways to a small island, the two generals, both too exhausted to continue, fell asleep beside a hedge even as their engineers were at work and the enemy was firing upon them and their workers. Rochambeau later recalled the incident: "The first to awaken by the wizzing of the balls which they fired down upon us to impede our operations, I hastened to call General Washington, and to remind him that we had forgotten the time of the tide. We quickly returned to the Mill Dam, on which we had crossed the inlet of the sea which separated us from the main land; but we found it overflowed. Two small boats were brought to us, in which we jumped with our saddles and other accoutrements; two American dragoons then led their horses, who were known as good swimmers, into the sea, and the remainder quickly followed, excited by the cracking of the whip by some dragoons on the other shore, to whom, by this time, our boats had returned. This maneuver, which lasted nearly an hour, was, fortunately for us, unseen by the enemy."[73]

In the course of the three-day Grande Reconnaissance Berthier noted, "Generals Washington and Rochambeau, with their respective engineers, aides and myself [Berthier] made a reconnaissance of all the English works along the Harlem River between King's Bridge and Morrisania."[74] The important work had been accomplished. These reconnoitering trips proved to Washington that the enemy was more substantial than he had previously estimated.

INDECISION OF CLINTON AND CORNWALLIS

General Clinton could only surmise from the activity of massed troops around New York that the allies were about to attack the city. (The attack never happened.) In fear and trepidation, he sent envoys to Cornwallis requesting reinforcements, which never came. Despite his larger force of twelve thousand, Clinton became increasingly nervous. With such an apparently menacing force at his doorstep, Clinton had sent a series of messages to Cornwallis. On July 8, he had requested that Cornwallis send three thousand troops to Philadelphia. (He did not comply.) On July 17, he requested that these same troops be sent to New York. (Cornwallis did not do so.) On July 20, Clinton asked him to retain these troops in Virginia in order to guard a naval port to be used later to land reinforcements from British ships. (Cornwallis moved to Yorktown and prepared to hold it.) Author Lee Kennett described results of the correspondence between Clinton and Cornwallis in this way: "Clinton thought that Cornwallis was being obtuse and ignoring his orders, while Cornwallis believed those directives were obscure and contradictory. The exchange between the two was a dialogue of the deaf."[75]

And so, at the beginning of August, all fronts were poised and marking time: in Newport, Barras would not move with his fleet until he heard from De Grasse or Rochambeau; in New York,

Clinton would not budge until he received reinforcements from Cornwallis; in Gloucester and Yorktown, Lafayette's small army stopped dancing with Cornwallis and stood pat. Cornwallis, having marched himself into a corner, waited for Clinton to send him aid by ship. Rochambeau and Washington would continue their charade in front of Clinton, feigning preparation for an attack on New York. De Grasse was in the Caribbean readying his fleet to move north, gathering additional troops and funds, all of which Rochambeau had previously requested. At that point all military components on both sides were, in Kennett's words, "suspended, caught in some delicate equipoise" before the final act of the War of American Independence began.[76]

Gradually Washington's thoughts turned toward Cornwallis as an objective, for he wrote on August 1, "I could scarce see a ground upon which to continue my preparations against New York, and therefore…I turned my Views more seriously (than I had before done) to an operation to the Southward."[77] That very day and the next, in Virginia, Cornwallis ferried his troops from Portsmouth to Gloucester and York. He had begun to dig in at Yorktown.

DE GRASSE COMMITS TO THE CHESAPEAKE

On July 28 De Grasse sent a message to Rochambeau, with letters also to Barras and La Luzerne, via the frigate *Concorde*. The letter to General Rochambeau stated, "I shall be obliged to employ the fleet promptly and to good purpose, so that the time may be spent to profit sufficiently against the enemy naval forces and their land forces; but I shall not be able to use the soldiers long; they are under the orders of the Spanish who will need them then."[78] That meant he would shortly be en route to the Chesapeake. In the same communication De Grasse included these words, flattering Rochambeau: "All this expedition having been arranged only on your [Rochambeau's] request and without being restricted by the French and Spanish Ministers, I have thought myself authorized to take everything on myself for the common cause; but I do not dare to change all the plan of their campaign by employing for a long time so considerable a body of troops."[79] De Grasse flattered Rochambeau by saying that he had been authorized by Rochambeau to accomplish this mission.

Rochambeau was too self-effacing to pat himself on the back for his timing and careful planning in the sending of this letter, which he did with enough time for De Grasse to arrange for the complicated three-fold task he was assigned by Rochambeau and Vergennes and even La Luzerne—bring ships, bring solders, and bring cash. The admiral stated that he was acting on the request of Rochambeau and undoubtedly also according to the wishes of French minister Vergennes. He clearly affirmed in the letter quoted above that he had the authority to complete this task in the West Indies and to transport aid to the allies at the Chesapeake. He agreed to remain there as long as he could work within the time frame set up with the Spanish, who wanted him to return the borrowed troops by October 15.

Even as the letter was on its way to Rochambeau, the admiral was in the midst of troop, ship, and specie gathering, which were the essential ingredients needed to beat the British. The Spanish came to his aid on all accounts. Raising the money needed by De Grasse was not an easy process in those days. The route the money took was, by necessity, circuitous. To eliminate the hazards associated with Spain shipping gold from South America to Spain and then France shipping gold across the ocean to the Caribbean, the French and Spanish devised a secure scheme to move funds. The French fleet would borrow gold from Spanish merchants in Cuba to buy supplies from Spanish merchants in the Caribbean, and then the French government would repay the debts by sending gold across the Pyrenees to the merchants' families in Spain. In this way, France and Spain could eliminate the risk of losing ships with holds full of specie.

As Admiral de Grasse made preparations for the campaign, he went so far as to offer to pledge his own plantations in Saint-Domingue and his estate in France. In the end, this extreme measure was not required as De Grasse found the money in Havana. Francisco Miranda, a lieutenant colonel in the Spanish army, recently involved in a campaign against the English to capture Pensacola, Florida, procured the large sum requested by Rochambeau. It was said that Cuban ladies, fond of the popular warrior Miranda, gladly offered him their diamonds and precious jewels to assist the Spanish in beating the reviled British.[80]

Havana was, for over 250 years, a golden stepping stone to the Western Hemisphere. Serving as the pivotal trading hub between Europe and the colonies in North America, Havana was indeed gold-encrusted during that time. The American rebels needed Spain's support, and Spanish financiers sought them as a new trading partner par excellence. Thus, Spanish aid to the United States, often under-reported by historians, was based on extraordinary profits from worldwide trade with this thriving center. Like Havana, the West Indies was the "exchange point for cash transactions between the French and Spanish courts."[81]

Despite the fact that expected specie did not arrive in time from Mexican mines, it was no surprise that De Grasse had little trouble amassing the funds required by Rochambeau in record time. Francisco Savedra de Sangronis, cultured and capable Spanish emissary to the West Indies, wrote that in De Grasse's haste to gather specie he had posted notices on the street corners of Cap Français, looking for contributions to the American cause. He pledged that notes so given would be redeemable in Paris with interest. Months later, after the American victory at Yorktown, in a gesture of mutual thanksgiving, on Christmas 1781 Francisco Rendon, the Spanish minister to Philadelphia, graciously hosted George and Martha Washington in his home for a traditional Spanish feast. King Carlos III was well pleased with his part in the funding of the American Revolution.[82]

Finally, at Cap Français, Saint-Domingue (Haiti), on August 5, Admiral de Grasse weighed the anchor of his flagship, *Ville de Paris.* Initially he sailed with twenty-six ships of the line. De Grasse directed the fleet on a heading through the narrow Old Channel (known today as the Old Bahama Channel) between Cuba and the Bahamas.[83] After two days at sea the admiral rendezvoused with the *Bourgogne* and the *Hector.* The addition of these two ships brought his flotilla to the full complement of twenty-eight ships. With the entire fleet assembled for the voyage north, the admiral carried about 3,200 of the Marquis de Saint Simon's troops: "The Agenais Regiment (1000), Gâtinais [Royal-Auverne] (1000), Touraine (1000), a detachment of the Metz artillery (100), and Navy volunteers (100)."[84] These soldiers were ready to assist on land at the Chesapeake.

De Grasse chose the Old Channel for two reasons: 1) Since it was the more dangerous, less frequented route, the French were unlikely to encounter the British there; and 2) He planned to meet up with the frigate *Aigrette,* which carried the precious cargo of the equivalent of 1,200,000 livres in Spanish gold piastres collected in Havana.[85] On August 17 they met at a location thirty leagues off the coast of Cuba near Matanzas to bring the money aboard.[86]

Having met all the requests set forth by General Rochambeau, the French fleet was well on its way and would arrive at the Chesapeake by the end of August.[87] Originally, De Grasse promised to leave part of his fleet in the Caribbean to guard French interests when he sailed north. Since De Grasse preferred to sail with his entire fleet in order to deter the formidable British at the mouth of the Chesapeake, he left the islands in the good hands of the Spanish and consequently was able to sail with his entire fleet.

By August 12 De Grasse's letter to Rochambeau saying that he was headed for the Chesapeake was received in Newport by Admiral de Barras. Barras promptly forwarded the message from De Grasse to Rochambeau in New York.

The Odell House

Rochambeau (L) meets with George Washington (R) at the Odell
House, Hartsdale. August 14, 1781. Artist: David R. Wagner.

On August 14, 1781, a pivotal day in American and French
history, Rochambeau received the excellent news that De Grasse
was headed for the Chesapeake. Rochambeau immediately sent a
message to Washington at the Appleby farm. The two commanders
met at the Odell House, Rochambeau's headquarters, to read the letter
together. Barras received a joint communiqué dated August 17 from
Rochambeau and Washington instructing him to bring the heavy
artillery siege guns to the Chesapeake. These would be an essential
element of surprise when the battle commenced against Cornwallis.
Admiral de Barras would bring as many men as possible from
Rhode Island, such as those serving under Choisy. De Grasse said
he would arrive close to two weeks from when his note was received.
Therefore, the point of battle would have to be Virginia. The generals

also received news that Cornwallis was already digging his redoubts at Yorktown while waiting for rescue. Redoubts were earthworks enclosed on all sides except for a narrow passageway built to protect soldiers in the way of a siege. Lafayette, the young Frenchman who wore the uniform of a major general in the American Continental army, was holding Cornwallis in place. No escape to the Carolinas would be possible for Cornwallis.

This was the good news that Rochambeau had waited patiently to hear. Everything was finally lining up to the advantage of the American and French allies. The time had come to follow through on the biggest coordinated military operation of the Revolutionary War that included movement over land, rivers, and sea. The wheels would at last be in motion toward a common focal point, Virginia.

Next, Rochambeau approached Washington one last time. Surely he would see the advantage in marching south! Jean-Nicolas, Vicomte de Desandrouins, colonel in the corps of engineers in Rochambeau's army, gave this account in his *Papiers*. He described a rare, unpleasant discussion between Rochambeau and Washington. Desandrouins attested to "sharp disagreement between them as to whether they should go after Cornwallis or attack New York.... Rochambeau had to emphasize that De Grasse was not under his [Washington's] orders before he could bring him to terms."[88] Fearing that Rochambeau's words might not be believed, Desandrouins added, "I put this all down the moment M. Rochambeau told me about it."[89] It later came out that the French general was reticent to admit that this altercation had occurred.

Alexander Hamilton, who worked closely with Washington, believed that Cornwallis would certainly escape into the Carolinas and that the whole thing would be a wild goose chase. It made Washington depressed to ponder the magnitude of the situation. He was thinking that if he could not do what he wanted to do, at least he would do the next best thing, and no matter what, he would not let the British profit in any way.[90] Washington wrote in his diary that everything had changed since Admiral de Grasse was sailing to the

Chesapeake with soldiers and cash. As a result, he determined that the best course of action would be for the combined French and American allies to begin their march to Virginia as Rochambeau had originally suggested. In turn, Rochambeau had promised the king that he would take his orders from Washington and keep his army together as much as possible. He would do both with a clear conscience. After hours of perplexity and consternation, which nearly paralyzed them, Rochambeau and Washington were ready to move. Washington gave the command to march south and Rochambeau complied.

CHAPTER SEVEN

Rochambeau vis-à-vis Washington

"I am every day more and more dubious of our being able to carry into execution the operations we have in contemplation."

—GEORGE WASHINGTON

LEADING UP TO THE MARCH of the allied armies to Virginia, a tug-of-war was waged between General Rochambeau and his commander in chief, George Washington. It revolved around Rochambeau's proposal to bypass New York and move directly to Virginia and Washington's obsession to target the British at New York. The working relationship between Rochambeau and Washington evolved gradually from the time the French troops landed in Newport until the eventual turnabout in Washington's long-held strategy. The two generals, by chance or by Divine Providence, were destined over time to find ways to work together harmoniously for the cause of American independence. Although they began oceans apart in every sense of the word—with each man bringing specific skills, characteristics, and life experience to the table—they exhibited the persistence of true leaders when faced with overwhelming disadvantages and were eventually able to agree on a winning plan.

To fully understand the relationship between Rochambeau and Washington, it is important to be familiar with Washington's military experience prior to joining forces with the French general. George Washington's first military experience was with the Virginia militia, which he joined in 1753 at age twenty-one. Having discovered that the French were advancing into the Forks of the Ohio, in the area of Pittsburgh, he fought for the British crown in its attempt to defend the territory. George Washington's actions in the Ohio Valley at that time may have lit the spark that ignited the French and Indian War.

Although as a young officer Washington made some tactical errors while serving in the Virginia militia, his courage and tenacity were deemed heroic. In late 1758 he resigned because he was frustrated by defeat, with the British treatment of colonial officers, and with the lack of political support for the war. This allowed Washington to return to Mount Vernon, the estate that he had inherited from his half-brother, Lawrence. He was then elected to Virginia's House of Burgesses for a period that lasted from 1759 to 1774. In 1759 he married Martha Dandridge Custis, a wealthy widow with two children, Martha ("Patsy") and John Parke ("Jacky").

During Washington's tenure as a Virginia politician, his interest in advancing the cause of independence came to the fore. He served as a delegate to the First and Second Continental Congresses in 1774–75. On April 19, 1775, British troops fired on Americans at Lexington and Concord, and on June 15, 1775, the Second Continental Congress appointed Washington as commander in chief of the Continental army. When Washington was appointed commander in chief, he confessed that he did not believe he was equipped for the task, saying, "I do not think myself equal to the Command I [am] honoured with" but that he would do the best he could.[1] The serious trouble that was escalating between Britain and her colonists led to rebellion and to the Declaration of Independence in July 1776.

Then serving as ambassador in Constantinople, Charles-Gravier Comte de Vergennes, who played an important role in moving France to support American independence, made an insightful prediction regarding England and her relationship with the American colonies. He declared, "England will soon repent of having removed the only check that could keep her colonies in awe. They stand no longer in need of her protection. She will call on them to contribute toward supporting the burdens they have helped to bring on her, and they will answer by striking off all dependence."[2] In other words, Vergennes forecast that England would ask her colonies to share her heavy war burden in the form of increased taxes following the French and Indian War (fought in America) and Seven Years' War (fought in Europe). Ambassador Vergennes also saw that it was a foregone conclusion that the colonies would eventually rebel against Mother England. A few years later, when working closely with Louis XVI, Vergennes would convince him, as well as Beaumarchais, Lafayette, La Luzerne, and the Count d'Aranda, to take action against the British where they were vulnerable in America.

On July 3, 1775, Washington took command of 14,000 American troops in Cambridge, Massachusetts, where they had surrounded British-occupied Boston. He began to train and prepare the troops for the takeover of Boston, which would occur in early March 1776. In January of that year, Washington wrote to Colonel Jonathan Trumbull, relaying to him the troubling news he had received: "Undoubted intelligence, of the fitting out of the fleet at Boston and of the embarkation of troops from thence...There is great reason to believe that this armament, if not immediately designed against the City of New York, is nevertheless intended against Long Island, and it is of the utmost importance to prevent the enemy from possessing themselves of the City of New York and the North River which would give them Command of the Country and Communication with Canada."[3] Thus began the fight for control of New York.

Washington immediately dispatched General Charles Lee to New York.[4] On February 4, 1776, both General Lee and British General Henry Clinton arrived in New York City. Clinton then headed south in March, and by April, with the British ousted from Boston, Washington took his army to New York as well. In late June 1776, after having abandoned Boston, the British, under the command of General William Howe and his brother, Admiral Richard Howe, established themselves on both land and sea in New York. At the same time, the British were strengthening their position in the South. By July 1776, while in New York, Washington celebrated by reading the Declaration of Independence to the troops. His celebratory mood would soon be quashed.

Whoever dominated New York would control the territory as a whole. In August 1776 the British forces initiated a battle against Washington at New York. Unfortunately, Washington bungled his response, and with the enemy breathing down his neck, he fled from Long Island to Manhattan and then to Harlem Heights. The effective coordination of the Howe brothers, along with that of Lord Cornwallis, swiftly prevailed over the inexperience of George Washington and his troops. During the evacuation some brave men held off the British, preventing what could have been an even more devastating blow to Washington. He took time to write to his cousin, Lund Washington, who managed his estates at Mount Vernon: "If I were to wish the bitterest curse to an enemy...I should put him in my stead...I do not know what plan of conduct to pursue. I see the impossibility of serving with reputation...In confidence I will tell you that I never was in such an unhappy, divided state since I was born."[5]

It was plain that Washington lost a significant battle to the British at Manhattan. As a result, the American cause lost momentum. Following his retreat from New York, questions were raised as to the validity of his appointment as commander in chief: "Some congressmen believed Washington to be incompetent; he was thinking much the same thing."[6] He had lost control of much of three states, and most of his army had fallen into panic and despair.

Washington's personal involvement in battles lost to the British, combined with the disturbing fact that the British had established their headquarters in the prime location of New York, reinforced his determination to defeat the enemy there.

By September 1776, meetings continued in an attempt to establish a diplomatic relationship with France; Benjamin Franklin and Silas Deane were sent to France. Their work would come to fruition on February 6, 1778, with the Treaty of Alliance, in which France recognized America's independence and pledged to help the rebel colonists in their fight against the British. Deane's role during this period was valuable to America. Unfortunately, in later years his reputation was tarnished due to claims made by Arthur Lee, and he was accused of being a double agent. These accusations were never proven. Before the year was out, bound by the moral strength of a just cause, Washington and his men turned the tide with two wins at Trenton, New Jersey, followed by success at Princeton in early January 1777.

After six years of fighting during trying times, Washington must have battled with severe self-doubt. Prior to Rochambeau's arrival, George Washington felt the threat of imminent loss to the British. Moreover, he could not be expected to continue much longer without extensive outside help. Hope was fading, especially as Washington and his men struggled to recover after the devastating winter of 1779–80 at Morristown. Washington admitted this in his correspondence. In a letter to Lafayette, Washington conceded, "Unless we secure arms and powder from the Count [de Rochambeau], we certainly can do nothing. With every effort we shall fall short at least four thousand or five thousand arms and two hundred tons of powder."[7] And Arnold Whitridge in his book, *Rochambeau, America's Neglected Founding Father,* agreed, "After six years of fighting [the] men were weary of pouring out blood and treasure in a struggle that seemed to lead nowhere."[8] All the same, Washington knew in his heart that his was a just cause that he could not abandon.

COMBINING SKILLS FOR A COMMON GOAL

Although living on separate continents, Washington and Rochambeau had been following a similar course. Since the death of his older brother, Rochambeau had pursued a purely military career and while Washington, too, was clearly involved in the military, he, unlike Rochambeau, was also establishing himself politically. Rochambeau had joined the army at age sixteen and commanded his own regiment by the age of twenty-one on March 3, 1747. In

1748 George Washington, at age sixteen, was surveying for a wealthy Virginia landowner, and in 1753, at age twenty-one, he joined the Virginia militia. Rochambeau had about seven to eight years' head start in his military experience. He fought in both the War of Austrian Succession and the Seven Years' War in Europe. It would later seem ironic that the French, once enemies of the Americans in the French and Indian War, would be the allies who would help the Continentals finally defeat the British. The French had their reasons, not the least of which was revenge against the British.

It was Rochambeau's training, character, and patience that would in the end be indispensable to Washington in bringing about a favorable outcome. Rochambeau's thirty-seven-year career in service to his country complemented Washington's years in politics and the military. They would need to draw on their combined careers to resolve the long drawn-out war for independence. Only seven years Washington's senior, Rochambeau had a distinct advantage in military skill and objectivity. Going forward, he would be an agent for change in aiding Washington to find the best strategy for success.

Rochambeau's top priority was to convince Washington to commit to a plan of action that he had not seriously considered prior to the Frenchman's arrival: to change his focus from New York to Virginia. It was Rochambeau, his subordinate, who in concert with French minister to Philadelphia, La Luzerne, as well as King Louis XVI's foreign minister, Vergennes, and Spain's ambassador to France, D'Aranda, pushed for concentrating on the southern strategy. Despite the difficulties that greatly complicated such a strategic shift, namely, lack of funds, low troop levels, unconfirmed naval support, and an arduous march of four hundred miles under the hot sun, Rochambeau waited patiently for favorable conditions to evolve.

From the time General Rochambeau made the acquaintance of General Washington in 1780 until he joined forces with him nearly a year later on the Hudson, it became evident to him that Washington was harboring punishing memories of the humiliating defeat he had suffered at the hands of the Howes in New York. Even though

William Howe was soon replaced by General Clinton as commander of the British headquarters, Washington's focus remained fixed on New York. The British chose New York as their strategic center of operations in America. No question, it was an obvious objective for the rebel forces; they needed a strong victory there to convince the states and Congress that this was a war worth funding and to raise the morale necessary to carry on the fight. Washington's thinking was that a decisive win over Clinton at New York could put an end to the interminable war.

So when Rochambeau and his four divisions of well-trained and war-tested soldiers landed in Newport, Washington's confidence took a giant leap forward. He envisioned that with the help of the French his chances of assembling the required force to conquer Clinton at New York were greatly enhanced.

Over the winter of 1780–81, Rochambeau and Washington carried on their correspondence regarding the best plan of action. They had met once at Hartford, then later at Rochambeau's winter headquarters at Newport, and in the spring at Wethersfield, where Rochambeau encouraged the American general to weigh the possibility of a combined strike in Virginia. There was one essential point upon which they steadfastly agreed: their cause was doomed without French naval support. General Rochambeau was influential in the shift of Washington's objective from New York to Virginia, but it took until August 1781 for the shift to occur. In the interim, General Rochambeau and General Washington continued to work out their differences on a path of shared destiny.

Washington did not try to conceal from Rochambeau that his raison d'être was to avenge his losses to the British at New York. He had brought it up for discussion with Rochambeau at their first, second, and third meetings as well as in their correspondence, but as the French general suggested, there might be alternatives worth considering. For six years following his defeat at Manhattan, Washington yearned for a day of retribution when he could turn the tables permanently on the British and thereby banish them from

American shores. This was a tall order, especially given that even with French aid, Washington and his ragtag army were fighting a behemoth.

The depth of Washington's frustration sometimes came to the surface during trying times. His soldiers knew he was prone to angry outbursts, especially in battle when results turned sour. In the early summer of 1778 he had ordered an attack on the British at Monmouth, New Jersey, only to find that his first line of attack had made a sudden retreat. This act of cowardice in the face of the enemy filled him with fury. He yelled, "You damned poltroon [coward], you never tried them."[9] An unnamed general who witnessed the scene described the American commanding officer as "shouting till the leaves shook on the trees."[10] Washington's frustration energized him to enter the battle himself on his charging horse, brashly leading his troops back into battle, winning the day.[11]

Rochambeau did not experience the intense outrage his American commander had exhibited at Monmouth. Although their debates over strategy were sometimes contentious, the French general used his diplomatic skills to keep their discussions of tactics in a polite tenor. Rochambeau knew his place; he knew also that he had to be patient waiting for time and events to line up in favor of the southern theatre. He withheld his direct challenge for the time when there would be no other choice.

AMERICAN REBELS FACE A GIANT

It was obvious to Rochambeau early on that Washington and his rebel army had pitted themselves against a world power yet had no standing army, no regular navy, no draft, no uniforms, and no reliable funding to pay them for their efforts. Neither the newly formed Congress nor the states could offer Washington and his bedraggled army the support they so desperately needed. As an example, Washington had to combat the Tories, who were constantly trying to undermine his progress and sabotage his supply lines, along with the ever-present threat of desertion and mutiny among his troops. On top of all these negatives he and his army had to deal with the frightful winters at Valley Forge and Morristown, which they barely survived.

In many ways, Washington and Rochambeau resembled David of the Old Testament, fighting the giant, Goliath. They had few resources compared to the strong and capable British who held sway over the land and sea on both sides of the Atlantic. Also, they were relegated to doing what they did best with what they had at hand. General Rochambeau sought a way to surprise the huge Goliath, the British. He proposed hitting them where they were most vulnerable, not at the heart of operations at New York, but where the eye of the giant was less fortified, in the South. Rochambeau would strike the British eye in Virginia, namely Cornwallis. He recognized that the center of King George's forces in New York was far too strong even for the combined American-French forces. The Grande Reconnaissance had proved that.

Rochambeau saw the wisdom in marching south. Lord Cornwallis, with his army moving into Yorktown, and with his back edging toward the sea, represented a more assailable enemy than Clinton at New York. Rochambeau readily perceived this fact. Lord Cornwallis, Clinton's second-in-command, would be the perfect, unsuspecting target. The veteran military tactician, Rochambeau, took this long-range plan as his central purpose.

After Rochambeau arrived in Newport, his correspondence with the French minister, La Luzerne, commenced. Lee Kennett in his book *The French Forces in America, 1780–1783,* refers to La Luzerne's letter, written August 4, 1780, addressed to Rochambeau: "If the operation against New York was not feasible, La Luzerne raised the possibility of a winter campaign in the South. Even so, the diplomat left the decision to the commander at Newport."[12]

Therefore, at his first meeting with the American commanding officer at Hartford in September 1780, Rochambeau planted the seeds of his strategy to reinforce Lafayette in Virginia and attack

Cornwallis. From then on Rochambeau watered the seeds, never pestering Washington on the subject, instead subtly pointing out the advantages of bypassing New York and marching south to Virginia.

The allied generals did find common ground at their first meeting. They had agreed that the allies could not prevail without superior naval support from the French. On this point they did not waiver. Accordingly, Rochambeau waited for his king to send the promised reinforcements of soldiers and ships.

Rochambeau's second division had been left at the port of Brest when he and Admiral de Ternay embarked from France in May 1780. His Most Christian Majesty, King Louis XVI, had sent Admiral de Guichen's fleet to the West Indies with the second division. As winter took hold in the new year of 1781, General Rochambeau had no word as to when the reinforcements would be sailing to North America to aid the allies. Instead of Guichen's fleet, British Admiral Rodney's fleet of thirteen vessels arrived at New York.[13] According to Rochambeau's memoirs, on September 20, 1780, the advent of Rodney's fleet tripled their numbers.[14] The allies could not hope to equal that show of force. Commanders Rochambeau and Washington were left at an impasse for the fall and winter of 1780–1781. All these events or non-events gave weight to Rochambeau's argument not to attack General Clinton at New York.

George Washington was naturally reluctant to place his full confidence in a Frenchman no matter how sterling his credentials, no matter how glowing his recommendations from the French king and his foreign ministers, Vergennes and Montbarrey. It was not that long ago that young Colonel Washington served under the British aegis and fought to banish the French from the Ohio territory. By 1780, a much more seasoned George Washington knew, as Joseph J. Ellis so eloquently put it in his *Founding Brothers,* "There was no such thing as a permanent international alliance, only permanent national interests."[15] Case in point: both Washington himself and Rochambeau were drawn together by the winds of Providence for this single high purpose, each man and each nation—serving the common purpose of ousting the British from America.

Washington's doubt turns to trust

Washington "was forever on his guard in the face of the French," but over the next months through meetings and prolific correspondence, Washington gained confidence in General Rochambeau, an essential first step before he could contemplate altering his six-year strategy.[16] The two generals became more candid with each other and found they were able to share their many worries and problems. Rochambeau and his army camped in close proximity to Washington; the two men attended daily briefings and planning sessions, all of which tended, over time, to break down barriers that stood to divide them. They were becoming true allies. Washington began to lay aside any pre-conceived ideas he may have held against the French up to this time. Despite the fact that they held differing views on strategy, as the two commanders worked hand in hand toward a common goal taking part in reconnaissance sorties, Washington's doubts were soon replaced by a growing respect for Rochambeau's ability, experience, and professionalism.

Little by little, according to Jean Jules Jusserand, French author and ambassador to America from 1902–1925, Washington's heart was won. The former wrote, "We did not, in that war, conquer any land for ourselves, but we conquered Washington."[17] On May 1, 1781, Washington made an entry in his personal diary referring to the French as "our generous allies."[18] For the American general, often stoic and rarely expressing positive feelings, these words spoke volumes in appreciation of his new French friends, especially Rochambeau. Gradually, they built a solid trust. In so doing, Washington began to fully appreciate that Rochambeau's intentions ran parallel to his own. At the same time, Rochambeau knew that it fell to Washington to make the final decision and to issue the final orders. No decision on future strategy was made during the winter except to join forces on the Hudson in milder weather.

Rochambeau and Washington found ways to work together, and the subtle beauty of Rochambeau's role as Washington's lieutenant emerged when coupled with Rochambeau's own strength of character, honesty, and experience. Gradually a climate of comfortable compatibility grew between the two men, and upon that state of mutual understanding was laid the foundation on which to base the final decision.

Leading up to the time of Washington's final determination to march south in August 1781, Rochambeau had proven himself "strong as an oak with the bending qualities of a willow."[19] For example, referring to the Hartford meeting of September 1780, Rochambeau yielded to his commander's will yet remained strong in his convictions. Acting as Washington's ideal lieutenant, he had agreed to go along with Washington's plan to lay siege to New York but used his influence over the next eleven months to convince his commander in chief to adopt a different strategy. Rochambeau's flexibility and perseverance were two of the very assets that prompted the twenty-six-year-old King Louis XVI and his minister of foreign affairs, Charles de Vergennes, to go along with his minister of war, Prince de Montbarrey, in choosing Rochambeau to lead the *expédition particulière*. According to Michele R. Morris, author of *Images of America in Revolutionary France,* Montbarrey preferred him, despite the fact that he was neither in his circle of friends, nor did he speak a word of English.

The prince chose Rochambeau for his strength of character, the precision of his military orders, his military insight, and his equanimity, all of which are indisputable.[20] Likewise, they chose Comte de Rochambeau because of his ability to listen, to make keen observations, and to strategize successfully. In addition, Rochambeau was well known for the exemplary manner by which he interacted with his peers, his troops, and his military opponents. All these qualities put Rochambeau, the equal but subordinate officer, in good stead for working with General Washington.

The French king and his advisors showed great wisdom not only in selecting Rochambeau, but also, under the recommendation of the Marquis de Lafayette, placing him under the command of General Washington for the American campaign.[21] Because an outsized ego is part of the job requirements, very few generals could abide such a role, especially so far from home base. "Never in French history had an expedition force been placed under an unknown and foreign commander who had not even been introduced to the king. However, this is to the credit of Lafayette that such trust was placed in George Washington."[22] Rochambeau had never been ordered to serve under a foreign general in a foreign land, but he did so with grace and aplomb. Although it was highly irregular and most likely not found in the French army's tactical manuals of the day, the strategy proved successful. The young divine-right French monarch had taken a calculated risk in sending one of his best generals across the Atlantic to serve in a foreign land under a foreign commanding general. From the American point of view, it may have been the most brilliant move in his reign. In the long run, the expedition would be credited for the throwing off of a foreign mantle from the newly emerging country, the United States of America.

Rochambeau had devoted much time and energy to implementing improvements for the reorganization of the French army before leaving for America, yet it was unlikely that he foresaw himself in such a unique military position. The American campaign was the first time Rochambeau was cut off from his supply lines. Because the Atlantic Ocean lay between Rochambeau's army and home base, there was even more reason for the French and American generals to find common ground on which to build trust. Good faith was essential between them in order to work well together and thus avoid prideful posturing.

Thus, the confident Rochambeau watered the seeds of concentrating the campaign in the South and gently nourished them through the fall, winter, and spring following the original planting. A seed cannot be forced to sprout. It does so in its own time. The same was true with the evolving plans for the next stage of the American Revolution. Rochambeau continued to discuss the pros and cons of the southern campaign with George Washington when the occasion permitted.

In the early spring of 1781, M. de La Luzerne voiced his advocacy for Rochambeau's point of view toward the advantages of taking the army to Virginia. "From his [La Luzerne's] pen came a steady stream of pleas..." to agree with Rochambeau's southern strategy.[23] La Luzerne had been working closely with southern delegates to Congress who were meeting at Philadelphia. He encouraged them to maintain a pro-French attitude because taking the battle south would bring about improvement of relations in that sector. La Luzerne was also preoccupied with the increasingly dangerous position that Lafayette faced while tailing Cornwallis in Virginia.[24]

Examining the results of the May 1781 conference at Wethersfield, Connecticut, between Washington and Rochambeau, consider the following observation by Walter W. Woodward, Connecticut State Historian: "The flexibility of the strategy planned at Wethersfield was what made the victory in 1781 possible."[25] In making this statement, Woodward intimated that it was the flexibility of Rochambeau's unique position that, in part, kept the decision from being wrongly nailed down too early in the strategy game.

Granted, Washington still did not wholeheartedly accept the proposed plan to take the battle south, but he was willing to see that events were beginning to point in that direction. He was waiting for more recruits, the reinforcement of the French fleet, and money to prepare and supply the troops for either the siege of New York or the long march to Virginia. It must have taken extreme patience and diplomacy for Rochambeau to remain amenable to Washington's lead, yet stand firm in his convictions.

At the Wethersfield meeting General Washington wrote a letter to Montbarrey in Paris, revealing his continued interest in New York. The gist of the letter appears in Bonsal's *When the French Were Here.*

It reads: "I should be wanting in respect and confidence were I not to add that our object is New York."[26] In the same vein Washington made an entry on May 22 in his newly resumed diary, proclaiming his continued fixation on laying siege to New York: "Fixed with Count de Rochambeau upon a plan of campaign in substance as follows: that the French Land force…should march, so soon as the squadron [French fleet] could sail…to the North River, and there in conjunction with the American army commence an operation against New York (which in the present reduced state of the Garrison would fall unless relieved) the doing which would enfeeble their Southern operations and in either case be productive of Capital advantages, or to extend our Views to the Southward as circumstances and a naval superiority might render more necessary and eligible."[27]

Colonel Jonathan Trumbull of Connecticut, with whom Washington discussed his plans freely and who was privy to the general's thought process, revealed still another side to his chief's thinking at that juncture. Trumbull maintained that the siege of New York "from its first contemplation had been deemed eventual and contingent…upon the exertions of the states and the place of arrival of the French fleet."[28] The key words, "eventual and contingent," were uttered by Trumbull in describing the evolving military scene as it played out in early summer 1781. Rochambeau persisted and endured.

Washington considers Southern theatre

"There are clear indications in Washington's own correspondence throughout that summer that his mind was far from closed to a Southern campaign,"[29] contends author Lee Kennett. In diary entries from early summer of 1781, the commander in chief began to show that he was seriously considering moving the siege to Virginia for the first time. In a missive on June 21, he told the Board of War "that circumstances might oblige the allies to 'transfer the weight of the war to the southward.'"[30] Soon after, Washington confided in

General Knox, saying, "I am every day more and more dubious of our being able to carry into execution the operations we have in contemplation [against New York]."[31] Again, more sure of himself, on July 30, 1781, Washington warned Lafayette, "It is more than probable that we shall also entirely change our plan of operation,"[32] indicating that the march south was becoming increasingly likely.

Over the next two weeks, Washington evaluated the two opposing plans. Rochambeau and his commander were together at New York, camped in proximity to the British forts. What series of events finally convinced Washington to shift his focus away from New York? In July and August 1781, three things happened that gave Washington no choice but to accept the French plan relayed via Rochambeau and French Minister de La Luzerne.

The first of these events was at the end of July when the Grande Reconnaissance of July 21–23 was completed, revealing that General Clinton possessed a greater number of troops than previously surmised. In late June, a garrison had arrived from Pensacola, Florida, followed by Hessians from Germany.[33] As a result, the reinforced enemy position was too formidable to attempt an attack at that time.

The second event was the report received from Washington's chief military engineer, Duportail. The commander in chief had requested that he conduct a thorough investigation of a possible plan of attack on the British defenses at New York. Duportail presented this report to his general on July 27, submitting that the attack would require *"beaucoup de temps et beaucoup d'hommes"* (much time and many men).[34] In Duportail's summation, an army of no less than twenty thousand would be needed to successfully take over New York.[35] At that point, Washington had only roughly two thousand soldiers available to fight, with another two thousand having arrived about this time from New England militias. Rochambeau had four thousand soldiers. Official numbers for the British were approximately 14,000 soldiers, though Rochambeau in his memoirs estimates the figure at more than 12,000 men.[36] The combined American-French armies consisted of just under 9,000 men.[37]

Rochambeau, in his memoirs, counts the allies' combined numbers in this way: "…General Washington and my own formed together but nine thousand men, which comparatively small force began already to annoy the enemy."[38] Surely, as Kennett had surmised, there was no equality in numbers.[39] Duportail, therefore, could not recommend taking up a siege that would require more men and more time than even the combined allies could muster.

The third event unfolded when Rochambeau received welcome news, which he had shared with Washington on August 14, stating that Admiral de Grasse was leaving the West Indies bound for the Chesapeake, not New York.[40] There were two valid reasons for De Grasse's choice. His time was limited for the roundtrip voyage, and his ships could not cross the bar into New York Harbor. He estimated his arrival by the end of August. The rest of the good news was that he would be bringing with him the much-needed ingredients for success: a good-sized fleet of twenty-eight ships of the line, plus four frigates, extra fighting men, and the equivalent of 1.2 million livres in Spanish specie to continue the fight. With De Grasse entering the picture, there was hope that the allies could meet the enemy on equal footing and with luck and good timing, take the advantage.[41] The allies needed De Grasse's fleet to complete the blockade of the British in Virginia. Rochambeau knew that without De Grasse, the attack would fail.

Even if the French fleet were to sail farther north to New York, it would not be able to cross the shallow waters at the bar near Sandy Hook leading to New York Harbor as evidenced in Rochambeau's memoirs. The British held the advantage in this respect because their ships drew a shallow draft, allowing them to navigate the bar, while the French ships, with their deep draft hulls, would find entry there far too risky to attempt.[42] "I then suggested," wrote Rochambeau to De Grasse, "as my own opinion, the propriety of attempting an expedition to Chesapeak[e] against the army of Lord Cornwallis, and which I consider more practicable, and less expected by the enemy, on account of the distances of our positions."[43]

If Admiral de Grasse were to sail as far north as New York, he would be hard pressed to return to the West Indies within the window of time the Spanish had allotted for him to be absent from his duties in the Caribbean. He also had to consider the approaching hurricane season. Therefore, De Grasse was truly working against the clock. He had promised the Spanish he would adhere to their timetable, and his arrival in Chesapeake waters was critically important to the allies whose plan to entrap Cornwallis at Yorktown was also time sensitive. De Grasse had to arrive early enough to prevent aid from reaching Cornwallis by sea while the allies tightened the noose around Cornwallis by land. In order to be successful, both components of Cornwallis's entrapment had to fall into place at the same time. Only after hearing of this series of events could Washington safely jump the gulf of indecision to stand firmly on the side of Rochambeau in favor of the southern campaign.

THE INVINCIBILITY OF WASHINGTON

With these three events lined up in the allies' favor, directing them away from certain failure at New York, some believed that God in his providential care and guardianship over his creatures once again guided Washington as he sought to pave the way to a free and secure foundation for America. More than once during his career Washington had been aware that Divine Providence protected him in battle and that he was guarded from certain death as those around him died. A few days after Washington's first encounter with enemy fire at Fort Necessity in the Ohio Territory, the opening battle for the control of the New World fought in 1754, he wrote to his brother, "I heard Bullets whistle and believe me there was something charming in the sound."[44] On July 9, 1755, a year after his defeat at Fort Necessity, he had two horses shot from under him at Fort Duquesne and numerous holes shot through his clothing, yet he emerged from that battle with no wounds.[45]

George Washington

French engraving after portrait by Piehle
with illustration of Yorktown surrender. 1783.
Anne S. K. Brown Military Collection, Brown University Library.

At Fort Duquesne, 977 of the 1,459 British troops under General Braddock died or were wounded in the three-hour surprise assault. The French, on the other hand, counted only seventeen dead or wounded while around a hundred Indian warriors lost their lives. Washington later wrote to his brother, contradicting the news that he (Washington) had died in the battle: "By the all-powerful dispensation of Providence, I have been protected beyond all human probability & expectation for I had 4 bullets through my Coat, and 2 horses shot under me yet escaped unhurt."[46]

Washington seemed invincible at Fort Duquesne. On the day that General Braddock was killed in the confusion of the attack, Washington "miraculously escaped without a scratch," though, as Washington observed, "death was levelling [his] companions on every side of [him].[47] Washington did not know why he was being saved, but it was no secret to him that his life was being preserved for a purpose beyond his knowing.[48]

Amidst the chaos that followed Braddock's death, Washington assumed the role of chaplain, officiating at the burial of his fallen chief. In the fading light he read from the 1662 Anglican *Book of Common Prayer*:

> I AM the resurrection and the life, saith the Lord: he that believeth in me, though he were dead, yet shall he live: and whosoever liveth and believeth in me shall never die. St. John xi. 25, 26. I KNOW that my Redeemer liveth and that he shalt stand at the latter day upon the earth. Grant this, we beseech thee, O merciful Father, through Jesus Christ, our Mediator and Redeemer. Amen.[49]

The prayer book Washington used was one he had printed especially for himself at the same time that he had prayer books printed for his whole family. He had asked that his copy be made to fit into his pocket so he would always have it with him. This was one such occasion when he needed the prayer book.[50]

The British, on the other hand, felt they were jinxed, so to speak, at times and that the battle would never be won against the rebels. Perhaps they were tiring of the protracted war. Or did the British think that fate was against them? Their predicament came up in conversation in the summer of 1780 while the British Admirals Graves and Hood and General Clinton were discussing a possible plan to attack the French fleet at Newport. According to Larrabee in his *Decision at the Chesapeake,* Admiral Hood remarked on "the strange fatality which seems to hang over us."[51] The admiral expressed anguish at not having had enough ships at the ready when he needed them. He was conducting a "would have, should have" analysis over poor planning, which was not uncommon after losing a skirmish. Hood could see that with the coming of Rochambeau and the French fleet their days were numbered. Despite recent successes at Savannah and Charleston, they had lost crucial headway earlier at Saratoga and eventually there would be a face-off with the French fleet. In speaking of fatality, he may have sensed their doom. If so, was his sense of eventual defeat the counterpoint to Washington's sense of eventual triumph?

Washington had emerged as the chosen one to lead his country to freedom. Divine Providence, thought of as the hand of God intervening in history, may well have guided him toward the fulfillment of the rebels' dream of a free America. For this reason, Washington may have enjoyed a certain sense of confidence. If so, any pride he might have possessed was overshadowed by his show of grace and humility. When asked to take on the challenge of becoming commanding general of the American Continental army, he admitted to himself and others that he was not qualified. When pressed, Washington accepted the post and offered to serve without pay, saying that he did not deserve the honor. Ultimately, he assumed the role because of the importance of getting the job done and because no one else was willing to bear the burden. He was, therefore, a man of contradictions in character while exhibiting an unrivaled sense of responsibility and undaunted courage in spite of the occasional appearance of low self-esteem.

During this extended period of equivocation, Rochambeau had formally agreed with his commander's wish to attack Clinton while not wholeheartedly believing in the viability of the plan. He would wait to see how events played out. Rochambeau was proven "the ideal lieutenant" when, after giving his own opinion, he deferred to Washington's preference for New York.[52] Rochambeau did this respectfully, not with resentment, in spite of his disagreement.[53] While Rochambeau had let his commander know his opinion as far back as their first meeting, he was meanwhile committed to carry out his commander's orders to the best of his ability.[54] Mathieu Dumas, one of Rochambeau's aides, made an astute journal entry regarding "his commander's 'perfect subordination' to General Washington."[55] Rochambeau's ability to bend was critical to working with George Washington. Rochambeau listened well, offered his suggestions, and followed orders even if he did not agree all the time, as a good lieutenant should; the best example was after the Hartford meeting when the two generals agreed that New York would be their prime objective. It is well known that Rochambeau did not agree but did acquiesce.

Meanwhile, Washington tried in vain to bolster his troop numbers. He wrote numerous requests to Congress and to the individual states, but neither Congress nor the governors came to his aid, some not even giving him the favor of a reply. Rochambeau watched and waited, noting that the British in New York still maintained superior numbers as compared to the allies. In fact, those numbers had recently increased with the addition of German recruits and the Florida garrison.

The following negative developments could have been counted as serious stopgaps in Rochambeau's strategy. The last division of French troops, for which Rochambeau waited a year, would not be sent from France. Even though the French king continued to send specie, it appeared that he had lost interest in sending more ships and men. In addition, to insure that neither ships nor soldiers left France for the New World, the British had blocked the harbor at Brest. Likewise, the enemy continued to block the harbor at Newport, making it difficult for the French fleet to exit in support of an attack on New York.

Unfortunately, the newly formed United States of America had not yet created or funded a full-fledged navy. Harassing British ships fell to the many privateers along the American coast and elsewhere in Atlantic waters. The American insurgents had neither the time nor the treasure to build that much-needed asset. They would have continued to be at the mercy of the British navy had the French not decided to send aid in the form of ships, soldiers, and supplies via De Grasse from the West Indies. It became even more apparent as time went on that the role of the French navy would be the crucial ingredient for an allied victory. These tactical deterrents were not insurmountable, however, from Rochambeau's point of view. Through careful planning, they were either avoided or overcome.

Rochambeau approached his general one more time, seeking his final answer. Would they march south, or would they stay and be humiliated again, or even worse, have to give up the fight? Rochambeau, in speaking with his commander, was emphatic that De Grasse was under his (Rochambeau's) command; he did order the admiral to sail to the Chesapeake after all. For the first time, there were words of open disagreement, for Washington loathed changing his mind on this subject.

Due to the aforementioned events, the French general was correct to point the conflict toward Yorktown since Cornwallis was already there with Lafayette backing him up to the sea. For the first time, there was obvious tension in open dispute, although brief, between them.[56] Washington finally admitted that the scale had tipped, conceding to Rochambeau that the southern strategy was the best plan, even though the American troops would balk at the idea of a long march.

C . F . COMTE DE ROCHAMBEAU .

Lieutenant Général des Armées du Roy

Commandant l'Armée Françoise en Amérique

Comte de Rochambeau

Lieutenant General of the Royal French Army in the American
Expedition with trophies, left and right. c. 1783. (Artist Unknown)
Anne S. K. Brown Military Collection, Brown University Library.

After working with General Rochambeau for a little more than a year, Washington saw that all the necessary components of ships, soldiers, and funds had fallen into place. He was wise to wait as long as he did, for the timing was perfect, and only at this point was he fully convinced he should order the French and American troops to march to Yorktown. By August 17, George Washington gave the command to march the allied armies to Virginia.[57]

The two generals had worked through their differences to initiate the great campaign that was to end in the finest hour of their combined destinies.

While still at his camp at Philipsburg, Washington made this entry in his diary, which explained his change of course: "Matters having now come to a crisis and a decisive plan to be determined on, I was obliged, from the shortness of Count de Grasse's promised stay on this Coast, the apparent disinclination of their Naval Officers to force the harbour of New York, and the feeble compliance of the States to my requisitions for Men…to give up all idea of attacking New York; and instead thereof to remove the French troops and a detachment from the American army to the Head of Elk… to be transported to Virginia for the purpose of co-operating with the force from the West Indies against the Troops in that State."[58] With the southern strategy firmly in place, the allies secretly prepared to move south, bypassing Clinton who was fully ready to fend off the presumed allied attack at New York.

CHAPTER EIGHT

The Secret March to Virginia

"George Washington was impatient to get all the troops across the river. He sent me back to tell the Comte de Rochambeau to send his army up as quickly as possible."

—Louis-Alexandre Berthier

THE APPEARANCE OF THE FRENCH ARMY on Clinton's doorstep forced him to prepare for an imminent attack. The British had been kept at high alert since Rochambeau's arrival on the Hudson Highlands in early July. It was already mid-August and still there had been no full-fledged incursion on the part of the combined armies. Clinton was beside himself with aggravation and confusion. He did not know whether to send for additional troop support from Cornwallis or to send him support should Washington and Rochambeau decide to march south. For Clinton the equipoise mentioned earlier drew on unmercifully.

Washington's message to De Grasse, written from Philipsburg on August 17, stated, "We have determined to remove the whole of the French army and a large detachment of the American army to the Chesapeake to meet your Excellency in Virginia." Washington and Rochambeau signed the message jointly.[1] Concerned with funding the march, Washington consulted with Robert Morris, superintendent of finance, and Richard Peters, secretary of the board of war, who were visiting the commander at his headquarters at the

Livingston mansion. "What can you do for me?" he asked. Peters replied, "With money, everything; without it, nothing." They had no money, so Morris and Peters had nothing to offer.[2] They did not know that on August 24 additional funds would arrive from France, giving Rochambeau and Washington the specie needed to begin the march.

On August 18, General Rochambeau ordered the French artillery and paymaster's wagons to march to King's Ferry, New York, where the artillery and soldiers crossed the Hudson.[3] Berthier and Crèvecoeur marched with them at the head of the forward column. Crèvecoeur wrote that it took six days to march forty miles from Philipsburg to King's Ferry, because of "terrible weather and incredible roads."[4] He added, "I have no doubt that had the enemy been able to predict our march, he would have caused us much anxiety."[5]

BREAD OVENS FOOL CLINTON

The next day "the call to arms was beaten," and George Washington ordered his troops to move out from Philipsburg.[6] Column by column, the whole army moved out of camp; soldiers were sent ahead to "establish ovens and commence victualling" in Chatham, New Jersey.[7] This was done in view of the British, "so as to feign an attack on New York by States Island [Staten Island], which doubly excited the anxiety of the enemy's General."[8] At this point, only the top officers knew that Washington had accepted Rochambeau's plan to march to Virginia to rendezvous with Lafayette and De Grasse. Washington knew that many of his troops would not relish such a difficult march, particularly when they did not know where they were headed. Unlike the French army who rarely, if ever, questioned orders, the Americans were used to a more relaxed method of marching and fighting. The American troops, however, would have to adapt to the current plans to move south. Washington told General Lincoln "that from now on his men 'were to consider themselves as light troops who are always supposed to be fit for immediate action' and that they should free themselves from every encumbrance which might interfere with activity of movement."[9]

The French split into two parts: Section A returned to New Castle (Mt. Kisco) and Section B passed through Thornwood, Pleasantville, and Chappaqua, along what is now the Saw Mill River Parkway. Rochambeau described their departure from Philipsburg: "We led our armies to the Delaware: we were fortunate enough to find its water low and were able to ford it near Trenton. It was not until then that Clinton could have seen clearly into our intended plans; but it was then too late to impede them."[10] General Clinton had been deceived, not only by the Grande Reconnaissance and the fake bake ovens, but also by a letter purportedly written to fool the British. It was signed by Washington and had been intercepted by Clinton's men. The letter clearly stated the American general's intention to attack New York. The ruse was so effective Clinton did not know he was tricked until they had crossed the Delaware.

The Continentals who marched south with the French consisted of the following: the New Jersey Continentals (two regiments), the First New York Continentals, Colonel Hazen's regiment (Canadians), Colonel Lamb's regiment of artillery (New York), and Colonel Scammel's light troops (New Hampshire).[11] "The Jersey Line and Hazen's regiment were ferried across the Hudson River from Dobbs Ferry to Sneeden's Landing."[12] They marched toward the Watchung Mountains, not far from Chatham, New Jersey. The rest of the Continentals moved north, following the Hudson, and crossed the Croton River at New Bridge near Van Cortland Manor House and on to Verplanck Point and King's Ferry.[13]

Washington assigned General Heath to remain in New York with 2,500 Continentals plus thousands of local militia to keep Clinton guessing while feigning ferry crossings and to fool him into thinking that the allies were preparing to attack.[14] Heath's second job, just as important, was to prevent Clinton from reinforcing Cornwallis in Virginia at all costs. Thirdly, Heath stood guard over

West Point, a pivotal position on the long river that connected New York with Canada.

On August 20 the Comte de Vioménil left the French camp with the grenadiers and chasseurs to take up the rear guard for the overland march. Rochambeau dispatched Count Fersen, his first aide, to Newport to hasten the preparations of Admiral Barras, who awaited a signal to join them at the Chesapeake. Barras would play a crucial role in transporting the heavy siege artillery to the point of battle. Rochambeau ordered his troops to pack up quickly and set out for their previous camp, North Castle. After a day's march, the French arrived at North Castle. The same day, Washington's troops moved north to cross the Hudson at King's Ferry.

BRITISH INERTIA

Clinton, seemingly frozen in place, did not pursue the combined American and French armies, even when he suspected they might bypass New York and march southward. He seemed incapable of taking a simple step of action in an obvious military maneuver. The British, by their inaction, may have foreshadowed that they would not have the staying power to match that of those still willing to fight fiercely for independence. Even Clinton's superiors, such as Lord George Germaine, secretary of state in charge of American affairs, was as incapable of initiating action as Clinton.

In his journal entitled *My Campaigns in America,* Colonel Guillaume de Deux-Ponts pointed out his surprise at the lack of British action at this pivotal, even vulnerable time, as the allied armies began their move southward. He wrote, "On the 22nd of August I formed the immediate advance guard of the army at Verplanck's Point on the North River. The grenadiers and chasseurs then received orders to return to their regiments, and we prepared to pass the river with all possible dispatch...the 23rd of August has been employed in embarking and taking across all the trains. An enemy of any boldness or any skill would have seized an opportunity so favorable for him and so embarrassing for us, as that of our crossing the North River. I do not understand the indifference with which General Clinton considers our movements. It is to me an obscure enigma."[15]

Inclement weather may have played a part in the stagnation of the British. Yet even with the arrival of three thousand German recruits on August 11, Clinton did nothing to deter the departure of the allies. As Arnold Whitridge put it quite succinctly, Clinton was at that point his own worst enemy. He risked nothing and lost all at New York.[16]

ROCHAMBEAU AND WASHINGTON VISIT WEST POINT

By August 23, the allied armies were combined once again. They camped on high ground over the Hudson about nine miles from West Point. According to his aide, Cromot Du Bourg, Rochambeau was curious about West Point and took a detour to visit the stronghold of the Hudson. He and Washington traveled by boat to the famous fort, which Benedict Arnold had tried to hand over to the enemy less than a year before. Surely, Divine Providence was with Washington that day when Arnold's plot was uncovered in September 1780.

Forty miles upstream from New York, West Point stands high above the Hudson, perched on high rocks with very steep sides above a plateau on which 1,200–1,500 men can deploy in line of battle. Six forts, raised one above the other, defend the approach and protect the troops below. Several fine batteries overlook the river, which at that point makes a wide elbow turn. To protect the Hudson River from British ships further ravaging the interior of New York State and Connecticut, two army posts were built on either side of the Hudson; one at Fort Washington on the East side and the other at Fort Lee on the West side where the George Washington Bridge now stands.[17] But these cannon-fortified forts were not enough to stop the passage of British ships. It was decided that forts alone were inadequate when it came to protecting a river. George Washington wrote to his brother

John in Virginia saying that creating an obstruction was absolutely necessary.[18]

Well before Rochambeau joined Washington on the Hudson, the British observed what was supposed to be a secret effort to blockade the Hudson. At first they thought the rebels were planning to use fireships. Instead they saw that the Americans were sinking vessels to obstruct the river. There were, however, problems associated with this defensive strategy. The tides, much stronger than calculated, moved the sunken ships out of line and presented dangers to both sides.

Then, in response to the need, Philadelphia carpenter Richard Smith developed *chevaux-de-frise,* a defensive obstacle with sharp spikes, to be deployed underwater unlike on land as they had been used in the past. He presented this plan to Benjamin Franklin and to the Pennsylvania Committee of Safety in July 1775. When used underwater, the chevaux-de-frise could do serious damage to a ship. The device would be sunk in the Hudson between Fort Washington and Fort Lee.[19] A secret gap would be left open for safe passage of friendly ships. Another would be installed in the Delaware River between Fort Mifflin and Fort Mercer. The latter was eventually removed intact from the Delaware in 2007.[20] Unfortunately, the British somehow managed to navigate around the obstructions.

Because the chevaux-de-frise was not effective, another deterrent had to be found. Thomas Machin, captain of the artillery and a leading member of the engineering corps of Washington's army, designed the specifications for a chain that would bring boats to a halt and a specialized boom to float the chain. "On the slack side of April 20, 1778, the chain—made fast to a huge rock crib in Chain Cove between Horn Point and Love Rock on the west bank—was slowly winched across the 25-fathom-deep river to a similar structure on the east bank by exuberant teams of soldiers straining at the Constitution Island capstan."[21]

The chain was 1,700 feet of iron links, a little longer than the width of the river between West Point and Fort Constitution, which stood on an island in the river.[22] Each link was two feet long and weighed 114 pounds. A special Fortifications Commission was created, with five commissioners chosen by the New York State legislature; the five would coordinate with the Continental army and be headquartered in Poughkeepsie. They decided on this particular point in the river because it was at a bend that caused the ships to slow down, riding lower in the water.[23]

The plaque at the west bank chain anchorage reads:

THE GREAT CHAIN WAS ANCHORED IN THIS COVE 1778–1783.
IT WAS FORGED AT THE STERLING IRON WORKS
IN ORANGE COUNTY. IT WAS FIRST STRETCHED
ACROSS THE RIVER UNDER THE DIRECTION OF
THOMAS MACHIN, CAPTAIN OF ARTILLERY IN
APRIL 1778.[24]

In the winter, the chain, boom, and floats were hauled up on the western shore at West Point to avoid ice damage. The salvaged West Point boom timbers with chain connectors have been on display at Washington's Headquarters Museum in Newburgh, New York, since 1985. However, in September 1780, John André sailed up the Hudson on the British ship H.M.S. *Vulture* past the chain and boom to Haverstraw for his clandestine meeting with Benedict Arnold. Later the same ship rescued Arnold and successfully skirted the chain again on the trip south.

In August 1781 the French army, still in the area of the Hudson River, made a two-day bivouac above the river. Crèvecoeur was hard at work ferrying the artillery and wagons across the river on flat boats. It was a tedious and slow process due to the limited number of boats and the two-mile-wide river. Crèvecoeur wondered why the redcoats did not deter them by sending some frigates up the river.

Commissary Claude Blanchard watched the American army cross the Hudson and remarked on the miserable state of Washington's men. He was stunned at the deplorable condition of the soldiers, yet amazed they found the strength to carry on. Blanchard wrote, "The

[American] soldiers marched pretty well, but they handled their arms badly…many who were small and thin…They have no uniforms and in general are badly clad."[25]

While passing through New Jersey with the combined armies, Du Bourg "dwelt on the fact that supplies came in, not brought by farmers or hucksters, but by ladies, 'with their heads dressed and adorned with jewels, driving their own rustic wagons drawn by spirited horses in double and sometimes triple front.'"[26]

On August 24, the second day of the French army march, they crossed into New Jersey. The news was optimistic. Admiral de Barras, new commander of the French fleet in Newport, had slipped past the enemy threat in the waters near Newport and, as ordered, was en route to the Chesapeake. Barras, older than De Grasse yet for the present campaign under this younger admiral's command, brought eight ships of the line, four frigates, and eighteen transports.[27] He knew the mission was dangerous and had to be extremely cautious to avoid being intercepted on the way to the Chesapeake. Once again, Clinton delayed and was thwarted, for he had thought, albeit too late, to send Admiral Graves to capture the French squadron at Newport.

The merging of the French and American armies on the Hudson and the subsequent feint of those armies bypassing Clinton's headquarters was reminiscent of the massing of French troops at Calais, France, just prior to the surprise taking of Minorca from the British, a small island near the mouth of the Mediterranean, in 1756. Rochambeau played a role in both military ruses. Likewise, in 1781 the British were caught off guard once again dealing with what they perceived to be an imminent threat—a threat that evaporated in the night when the allied forces marched south around New York, calling their bluff. Likewise at Calais, in 1756, the French led the British to believe that they would cross the English Channel to attack at any moment. Instead, they moved to the south to capture Minorca.

Also on August 24 came the influx of much-needed hard currency that had just arrived from France. John Laurens returned from a special mission to France on the frigate *Magicienne* and brought into Boston "2,500,000 livres as an installment of the King's bounty of 6,000,000 livres recently donated to the United States."[28] Blanchard, on the other hand, recorded that 1,800,000 livres had been delivered to Boston by the frigate *Magicienne;* the news reached his ears while he was in the area of Chatham, New Jersey.[29] Whatever the amount, the soldiers, both French and American, were better supplied for the rest of the march.

Regarding the newly arrived funds, which were now on their way to the everyday soldier, the following was one man's account of its impact. The American enlisted man Joseph Plumb Martin, in his *Narrative of a Revolutionary Soldier,* revealed the sorry state of a dedicated military man fighting for independence and traveling with the combined French and American troops on the march south. He was not a complainer, but after passing through Philadelphia he wrote, "We, that is, the Sappers and Miners staid here some days... While we staid here we drew a few articles of clothing, consisting of a few tow shirts, some overalls and a few pairs of silk-and-oakum stockings; and here, or soon after, we each of us received a MONTH'S PAY, in specie, borrowed, as I was informed, by our French officers from the officers in the French army. This was the first that could be called money, which we had received as wages since the year '76, or that we ever did receive till the close of the war, or indeed, ever after, as wages."[30]

SOUTHWARD BOUND

Martin and his fellow soldiers were fortunate to board a schooner that took them to the mouth of Christiana Creek, albeit with a hold packed with gunpowder. Martin spent some uneasy days and nights sitting on the volatile powder keg of a ship, praying that the nearby British cruisers would not fire upon them, sending him sky high. They wound their way up the creek "fourteen miles... through a marsh, as crooked as a snake in motion."[31] At one point, he mentioned that to gain the comparatively short distance of forty rods on land they had to sail four miles through the winding creek. They disembarked when their ship went aground, and they marched overland to the Head of the Elk, Maryland. Later Martin was fortunate to find space on the schooner *Birmingham* to make the trip to the Chesapeake, while most of his corps were forced to travel overland due to lack of ships. When his conveyance reached Lynnhaven Bay, Martin recalled passing the French fleet, which anchored there.[32] He observed, "They resembled a swamp of dry pine trees."[33]

Joseph Plumb Martin recorded the story of his "mosquetoe" fleet as it sailed downriver toward Annapolis. He was one of the few who were able to float rather than march to Virginia. He told of the commissary (probably Blanchard) who traveled with them on the schooner and who was in charge of a "small quantity of stores [and] …a hogshead containing twenty or thirty gallons of rum."[34] It was the duty of the commissary to guard the supply of hard liquor which the soldier Martin called the "good creature" during the voyage.[35] He had the barrier removed between the hold and his cabin before nailing the barricade up again on the other side. In this way it was supposed that only the officers had access to the contents. Little did the commissary know, the soldiers found a way to broach the barrel of rum from the opposite end, "so that while the officers in the cabin thought they were the sole possessors of its contents, the soldiers in the hold had possession of at least as good a share as themselves."[36]

In his commentary, the commissary Blanchard made a comparison of the Delaware and Loire Rivers, in the United States and France respectively. Having just crossed the Delaware on a ferry, he observed that it was neither broad nor deep, but that at a distance of forty-four leagues it became as broad as the Loire. Some Americans had told him the Delaware did indeed resemble the Loire due to "the colors of the white and limpid waters."[37]

Rochambeau and Washington rode ahead of the troops to arrive at Philadelphia on August 30. They were met with great acclaim by the Light Horse Troop of the Quaker City and escorted into town. The allied generals alighted from their horses at City Tavern and were invited to dine with Mr. Robert Morris at his home. Also among the dinner guests were the Chevalier de Chastellux and Generals Knox and Moultrie, along with the two commanders' aides-de-camp.[38]

Their host in Philadelphia, Robert Morris, played a critical role in financing the Revolution. Born in Liverpool, England, Robert Morris became a banker and wealthy merchant in Philadelphia. He signed the Declaration of Independence and was known as the financier of the Revolution. He also served as a member of the Continental Congress and the Pennsylvania Legislature.[39] Until 1781, he had raised funds to supply Washington's army. Unfortunately, when he had seen Washington at Livingston Manor in New York, just prior to the march south, he was in no position to provide further aid. Although he had nothing to offer, he did manage to help Washington by securing a timely loan from Rochambeau, which made the march possible. Fortunately for the allies, there was one ready source for hard currency: King Louis XVI's war chest. Rochambeau made a gracious loan to the American general of $20,000 in coin. It was to be paid back by Morris in October 1781.[40] Because of French largesse, there was money "to pay Washington's men some of the money they were owed."[41] General Washington made the announcement that the soldiers in good stead, not the deserters or the backsliders, would be given one month's back pay.[42]

By September 1, the main body of the armies of Rochambeau and Washington had passed through Princeton into Trenton, and the next day they reached the Red Lion Tavern (sometimes called the Redline Inn by the French). On September 3 they camped near the Schuylkill River in the vicinity of Rittenhouse Square. Crèvecoeur described Pennsylvania simply as being flat country.[43] The French army made an impressive entrance into Philadelphia, then the capital of the colonies. Just outside town they halted and the "troops spruced up," wrote Crèvecoeur, and they entered Philadelphia "with drums beating and flags unfurled."[44] Only when the French and Americans reached Philadelphia did Clinton finally understand their southern goal. The allies were too far afield at that point for him to catch them. He could do but one thing: warn Cornwallis.[45]

At the head of the line into Philadelphia marched Lauzun's cavalry and infantry, followed by the artillery of the Bourbonnais and their regiment. Then came the Royal Deux-Ponts and their regiment, the artillery, and finally the artillery of the park, escorted by pickets of the cavalry and infantry.[46] The next day, the second division followed in the same order.[47] The streets were crowded with locals, observed Crèvecoeur, who were "absolutely amazed to see such a fine army" in such good condition after a long march. He also noted, "The prejudices the English had aroused in them against our country were soon dispelled, for they saw superb men."[48]

The army passed Independence Hall where they marched in review before "the President and the Honorable [sic] Congress of the United States…The President was covered [wore his hat], his Excellency General Washington…[and] the Count de Rochambeau…stood on his left hand, uncovered [did not wear his hat].…The orders of his most Christian Majesty are to pay the same honors to the President of Congress as to the Field Marshal of France and a Prince of the Blood, and to Congress the same as to himself."[49] On September 8, 1781, *The Pennsylvania Packet* (the first newspaper in Philadelphia) told of the onlookers' "gratitude to the brave, noble, and virtuous prince, who so happily governs the French nation; whose shining reign and magnanimous acts are rather to be conceived than recorded. Angels envy him his acquired glory."[50] The eighth president of the Continental Congress, Thomas McKean, wrote a most complimentary letter of welcome to Rochambeau.

Following the fine reception, the French army camped a mile from town on the Schuylkill River, which flows into the Delaware. That night the whole city was illuminated in celebration. Du Bourg, partial to the Soissonnais regiment, described their colorful coats with rose-colored facings "and their grenadier caps with white- and rose-colored feathers, which struck with astonishment the beauties of the city."[51] Performing in front of a crowd of "at least 20,000 persons and a vast number of carriages, remarkable for their elegance," the Soissonnais regiment "gave an exhibition exercise of the manual of arms."[52] The Honorable Thomas McKean, in a black velvet suit, lent his luster to the performance.[53]

While in Philadelphia, Commissary Blanchard wrote in his diary that he spoke with some Tories who were enjoying the demonstration by the Soissonnais. They alleged that the regiment must have been "recruited in England" since they were so fine.[54] He continued by admitting that the "English had described us [the French] to the Americans as pigmies."[55]

Enthralled with every new scene, Crèvecoeur reported that Philadelphia had a population of forty thousand, the houses were made of brick, and the streets were wide and straight with sidewalks. He described the markets in downtown Philadelphia and the sizeable port, remarked that the State House (Independence Hall) was without decoration, and observed that the furniture in the main hall was simple and plain.[56] He noted a university, a hospital, and Protestant and Catholic churches, though most inhabitants were Quakers. All the buildings were, per Crèvecoeur, "of simple architecture and not especially handsome."[57]

Crèvecoeur was amazed that even a locksmith, a cobbler, or a merchant could become a member of Congress. "They all believe themselves equal."[58] He also observed that they "scramble for the lucrative posts" and marveled that the lowest man could become a general in the army if he met the qualifications.[59] When that same man left the service of his country, he went back to his original status in society. These practices were remarkable to a Frenchman, since in France only men of noble birth commanded posts of high rank in the army. The lowborn remained in the inferior category in service to their country and rarely, if ever, moved up through the ranks to become an officer. The elevated status of the French nobleman would undergo drastic change at the time of the French Revolution, beginning in 1789.

In America, certain uncomfortable situations arose from discrepancies in terms of military hierarchy. For instance, Crèvecoeur revealed that the rank of lieutenant was scorned in America, but revered in France. It was the practice in the American army not to include lieutenants on the invitation list along with generals. He added, "Our generals were surprised at this discrimination and somewhat offended. General Washington excused himself by saying that, since it was not the custom to invite his own lieutenants, he could not, for political reasons, invite those of the French army, though he knew that ours were selected differently than his."[60]

However, Crèvecoeur could not help admitting that the rich did receive preference in most things in America as well as at home. That was the same the world over. On the other hand, he remarked that even the young girls of poor origins in America dressed in a manner similar to those of high station, making it difficult to distinguish between the two. The local American girls, he said, whether from town or country, wear their hair "in the French fashion" with curls around the face and flowers in their hair.[61]

Chastellux related that Chevalier de La Luzerne, French minister to the colonies in Philadelphia, received his visiting countrymen in fine form.[62] He invited the officers to dine *à la française* at his table in complete elegance. Washington and Rochambeau had gone on ahead and were absent from the dinner party. Nonetheless, Commissary Claude Blanchard was among the eighty invited guests.[63] No sooner was everyone seated at the table than a hush fell over the guests as the Express handed an important-looking letter to La Luzerne. He quickly eased their fears as he read aloud: "Thirty-six ships of the Line commanded by M. le Comte de Grasse have arrived in the Chesapeake. Three thousand soldiers [of Saint-Simon] have been landed and are now in communication with the Marquis de Lafayette."[64] In jubilance, toasts were raised to De Grasse, to Washington and Rochambeau, and to the officers of both armies. In the city, when the news spread, "funeral orations were pronounced over Cornwallis" in anticipation of his demise.[65] They mimicked the lamentations of the Tories. People from the street entered the house of La Luzerne shouting, "Long live Louis the Sixteenth!"[66] De Grasse's fleet had anchored safely at Lynnhaven Bay at the entrance to the Chesapeake on August 30.

Meanwhile, the two commanding officers who were still in Pennsylvania were "more interested in boats than banquets" and had the heavy business of war on their minds.[67] They sought to move swiftly by means of water toward their ultimate goal. They wanted to find the speediest way to the heart of the matter: Yorktown. First, they concentrated on their immediate destination, the Head of the Elk, the uppermost tip of the northeast section of Chesapeake Bay where they would transfer as many troops as possible onto ships headed for Williamsburg at the mouth of the bay. This would be their assembly point before marching the last leg of the trip into nearby Yorktown.

JOYFUL NEWS FROM DE GRASSE

General Washington, then at Chester, Pennsylvania, had received the news of De Grasse's safe landing just prior to the message being delivered at La Luzerne's grand dinner party. He and Rochambeau were separated for a portion of the route as the French general took a boat down the Delaware River from Philadelphia to Chester, just south of the city.[68] After arriving at Chester, Rochambeau "beheld a very tall American officer on shore, waving his hat, twirling a white handkerchief over his head, and capering while bellowing something indecipherable."[69] Rochambeau and Washington then met in a hearty embrace.[70]

Rochambeau recalled, "When I reached Chester I caught sight of General Washington waving his hat at me with demonstrative gestures of the greatest joy. When I rode up to him he explained… that De Grasse had arrived in the Chesapeake with twenty-eight ships of the Line and Lauzun, who was also present, said, 'I never saw a man more thoroughly and openly delighted than was General Washington at this moment.'"[71] The number of ships in De Grasse's fleet varied according to the reporter. In his memoirs, Rochambeau incorrectly stated that there were twenty-six sails of the line.[72] In fact, there were twenty-eight.

The carefully laid plans were coalescing as each part of the puzzle fell into place. Time was of the essence as the French and American armies pressed onward. Rochambeau foresaw only one possible snag in De Grasse's momentous message. De Grasse warned Rochambeau that he could remain in the Chesapeake area no later than October 15.[73]

Another witness to this emotional scene, Colonel de Deux-Ponts, expressed it this way: "I was surprised and affected by the great and true joy which General Washington showed. Of a natural coldness and a noble approach, which so well adorns the chief of a whole nation, his features, his whole bearing and deportment were now changed in an instant. For the moment he put aside his character as arbiter of North America and contented himself with that of a citizen happy beyond measure at the good fortune of his country."[74]

Immediately Washington passed the good news on to the army so as to encourage them in their march that all was going according to plan and that "no circumstance could possibly happen more opportunely in point of time, no prospect would ever have promised more opportunely of success."[75] In that moment he was reassured that his decision to follow Rochambeau's plan was well advised, indeed. This news brought a change of heart to the naysayers in Washington's army of the North who had been grumbling that the march south was a fool's errand. According to Arnold Whitridge, "More than ever, they both [Washington and Rochambeau] thanked God that De Grasse had brought with him, as they had already heard at Chester, the generous supply of hard cash [Rochambeau] had requested."[76] Learning that the French admiral had arrived on American shores bringing his full fleet, additional troops, and significant funding, joy was felt from the allied high command to the foot soldiers.

Then, to further encourage his officers and men, General Washington wrote this touching appeal to them: "The General calls upon the gentlemen officers, the brave and faithful soldiers he had the honor to command, to exert their utmost abilities in the cause of their country, to share with him, with their usual alacrity, the difficulties, dangers and glory of the enterprise."[77] The chief military engineer, M. Duportail, who had gone ahead of the armies en route to Virginia, was fully apprised of the happy event. He sent a message to Rochambeau telling him to "Hurry, hurry, come quickly!...We shall content ourselves. And that will be glory enough if we are successful, to prepare the way for victory and to prevent as far as possible the enemy from assembling further means of defense."[78] A renewed sense of purpose energized the French and American troops.

The allied forces passed through the three towns of Wilmington, Newport, and Christiana, Delaware, in a single column. The French troops comprised two brigades, each consisting of thirty companies. Each company was comprised of sixty-four men and eight officers. They marched four abreast and covered about a mile in length. Following the same plan as they had used in crossing Connecticut, the columns were spaced a day's march apart, averaging around sixteen miles per day.[79]

The gathering of supplies for the army never ceased: "Quartermasters and purchasing agents would bargain with local farmers and merchants to buy food and other wares and provide for pasturage for the hundreds of horses and cattle accompanying the army. The Continental army often paid with IOUs, but the French Army paid in silver."[80] Their campsites were best located by a stream of ample flow to allow for usage by twenty-five hundred soldiers.[81] And as they had done in their march from Rhode Island, the army generally began their march each day well before sunrise to avoid the hot summer sun.

Rochambeau's army may well have had over 2,000 horses and oxen—855 horses for the wagon train, 500 horses for the artillery, upwards of 300 horses for Lauzun's Legion, and as many as 800 oxen. Imagine that many horses and oxen grazing outside Wilmington on the evening of September 6, 1781.[82]

The bustling town of Wilmington, located on the Delaware River, is described by author Anna Lincoln in *Wilmington, Delaware: Three Centuries under Four Flags,* as a town with "335 houses and 1,229 inhabitants."[83] It was the largest town in Delaware at the time. For the sake of comparison, there were "about 200 fewer than the 1,432 persons on board the *Duc de Bourgogne* at the time of departure from Brest for Newport in 1780."[84] In Delaware they passed "Christiana Hundred, of which Wilmington is a part, [which] had a total of 3,305 inhabitants in 1782."[85] Christiana, situated between Philadelphia and Baltimore, was an important shipping and trading center along the Delaware River. In the state as a whole, "the population [was] estimated at 42,500 whites and 7,000–8,000 African-Americans in 1781."[86]

The French fleet of Admiral de Grasse, having set anchor in the Chesapeake at Lynnhaven Bay on August 30, enjoyed a curious occurrence. A boat came out to meet the flagship. A man who identified himself as "one of the principal citizens of Virginia" inquired which ship was Lord Rodney's.[87] A crewmember who was fluent in English invited him aboard. The Virginian was taken aback when he saw soldiers in white uniforms. When the visitor reached the admiral's cabin, he realized he was terribly mistaken. His boat was confiscated, and he was taken prisoner. The French soldiers and sailors relished the melons and other foodstuffs sent out to the supposed English.[88] This story is not of much consequence except to prove that the coming of the French fleet had been a guarded secret! In other words, none of the ships carrying messages between Rochambeau, Barras, and De Grasse had been compromised. It was another stroke of good luck for the allies.

The safe, undetected arrival of De Grasse's fleet at the precise time and place suggested by General Rochambeau was the first facet of his plan to fall into place. Thanks to his foresight in sending messages to De Grasse as early as May, marking the Chesapeake as the point of rendezvous, and the subsequent diligence with which the admiral carried out his orders, this part of Rochambeau's strategy went smoothly.

There still remained unsolved dilemmas ahead as the allies pressed on toward the Head of the Elk and Baltimore in search of water transport. Moving the thousands of soldiers down the Chesapeake into Virginia was a daunting task. There was the added pressure of timing that compounded the stress. Still unresolved was the crisis facing the Virginia militia and Lafayette's scant army, both of which were in dire need of reinforcements to prevent Cornwallis from escaping.[89]

Rochambeau found that viable boats were in short number on every waterway they approached. He noted, "The English, in their different incursions, had destroyed nearly all the American boats, so that we were scarcely able to muster a sufficient number to embark more than two thousand men, and the latter number would hardly include the two van-guards [sic], consisting of the Grenadiers and Chasseurs of the two armies."[90] Some of the troops were embarked at the Head of the Elk, but this was a small number compared with those who had originally planned to travel by water. The rest had no choice but to walk, and many walked the entire way to Williamsburg.[91] Because of the limited number of boats available, the Vioménil brothers and diarist Crèvecoeur continued by land with the French troops along the shore of the Chesapeake toward Baltimore and Annapolis, Maryland, according to Rochambeau's memoirs.[92] Later, at Annapolis, troops and field artillery would be picked up by a detachment of frigates and transports dispatched by De Grasse.[93]

When the main body of troops arrived at the Eastern Shore of Maryland, they were met with bad news and good news. British raiders had sunk or captured most of their pungies. The French and American commanders were met instead by a boat they did not recognize. After setting anchor, the captain came ashore to greet Washington. Incredibly, it was an emissary bearing dispatches from De Grasse, Capitaine de Pavillon, having come to their aid.[94] It was quite amazing that the ships from the West Indies and the soldiers from New York met almost as if it were timed to perfection, within an hour of each other at the Head of the Elk.

Two small detachments embarked downriver on September 8: one French detachment, to include "the grenadier and chasseur companies of all the French regiments" plus Lauzun's infantry led by M. de Custine, and one American detachment, led by General Lincoln.[95] When this group reached Annapolis on September 12 they were delayed by turbulent weather. The remainder encountered severe difficulties crossing the Susquehanna, farther south.[96]

Crèvecoeur complained in his journal that he had been unable to board at the Head of the Elk on small boats with many of the soldiers, but in the end he was fortunate not to have boarded the ships. The destination via ship was some three hundred miles south to the mouth of the Chesapeake. Later, he discovered that those who did embark there met with "weather...so terrible and the winds so adverse that the journey took them 18 days."[97] In fact, he arrived about the same time they did despite walking the overland route.

The route taken by Crèvecoeur included crossing the Susquehanna on September 10: "We crossed the Susquehanna River, the troops in boats...and the artillery and wagons 10 miles upstream by a ford 2¼ miles wide. [Crèvecoeur may have exaggerated the river width.] ...We were in water up to our waists, and the horses up to their knees.[98] Several horses were lost, as the rocks were large and dangerous for them to traverse. When they finally reached their camp that night, it was almost time to start out for the next day's march.[99]

More good news came announcing that Washington's good friends, Thomas Johnson, former governor of Maryland, and Sims Lee, the second governor of Maryland, answered his appeals sent out from Wethersfield months ago "under flying seals."[100] Three new Maryland regiments, numbering eighteen hundred men, were ready to march with the allies. Maryland's General Gist informed Washington that these volunteer sons of Maryland were fine fellows. They were sons and brothers of the men who had fought and died with him at Harlem Heights, Monmouth, and Camden: "They are young, terribly young, but they are lions' whelps and now they are under way... they will be there, General, before you are."[101]

Washington and Rochambeau, along with their senior staffs and guards, followed much the same route, with Washington preceding Rochambeau by one day. General Vioménil was in command of the remaining French force, which traveled overland and brought up the rear guard.[102] The unencumbered commanders on horse-back advanced at a much faster pace than the infantry columns. Baltimore, which had such a splendid maritime reputation, had been laid waste by the British whose gunboats leveled, sank, or captured most of the sailing craft that might have been put to good use by the allies to transport men and supplies faster and easier to the South. Vioménil and Deux-Ponts arrived to check out the availability of boats remaining afloat. They found few worthy craft.[103]

THE WASHINGTONS RECEIVE ROCHAMBEAU AT MOUNT VERNON

Washington informed General Gist that he hoped to stop at his home, Mount Vernon, to see his wife, Martha, and their four grand-children, who had been born while he was away at battle. Washington had not visited his home in six years and five months since he left to attend the assembling of the Continental Congress in May 1775. For him a homecoming was a most welcome advantage of the march to Virginia. This is not to say that he was deprived of seeing Martha for those six years he was away from Mount Vernon. Martha, like many military wives during the Revolution, spent the winters and many other months traveling with the army.

In his haste to reach home after such a long absence, Washington departed Head of the Elk and rode hard for two days straight. He rode ahead of Rochambeau and his entourage, covering an exhausting sixty miles each day. Even at age forty-seven, his pace was too strenuous for most of them. Incredibly, he even rode safely through unguarded towns known to harbor Tories. With little rest, he arrived home on September 9.[104] He made an entry in his diary that night: "I reached my own seat at Mount Vernon, distant 120 miles from the Head of Elk, where I staid until the 12th, & in three days thereafter, that is on the 15th reached Williamsburg."[105]

On the day following Washington's arrival at Mount Vernon he welcomed his friend and comrade at arms, General Rochambeau, who arrived the next day from Baltimore, for a short respite.[106] The two generals and their staffs had traveled separately from each other and from their armies most of the trip and almost entirely overland. Washington was proud to introduce Rochambeau and his French military comrades to Martha and their family and to entertain him, albeit briefly, under his own roof.

An elaborate feast was prepared in honor of Rochambeau in personal thanks for all the French general was doing to aid George Washington. It was harvest time, and the dinner table was laden with fresh produce grown on the Mount Vernon farm and in Martha's herb gardens. The conversation around the table was lively, with stories of the campaign thus far and plans for its successful conclusion. Chastellux was most fortunate to have been among Rochambeau's closest staff to join them at Mount Vernon. A few days' rest with clean, fresh linens and a comfortable bed did them all a world of good after the hardships of the march and all its attending hazards and deprivations.

Rochambeau and Chastellux must have been impressed with the breathtaking beauty of Mount Vernon, especially with the splendid panoramic view of the broad Potomac River from the mansion lawn high above the water. Rochambeau and his hosts undoubtedly sat on the gracious, wide veranda overlooking the river where they could benefit from the cooling breeze. In the fourteen months since leaving France, there had been no respite quite like this for the French general.

The allied generals assembled at Mount Vernon, not just for pleasure, but also to continue the important strategy talks concerning the crucial Battle of Yorktown. Everything depended on the simultaneous arrival of the allied armies and the French navy at Yorktown. The French and American troops planned to converge at Williamsburg first and then march into Yorktown. De Grasse's fleet was already in place offshore. The exact location of Barras's fleet was not clear at that time.

The feeding and supplying of these soldiers and sailors was an overwhelming task but accomplished by the grace of God in a land already ravaged by the British. Even with cash in hand, Blanchard and the other commissaries could not locate the necessary items locally. Resources often arrived just when most needed from father Louis XVI and distributed by Papa Rochambeau. Many of Rochambeau's men affectionately called him "Papa" amongst themselves.

The French suffered intense lack of provisions on the march south, especially when approaching the Susquehanna River. *Le Mercure de France,* a French newspaper, reported a year later on the "bareness of the country" on the last hot, miserable days of the march, saying, "This region resembles more a desert than a country fit for human habitation."[107] Along the way the men had much difficulty buying and cooking "a few beeves."[108] According to the *Mercure,* "Each officer and man alike was given a pound of cheese, a little rum, and a provision of biscuits for seventeen days," which was not much nourishment for over two weeks' time.[109]

While marching through Virginia, Blanchard, whose duty it was to guard the barrels of specie that the French took with them everywhere they went, related a most queer event in his journal on September 23. One night as he slept in a house along the route, with the barrel of silver in the adjoining room, he awoke to a sudden, horrible creaking followed by a deafening crash. The floor of the next room gave way under the incredible weight of the precious metal, landing on the floor below in the cellar. The barrel containing 800,000 livres in silver went barreling straight down to the cellar! "My servant," wrote Blanchard, "who lay in this room, fell down the length of a beam, but was not hurt."[110]

En route to Williamsburg near the mouth of the James River, Joseph Plumb Martin encountered the French fleet at anchor. Martin was sent in a small, borrowed boat with two men to fill a cask with water. He left at sunset, and had to cross the river at a wide point before passing through the anchored fleet to reach the shore. When he was ready to return, it was nearly dark and, unable to identify his vessel, he recalled, "I could not find her in the dark among so many."[111] He called out to each vessel as he passed. Each time he received an answer, but never the right answer. He rowed and rowed back and forth, in and out among the ships, not finding his own until nine or ten o'clock that night—"wishing every man in the fleet, except ourselves, had a toad in their throat; at length by mere good luck I found our vessel, which soon put an end to my trouble and fatigue, together with their mischievous fun."[112]

It was on September 10 that Admiral de Barras and his French transport ships entered Chesapeake Bay from Newport carrying the heavy artillery and soldiers. When the brothers Vioménil received word of Barras's safe arrival, they redirected their march to Annapolis.[113] Barras sent transports including some of his frigates, and the *Romulus* with her chief naval officer, Villebrune. Some of De Grasse's frigates were also assigned the task of transporting the troops.[114] They sailed up the bay and anchored at Annapolis. Because of the small number of boats available, Barras was asked to pick up the French infantry numbering four thousand, as well as their field artillery. They embarked on September 21. On September 24 they disembarked near Williamsburg, and converged on the town with the rest of the French and American armies.[115]

The overland march of troops, which was about three weeks ahead of the baggage train, was joined in Maryland by several Maryland Continental regiments (twelve hundred soldiers) under American General Clinton. Earlier, they met up with the allied forces in Baltimore and continued on toward their Virginia destination. At Fells Point in southeast Baltimore they boarded ships that had been locally commandeered.[116]

Washington and Rochambeau left Mount Vernon at 5 a.m. on September 12. They rode hard all day and spent the night in Fredericksburg, Virginia, where Washington had grown up. In Fredericksburg, several sites are reminiscent of Washington's parentage and his childhood. Kenmore, originally part of a nearly thirteen-hundred-acre plantation, was built by Washington's brother-in-law, Colonel Fielding Lewis, for Washington's sister, Betty. Colonel Lewis spent much of his fortune to build and run an arms factory during the Revolution.[117]

In 1731, Augustine Washington, a widower aged thirty-seven, married Mary Ball, aged twenty-three. George, the first of five children, was born a year later. Augustine moved his family to Ferry Farm plantation on the Rappahannock River, in Fredericksburg, when Washington was six years old.[118] This was but one of many farms his father, Augustine, owned. Augustine died after twelve years of marriage in 1743, leaving Mary at the age of thirty-five a widow with five children.

The Mary Washington House, 1200 Charles Street, Fredericksburg, was purchased by George for his mother in 1772. It was within walking distance to Kenmore, her daughter Betty's house. Lafayette visited Mrs. Washington there during the Revolution and found her in her garden pursuing her favorite hobby.[119] Mary Washington lived there seventeen years until her death in 1789.

Allied armies coalesce at Williamsburg

After leaving Fredericksburg, the allied generals continued their march, arriving in Williamsburg by the evening of September 14. The Marquis de Lafayette, the Virginia governor, Thomas Nelson, and Saint-Simon along with his 3,200 troops, which had been off-loaded by De Grasse, met them in Williamsburg. The land forces, having been funneled into Williamsburg, then prepared to block Cornwallis by land.[120]

It was a most happy occasion when the Marquis de Lafayette greeted General Washington for the first time in many months. St. George Tucker of Virginia, an eyewitness, reported their reunion: "At this moment we saw the Marquis, riding in full speed from the town, and, as he approached General Washington, threw his bridle on his horse's neck, opened both his arms wide as he could reach, and caught the General around the body, hugged him as close as it was possible, and absolutely kissed him from ear to ear once or twice as well as I can recollect with as much ardour [sic] as an absent lover kissed his mistress on his return. I was not more than six feet from the memorable scene."[121]

Meanwhile, still on the road on September 13, the rest of the officers traveled through Wideawake, Virginia, Villboro, and Bowling Green, stopping at Hanovertown for the night. They covered an incredible fifty-three miles on that day. On September 14 they traveled forty-seven miles, passing near Studley en route to Old Church and Tunstall, by Toana, Norge, and Lightfoot, finally arriving at Williamsburg.[122] The major portion of the route to Yorktown was behind them, Williamsburg being only thirteen miles west of their ultimate destination.

As noted on the Berthier maps, in Williamsburg the American troops camped along what is now Route 60 across from the Patrick Henry Inn on York Street. Some French troops were camped behind the inn where the railroad line runs while others were camped behind the restored capitol building. Lafayette's American troops were settled behind where the College of William and Mary's stadium now stands, and Saint-Simon's West Indian troops were not far from Richmond Road and Nelson Avenue.[123] "These French," as reported by Sol Stember in *Smithsonian Magazine,* "were all to be congratulated, not only for having survived all that walking, but for finding places to sleep in Williamsburg without reservations."[124]

The Berthier brothers, although late in joining Rochambeau's expedition, were on hand to map the entire route for use by the French and American armies as they traveled to Yorktown and back to Boston. In spite of difficult conditions on the road and the urgency of the march, the Berthiers found time to reconnoiter their locations and draw their maps. Their detailed maps are preserved and accessible for researching the routes of the French army in America.

As for Lauzun and his troops, at the Head of the Elk they boarded boats. In his memoirs Lauzun recalled that they "embark[ed] on all sorts of boats all the grenadiers and chasseurs of the army and all infantry of my regiment under the command of M. de Custine.... General Clinton followed us also by water at a little distance."[125] On their voyage they encountered foul weather, and Lauzun lamented, "The boats were awful, two or three turned over, and we had seven or eight men drowned."[126] Near Annapolis they landed and Lauzun waited for orders from Washington as to which way to proceed.[127]

When word came, Lauzun was told to re-embark his men and sail to the mouth of the James River. The retinue was water-born for another ten days under difficult weather conditions. Finally at their destination, Lauzun's Legion disembarked once again to await instructions. Lauzun was then summoned by Washington and Rochambeau, "who were not far off on a corvette" waiting for him.[128] Rochambeau informed Lauzun that Cornwallis had just landed a sizeable corps of troops on the Gloucester Peninsula. Was Cornwallis hedging his bets and securing a way of egress from Yorktown? Rochambeau ordered Lauzun and his men to Gloucester as a precaution. Once in place, Lauzun, along with his hussars who had arrived separately, would put himself under the command of American General George Weedon. The isolated British General Cornwallis had taken up a post on the bluff high over the York River and made no further attempt to impede the allied armies converging on him. With his back toward the water, his position became more hopeless each day. Admiral Graves did not come to his rescue, nor did General Clinton send any encouraging news. In fact, messages addressed to Lord Cornwallis were almost nil at this point since the French and American armies and the French navy finally had him hemmed in on all sides.

The gathering of officers, troops, baggage, wagons, livestock, supplies, and artillery at Williamsburg took a few weeks to assemble. It was estimated that an army of sixteen thousand men was rapidly converging on Williamsburg while two naval squadrons floated off Tidewater, Virginia.[129] With the massing of French ships and American boats in Virginia, the concentration of the Revolutionary War shifted dramatically from the North to the South.

In the long march south from the Hudson, Rochambeau had been separated from much of his staff. With the men once again united at Williamsburg, he and his aides showed honest pleasure at their reunion. Cromot Du Bourg wrote, "I was really delighted to see him again....I had been separated from him, and I can compare an aide-de-camp without his general to nothing but a body without a soul."[130]

Vioménil managed to secure boats to ferry his men across the Susquehanna River, but "they forced the horses across by making them swim in herds—a technique used by Americans (and probably the only local practice adopted by the French army during its entire sojourn in America)."[131] As the advance troops were collecting at Williamsburg, others were still moving south and would not arrive for several days. It had proved impossible for Baron de Vioménil and General Lincoln to find water transport for their troops at Trenton, Philadelphia, Head of the Elk, or Baltimore. At each juncture, they were forced to continue their march on foot. Finally, on September 21, Vioménil was able to embark his troops on ships sent in by De Grasse.

By September 21 only Lauzun's cavalry, along with the oxen trains, were left to the overland route. The route was grueling in the oppressive heat, and they had outrun their supply lines. "The French baggage-wagon train [made up of horses and oxen]...traveled south via Bowie, Bladensburg [both found in Maryland], and Foggy Bottom [now in Washington, D.C.], and Georgetown [in Maryland at that time]...The hussars...went from Annapolis to cross the Potomac River at Laidler's Ferry...MD to Dahlgren in VA."[132]

Imagine the sheer bulk and length of the troop and supply move-ment traveling from Annapolis to Williamsburg. The army wagon trains formed a column numbering 1,500 horses, 800 oxen, and 220 wagons.[133] They crossed the Patuxent, Potomac, and Rappahannock Rivers, no small feat in itself. This column was led and commanded by Assistant Quartermasters General Victor Collot and Alexandre Berthier. Despite a myriad of difficulties, they made the march of 230 miles in ten days. They arrived in Williamsburg on October 6. Much of their route was re-traced on the return trip north in 1782, putting Berthier's mapping to good use.[134]

Journal-keeper Saint-Exupéry, a second lieutenant in the garrison of the sailing ship *Triton,* one of De Grasse's convoy making up the blockade of the York River, witnessed the anger of Cornwallis. Saint-Exupéry and his crew had come to the aid of the men who had arrived from the Head of the Elk, starved and exhausted from their terrifying journey over water. The soldiers boarded some of the French warships anchored in the Chesapeake seeking rest and recovery when, during the night of September 22–23, Cornwallis, in desperation, attacked the allies with fireships. These deadly fire-ships "rained firebrands down on the crews all night and spread terror among them. By the greatest good fortune they escaped injury, though they were attacked by no less than 7 fire-ships."[135]

Saint-Exupéry detailed his terrifying fireship experience: "Six ships in flames and proceeding abreast offered a horrible spectacle, when a seventh ship...bore down upon the *Triton* [ship bearing French and American troops] and burst into flames at a distance of a pistol-shot. This sudden explosion made the sailors on the *Triton* lose their heads. Two hundred of them either jumped overboard or into various boats alongside....The *Triton,* during this night, lost 17 men, her bowsprit, and her stem."[136]

Berthier's wagon train was the last unit to arrive in the southern battle theatre. The march that set out from Philipsburg on August 19 was completed with the arrival of the last of the wagon trains at the allied camp at Yorktown on October 7.[137]

During the intense business of coalescing the French and American armies as they arrived at Williamsburg, the French fleet, commanded by Admiral de Grasse, was protecting the coast off the Virginia Capes. Admiral de Grasse had made good his promise to General Rochambeau to arrive approximately August 30. The second component of the French fleet in the Western Hemisphere under the command of Admiral Barras had managed to escape the British threat at Newport and sail south to rendezvous with De Grasse at the Chesapeake. The two arms of the French fleet were destined to join forces off the Virginia Capes while the allied land forces, the third component, prevented General Cornwallis from escaping from the encircling Franco-American land forces. Considering that the methods of communication in the eighteenth century were fraught with all manner of unpredictability, it was nothing less than a miracle that Rochambeau and Washington's plan materialized in a timely fashion.

CHAPTER NINE

Admiral de Grasse
Fights Pivotal Sea Battle

*"I consider myself infinitely happy to have been of some service
to the United States."*

—FRANÇOIS-JOSEPH-PAUL, COMTE DE GRASSE

FRANÇOIS-JOSEPH-PAUL, COMTE DE GRASSE stepped
onto the stage in the southern theatre in the War for American
Independence by landing much-needed troops to strengthen the
cause in Virginia. Only months earlier the up-and-coming French
admiral had been honored to walk on the arm of Marie Antoinette
during his February 1781 visit to the Palace of Versailles. He had just
been named commander of the French West Indies fleet with the
assignment of bringing provisions to the West Indies and the task
of eventually cooperating with Washington and Rochambeau in the
delivery of the second division of troops. By September of that same
year, he had sailed his fleet to the mouth of the Chesapeake River
in America where he was about to make his king and queen very
proud.[1]

Shortly after De Grasse's prestigious visit to the Royal Court
of France, Maréchal La Croix de Castries, Minister of Navy, had
promoted De Grasse to lieutenant general (rear admiral).[2] Thereafter
De Grasse received his command and flagship, the *Ville de Paris*,

the largest warship at the time to grace the seas under the French flag. Originally ninety guns when she was built in 1764, she was later equipped with ten more in her 1778 refitting. By the time De Grasse sailed, the *Ville de Paris* had a total of 104 cannon on her three decks. Such a large fighting ship was not built for agility, however, but as a "veritable floating fortress."[3] On March 22, 1781, she had sailed for the West Indies as Comte de Grasse's flagship in a fleet of "20 ships of the line, 3 frigates, and 156 transports." At the same time, Rochambeau's son sailed from France with cash for the allied forces in America. De Grasse arrived in the West Indies on April 28.[4]

On May 28, immediately following the Wethersfield Conference, Rochambeau had written to De Grasse at Cap Français, West Indies, saying, "That is the state of affairs and the very grave crisis in which America, and especially the states of the South, finds herself at this particular time. The arrival of M. le Comte de Grasse would save this situation; all the means in our hands are not enough without his joint action and sea superiority which he is able to command.... The southwesterly winds and the state of distress in Virginia will probably make you prefer Chesapeake Bay, and it will be there where we think you may be able to render the greatest service...."[5] As mentioned earlier, Rochambeau's letter strongly intimated that De Grasse should move briskly to the Chesapeake.

A second note dated June 6 also awaited De Grasse's arrival at Cap Français, spelling out the urgent details relating to the grave state of the army's finances. It was addressed to Rochambeau by M. de Tarlé, quartermaster of the French army, and forwarded to De Grasse. Tarlé warned, "The funds remaining in the military chest will be sufficient to support the army only up to next August 20...The funds that ought to arrive with the convoy [1.2 million livres] will only extend the time to October 20."[6] Like the first note, the second one to the admiral was essentially a not-so-subtle command. Funds were running out, and De Grasse was put on notice that timing was propitious once again.

When Washington was wrestling with the decision about whether to march south, he was not aware of all the correspondence between Rochambeau and De Grasse proposing that the latter rendezvous with the allies in Virginia. Nor had he been apprised of the message from La Luzerne, the French minister in Philadelphia, who had importuned De Grasse as well, pleading, "It is you alone who can deliver the invaded states from that crisis which is so alarming that it appears to me there is no time to lose."[7]

Meanwhile, correspondence had raced back and forth between Cornwallis and Clinton as they had tried in vain to discover what the allies were planning. On June 5, 1781, a letter had been intercepted on its way from George Washington to the Marquis de Lafayette stating that after the Wethersfield meeting it was decided that the allies would surely attack New York. It is a controversial point, but some believe the letter written to purposely mislead the British into thinking that Washington was preparing to attack New York. Intentional or not, the theft of this letter and two similar ones may have started the downhill slide of the British.[8] Accordingly, Clinton demanded Cornwallis send him at least two thousand men to help him defend New York. In England, Lord Germain countermanded the order and the troops stayed in Virginia.

In early July the *Concorde,* a very busy vessel ferrying messages between the allies, had arrived in the French Antilles bringing twenty-five American pilots to be used by De Grasse's fleet to aid them in navigating the waters off the east coast of America. This was but one part of the continual, essential planning that was carried on behind the scenes to assure a successful Franco-American outcome.[9]

The British occupied Williamsburg until July 4 when Cornwallis headed toward Jamestown. En route, on July 6, Lafayette and General Anthony Wayne engaged Cornwallis at Green Spring. The allies, greatly outnumbered, fought bravely but were forced to retreat. By August 1 Cornwallis reached Yorktown and began to prepare earthworks. On September 7, Lafayette arrived in Williamsburg to block Cornwallis's escape by land and with the addition of Saint-Simon's troops the noose tightened around Cornwallis. But along with the good news came the more serious consequence of maintaining a larger fighting force and the challenge of feeding them.[10] Complaining about the status of his army, Lafayette wrote to Governor Thomas Nelson Jr. of Virginia, "Few men in the field; not a sixth part of what is called for—a greater number without arms, the greatest part of whom live from day to day upon food which is injurious to their health, without six cartridges per man."[11] Lafayette wished to convey to Nelson his fear that if Cornwallis knew of the dwindling of both food supplies and military munitions in Virginia, he might well take advantage of the weakness. At this point, following Clinton's orders, Cornwallis was digging in for a long stay on the bluff over the York River.

DE GRASSE EN ROUTE TO CHESAPEAKE

Meanwhile, Rochambeau and Washington had received news on August 14 that Admiral de Grasse was heading north from the West Indies and would be arriving at the Chesapeake by the end of August. This was the best news that the Franco-American commanders could receive. The success of their mission depended on the French fleet assisting in tightening the noose on Cornwallis at the same time as the allied army arrived on the scene in Virginia. The admiral had made good on his promise. The safe, undetected, and unimpeded arrival of De Grasse's fleet at the precise time and place agreed upon by the allies was the prime feature of Rochambeau's campaign strategy.

On August 30, De Grasse's fleet was sighted in the Chesapeake. He sent the message that he had 3,200 soldiers. The soldiers and eight cannon were to be set ashore immediately, and if needed, De Grasse thought he could land 1,800 sailors for shore duty. This offer would have allowed Lafayette the opportunity to attack immediately. Lafayette briefly considered joining in a hasty frontal assault on Cornwallis. After an assessment of the situation, this was deemed to be unwise. The allies chose the more prudent course of using their strength to hold Cornwallis with their well-planned land ring. This decision demonstrated Lafayette's willingness to share the glory with Washington and Rochambeau, both of whom had been persistent in waiting for the right opportunity to wrap up this unending war.[12] Maybe the troops coming from the north, too, would appreciate an opportunity for action that would yield victory after the hardships they had endured on the long march.

The arrival of De Grasse's fleet in American waters brought three advantages to the allies: first, the French fleet introduced a formidable naval force equal to or surpassing the British navy; second, with the fleet came the extra troops needed to complete Rochambeau's *expédition particulière*; third, the French ships carried the hard currency to raise the morale of the American army and sustain both armies through the final battle.

De Grasse had originally informed Rochambeau that he could not bring his entire fleet north since it would interfere with his duty to protect the French and Spanish interests in the West Indies. It would not have been wise to leave them unprotected while he sailed to America. However, this dilemma had been readily resolved by De Grasse, and Lafayette had happily relayed the following message to La Luzerne: "The Spanish have behaved like little angels"[13] by offering to take over for the French admiral in his absence. De Grasse was free to move out with his complete fleet.[14] Spanish aid was furnished at the point of greatest need. Covering for De Grasse in the West Indies may have seemed inconsequential; however, in terms of making possible an increased number of ships available to the French in the Chesapeake, it was of utmost importance.

The full French fleet of twenty-eight ships of the line and four frigates, having sailed without hindrance from the West Indies, anchored in Lynnhaven Bay near Cape Henry to anchor closer to land in a strategic location.[15] In doing so, they captured the British frigate *Loyalist* and wasted no time in blocking the mouth of the York River. Cornwallis would not be escaping to the Carolinas as feared. Curiously, a year earlier the Marquis de Saint-Simon had written to Rochambeau in Newport, saying, "I should be delighted to be under your orders."[16] He had no idea he would be serving under Rochambeau so soon. Therefore, even if the king's second division of promised reinforcements would not be sent directly from France to Newport, Saint-Simon's troops, coming from the West Indies, would fill the gap.

Saint-Simon's troops were ferried up the James River to Jamestown where they disembarked. From there, they were sent immediately to bolster Lafayette's forces, further ensuring that Cornwallis would have no escape by land. Cornwallis committed an error in judgment by letting this influx of soldiers pass unchallenged.[17] He greatly underestimated the quality of Saint-Simon's army, labeling them "raw and sickly...undisciplined vagabonds... [who] would soon be conquered, were it only by the first attacks of cold weather."[18] Cornwallis had a dismissive attitude, and he talked himself out of any constructive action. He was indecisive and his timing was poor compared with the wise planning of the allies.

ADMIRAL RODNEY'S AVARICE AIDS DE GRASSE

Like De Grasse, the British fleet had been occupied in the Caribbean as well. At the request of King George III, Admiral George Rodney had captured the poorly fortified Dutch island of St. Eustatius the preceding February, gaining the incredible booty of 75–80 million livres (more than twice the amount that King Louis was sending to subsidize the American cause). St. Eustatius was reputedly "the richest island in the world."[19] As a trading center it had tremendous potential for England were it to come under her control. Rodney plundered the island and auctioned much of it at a loss, which angered the British crown. Rodney left his portion of the bounty in St. Eustatius to be shipped to London separately. Unfortunately for Rodney his loot was taken over by the French who, on November 26, 1781, repossessed the island.[20]

Then, unexpectedly, Rodney commandeered four of Commander Sir Samuel Hood's ships to protect the remainder of the loot as he traveled home to England. He left the island a sick man, but still hoped to make himself a rich man in order to pay off his many debts at home with his captured fortune. It meant everything to him to get his bounty-laden ships home safely to the detriment of the British naval presence in the Western Hemisphere.[21] Rodney, sick in body and ravished by greed, placed commercial and personal interests ahead of all else. Most of his spoils were taken when his convoy was captured by the French at sea.

Rodney had inadvertently assisted De Grasse by selfishly taking four of the best British ships for himself. At once, the French admiral recognized that Rodney's carelessness had given De Grasse the advantage over Hood in terms of naval power in the Caribbean. The moves in the West Indies played out like a chess game between the French and the British. The French were winning.

Back in England, John Montagu, First Lord of the Admiralty and Earl of Sandwich, estimated his ship count: "According to his Admiralty arithmetic, the New York and West Indies squadrons combined, plus Rear Admiral Digby's small escort on the way, amounted in all to thirty-one ships of the line. The French, he [Montagu] figured, had only eight at Newport under Barras; and De Grasse, he figured, may have had as many as twenty-eight in the Antilles. However, it was assumed he had to take care of the summer trade convoy to Europe, and surely would not take more than half of his fleet to reinforce Barras. Rodney and Hood commanded twenty-one at the Leeward Islands, and in the hurricane season they could be expected to take most of them northward to join Graves's seven, plus Digby's three, for a total of twenty-five or more. How, then, could England possibly be expected to lose command of the sea off the American coast?"[22] Unfortunately for the British, the Earl of Sandwich underestimated the strength of the French navy, and failed to take into account that several ships of the British fleet were in need of repair.

Unaware of these miscalculations Rodney had sailed for home on August 1 in the best ship of the fleet, the *Gibraltar*. Before leaving, Rodney ordered the *Pegasus* to New York to inform Admiral Graves of the latest intelligence that De Grasse's fleet "consisted of twenty-six sail of the line and two large ships armed *en-flûte* and I imagine that at least twelve of these ships, and in all probability a part of M. De Monteil's squadron [Commodore de Monteil sailed with De Grasse] will be in America; and it is not impossible they may be joined by some Spanish ships."[23] Rodney also wrote that he had sent Hood "to the Capes of Virginia where I am persuaded the French intend making their grand effort."[24]

At this point, two events favored the allies. First, the *Pegasus* did not arrive in New York until September 8, three days after the Battle off the Capes had already taken place. Second, Rodney did not convey to Hood the information he had sent to Graves, thereby putting Hood, who was on his way to the Chesapeake, at a disadvantage in preparing for the Battle off the Capes.[25] The allies, however, were well organized in their communication to one another and were fortunate that no key messages were intercepted revealing crucial strategy. The enemy was constantly defeating itself with poor communication, infighting, indecision, and bad judgment.

Hood left Antigua with fourteen ships on August 10, not the original twenty-one that Sandwich had estimated would be en route to the Chesapeake.[26] Hood's faster-sailing coppered ships took the usual sea-lane north, unlike De Grasse, who took the more difficult route but the one that was safer in terms of avoiding the enemy.[27] Hood arrived at the Chesapeake a few days ahead of De Grasse on August 25.[28] Oddly enough, Hood did not encounter any of the ships Admiral Graves had sent there to meet him. Was he Hood-winked? Encountering no ships, neither friend nor foe, in the Chesapeake, Hood sent messages to Clinton and Graves via the *Nymphe* and proceeded to New York.

BRITISH, OVERCONFIDENT, FOOLED AGAIN

Upon hearing Hood's news, Clinton was convinced the French fleet was not in the area of the Chesapeake. Hood had also been arrogant in assessing that his fleet could easily overcome anything

De Grasse could bring to bear. Preferring not to cross the bar with his fleet at Sandy Hook, New York, Hood made the long row ashore to meet with Graves and Clinton on Long Island on August 28. Fearing that fate was against him, Admiral Hood contemplated the realities of missed opportunities and miscalculations.[29]

Even as late as August 30, the British admirals had no word of De Grasse's arrival in the Chesapeake.[30] The only solid news they received was that Barras had left Newport on August 25, the same day Hood had arrived at the Chesapeake the first time. This news meant that the British admirals were woefully lagging behind. How would they protect Cornwallis from behind the bar at Sandy Hook?

When a favorable wind came up on September 1, the British navigated the bar at Sandy Hook to head seaward. Graves had just five functional ships of the line and some frigates. He combined his fleet with that of Hood after reaching open sea. Together they sailed a fleet of nineteen warships south to the Chesapeake under Graves's command. They covered the 240 nautical miles in three and a half days.[31]

Upon arriving at the mouth of the Chesapeake, they spied a fleet at anchor at Lynnhaven Bay and deduced it must be Barras since they counted only ten ships. They did not consider Barras a threat. Because of the manner in which the ships were aligned, it was difficult to count them correctly. Actually, it was De Grasse with a fleet of twenty-eight ships of the line plus four frigates. De Grasse's scout had seen the fleet approaching and thought it must be Barras as he counted only ten ships. In actuality, it was nineteen ships belonging to the British fleet. Both parties misread what they saw that day.[32]

Before long, Graves's lookouts re-counted the ships at anchor and decided that they were observing Barras and De Grasse combined. That would account for the twenty-four ships, they reasoned.[33] Graves guessed that De Grasse had sixteen, having left half his fleet in the West Indies, and Admiral Barras, eight. Both were wrong again in their estimations. Graves grossly underestimated the numbers and misidentified the fleets he was observing! At first, both sides were in error, thinking that Barras was there when in fact he was not. It did not take De Grasse long to reassess the incoming ships. He soon realized the number was far too great to be Barras. It must be the British.

The British actually had fewer ships, by five, than the French. The British had nineteen versus the French with twenty-four ships (having left four ships to guard the mouth of the York and James Rivers). They also had less firepower (i.e., fifteen hundred British guns to two thousand French guns). The British fleet included at least five ships in poor fighting condition. That tipped the scale even further in favor of the French. The British, however, did have the advantage in that all their ships were coppered, making them faster, sturdier, and better able to repel cannonades, while the French had only one-half of theirs coppered. In addition, the British ships were fully manned, but the French had dropped off soldiers and sailors both to assist in the disembarking and to reinforce Lafayette on land.[34] "Here, off the Virginia Capes," wrote Yale historian Jonathan R. Dull in his book *The French Navy and American Independence,* "began the major phase of the most important and most perfectly executed naval campaign of the age of sail."[35]

FRENCH ENGAGE BRITISH NAVY OFF THE CAPES

Unbeknownst to the allied generals, while they gathered their forces at Williamsburg, a crucial sea battle, known as the second Battle off the Virginia Capes (this second battle is most frequently referred to as the Battle off the Capes), was about to take place off the Capes of Virginia. On the morning of September 5 at 10:05 the British navy, favoring the windward position it usually preferred for battle, made a signal to clear for action and sent up the cry of "Up all hammocks!"[36] All hammocks, yards, and nets were secured to absorb flying splinters that resulted from enemy cannon fire landing above decks, and to catch broken spars or men falling onto the decks. Cordage was gathered to be used to repair damaged rigging. The ships' carpenters prepared plugs for holes made by enemy fire. Gun crews cleared their positions, getting powder and ball in place; decks were sprinkled with sand to prevent slipping on the gore, which would soon cover them.[37]

De Grasse did not have time to recall his well-trained boat crews, adding up to about ninety officers and seventeen hundred sailors. They had been off-loaded to assist in the landing of the soldiers at Jamestown and to guard the river entrances. Nor did they have time to take on the food and water De Grasse needed.[38] "It was reported that 'every vessel had a hundred men in the [long]boats,' which meant also that the French warships were virtually boatless [without dinghies or tenders] in going to sea."[39] In some ways this was not the disadvantage it might have seemed, in that having fewer boats on deck meant more space for action on the decks and less splintering of wood upon impact of cannon balls, which endangered the sailors. The French admiral sent a message for the sailors and soldiers to return to the ships, but too late. Therefore, the *Citoyen* was short five officers and two hundred seamen, which caused her crew to be unable to man their tier of guns on the upper deck. Luckily, the British were not aware of these shortfalls.

There was no time to waste, but the tide and the wind were not yet favorable for the French to exit the bay. The French finally slipped their anchor cables at eleven-thirty in the morning, September 5, and set out to meet the adversary.[40] De Grasse chose to go out to meet the British beyond the Capes. There was a sound reason for that decision: by moving outside the Capes there would be room for Barras, should he arrive soon, to skirt the battle and enter the bay with safety to resume the blockade of Cornwallis. On the other hand, if De Grasse had chosen to remain on the defensive at Lynnhaven, it would have meant almost certain obliteration for Barras's squadron given their small number.[41] It was of paramount importance to secure the way for Barras as he carried with him the siege artillery and auxiliary troops needed for the impending battle at Yorktown.

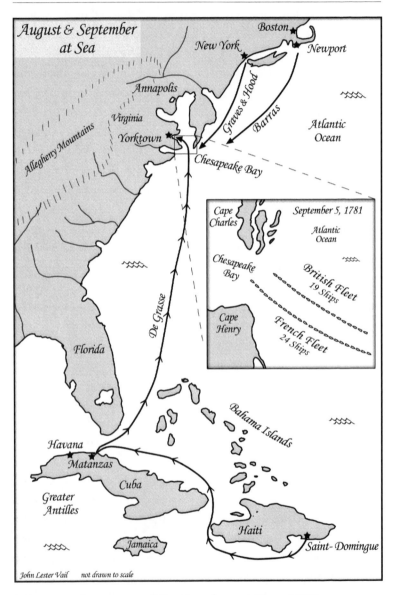

August and September at Sea, 1781

Ocean routes of French and British admirals.
Inset: French and British fleets at Second Battle Off Virginia Capes.
September 5, 1781. Artist: John Lester Vail.

Admiral de Grasse and his fleet set their sails to best advantage against a testy wind and began the struggle for superiority of the seas. No, this was not Yorktown, but it was the onset of combat in the last great battle of the American Revolution. Rochambeau had foreseen that to win this war much would depend on supremacy at sea. De Grasse was going to serve up the British fleet on a silver platter!

At eleven-thirty, with the tide nearly full and the wind still not in their favor, the French fleet moved out. Even though the bay was ten miles at its broadest point between Cape Charles and Cape Henry, the boat channel was only three miles wide between Cape Henry and the Middle Ground Shoal. It was a slow and disorderly exit. At twelve-thirty the signal was given to form the line of battle.[42]

The twenty-four French ships gradually moved into line in a somewhat unfavorable wind, with the last ship standing out of the bay by two in the afternoon in the following order: *Pluton, Bourgogne, Marseillais, Diadème, Réfléchi, Auguste, Saint Esprit, Caton, César, Destin, Ville de Paris, Victoire, Sceptre, Northumberland, Palmier, Solitaire, Citoyen, Scipion, Magnanime, Hercule, Languedoc, Zélé, Hector,* and *Souverain.*[43] The French van was commanded as follows: Louis-Antoine, Comte de Bougainville, on the *Auguste,* was in front; the rear was under the command of Baron de Monteil on the *Languedoc;* and Francois-Joseph Paul, Comte de Grasse, was in the center with his flag flying high on the *Ville de Paris.*[44]

At one o'clock Admiral Graves's fleet of nineteen formed their line of battle on an east-west bearing with spacing between ships fixed at a cable's length (608 feet) in this order: *Alfred, Belliqueux, Invincible, Barfleur, Monarch, Centaur, America, Resolution, Bedford, London, Royal Oak, Montagu, Europe, Terrible, Ajax, Princessa, Alcide, Intrepid,* and *Shrewsbury.*[45] The British van was commanded as follows: Admiral Sir Samuel Hood in the *Barfleur* leading; Francis Samuel Drake, in the rear, in the *Princessa;* and Rear Admiral Thomas Graves, in the center, in the *London.*

The French fleet carried a total of "1,794 guns in one three-decker of 104 guns, three 80's, seventeen 74's, and three 64's."[46] The

British totaled "1,410 guns in two three-decker 98's, twelve 74's, one 70, and four 64's."[47]

As the French fleet finally sailed out of the bay at one o'clock in the afternoon, the 104-gun flagship, *Ville de Paris,* the largest ship afloat and eleventh in line, exited the channel. The fleet moved too quickly and became spread out beyond the British line, which was not advisable. Graves could have cut off the stray ships then and there and fought them two on one, but he did not. De Grasse ordered his commanders to tighten up their line.

Looking back at the battle, Louis-Antoine de Bougainville, the first Frenchman to circumnavigate the globe (1768), could not recall which ships were actually involved in the fighting. There were a variety of reports on the event, but the details are not all in exact agreement regarding the placement of the ships in the van.[48] Not all ships were involved since some had no opposites to fire upon, and furthermore, it was difficult to see more than a few of the ships on either side, for the lines were spread out in irregular formation over a distance of five miles. Being at the mercy of the wind made maneuvers slow and cumbersome.

The English, in accordance with the British admiralty's fighting manual, strove for a close line formation with each ship engaging its opposite ship. At one o'clock Graves had called for the line-ahead formation.[49] This was in order to face the French line and bring his ships out from the shoals and into a parallel position with the French. At 2:15 Graves called for a wear together.[50] The British fleet then turned their entire line almost 180 degrees to change their course to east-southeast with the wind, north-northeast.[51] The two fleets were then on the same tack and nearly parallel. This maneuver took about ninety minutes and was accomplished by 3:46 in the afternoon.[52]

After the turn, the fastest British ships, originally at the front, were at the end of the line. That included Hood, who had been fourth in line, who then moved near the rear with fifteen ships ahead of him. Drake, who had three 74-gun ships, which were leaking when they left New York, had originally taken up the rear, but soon took the lead.[53]

Also, according to strict admiralty fighting instructions, Graves then ordered his squadron to wait for the French to draw even with their line, center to center. His officers were not pleased with this tactic. De Grasse, to the contrary, was happy to have more time to line up to his advantage. In the new formation, the French fleet's best and fastest ships were opposite the weakest and slowest of the enemy.

These rules of engagement for the British Royal Navy were reminiscent of their battle formations on land. The redcoats were famous for their straight-line marching technique, in which they headed directly toward the enemy in open fields with no thought of defensive strategy.

It became evident that Graves was trying to avoid the more numerous French ships from doubling his, that is, getting caught between two lines of firing ships. Graves and his commanders passed many messages before commencing to fire. It took nearly six hours for the two fleets to line up and the British to signal their commanders to bear down and engage their opponents from the time when the French first noticed the enemy fleet arriving at ten in the morning.[54]

Graves saw that the French were approaching and that dusk would be closing in soon, so at 4:03 the same signal was raised "to engage the enemy closely."[55] The signal for line ahead was hauled down so as not to interfere with the first signal. At 4:15 the British van at the center initiated the action. At 4:22 the two signals were hoisted once more and five minutes later the line ahead signal was dropped again. These were confusing signal flags for Graves's men to interpret. The French were not able to attack, as the British, who had the weather gage, had the advantage of better positioning and maneuverability in terms of wind direction because one vessel's windward position had an effect on the other vessel's ability to maneuver. The British fired the first volley, as it was the Royal Navy's tradition to begin the fight in order to get an early advantage. As a result, the French took the first punishing volleys broadside. It was only at the first volley that all the ships fired at once, usually at broadsides if possible. After that, each cannon was fired when ready.

The fifth French ship in her column, the *Réfléchi,* did indeed take the first broadside, killing Captain M. de Boades. The *Réfléchi* and the *Caton* bore away with heavy damage. Admiral Drake's flagship, the *Princessa,* hit the *Diadème* and set her afire. Bougainville was too distant to assist her. In return he turned the guns of his flagship, the *Auguste,* on the British ship *Terrible* with such fury that she had to be sunk the next day.[56]

Lieutenant Karl Gustaf Tornquist, a Swedish officer serving in the French navy, reported an incident that proved the French devotion to honor in battle. Admiral Bougainville "twice had his foretop bowline shot off" during the battle. Twice his men tried of their own volition to repair the bowline during the thick of the fighting. Both men were shot. No one else volunteered for the dangerous job. Bougainville then "offered his purse" to the one who would repair it. Tornquist added, "A common sailor immediately went out on the yard and called back, 'My Admiral, we do not go there for money'; whereupon he tackled the work and fortunately carried it through."[57]

Admiral de Grasse "was extremely desirous that the engagement should become general [as opposed to fighting in line] and to tempt the enemy a second time ordered his leading vessels to attack."[58] The fiercest fighting of the day was between the vanguards of the two fleets; Drake's squadron suffered severely.[59] By five o'clock, the wind had shifted in favor of the French, taking away the British advantage. This also gave Graves a chance to re-form his column contingent on the center and the rear. The vans continued to fight at close range.

"At 6:23 Graves ordered the signal for close action to be hauled down and the signal for line at one cable distance to be hoisted. At half past six 'the fire ceased on both sides.' At 5:45 the French van was ordered to bear away; at 6:00 the ships were signaled to move closer together, and as they were then 'out of range of the enemy, firing ceased'; and at 6:30 ships were ordered to reform the line. At a quarter to seven, Graves had the night signal made for the line ahead at two cables' distance. At sunset, Cape Henry was to the west-north-west at a distance of three leagues."[60]

Admiral Comte de Grasse

Copper engraved plate from *London Magazine* (1782).
1782. Anne S. K. Brown Military Collection,
Brown University Library.

At 5:45 the French van was ordered to bear away, while at 6:00 they were signaled to move tighter together. They were out of range of fire, so firing ceased, and at 6:30 they headed for open sea to re-form their line. Both sides were left to assess the damage and to see what could be repaired overnight. The British suffered heavily. Three of their ships were out of the line for good. Several others had mast damage, which precluded full sail; masts were hanging precariously over the decks. There was plenty of topsail damage, yards shot down, and serious leaks. All ships but Hood's and the *America*, which was at the rear, had casualties. "The British casualties were 90 killed and 246 wounded... Captain Robinson of the *Shrewsbury* lost a leg, and his First Lieutenant was killed."[61] As for the French, only the *Diadème* and the *Caton* were unable to keep the line, and the *Pluton* suffered mast damage. "The French lost three officers killed and eighteen wounded and about 209 men killed and wounded."[62] In roughly two and one-half hours of fighting much damage was wrought, and blood spilled aplenty.

DE GRASSE PREVAILS IN SEA BATTLE OFF THE CAPES

Repairs were underway immediately after the fighting ceased. The two fleets remained within sight of each other, though out of sight of land, for the next few days with no action taken to resume the fight. Nevertheless, it became clear that the British were in no condition to undertake further action at sea. The French admiral was content to keep the Capes clear of the enemy. That was his greater goal, not to win a bloody battle for the sake of winning. De Grasse proclaimed afterwards to the allied generals that "the laurels of the day belong to De Bougainville...for having led the van and having personally fought the *Terrible*."[63] The British and the French fleets, after serious fighting all day September 5, bore away to assess damages and make repairs.

The people of Williamsburg were not aware that a sea battle was underway, but according to Rochambeau's memoirs, they "were much alarmed...[when] the firing had been distinctly heard."[64]

Returning from the sea battle, De Grasse and his fleet sailed back to Lynnhaven Bay and to their surprise discovered that Admiral Barras had arrived from Newport with his fleet on September 10.[65] On his way into port, Barras had encountered and captured two British frigates that were up to no good in the bay at Lynnhaven. While the ships were out at sea, the British had cut all of De Grasse's anchor cables and made off with the buoys, making the return of the fleet most inconvenient. Repairs took hours of work fishing out the anchors and re-fitting them with cables and buoys.

TARDY EFFORT TO RESCUE CORNWALLIS FAILS

After several days of indecision, on September 13 Graves called a council of war to assess damages and formulate a strategy. Succumbing to the superiority of the French fleet, the British determined they would be unable to help Cornwallis. Admiral Graves gave up his option for further engagement with De Grasse at that time. Besides, the British ships were in need of repair, and both the equinox and the hurricane season were approaching. They admitted defeat, a rare occurrence for the British, and returned to New York.[66] In effect, the battle was fought and won in one day.

After returning to New York, the British navy decided to make use of the three additional ships of the line, which arrived from England with Rear Admiral Digby on September 24. They gathered supplies, made repairs on their ailing ships, and prepared to sail to Yorktown. They knew they had to do this, but they were not sure they could muster enough in the way of ships, supplies, and men to be of much help to Cornwallis. They would not be ready to set sail until October 19. It would be too little, too late.

A message arrived in Williamsburg on the evening of September 14 addressed to Rochambeau, bringing news from Admiral Comte de Grasse. On September 5, 1781, the French fleet had defeated the British fleet at the Battle off the Capes. As a result, Cornwallis had no escape route left. It was very good news indeed.

After the battle there was much criticism of the way the British handled themselves. In letters and memoranda Hood pointed out Graves's faults, from not attacking the enemy's van as it came out of Lynnhaven, to Graves's confusion regarding signal flags that resulted in his lack of timely action against the French. Graves's logs do not match Hood's complaint. French E. Chadwick states, "It is impossible, however, to avoid the impression, that Hood did not do his duty as, had he been in chief command, he would have expected a subordinate to do."[67] Graves contended that the signal flags did not contradict each other and may have overlapped only a few minutes. Some said that Hood may have held "contempt" for his commander prior to the battle and therefore "did not wholeheartedly aid his chief" on the question of signal raising.[68]

Sir Julian S. Corbett (1854–1922), British maritime strategist, criticized Hood, positing, "Had he been a man of less influence, he… would have been court-martialed for not doing his utmost to engage the enemy. In fact he did nothing."[69] Corbett also commented, "The British van was cut to pieces before Graves got into action at all."[70] It has been suggested that had Hood been the senior officer, the battle would have turned out differently.

In a communication to Lord Sandwich, Graves wrote, "Your Lordship will perceive my constant attention by the Minutes was to press the enemy close. And to prevent the signal for the line becoming an impediment to the rear, I took in the signal for the line before any firing began and urged the close action, and only resumed the signal for the line who were for about five or seven minutes to push the ships ahead of me forward, and who were some of them upon my off beam."[71]

After the Battle off the Capes, De Grasse became more and more impatient about returning to the West Indies, and he was difficult to deal with because of his determination to leave. He wanted to sail before hurricane season became especially volatile, and he was eager to head back in order to honor his commitment to Spain by resuming his coverage of the islands that the Spanish had taken over for him in his absence. It was not easy for the allies to reason with him on these points.

Rochambeau was afraid if De Grasse left the Chesapeake before the end of October, the allies would be left unprotected. He feared the possible return of the British fleet. True, Admiral Graves and Admiral Hood had sailed to New York, but it was unclear if and when they might return with a larger force to resume the sea battle with De Grasse in the Chesapeake. It was of prime concern that if the French fleet were to leave too early, before the campaign was concluded, the chances of Cornwallis trying to escape from Yorktown would be multiplied. Thus, the consensus was that a meeting with the admiral was essential.

While on his mission to the Chesapeake, Admiral de Grasse never left his ship nor set foot on dry land. He was reluctant to leave his post while on duty. With this fact in mind, the allies went to him on his ship for this meeting. They had to reaffirm with him that he was needed in the Chesapeake through the entire month of October.

Accordingly, on September 17, Washington, Rochambeau, Duportail, Lafayette, Chastellux, Knox, Hamilton, and Governor Benjamin Harrison went to Hampton, Virginia, where they boarded the *Queen Charlotte,* a prize captured by the French, and sailed a few hours out into the Chesapeake Bay to Admiral de Grasse's ship. Alexander Hamilton was fluent in French since his mother was a French Huguenot (French Protestant). This was very helpful in their meeting because Washington knew little French.

The allied generals must have had an enormous feeling of pride as they wended their way through the massive convoy of nearly thirty warships to De Grasse's flagship. They must have felt proud that this was the fleet that had defeated the British less than two weeks ago and sent them packing to New York. This was the fleet that had successfully tightened the noose around the British army by sea, blocking Cornwallis's last avenue of escape. This was the fleet that both Rochambeau and Washington had agreed they needed to win the last, great battle. They were thankful to be surrounded and protected by these impressive French warships.[72]

According to William Hallahan's book, *The Day the Revolution Ended,* when the envoys, including Washington and Rochambeau, reached the *Ville de Paris,* they climbed aboard in the midst of a thirteen-gun salute and were very surprised at the way De Grasse received them.[73] The Admiral (six feet two inches) went up to George Washington (six feet three inches) and gave him "a mighty bear hug" as well as the traditional French *bises,* which were kisses on both cheeks.[74] Then he shouted, "My dear little general!" This gave great glee to all those around him.[75] "The Frenchmen, governed by the rigid etiquette of the *ancien régime,* controlled their mirth as best they could; but our own jolly Knox, heedless of all rules, laughed, and that aloud, till his fat sides shook again."[76]

It was the first time the American general and the French admiral had met. The latter was an overly proud, overly loud, self-assured but courteous, colorful character born and bred in Grasse, Provence (a province in the south of France). He used his origins as an excuse for his brashness, saying that he was a Provençal first and a sailor second. He did, however, serve a memorable feast to his guests that night. "The fleet was dressed with flags, and the health of the King, the Congress, and the commanders was drunk with salvos."[77]

Washington had a few goals in mind for this visit. First, he asked De Grasse to extend his stay until October 30, and second, he needed men from De Grasse's fleet to help short-term.[78]

During the on-board conference, the mercurial De Grasse gave his word; he would stay through the end of October, to the delight of Washington and Rochambeau. He also conceded that he could spare as many as two thousand of his men from the fleet, but only for a temporary role, a "coup de main" as well as some cannon and powder.[79] This news greatly lessened the anxiety on the eve of the Battle of Yorktown.

Their mission accomplished, their return was not a very speedy one and, according to Washington, "by hard blowing and contrary winds did not reach Williamsburg again until the 22nd."[80] They could ill afford to lose this much time due to bad weather. On the day following his return to army headquarters on the 23rd, Washington sent the following dispatch to the president of the Congress, announcing that all was well. He is quoted as writing, "I am happy to inform Congress that I found the French Admiral disposed in the best manner to give us all the assistance in his power and perfectly to co-operate with me in our present attempt."[81]

French Admiral De Grasse successfully prevented the re-supply and rescue of Cornwallis by sea. The second Battle off the Virginia Capes was fought out of sight of land with no American ships or American sailors involved. Although few military and even fewer civilians were aware of the crucial ocean battle fought within earshot of Williamsburg, the effects carried important implications for the outcome of the insurgents' seven-year struggle. Rochambeau's decision to emphasize the need to move south, involving De Grasse at sea in lieu of engaging Clinton at New York, had thus far produced the positive effect he and Versailles had intended. With the British fleet having returned to New York, the allies gained a window of time in which to move their armies from Williamsburg into Yorktown. There they would continue to tighten the noose around Cornwallis by land and prepare defenses for the upcoming battle.

After the four-hundred-mile march of the combined armies from New York and the even longer six-hundred-mile march of Rochambeau's army from Newport, Washington and Rochambeau and their men were eager to commence what they hoped would be the decisive battle of the American War of Independence.

CHAPTER TEN

The Battle of Yorktown

"The Yorktown siege was essentially an exercise in engineering, which happened to be one of the Continental army's major weaknesses. Fortunately, the French army included the best military engineers in the world."

–JOSEPH J. ELLIS

ON SEPTEMBER 28 Generals Rochambeau and Washington ordered the allied armies from Williamsburg to Yorktown on the last leg of their march south. It was a relatively short journey of twelve miles that became known as the "Grand Approach."[1] On the eve of the march, in deference to military standards of the smartly turned-out French officers and troops, Washington's officers ordered the commissary to issue at least twelve pounds of flour per brigade for the men to powder their hair *à la française.* The men were also ordered to be clean-shaven for the march. The Americans wanted to look as stylish as the French while at the same time creating the air of the conquering army.[2]

Although they began their march at four in the morning, the army could not avoid the extreme heat of the day. According to his journal, Crèvecoeur, along with other officers and even some generals, had to make the journey on foot in the midday sun since their horses had not yet arrived. He explained that the heat was so excessive that two men actually died at Crèvecoeur's feet during the march. On that first gruesome day out of Williamsburg, the troops did not arrive at Yorktown until six in the evening.[3] It was so hot that the flour must have baked on their hair. The allies had to stop frequently because of heat exhaustion, and eight hundred soldiers had to be left at the hospital in Williamsburg as a result.[4] Crèvecoeur expressed his distress during that day in this way: "I can testify to having suffered every affliction imaginable."[5] Rochambeau reported that Virginia had "the burning heat of the coast of Barbary."[6] Barbary Coast was a term used by Europeans at the time to refer to the mid and western coast of North Africa.

Taking up three columns, the Americans formed the right-hand column of the march and the French formed the other two columns. Although it was a mere twelve-mile march, compared to the nearly six hundred miles the French had already come and the four hundred miles for the Americans, it took a few days for the entire army and support systems to assemble at Yorktown.

The French and American armies had a great deal of difficulty maintaining and moving their stores into place as the British tried every day to undermine their supply route. The enemy captured boatloads of food and rations that were either being shipped or hauled along the road toward Williamsburg and Yorktown. The British captured a small vessel, which was loaded with flour and carried twenty-five hundred rations for the army. This loss was very damaging to the allies as their food supply was greatly limited in Virginia.

Cornwallis had written to Clinton, telling him that he had food supplies to last six weeks.[7] However, by September 11, a German soldier in the British army, Johann Doehla, wrote in his journal that the soldiers ate "putrid ship's meat and wormy biscuits."[8] Later, just before the allies' march into Yorktown, Cornwallis raided the Lower Peninsula for grain, meat, and fodder in desperation for provisions.[9]

From their headquarters in Williamsburg, the generals strategized and planned up to the last minute. Rochambeau made his headquarters in the frame house of the widow of Peyton Randolph, the late first president of the Continental Congress. The Marquis de Lafayette also used this house during the Revolution. The Randolph House was located at the corner of Nicholson and North England Streets and was built in 1715 by William Robertson. The large clapboard house was built as two houses in one, called the east and west wings. Sir John Randolph purchased the west wing in 1721 and built the east wing in 1724. Sir John's son, Peyton Randolph, built the center section with a grand staircase that connected the two wings.[10]

Prior to the battle Washington settled into the Wythe House (pronounced "with") not far away. Built in the 1750s, the Wythe House stands on the Palace Green next to the Bruton Church and is one of the few brick mansions still standing from the Revolutionary War period. The original owner was George Wythe, "the foremost classical scholar in Virginia."[11] He was the leader of the patriot movement in Virginia, a delegate to the Continental Congress, and a signer of the Declaration of Independence.[12]

Dr. Goodwin, who encouraged John D. Rockefeller Jr. to begin the restoration of Williamsburg, bought the historic Wythe House in 1926. In 1927, Rockefeller adopted Goodwin's plan of revival for the town. The Wythe House became the parish house for the Bruton Church.[13] Today it is known as the George Wythe House and is furnished as it would have been in the period when George and Elizabeth Wythe resided in the home. Following the Battle of Yorktown, General Rochambeau used the Wythe House as his headquarters until his departure from Virginia.[14]

General Rochambeau met with General Washington each day, not only to review the events of the day, but also to plan for the next one. In the midst of all the excitement and hurried activity to prepare for the siege, Rochambeau became ill with what was called a tertian fever.[15] There is not much documentation on his illness and how it affected Rochambeau during the siege of Yorktown. The French general did not mention this ailment in his memoirs, but one can assume it was problematic for him and that he downplayed it as much as possible. It is also known that General Rochambeau continued to suffer from his old thigh injury, but as a stalwart French officer, he said little about it even as he continued to travel endless miles on horseback.

While on the last portion of the march, General Washington ordered that if the British attempted to stop them they should use their bayonets "that they may prove the vanity of the boast which the British make of their peculiar prowess in deciding battles with that weapon."[16] It was widely known that the French excelled in close fighting with bayonets and were well prepared to fend off the British.

Washington encouraged his men with these words: "The justice of the cause in which we are engaged and the honor of the two nations must inspire every breast with sentiments that are the presage of victory."[17] The commander in chief wrote to General Heath in New York, "Lord Cornwallis is incessantly at work on his fortifications, and is probably preparing to defend himself to the last extremity; a little time will probably decide his fate; with the blessings of Heaven, I feel it will be favorable to the interests of America."[18]

When the allies arrived at Yorktown, they encountered some British soldiers who had been sent out in a forward column to scout the French and American troops. There were some shots fired; some Englishmen had their horses shot from under them. The British retreated quickly.[19]

Cornwallis received a message on September 29. The letter, dated five days earlier, was from General Clinton in New York, stating that he and the other officers had decided to send a task force of twenty-three warships that would set sail in "a few days."[20] Cornwallis was heartened by this message. He calculated that he would be rescued by October 5. Further, the general believed he would be safe until that time because he had not yet seen the Americans bring in their siege artillery. Any additional messages to or from Cornwallis would be scarce because the allies controlled the roads in and out of Yorktown, and there were so many allied ships in the area that it would be very hard to get a message through by water. It was also true that anyone who was caught carrying a message to the British was to be shot immediately.

Knowing that Rochambeau and Washington were closing in around Cornwallis, in desperation, General Clinton asked Major Charles Cochrane to get a message through to Cornwallis. This request prompted Major Cochrane to set forth from New York Harbor in a whaleboat with "a crew and twelve oars."[21] The plan was to row several hundred miles to Yorktown despite high seas in stormy weather because Clinton was desperate to get a message to Cornwallis.[22]

CORNWALLIS ABANDONS FIRST LINE OF DEFENSE

In the course of the next two days, Rochambeau investigated the English works. A few of his men were killed and a few wounded. On September 30 he discovered that the British had already retreated from their entrenched camp at Pigeon Hill. The camp consisted of some well-built redoubts.[23] When Cornwallis saw that he was outnumbered three to one, he abandoned the outer works at Pigeon Hill in favor of consolidating his army.[24] This was a promising development for those plotting the siege.[25]

The allies were suspicious when they discovered that Cornwallis had abandoned the first ring of earthworks, consisting of three redoubts and one redan.[26] Not expecting such good fortune, Washington suspected that as Cornwallis retreated, he may have left behind a Trojan horse to surprise the allies as they advanced into Yorktown.[27]

Why would Cornwallis give up redoubts that were in an excellent position on a high place, each one facing in a different direction? The allies could easily move into them, saving the time, energy, and blood it would have taken to capture them.[28] Rochambeau and Washington made haste to profit from this unexpected retreat. They reinforced the old earthworks and added new ones to strengthen their position. This new set of earthworks became the allies' First Parallel, and it stretched in an arc from Pigeon Hill to the York River.[29] In his journal Crèvecoeur wrote, "We converted a redan they had also abandoned into a redoubt and built a fourth to tie them all together."[30]

There were several cannon shots that day, which rained down on the allies as they were moving into the captured British redoubts and rebuilding them for their own benefit. Crèvecoeur went on to describe the casualties: "We lost only 4 or 5 men during the course of its construction…M. Drouilhet, an officer of the Agen[a]is Regiment, had his leg shattered. One hussar was killed and another wounded."[31]

Upon their arrival in Yorktown, it was evident to both Rochambeau and Washington that a great deal of engineering would be necessary before the actual battle could begin, as the allied generals had previously expected. "Fortunately, the French army included the best military engineers in the world. As a result, though Washington was officially in command, the Yorktown siege was primarily a French operation…Washington issued a fifty-five-point memorandum to his officers clarifying their respective duties."[32]

Soon thereafter, Rochambeau and Washington rode out to examine the British fortifications in Yorktown. Later Washington rode out again "on his new horse, Nelson, a light sorrel, sixteen hands high, with white face and legs."[33] According to Baron von Closen, Rochambeau had taken part in fourteen sieges in his career, so the planning of the Battle of Yorktown came easily to him.[34] The rules for the taking of a city were condensed into "an exact science."[35] What's more, the lay of the land was familiar to the American general. The two generals each had their own expertise in approaching the planning of the assault. That night, since the tents had not yet arrived, Washington spent the night under a mulberry tree.[36]

Ironically, Yorktown was founded in 1691 on land owned by an ancestor of George Washington, Nicholas Martiau (1591–1657). He was a French Huguenot or Walloon, a name referring to the people and the language of these inhabitants of southern Belgium and northwest France who immigrated to America in 1620.[37] On the high bluff overlooking the York River, where the Battle of Yorktown was to take place, Martiau had purchased fifty acres of land in 1635.[38] After his death, this land was designated by his heirs as part of the port at Yorktown, the biggest port on the Chesapeake until 1750.[39] It seemed only fitting that the French General Rochambeau and Martiau's descendant, General George Washington, an American soldier of French heritage, should together re-claim this ground for a free America.

Considering the geography of Yorktown, it seemed strange that Cornwallis chose it as his last defense against the rebels. The only advantage of the location lay in the fact that he could easily have been rescued by sea had there not been a barrier of two French fleets anchored in the harbor. Cornwallis's fortifications were situated about thirty feet above the York River, and from there, heading inland, the terrain was virtually flat. Because it was flat, Cornwallis was forced to dig many redoubts in the weeks leading up to the arrival of the French and American armies. They were his only defense.

In the end, the bluff overlooking the York River proved to be virtually indefensible for Cornwallis and his hungry army of eight thousand. As he waited in vain to be rescued, with his back to the sea, his elaborate earthworks turned out to be his last-ditch effort. "He [Cornwallis] had made up his mind he was going to be relieved and that comfortable assumption blunted his initiative."[40] In other words, the only initiative that he showed for this battle was in creating earthworks. Most of the time, he simply sat and waited to be rescued by the British fleet. He really did not believe there would be a decisive battle at Yorktown.

Noose tightens around Cornwallis

Cornwallis was feeling the pressure on all sides and growing most uncomfortable. He had no place to run or swim! The only action the British general could take was to continue to fortify his position on the bluff at Yorktown between the ravine that extended up from the river onto the high ground and Wormley's Creek.[41] Governor Thomas Nelson Jr.'s father, also named Thomas Nelson, had served as secretary of the Colonial Council of Virginia before the Revolution. He lived in the family home, a Georgian brick mansion atop the Yorktown bluff. Known as the Thomas Nelson Jr. House, it stands at the corner of Main and Nelson Streets. From the front steps, there is an unobstructed view of the York River, and it is not far from the battlefield where Cornwallis would make his final stand.[42] Cornwallis and Secretary Nelson had been friends under British rule, so when the Revolution began, the elder Nelson chose not to take sides in the fight. Later, when Cornwallis arrived in Virginia with his troops, Secretary Nelson invited him to make his headquarters in the Nelson home, while he remained in residence. However, on October 10, when the fighting moved dangerously close, they moved out—Cornwallis to a cave below the bluff on the bank of the York.[43] At the same time, Governor Nelson supplied Washington's army and led the Virginia militia in battle.

As the allies prepared for the coming battle, they knew that everything hinged on winning this campaign. If the allies failed, the American Continentals could not put together another army. This would be their last chance to win the war against the British.

On the other hand, no one would ever have imagined that the British would have lost the recent Battle off the Capes. They had been supreme on the seas for many years, rarely experiencing defeat. On September 15, British Lieutenant MacKenzie wrote in his diary, "Should our fleet be defeated, the loss of the whole army under Lord Cornwallis is much to be dreaded."[44] He forecasted that if the British fleet should lose on the ocean to the French, the rest of the dominos would fall accordingly. History proved MacKenzie correct in his assumption.

Although the British were constantly working to sabotage the allies' march onto the battleground, the Franco-American forces converged on Virginia unscathed. Thanks to the assistance of

Rochambeau, De Grasse, and Barras, after arriving in Williamsburg, Washington could at last be truly "hopeful, more hopeful than he had been at any time since the war began."[45]

There remained one elusive factor. Would Clinton be able to send his fleet back to Yorktown to extract Cornwallis from certain defeat? The British fleet under the command of Graves and Hood had just limped back to New York, sorely beaten by the French. Rochambeau, nonetheless, could not discount the possibility that the British might soon be restored to fighting status with the help of Rear Admiral Robert Digby, who had recently returned from England with a small fleet "vaguely reported as from three to ten" warships.[46] Rochambeau, in his memoirs, stated that Digby sailed into New York with "three ships of the line and a body of troops on board with Prince William-Henry, one of the king of England's sons, [sent by his father]… to retake possession of the Government of Virginia."[47] This news posed a great threat to the allies. Once again, the outcome would depend upon the continued support of the French fleet as agreed upon months ago by Rochambeau and Washington. Even as Rochambeau marched toward Yorktown, the British fleet might have been beating its way down the coast toward Virginia. Washington impressed upon De Grasse, "You will have observed, whatever efforts are made by land armies, the navy must have the casting vote in the present contest."[48]

The allied forces were pressed for time; food supplies were running very low in Virginia, and De Grasse had to leave soon. The Franco-American campaign had to commence its decisive battle before the British fleet arrived by sea, provoking renewed action on the Chesapeake. If this were to happen, it would draw De Grasse out of the channel into another sea battle off the Capes. However, Admiral Barras was presently on the scene, also guarding the mouth of the Chesapeake. This time Barras could guard the Chesapeake while De Grasse exited to fight a battle.

"MOST AMIABLE ADMIRAL" REMAINS IN CHESAPEAKE

Rochambeau considered all these possibilities while preparing for the final battle against Cornwallis. De Grasse, already proven feisty and quick to come to his own decisions, heard the unpleasant news that Digby and company might be en route. He hastily suggested to Rochambeau that he should depart his post to meet the English fleet at sea. Rochambeau and Washington, of one accord, agreed that the French admiral should remain on guard at the Chesapeake because they needed him there in order to succeed with their offensive strategy. Without his protection, Cornwallis might slip the noose, and all would be lost.

Baron von Closen, who carried the message about Digby to De Grasse, recorded this in his diary: "The news of Digby's arrival and of the approaching departure of Hood's fleet from New York alarmed and disquieted these excitable gentlemen of the navy, who think only of cruises and battles and do not like to oblige or to cooperate with the land troops."[49]

When Rochambeau received the answer from De Grasse, again carried by Closen, he was quick to respond, using his most diplomatic verbiage. He began, *"Mon cher A[d]miral"* (My dear Admiral), a phrase he repeated several times in the letter to impress upon the admiral that he was shocked at De Grasse's suggestion.[50] Rochambeau wrote that under no circumstances should he leave the Chesapeake, couching his order in the most polite but firmest terms possible. Washington also addressed a letter to De Grasse at the same time; both generals expressed their horror that the admiral had considered leaving his post to meet the enemy on the high seas.

Rochambeau received word back from De Grasse after the admiral called a council of war with his officers. Rochambeau was greatly relieved that De Grasse agreed to remain in the Chesapeake. Rochambeau cheerfully replied, "You are the most amiable admiral I know."[51] In a similar vein but in a more formal tone, Washington wrote the admiral, "The Resolution that your Excellency has taken in our Circumstances proves that a great Mind knows how to make personal Sacrifices to secure a general Good."[52]

Continuing with battle preparations, Rochambeau visited the troops of Generals Saint-Simon and Vioménil with the Marquis de Laval's chasseurs and grenadiers. Following the initial retreat of the British to the first parallel that first evening, the Americans settled into the place of honor on the right while the French covered the left, both facing the water. From a soldier's point of view, facing the York River, the Americans took up their position to the right of Cornwallis's post and the French, to his left. The allies fanned out, filling the entire semicircle in front of Cornwallis. He was locked in.

Washington's brief order that evening was, "The whole army, officers and soldiers, will lay on their arms this night."[53] General George Weedon from Virginia wrote to Nathanael Greene, major general of the continental army, "I am all on fire...By the Great God of war, I think we may all hang up our swords by the last of the year in perfect peace and security!"[54]

FRANCO-AMERICAN ALLIES MARCH TO BATTLE

The battle was about to begin. "Fifes and drums sounding, banners streaming, three divisions of Continentals under Generals Lafayette, Lincoln, and von Steuben led the way. General Wayne and his brigade of Pennsylvanians...marched with heads up under General von Steuben's command."[55] Then marched Yorktown native General Thomas Nelson Jr., now also a governor, who led an assembly of more than three thousand Virginia militiamen. General Nelson had assumed the governorship of the state of Virginia after Thomas Jefferson. Nelson's home proudly carries the battle scars of the Yorktown battle; bullet holes can still be seen in the side of the house.

Next came the Second Canadian regiment. There were only two hundred men, due to attrition and casualties suffered since 1775 when they had numbered eight hundred. The First Rhode Island regiment also marched with the allies. Their regiment consisted of black troops with white officers. On several occasions, they distinguished themselves during the Revolution. The order of march continued with the artillery brigade of General Henry Knox and his two hundred cavalry men followed by the sappers and miners, including Sergeant Joseph Plumb Martin. They were followed by the French troops with their seven regiments commanded by the two Vioménil brothers, Chastellux, Saint-Simon, and Choisy. Three of these regiments—the Gâtinais, the Agenais, and the Touraine—had come by sea with De Grasse while the other four—the Bourbonnais, the Saintonge, the Soissonnais, and the Deux-Ponts—had marched from Newport. All of the troops were "smartly stepping, superbly tailored soldiers."[56]

The National Park Service in its *Statement of National Significance* gives figures for the three armies and the naval forces involved at Yorktown.[57] They are:

American Army	9,150 Continentals and Militia
French Army	9,300 Armies under Rochambeau and Saint-Simon
French Navy	28,400 French marines and ship crews
British Forces	9,700 (Includes 840 naval personnel)[58]
Total Forces	56,550

Rarely mentioned is the fact that the Americans were in the minority at the siege of Yorktown, the battle that would profit them most directly.

LAUZUN'S LEGION DEFENDS GLOUCESTER

For Lauzun the march from New York had been long, scorching hot, and dangerous. He and his infantry had embarked in boats to travel down the Chesapeake, all the time fearing bad weather and British fireboats, which could be launched at them at any moment. The hussars forded the Susquehanna and Rappahannock Rivers with their horses nearly being swept away into the current because the footing was very slippery, and then they rode directly to the Gloucester peninsula. The infantry disembarked on September 23 at Jamestown (near Williamsburg), and Lauzun received orders from General Rochambeau to march down the Gloucester Peninsula to join his cavalry and reinforce American General George Weedon and his fifteen hundred Virginia militiamen there.[59] Together they would hold the British to their position on the Gloucester shore. They dug in around the British encampment on Gloucester as first defense against an escape attempt by Cornwallis.

Defending the peninsula was part of a carefully thought-out strategy. Should Cornwallis endeavor to make a getaway, this would likely be the route he would choose. To do so he would have to cross the York River silently under cover of darkness in order to make his way out of the danger zone at Yorktown.[60] This method would be fraught with insurmountable problems. Where would he get the boats without being noticed? How many of his officers and men could he ferry across the river to safety? Once across the water, how could he hope to penetrate the allied defenses on Gloucester? Choisy, who commanded the allied forces at Gloucester, would see to it that Cornwallis did not use Gloucester as an escape route. Unless Clinton's fleet could extract him from his vulnerable position on the bluff at Yorktown, there was no viable means of escape.

Under Cornwallis the British had fortified Gloucester Point with four substantial redoubts, twenty guns, and three batteries plus a stockade spanning the beach.[61] Gloucester was a small community consisting of only four houses at that time.[62] The negligible size of the community paled in comparison to its strategic importance in the impending battle.

Cornwallis put Colonel Thomas Dunda's garrison in place to guard the peninsula. It numbered about 1,100 men, including some 500 cavalry.[63] The British soldiers at Gloucester were a mixed bag of nationalities including Scots, Hessians, Welsh, and North Carolina Loyalists.[64] Of most interest to Lauzun, however, was British Lieutenant Colonel Banastre Tarleton who commanded 240 men including the cavalry of the British Legion. Tarleton was the closest to being Lauzun's counterpart, that is, the soldier most like him in America who would fight opposite him on horseback.

Lauzun, ever ready for a good fight, was wary of working with General Weedon, who had distinguished himself at Brandywine and was his senior, but who had the reputation of being "in deadly fear of coming under fire."[65] Lauzun made it known that he needed more experienced men to hold the peninsula. When Rochambeau heard these complaints, he reasoned with Lauzun concerning his doubts about serving under Weedon, but decided to send French Major General Claude Choisy to assume command of the allies at Gloucester. Pursuant to Lauzun's request on September 29, Rochambeau sent Choisy with eight hundred men borrowed from De Grasse and fifteen hundred militia.[66] Choisy, who had recently sailed from Newport to the Chesapeake with Admiral Barras's fleet carrying Rochambeau's heavy artillery, began his assignment by building defenses on Gloucester Point.

Crèvecoeur offered his view of events during the first days of digging redoubts in Gloucester and Yorktown. He reported that on October 1 the English kept the allies "under continuous fire, killing many men."[67]

On the morning of October 4 Choisy chose to lead an expedition to seize a defensive position on Gloucester, which he believed to be vacant, but he was surprised to find still in enemy hands.[68] Choisy had set out with Lauzun's Legion of 330 cavalry and 360 infantry and American Lieutenant Colonel John Mercer's best Virginia militiamen. They continued their march, but Tarleton had been warned of their approach and had hidden in the woods to surprise them as they marched into view.[69] When Tarleton saw a battalion of the despised American militia approaching, he responded with a violent assault.[70] Lauzun returned fire and charged without hesitation.[71] He attacked the British at least three times, eventually pushing the enemy back to their small outpost on Gloucester Point.[72]

Tarleton discovered that the Virginia militia was indeed more formidable than he had anticipated. To his detriment the militia consisted of seasoned fighters, most of them former Continental army regulars led by Lieutenant Colonel Mercer. Just as the French and Americans were readying for another attack on Tarleton, the latter suddenly and unaccountably withdrew.

It was a successful day for the allied campaign on the peninsula. Choisy called a retreat, but as they were pulling back, Lauzun noticed "one of his hussars assailed by three of Tarleton's cavalrymen."[73] In an act of selfless bravery Lauzun moved quickly to defend his hussar. Together they fought side by side and then got away safely. Crèvecoeur learned about the incident from the hussar, but Lauzun did not speak of it.[74]

There is another, more detailed description of the clash between the combined French and American armies and the British on Gloucester. It is the firsthand account of "Light-horse" Harry Lee on a mission from General Nathaniel Greene. Early on October 3, Lee saw that Tarleton had stopped to speak with a local farmwoman. He had told her unabashedly that he wanted to shake hands with the famous Duc de Lauzun. Only a few minutes later, by chance, Lauzun spoke with the same woman asking for the location of Tarleton and his cavalry. Her answer sent him off in a cloud of dust as he rode quickly away in pursuit of Tarleton.[75] Farther down the peninsula the allies met up with Tarleton's foraging party loaded with corn. The skirmish that followed was a serious one with casualties on both sides.[76]

A hussar drove a lance into the side of a British horse, causing the horse to rear and creating a pandemonium of falling men and horses. In the scuffle it appeared that Tarleton had been killed when he was thrown from his horse just as he was drawing a bead on Lauzun. Although wounded, he did find the means to mount another horse. Due to the strength and perseverance of the Virginia militia and Lauzun's Legion, Tarleton was forced to retreat to the British defenses at the village of Gloucester.[77] Weedon did not participate in this, the only battle on Gloucester due to lack of transportation.[78]

Tarleton's reputation for "vicious behavior in the Carolinas... including the depredation of civilian property and the massacre of prisoners of war" had preceded him, but nonetheless Lauzun and the Americans had bested him.[79] Tarleton finally got his wish to meet Lauzun face to face for he had, in a manner of speaking, shaken hands with him on the battlefield.

"The next day Washington saluted both Lauzun and Mercer and pinned the laurel of praise on them for their victory."[80] Within a matter of days Gloucester would be secured and all would be in readiness for the larger battle expected to encompass both Gloucester and Yorktown.

After the surprise ambush by the British on Gloucester, Choisy requested more artillery and more men to better defend the Gloucester Peninsula. Rochambeau complied and sent "4 field pieces with 2 artillery officers and 32 gunners."[81] Unfortunately, after all was said and done, Lauzun lost two hussars in the fray.[82] Following the battle the allies continued to establish their post on Gloucester, including a hospital and storage depot.

The outcome of the battle on Gloucester was as follows:

Casualties:

British:	12 of Tarleton's men and an infantry officer killed
American:	2 killed and 11 wounded
French:	(from Lauzun's Legion) 2 killed in action and about 15 wounded, of whom 3 died from their wounds.[83]
Result:	Choisy had successfully moved the allied line to one mile from the outpost of Gloucester held by the British.[84]

ALLIES STRENGTHEN FORTIFICATIONS

October 5 was a washout, for just as the sappers and miners on the York bluff began to lay out their laths of pinewood end to end to show the line of digging for the trenches, it began to rain and they were ordered back to their tents. Sergeant Joseph Plumb Martin was among them.[85]

The next night, October 6, they began digging in earnest despite the soggy ground. On the American side, according to tradition, General George Washington lifted the pickaxe and made the first cut to open the trenches.[86] The allies first laid out *toises* on the ground to indicate the location and size of the trenches to be built. "That on the right [referring to the American trenches] was cut to a length of six or seven hundred toises, and was flanked with four redoutes [sic]."[87]

After laying out the perimeters of the trenches, the sappers and miners aided the engineers with fifteen hundred men carrying shovels, *fascines, saucissons,* and *gabions.* Gabions were highly portable and could be brought to the defensive positions and filled with earth and stones. They were used as we would today use sand-bags.[88] A soldier could make but one gabion a day. The French soldiers were paid for each gabion they made; the Americans were not paid.[89]

Surprisingly, while the allies were stealthily digging and making preparations, behind the enemy walls could be heard the strains of popular tunes being played by the British regimental bands. The most recognizable was "Yankee Doodle Dandy."[90] The British felt secure and were celebrating with music because they had doubly fortified themselves in fewer redoubts. Moreover, they were still hoping for their rescue from the British fleet. In addition, although they were firing at the French trenches, not yet knowing exactly where their batteries were located, the allies did not return fire. They were not yet ready to let Cornwallis know where their batteries were located.

The French and Americans built fires at night to distract the British into thinking that the allies were up to some "secret mischief," while digging their redoubts as swiftly as they could, right under their noses.[91] They continued as quietly as possible through the night of October 6 and into the day and night of October 7.

During this two-day stretch General Rochambeau was ailing physically and was so unwell that he was confined to his bed. Weelen aptly described the inconvenience of the general's illness as having "nailed him to his bed."[92]

To make the best use of time, the American and French divisions took turns digging and resting to maintain the frantic pace. By daylight, there was no disguising their intent from the British. The digging operation took place in the open within easy shooting distance of the enemy. Since the allies needed these redoubts for protection, the pressure was intense to complete the project. The French constructed their First Parallel of defensive works on the left flank, which would bring them up to five hundred meters from the British lines.[93] According to Rochambeau's memoirs, no one was hurt during this crucial time of building fortifications.[94]

BATTLE JOINED AT LAST

The French completed their works slightly ahead of the Americans and waited for both armies to be ready before beginning the siege. By the afternoon of October 9, the French and American troops had finished digging their First Parallel ring of trenches. "At three o'clock on Tuesday, October 9…the French flag slowly rose up its pole and stirred in the breeze. Then the American flag matched it. Everyone was in place for the official ceremony that traditionally opens a siege, commencing with martial music."[95] The allied soldiers felt a rush of pride and excitement as they watched their flags rise above the trenches to signal their readiness to commence battle. Sergeant Martin saw it as "an omen of success to our enterprise…the French troops accompanying it with 'Huzza for the Americans!'"[96]

General Washington gave the honor of firing the first gun at three o'clock on October 9 to French General Saint-Simon. The first allied shot thundered from the barrel of a "wall-crushing twenty-four pounder" and scored a direct hit.[97] The troops cheered. Then it was the Americans' turn.[98] A Massachusetts doctor, James Thacher, wrote a description of this event, saying that General Knox was to do the honors by firing off the first ceremonial shot for the Americans. Knox took the touchhole match from the gunner and, instead of doing it himself, handed it to General Washington, who put the match to the touchhole and sent the first American volley into the British camp at five o'clock.[99]

Their first shells hit a British-occupied house where the secretary of state was meeting with his men over dinner. Several were either killed or wounded according to Martin's account.[100] He named it a "warmday [sic] to the British."[101] The battle officially began.

Washington Gives Last Orders at the Siege of Yorktown

Washington and Rochambeau confer outside field tent.
Mezzotint by E. Massard after Couder. 1785.
Anne S. K. Brown Military Collection, Brown University Library.

A key component in the allied success at the Yorktown battle was the French heavy-duty siege artillery. As a part of Rochambeau's detailed pre-expedition planning, the French general shipped the heavy siege artillery from France to Newport. These same armaments were carried on Admiral Barras's ships from Newport to the Chesapeake and had been unloaded near Williamsburg on September 10; teams of oxen had waited at the James River port for the guns to be transferred from the boats to the oxen train. The dependable teams then pulled the drays the last stretch of road to the battlefield. This was quite a journey for heavy siege guns and might have established a distance record for the hauling of heavy weapons over land and sea. It had been worth the effort to transport the weaponry, as it proved critical for the success of the allied offensive.

Cornwallis had not anticipated the French heavy artillery, and his inferior guns and flimsy earthworks were no match for their big guns. The allies were able to shoot from a longer distance with these cannons, which gave them an upper hand since they were less vulnerable as a result. The cannon were in place and shelling the British by October 10. In addition to the ninety French pieces of artillery, including thirty-six heavy siege guns, there also were sixty American pieces of artillery.[102] Their incredible firepower pounded the enemy for twenty-four hours.

On the evening of October 10 a gun installed by the French close to the York River "gave a spectacular demonstration of [French] virtuosity. They had constructed an oven for heating cannon balls. Now they fired their oven and loaded the heated balls into cannon with special tongs brought all the way from France. This 'hot shot' set fire to the British vessel *Charon*, which burned on into the night."[103] Coincidentally, this was the same ship that carried traitor Benedict Arnold to Virginia, where he pillaged and burned his way across the state. Ironically, the *Charon* had been stripped of its cannon and artillerymen early on by Cornwallis in order to strengthen his land batteries.[104]

Later that night the twelve-oar whaleboat sent down from Clinton with a message for Cornwallis entered the Chesapeake with muffled oars, managing to slip quietly past the French convoy anchored at Hampton Roads in the York River. Major Charles Cochrane went ashore to deliver the letter. He and his crew had been at sea for only seven days. The dangerous trip was to no avail, because Clinton's note was full of vagaries and stalls with no promises. Cornwallis's reply was more to the point, pleading that his only hope would come with a full fleet on the York River.[105] If indeed the whaleboat could make it back to New York undetected, it would take at least seven more days until Clinton could possibly read Cornwallis's reply.

On Thursday, October 11, as described by American Captain Benjamin Bartholomew in his diary, "The Baron's [Vioménil's] division Relieved the Marquis [Lafayette] and some of our Cannon split, but were Replaced."[106] The captain also described the heavy rain that occurred as they started to dig the Second Parallel. The troops continued to work in stages and used a system of relieving each other every eight hours or so to keep the work underway.

The French and American troops worked in full view of the enemy and did not want to be left in an undefended position any longer than necessary. They worked day and night without ceasing until October 13 when the Second Parallel of earthworks was finished, bringing them up to three hundred meters from the enemy. In all, they dug three miles of trenches before they were done.

Crèvecoeur wrote, "On the night of 12th–13th three redoubts were built in support and batteries emplaced. There were 3 in all, composed of 6 guns each. They were mounted in a semicircle so as to cover a wider field and were placed 160 yards from the *place d'armes* [center of enemy defenses]. A mortar battery containing 10 mortars and two 8-inch howitzers was placed in the center to deliver shells and bombs to all the enemy works."[107] It was these powerful howitzers that surprised Cornwallis when the barrage began. Their range is ten and a half miles, but the beauty of these heavy artillery armaments was that they did not need to be moved to change their trajectory, unlike most of the cannon used in the eighteenth century. They required fewer men to operate them and could be lowered or raised to change trajectory, saving precious time in the midst of battle operations.

The fighting that ensued was bloody and fierce. Musket smoke filled the air; the sound of battle was deafening. Georg Daniel Flohr, a German-born member of the Deux-Ponts regiment who left a complete journal account of the attack, wrote, "We could see from our redoubt the people flying into the air with outstretched arms."[108] Flohr, who devoted forty pages to the Battle of Yorktown, continued in his descriptive style, "There was a misery and lamenting that was horrible…the houses stood there like lanterns shot through by cannon balls."[109] A few Yorktown homes had the misfortune to stand in the line of fire.

Mathieu Dumas told of an event that occurred on the night of October 13—Rochambeau had argued with Baron de Vioménil, insisting that they were not yet ready to attack the two remaining British redoubts. Vioménil was eager to join the battle, but Rochambeau was reluctant to commence until proven beyond a doubt that the British lines had been softened up enough to be taken by the infantry. The only answer was to inspect the British fortifications to see if they had been sufficiently damaged during the bombardments. General Rochambeau and his son—not wishing to take anyone else with them—stole into the adjoining ravine and up the far side to do their nighttime reconnaissance.

The Rochambeaus discovered that the British *abatis* and *palisades* were still intact. Returning unobserved by the enemy, Rochambeau and his son determined that "the artillery fire must be redoubled in order to level the parapet."[110] After more pounding of the enemy defenses on October 13, Rochambeau predicted, *"Nous verrons demain si la poire est mûre"* (We shall see tomorrow if the pear is ripe).[111]

By eight in the evening of October 14, Rochambeau had made up his mind that all was in readiness to attack the two British redoubts. The French and Americans led separate, simultaneous attacks on Cornwallis's last and strongest redoubts, numbers 9 and 10. The French took number 9 and the Americans, number 10. redoubt 9, located near the road that led to the nearby Moore house, was a five-sided stronghold protected by about 125 men. Redoubt 10, closer to the river, was a square position guarded by only seventy men.[112]

Just before the army stormed the two British redoubts, the sappers and miners were sent out once again to clear the way. American Sergeant Martin was among those who were, in his words, "furnished with axes, and were to proceed in front and cut a passage for the troops through the abatis."[113]

The sappers and miners lay flat on the ground in the silence of the dark night of October 14, waiting for the signal to begin the assault. Sergeant Martin reported that they listened for a spoken signal as well as a signal to be fired from a nearby battery. There would be three shells fired in quick succession. The first signal was simply the word "Rochambeau!" shouted aloud. Martin recorded that it sounded like "Ro-sham-bow" that was translated to his American ear as "Rush-on-boys."[114]

When Martin saw the flash of the three shells in the night sky and heard the spoken signal, he and his men, who had soundlessly crawled out in advance of their trenches, were the first to leap to their feet and rush to the enemy's abatis. It was their job, under a hail of enemy fire, to cut the abatis down with axes and saws so that the soldiers could scale and enter the redoubts without being impaled on the points of the trees.[115]

Four hundred French grenadiers and chasseurs of the Deux-Ponts and Gâtinais regiments stormed redoubt 9 under the command of Baron de Vioménil and his second-in-command, Guillaume de Deux-Ponts.[116] According to Rochambeau's memoirs, Deux-Ponts personally led this attack.[117] Georg Daniel Flohr reported, "The camp of the [English] army in and about the city resembled a veritable scene of destruction."[118]

As the grenadiers of the Gâtinais rushed toward redoubt 9, they heard a familiar voice above the din: *"Auvergne, Auvergne sans tache* [untarnished]!"[119] It was Papa Rochambeau inspiring the men of his precious Auvergne regiment with whom he had fought and won the bloody battle at Clostercamp. After the Seven Years' War Rochambeau's favored Auvergne regiment had been divided into two regiments, one retained the Auvergne name and the other given the name Gâtinais. The veterans of Rochambeau's old regiment yelled back to him: "Give us back our old name, ...and we will fight till the last man."[120] "They kept their word," said Rochambeau after the storming of the objective, and they "charged like lions, and lost a third of their effectives."[121]

Redoubt 9 was taken in the French style of close fighting with bayonets as the French infantry leapt into the enemy trenches. Flohr left his written observation of the French assault: "Things went very unmercifully that night...One screamed here, the other there, that for the grace of God we should kill him off completely. The whole redoubt was so full of dead and wounded that one had to walk on top of them."[122] Crèvecoeur, in the thick of the bloodiest battle of the siege, was ordered to set up a detachment of two four-pounder cannon between the two redoubts.[123]

Lafayette led four hundred Americans, who marched on redoubt 10, located nearest the river, and captured it.[124] Although Lafayette commanded the American right column, it was Lieutenant Colonel Alexander Hamilton and Lieutenant Colonel Gimat who were on the ground, leading the American flank of the attack.[125]

During the planning of the attack on redoubt 10, there had been bickering behind the scenes. On October 14, Hamilton was named field officer of the day. Hamilton, who had been Washington's aide-de-camp, penned the general's letters. He had long wanted to get into the action, even as far back as New York, but Washington had other work for his young aide. Since Hamilton was endowed with fine handwriting and French language skills, the general, a prolific correspondent, preferred to keep him close at hand.

On the eve of the Battle of Yorktown, in protest, Hamilton submitted his resignation as aide-de-camp and asked that he be put into the battle. Reluctantly, Washington assigned him to Lafayette's command. Hamilton, so long sidelined, demanded that Lafayette give him command of a light infantry division, the one that was to storm enemy redoubt 10. Hamilton said it was his right to ask since he was "officer of the day."[126] Lafayette, however, refused, as he preferred that his aide, Colonel Chevalier de Gimat, command the vanguard, for he had served in the American army for two years with an excellent reputation.[127]

Without hesitation, Hamilton went directly to Washington with his complaint. Washington granted Hamilton his wish, naming him to the commanding position in the all-important assault,[128] but granting Gimat's battalion the honored point position of extreme danger.[129] Unfortunately, Gimat was wounded at the outset of the siege and sent to the rear. After that, there was no further jealousy between the young officers.

Hamilton kept an exemplary account of the attack on redoubt 10. He commanded two American columns: one led by Major Gimat and the other by Major Fish. A third column, led by Lieutenant Colonel Laurens, was assigned to intercept the possible retreat of the enemy from the side or behind. An advance guard of sappers and miners led by Lieutenant Mansfield and commanded by Captain Gilliland prepared the way for Gimat's column by removing obstructions.[130]

Redoubt 10, the American objective, was under the command of British Major Campbell and his detachment of British and Germans; the best they could muster was a weak defense. American Colonel John Laurens, although ready to intercept the enemy in retreat, was the first to reach redoubt 10. He executed his part of the plan precisely and captured Campbell. "Lt. Mansfield," according to Hamilton's report, "conducted the vanguard with 'coolness, firmness and punctuality.'" Hamilton also applauded Gilliland, who with the sappers and miners "acquitted themselves in a manner that did them all great honor."[131]

With redoubts 9 and 10 under allied control, the allies immediately resumed digging on the Second Parallel, which had been started on October 11 by Baron von Steuben and Vioménil's divisions. Now able to join the sections of the Second Parallel, the earthwork was completed by the morning of October 15. The Second Parallel of works brought the French and Americans much closer to Cornwallis's shrinking base. He was in an untenable position on the edge of the bluff, hemmed in place by the ever-tightening noose. No fleet from Clinton was in sight to pluck the humiliated Lord Earl Cornwallis from his impending demise.

As for Cornwallis's tiny fleet, his ship, the H.M.S. *Charon*, was a charred heap resting in shallow water. The two other British transports had been sunk nearby. All three were eliminated early on by French gunfire. Only the *Guadeloupe* remained afloat. She had struggled over to the Gloucester shore.[132]

The advantages of taking the last two British redoubts were many. The allies were able to "fire...at point blank range" at Cornwallis's remaining position. Cornwallis and his army were reduced to one position on the bluff at Yorktown.[133] The Americans suffered fewer losses than the French, taking their targeted redoubt faster at one-third the cost in lost lives.[134] Fifteen French soldiers were killed and 77 were wounded.[135] The Americans lost six men according to Blanchard's report. Since he was stationed in the hospitals at Williamsburg and not at the battlefield, he may not have gotten the full count of the dead. He probably had accurate figures for the wounded, but he did not mention the numbers.[136] An official account states that the Americans lost nine men while twenty-five were wounded.[137] From both redoubts, the British lost more than seventy men, while seventy-three, including six officers, were captured by the French.[138] The assault on British redoubts 9 and 10 on the night of October 14, 1781, became the most-reported, most-remembered battle of the entire siege at Yorktown.

On October 16, under cover of darkness before dawn, the British, commanded by Lieutenant Colonel Robert Ambercromby, retaliated under heavy fire, entering a French trench that was temporarily deserted.[139] Some of the French Agenais soldiers, who held that redoubt, were on a sortie to retrieve some overturned guns, leaving only a skeleton crew to defend the trench. The British took the French captain by surprise. The enemy spiked four of the French's largest guns, which put them temporarily out of action by hammering a spiked implement into the touchhole, by reaming the touchhole (which makes it larger and decreases its efficiency), or simply by blocking the hole. Blockages could be restored, but a spiking usually rendered the cannon useless for the duration of the battle. New plugs could be added to the widened touchhole, but such an operation took time and resources.[140]

The Vicomte de Noailles, commander of the Soissonnais regiment, quickly saw the danger and repulsed the enemy. The French crushed the British spikers, killing most and taking some prisoners. The French lost eleven men, with thirty-seven wounded including five officers.[141] Rochambeau, in his memoirs, added that the spiked guns were "rendered fit for service six hours afterwards, and were again used against the place by our artillery in command of General D'Aboville."[142] Adding particulars not recorded by others, Crèvecoeur reported that most of the British troops had over-imbibed the night of October 16, which accounted for the fact that the attack did not go well for them.[143]

The repaired siege guns were put to good use later on the 16th, using a battle tactic called "ricochet projectiles," whereby guns are aimed offsides in order that the balls or bullets then bounce back, sometimes sideways, onto a target not accessible with front-on fire.[144] They steadily bombarded the British lines from the two new batteries of the Second Parallel.[145]

For successfully commanding the attack of redoubt 9 and repairing the spiked guns so they could be put in working order once again, Guillaume de Deux-Ponts, wounded during the capture of the redoubts, was made a Chevalier of the Order of St. Louis. This honor took place in December 1781 and was presented by King Louis XVI.[146]

Claude Blanchard recorded in his journal that on October 16 he was invited to dine with Washington, but he had to decline due to his responsibilities concerning the wounded under his charge at the battlefield hospitals in Williamsburg.[147]

On the night of October 16, Cornwallis, fearful for his life, began to spirit his troops across the York River to Gloucester in the dark. His careful plan included the use of sixteen large flatboats. Upon arrival at the opposite shore, Cornwallis would have been received by Tarleton but would still have had to face to Lauzun's cavalry and the Virginia militia. In short order, however, his last hope was dashed when the weather turned foul. After one boat made it to safety, a sudden squall blew up over the river, making it impossible for the other boats to make the crossing. The stranded British boats had no choice but to return to Yorktown just before daybreak. Providence intervened once more in worldly affairs by sending a storm to prevent Lord Cornwallis from escaping the battle at Yorktown. He would have liked nothing better than to avoid such a defeat.

This was not the only time when weather intervened to alter the course of a military campaign. There were three such storms over the English Channel. The earliest such incident worthy of note was in the year 1066 at the time of the Norman Conquest of England by William the Conqueror. In August of that year, as William was preparing to cross the channel with his army, he was prevented from doing so by inclement weather. Had he been able to attack at that time, he would surely have lost the Battle of Hastings to King Harold, who was ready and waiting for him. Instead, Harold turned north to face the more imminent threat of a Norwegian invasion. Then, on October 14, William sailed to England to attack Harold at Hastings, winning the battle and bringing England under Norman rule for centuries to come.

Later, in 1588, weather again changed the course of history when the Spanish armada sailed into the English Channel with 160 ships to storm Queen Elizabeth I. Elizabeth, with no standing army, was ill prepared for such an invasion and would have lost England to Spanish control under King Philip had fair weather prevailed. Instead, the once formidable armada was scattered and scuttled until it posed no threat. England remained supreme and free from Spanish rule.

One other noteworthy example was in June 1944 when France was suffering under Nazi occupation and waiting for Eisenhower to initiate the storming of Normandy to free the French. American and British allied forces waited for the perfect time to attack; their convoy of 5,000 ships eclipsed the Spanish armada. On the evening of June 5 a storm whipped up over the English Channel. The German generals determined that the bad weather would preclude an invasion that day or the next. So, they attended a birthday party instead of manning their posts. In the wee hours of June 6 General Eisenhower counter-manded the weather report and ordered the invasion of Normandy. Although the invasion was devastating for both sides, the Germans were caught unprepared and the allied forces won the day, eventually freeing France.

Cornwallis, too, was thwarted by inclement weather. He was left with no alternative but to return to his command on the Yorktown bluff and await his fate.

CHAPTER ELEVEN

British Surrender and Aftermath

"America is lost! Must we fall beneath the blow?
Or have we resources that may repair the mischief?"
—GEORGE WILLIAM FREDERICK III, KING OF ENGLAND

ON THE MORNING OF OCTOBER 17 the fighting stilled at ten o'clock, when out of the musket smoke "a small drummer boy in a red coat who stepped up in clear view of the British hornwork" drummed out a message that clearly indicated "parley."[1] The boy was followed by a British officer waving a white handkerchief. An American met the British officer on the field after directing the drummer boy back to his trench. The soldier then blindfolded the man carrying the white flag and led him to General Washington's tent where Cornwallis's aid handed Washington the message requesting a twenty-four-hour ceasefire to prepare for England's surrender. Cornwallis also suggested that each side send two men to negotiate at a Mr. Augustine Moore's house to settle terms for surrender of York and Gloucester. He signed his missive, "I have the honor to be Sir Your most obedient and most humble Servant, Cornwallis."[2] He was indeed humbled. Much of his army lay dead at his feet and the rest were mortally ill of disease.

George Washington sent his response: "An Ardent Desire to spare the further Effusion of Blood, will readily incline me to listen to such Terms for the surrender of your Posts and Garrisons of York and Gloucester are admissible. I wish previously to the Meeting of Commissioners, that your Lordship's proposals in writing may be sent to the American Lines: for which Purpose a suspension of Hostilities during two hours from the Delivery of this Letter will be granted."[3] Washington tightened the length of time to halt the fighting, giving Cornwallis only two hours to make up his mind. Washington did not care to wait an extended period for the British to decide to capitulate. What if Clinton's rescue fleet appeared overnight during the cease-fire? He was not willing to take that gamble.

The last few days in the endgame at Yorktown are worth noting. First, it had been exactly four years to the day, October 17, since a similar British surrender had taken place, that of General Burgoyne at Saratoga. Second, unbeknownst to the British as they proffered the white flag at the same moment the drummer boy emerged on the field above the York River, the long-awaited British fleet, commanded by Admiral Graves, was crossing the bar heading out of New York Harbor to rescue Cornwallis at Yorktown. Providential timing is reckoned best by hindsight.

Back on the battlefield, after a little less than two hours of silence, Lord Earl Cornwallis sent his reply.[4] He asked for full military protocol for his army. He also wanted them returned to England and to be placed on parole there.[5] He dared to request terms of special honor for the Gloucester garrison under command of Lieutenant Colonel Tarleton, permission to send a ship to New York with private property.[6] Cornwallis also requested immunity for the Tories and British deserters.[7] Washington said he would use these requests as a basis for beginning the negotiation. In the end, most of these terms proved unacceptable to both Rochambeau and Washington.

Plans for the formal negotiations were made at the nearby Moore House overlooking the York River. According to the National Park Service, which now owns the house, the modest frame edifice had once been a part of York Plantation on a site first claimed by Governor John Harvey in the 1630s and later known as the five-hundred-acre Temple Farm. Robert Smith was the owner until 1760 when he sold the acreage to his brother-in-law, Augustine Moore. The home is on the edge of the battlefield not far from the center of action. However, in 1781, when General Cornwallis settled into town with his army, many locals moved out of town in anticipation of the battle. It is believed that the Moores moved to Richmond for the time being to escape the coming siege.[8]

Unlike that of the Nelson House, which was Cornwallis's head-quarters, the beautiful lines of the well-kept Moore house emerged in perfect condition from the battle at Yorktown, but it was marred during the Civil War. The National Park Service later bought and restored the building.[9]

Four negotiators were chosen to write up the terms of surrender. The two British commissioners were Lieutenant Colonel Thomas Dundas and Major Alexander Ross, Cornwallis's aide. Representing the Americans was Lieutenant Colonel John Laurens, and on hand for the French was Second Colonel Vicomte de Noailles.[10] Negotiations continued until midnight when the draft of the Articles of Capitulation was ready. A staff officer then corrected and delivered the document to Washington and Rochambeau for approval.[11]

On the morning of October 19, General Washington read the articles and wrote "Granted" by ten items and penned "Disallowed" by four provisions. He gave no immunity to the Loyalist citizenry or to American deserters who had sided with the British. He "insisted that British civilian merchants were prisoners of war, and he required Cornwallis to care for his own sick and wounded."[12] After a few changes were made, the document was revised and a copy presented to Cornwallis.[13] The fourteen articles gave directions for the handling of British troops and arms and the plans for the actual surrender ceremony that would take place that afternoon. British soldiers became prisoners of war. After the ceremony, some were sent to Frederick, Maryland, and the rest to Winchester, Virginia, to be incarcerated. Under the existing rules of engagement the British officers were allowed a certain amount of leeway to either return directly to Europe or to remain in America promising not to continue to fight until they were exchanged.[14] The Articles required that the British care for their own sick and wounded.[15]

At the close of the negotiations, Laurens frisked the commissioners and confiscated the British army's wallet held by Major Alexander Ross, in which he found eighteen hundred pounds of sterling. Ross passed it off as a trifling sum, as did De Noailles. Laurens, however, expressed a different opinion. "A subject of one of the world's great monarchs may think eighteen hundred pounds inconsiderable," said Laurens, "but in our new country with its poor currency, this means a great deal indeed."[16] Every penny was precious to impoverished Americans.

And so it followed that at Yorktown the French and American allies turned the tables on the British, treating them as the Continentals had been treated in their recent defeat in Charleston. There was little time to haggle over the details as the final draft had to be signed before noon on October 19. Cornwallis had no choice but to agree to the terms set before him. Near eleven o'clock on the morning of October 19 the Articles of Capitulation were signed, as they say, "in the trenches."[17]

During the negotiations for the final Articles of Capitulation the British army wasted no time. They destroyed as much of their armaments and supplies as possible. They scuttled their own ship, the *Guadeloupe,* by opening the seacocks and letting her sink slowly to the bottom of the York River. They hauled the H.M.S. *Fowey* close to the shore, drilled holes in her hull, and sent her to a similar watery grave. French cannon fire had already burned the *Charon,* which at the end of the battle was a skeleton of a ship near shore.[18]

In contrast to the previous days and nights of cannonades, the night of negotiations had been relatively quiet. A priest named St. George Tucker wrote to his wife of the beauty of the stillness. He wrote in a poetic tenor of the thousands of stars and countless meteors which illumined the clear sky that night and described how "the atmosphere afforded a pleasing resemblance to the bombs which had exhibited a noble firework the night before, but happily divested of all their horror."[19] Unfortunately, that same night the quiet was interrupted when a store of British ammunitions and gunpowder exploded, killing several of their own men.[20]

Barely three hours after the Articles of Capitulation were signed, the surrender ceremonies began. At two o'clock in the afternoon on October 19, the British filed out of Yorktown between the long columns of French and American armies. Across the York River at Gloucester, a mirror image ceremony was held, though on a much smaller scale.

The artist Louis-Nicholas van Blarenberghe (1716–1794) painted two pairs of gouaches, depicting *The Siege of Yorktown* and *The Surrender of Yorktown*. The first set was commissioned by King Louis XVI and hangs today at the Palace of Versailles. The second pair of paintings was a gift from the king expressly for General Rochambeau. *The Surrender of Yorktown* depicts the traditional Old World surrender ceremony with three lines of soldiers stretching from horizon to horizon—the French on one side, the Americans facing them on the other, and the vanquished British preparing to ground their arms in the center column—with the French and the British in their well-turned-out fancy dress uniforms. Of course, the American army was woefully lacking on this account, but they stood their ground clothed with pride.

Rochambeau's descendent Michel, Comte de Rochambeau, quoted Van Blarenberghe as saying that each of the hundreds of faces at the surrender was painted with an individual countenance. In fact, there was much emotion on the faces of the soldiers of the three countries as they turned out for the surrender. The French and Americans were pleased and proud. Some English were weeping; some were angry. It was clearly a red-letter, unabashed day of victory for the Continentals. Alexandre Berthier, who not only knew the details of the battle personally, but also was an accomplished draftsman, directly supervised van Blarenberghe's execution of the paintings.[21]

Regarding the surrender, George Washington would only accept terms similar to those forced on American General Lincoln at the fall of Charleston, South Carolina, May 1780. Specifically, the defeated Americans at Charleston had been made to march with their colors furled, a sign of defeat and humiliation. Their military band was required to play the tune of the victors.[22]

At Yorktown, the British, according to the Articles of Capitulation, walked somberly between the two allied columns. The vanquished troops marched with their flags furled or cased per surrender terms. They all carried their arms. The defeated were ordered, probably by Cornwallis, to march "eyes right," looking at the French column and ignoring their conquerors.[23] As they passed through the two lines, the British played a tune of their own choosing, "The World Turned Upside Down." This was a British nursery rhyme in the form of a march. "The last two lines of the song are, "'If summer were spring and the other way 'round then all the world would be upside down.'"[24] It probably would have been more appropriate had the British played an American tune. Lafayette was incensed by their disregard for courtesy to their captors and shouted "Jankey Dudle!" (Yankee Doodle) to the American band.[25]

The British soldiers then marched on to a specified location where each man stood before his conquerors in order to lay down his weapons. In effect he actually bowed before the French and American allies as they grounded their weapons. At the laying down of arms, one British soldier was seen crying, and one colonel touched his sword to his teeth before turning away with his hands covering his face.

CORNWALLIS AND HIS SWORD DEBACLE

Lord Earl Cornwallis, feigning illness, sent General Charles O'Hara as his deputy to the surrender. Did Cornwallis really suffer from dysentery so severe he was prevented from attending the ceremony of capitulation? O'Hara was instructed to hand over

Cornwallis's sword to General George Washington. As he neared the victors with the sword in hand, he mistook Rochambeau for Washington and gestured as if to surrender it to the French general, who in turn waved it over to Washington, who handed it off to his second-in-command, saying to General Lincoln, "Never from so good a hand."[26]

The above account is from the author Samuel F. Scott's perspective. He concentrated on the participation and evolution of the French army up to and including the Battle of Yorktown. Scott presents the sword surrender as a matter of fact, giving Cornwallis and his man, O'Hara, the benefit of the doubt. Even General Rochambeau in his memoirs gives no space to the handover of the sword, implying that, for him, it was unimportant. Rochambeau evidently did not feel it was a significant detail in the much larger event of the surrender itself to record for future generations.

Following is an entirely different version of the surrender of Cornwallis's sword as found in the book by Jean-Edmond Weelen titled *Rochambeau,* dating from 1930 and written in French. In addition, there is the account from Clermont Crèvecoeur, faithful diarist of the entire French expedition. The differences between these accounts and that of Scott stand out for the purpose of comparison and reveal how Weelen and Crèvecoeur fleshed out the fleeting but impressive scene of the passing over of the sword. They posit the real reasons for the way in which the sword was first handed to Rochambeau, then to the victorious General Washington.

Weelen theorizes that Cornwallis, *"fou de douleur,"* sick with grief, did not show up for the surrender, as he was too devastated with embarrassment to show his face.[27] He unwillingly shouldered the blame for the entire British nation in his defeat. In his stead, Cornwallis sent his second-in-command, General O'Hara, to surrender his sword at the ceremony of capitulation. O'Hara, who was escorted on horseback to the field by Mathieu Dumas, turned to him to ask which one was Rochambeau. He fully intended to surrender to the French general. Most likely, his commander Cornwallis, from his sickbed, had bade him give up his sword to Rochambeau. Dumas gave an innocent response, saying that the French general was on horseback on the traditional left at the head of the French army. Fully assured, O'Hara gave his horse a kick in the ribs to quicken his pace and headed toward General Rochambeau to present him with the conquered General Cornwallis's sword, though not as protocol dictated.

In giving up the defeated general's sword to the French general, Cornwallis was planning to bypass his longtime enemy, General Washington, for it was too painful to submit to him face to face. Thus, O'Hara was sent to do the dirty work. How degrading to General Washington for Cornwallis to send his second-in-command to surrender to the French and not to the Americans, whom they had been fighting for the last seven years.

In Crèvecoeur's version of the surrender, Dumas, who guessed what O'Hara was about to do, galloped over toward Rochambeau to place himself between Rochambeau and O'Hara in order to prevent the surrender of the sword to the wrong general.[28] Dumas noticed the signal that the British general was about to make an intended faux pas and a serious slight to the conquering general, Washington.

With a nod of his head toward the American commander in chief, Rochambeau graciously indicated that O'Hara should give the sword to Washington, who declared, "Never from so good a hand!"[29] He was referring to Rochambeau, not O'Hara. Not only was the British army late to the ceremony, but to add to the insult, the sword was being delivered by the second-in-command to Cornwallis, humiliating Washington. Washington clearly would only accept the sword from his long-time adversary, Cornwallis, and so directed O'Hara to his second-in-command, General Lincoln. Lincoln touched the sword as "a symbolic gesture of surrender received."[30] He then made it clear that O'Hara was to keep the sword.[31] The grand irony of this gesture was not lost on the principal players that day at the Yorktown surrender ceremony. For the American general Benjamin Lincoln, who received Cornwallis's sword, it was a moment of sweet revenge. Lincoln recalled May 12, 1780, when he was forced to surrender to the British after a devastating American defeat at Charleston. The surrender drama at Yorktown was played out in a matter of moments, but the interpersonal dynamics were enormous.

Still another viewpoint of the surrender is found in the narrative left by the American soldier Joseph Plumb Martin. In his words, "We waited with anxiety the termination of the armistice, and as the time drew nearer our anxiety increased… After breakfast, on the nineteenth, we marched on to the ground and paraded on the right hand side of the road and the French forces on the left. We waited two or three hours before the British made their appearance;…with bayonets fixed, drums beating, and faces lengthening; they were led by Gen. O'Hara, with the American Gen. Lincoln on his right… they [the British] eyed the French with considerable malice."[32] The handover is not mentioned, probably because Martin, a member of the sappers and miners, was too far removed from the center of action.

Blanchard remarked that the surrender was a most sad occasion for the British. Unable to be present himself at the grand surrender due to his pressing duties at the hospital, Blanchard learned secondhand that "Cornwallis said that he was sick…The general who commanded in his stead wished to give up his sword to M. de Rochambeau, but he made a sign to him that he ought to address himself to General Washington.[33]

SURRENDER AT GLOUCESTER

Once again, the Duc de Lauzun and his foreign volunteers were separated from the main body of the army who held their grand, official surrender at Yorktown. On the Gloucester Peninsula, Lauzun and Tarleton were set to meet at 3 p.m. on October 19 at their separate surrender. However, as if by design, the British Commander Tarleton, like Cornwallis, was absent from the ceremony. Tarleton had been fearful for his life leading up to the surrender so he appealed to Rochambeau for his protection. He asked Rochambeau to let him remain within the confines of the tiny town of Gloucester behind his beaten troops. "Though Rochambeau considered Tarleton a butcher and barbarian without merit as an officer, permission was granted."[34] The ceremony was carried out with 1,000 British, Scots, Welsh, Hessians, and North Carolina Loyalists all grounding their arms before the Duc de Lauzun, 100 of his legion, and 200 men of the Virginia militia. The losers were of very poor demeanor.[35]

After the surrender as on the opposite shore, the British and French officers met for their usual courtesy toasts. The British gave their remaining swords and other equipment to the French rather than handing over anything of value to the victorious Americans. Relations became tense in the days following the battle as old jealousies were vented.

The total casualties were as follows: the British lost 552 soldiers during the Battle of Yorktown and had over 2,000 sick and wounded in the Williamsburg Hospital; the French lost 253; and the Americans lost 130, not including the militia.[36]

Crèvecoeur and Verger related different casualty numbers and tallies for conquered supplies.[37] As bad as it was under fire on the battlefield, "fewer than a thousand men were killed or wounded," while the ravages of disease and illness were punishing to the soldiers on both sides.[38] Today, historians agree that "eight times the number of Americans died of depravation and disease in the Revolutionary War as did in combat."[39] Though these numbers seem large as stated, in comparison to other turning-point battles, they were few.

On the afternoon of October 19 the French and American armies took possession of the British position. General Rochambeau and George Washington, his commander in chief, were victorious. Cornwallis was defeated in a major, decisive battle at Yorktown, virtually ending the American Revolution.

CHIVALROUS MEETING OF OPPOSITES

Commissary Blanchard wrote that after the surrender ceremonies were over, Rochambeau paid a visit of grateful thanks to Admiral de Grasse aboard the *Ville de Paris*. It was not quite a month since his last visit with De Grasse, and since the admiral did not think it prudent to leave his ship to attend the surrender ceremonies, the generals came to him once again. This time Rochambeau came to express his grateful thanks for De Grasse's indispensable assistance and timely cooperation in bringing about the desired result in the Yorktown battle.[40]

In keeping with the times, the officers were chivalrous in their protocol after the battle, whether winners or losers. For instance, General Rochambeau visited Lord Cornwallis shortly after the surrender, and Rochambeau made a generous loan of 150,000 livres to help cover the expense of the return home for Cornwallis and his officers.[41] This loan was later repaid in good faith.[42] Apparently this good-faith loan was eschewed in American circles since they themselves were so needy after the battle and did not feel so kindly toward the losers. According to Jacques Bossière, Ph.D., Washington-Rochambeau Revolutionary Route (W3R) founder, there was an interesting epilogue to this meeting between the victor and the vanquished. Lord Cornwallis eventually made his way north to embark for England. He made a stop in Vermont to purchase a wheel of fine cheese for General Rochambeau as a thank-you gift for the latter's generosity.[43]

George Washington invited the vanquished leader for dinner, but the latter sent his regrets. However, Cornwallis did accept an invitation from Vioménil. Blanchard declined Vioménil's invitation because he had received one from the Chevalier de Chastellux. The French were a gregarious lot, and they had much to celebrate! Moreover, it was in keeping with the practice of the old regime in Europe for officers of both sides, since they were generally acquainted, to hash over the siege together after the surrender was signed.

On October 21 Commissary Blanchard, who during the battle had been stationed in Williamsburg near the hospital with the sick and wounded, wrote, "I went to see the city of York. I visited our works and those of the English; I perceived the effect of our bombs and balls. I made this visit with M. de Vioménil, who had been to see Cornwallis, who had not yet appeared;...I regretted that I could not be present at this first meeting of Cornwallis with the French and American generals. He...praised our troops, especially the artillery, which he said was the first in Europe."[44]

NEWS OF GLORIOUS VICTORY SENT TO PARIS

Soon after the surrender, on October 24th and 26th respectively, Rochambeau dispatched Duc de Lauzun on the frigate *Surveillante* and Comte Guillaume de Deux-Ponts on the *Andromaque* carrying duplicate messages to the French court to announce to King Louis XVI that his general, Rochambeau, had been victorious.[45] These envoys were not chosen at random. Rochambeau selected Lauzun for his excellence in the battle at Gloucester against Tarleton; Deux-Ponts was chosen for his successful performance in storming British redoubt 9. Both had discharged their duties heroically.[46] This *Andromaque* encountered the British at sea and had to return to port. It left again on November 1. Both ships later did succeed in relaying the message to the king, who proclaimed that a *Te Deum* be celebrated and sung all over France on the same day to thank God for his and Rochambeau's success.[47]

Lauzun was the first to reach Paris with the splendid news of the victory after the historic battle. When Deux-Ponts arrived a few weeks later, Parisians were eager to hear his stories of Rochambeau's six-hundred-mile march to victory, the massing of troops, French and American, in Virginia, and the success of Rochambeau, Washington, and De Grasse's combined siege of Yorktown by land and by sea. The British were finally defeated in the New World. Lauzun and Deux-Ponts carried with them stories of the march to Virginia and were bombarded with questions from the French people regarding life in America. Their stories piqued the interest of Parisian society.

Not long after the surrender of the British in America, King George III of England penned a letter, which began with one short statement of anguish followed by a rhetorical question, "America is lost! Must we fall beneath the blow?" No date is given, and no addressee is mentioned.[48] Surely the king must have seen defeat bearing down on his thirteen colonies. Some years after the defeat King George had to face another debilitating battle—that of mental illness.

Two months after the surrender at Yorktown, Caron du Chanset wrote a poem titled *La Double Victoire (The Double Victory)*. Shortly thereafter it was in the hands of Parisians. Addressed to Madame la Comtesse de Rochambeau, his words glorified the victory by land and sea, thus the reference to the double victory. The nineteen-page poem praises and glorifies the strength of France, naming the accomplishments of the major participants in the campaign, from George Washington and Rochambeau to Cornwallis. It closes with thanks to God for the birth of the Dauphin, son of Louis XVI, whose cradle, according to Chanset, was lined with the laurels and palms of the glorious war.[49] An excerpt from the poem gives a vivid description of the swift twenty-two-day voyage of Lauzun back to France:

D'un cours impétueux & semblable à l'éclair,
Il part, l'onde en mugit & son vaisseau fend l'air.[50]

[On a hurried course, much like a bolt of lightning, He left, waves booming and his vessel fairly slicing through the air.][51]

On October 29 the United States Congress at Philadelphia issued a resolution addressed to General Rochambeau, stating, "Resolved,...That the thanks of the United States, in Congress assembled be presented to his excellency, the count de Rochambeau, for the cordiality, zeal, judgment and fortitude, with which he seconded and advanced the progress of the allied army against the British garrison in York [and Gloucester]: That the thanks…be presented to his excellency the count de Grasse for his display of skill and bravery in attacking and defeating the British fleet off the Bay of Chesapeake, and for his zeal and alacrity in rendering, with the fleet under his command, the most effectual and distinguished aid and support to the operations of the allied army in Virginia."[52] Included in this auspicious document of praise to the French was an offer of two commemorative cannon to be inscribed and shipped to both the general and the admiral in France as a token of American gratitude. The Congress promised to build a monument at Yorktown, which is described later in this book.

There are follow-up tales regarding the gift of the cannon. As for the ones sent to Rochambeau, Michel, Count de Rochambeau exclaimed that they were graciously received and installed at the Château de Rochambeau where they stood guard over the premises until the French Revolution. They were considered a symbol of what the revolutionaries deemed excessive expenditure and an unhappy reminder of funds paid out from an already threadbare French trea- sury by King Louis XVI. Madame de Rochambeau, in her husband's absence (he was imprisoned at the Conciergerie in Paris at the time), tried to placate the revolutionaries by donating the two cannon from Yorktown to their cause. The cannon were carted off to Vendôme and never seen again. Many years later, under the restoration of King Louis XVIII, another smaller pair was sent to Madame la Comtesse de Rochambeau.[53]

On the other hand, there was also a problem with the two cannon sent by the United States Congress as a special gift to De Grasse "from consideration of the illustrious part he bore in effec- tuating the surrender."[54] The Americans who sent them discovered after the fact that the pair of cannon sent were not seized from the British at the Battle of Yorktown after all, but substitutes sent in error. In reparation for the mistake, Congress sent De Grasse two more cannon that were confirmed as authentic. Each piece was engraved as original to the Battle of Yorktown.[55]

Following the military siege, another battle arose, that of fighting off sickness and disease, hunger and deprivation. Crèvecoeur observed that the excessive fatigue to which the army had been subject, as well as the bad food, caused a great deal of illness among the troops: "We were short of nearly everything. Many officers also paid their toll in the form of serious illnesses. We lost many from bloody flux."[56] Beyond all that, many of the soldiers complained that they, namely Choisy's men at Gloucester, had few of the bare necessities following the siege. Virginia was an already ravaged and depleted area before the armies converged on Yorktown and Williamsburg. It stood to reason that conditions would worsen in the aftermath of the battle.

The English had many of the same complaints. The slaves that they requisitioned as workers were infected with the plague, which spread in Yorktown. It was rumored that the British sent these infected men into the allied camp. "These miserable creatures could be found in every corner, either dead or dying. No one took the trouble to bury them, so you can imagine the infection this must have engendered."[57] Amazingly, some survived. Many of the slaves who wandered away had been freed and were eventually hired as servants by the French at bargain rates or reclaimed by locals.

Abbé Robin, the French priest who had accompanied Rochambeau on the expedition, visited the battlefield to view the extent of the devastation. He saw rubble, books, broken furniture, and corpses of horses and men scattered in the sandy streets of the village. Abbé Robin passed by the moss-covered Church of England and its small graveyard, lamenting the death of so many near this sanctuary in the small town in Virginia where world history was made on October 19, 1781.[58]

ROCHAMBEAU AND FRENCH ARMY
WINTER IN WILLIAMSBURG

After the dispersion of the Americans and British, Rochambeau and the French soldiers stayed behind in Yorktown and Gloucester to dismantle the earthworks.[59] They also razed the earthworks that Benedict Arnold had built around Portsmouth, Virginia. Between November 15 and 19, having accomplished the major goal of the *expédition particulière,* the French army settled into their winter quarters in Williamsburg. Lauzun's Legion camped at Charlotte Courthouse in support of General Greene. They remained in Virginia to insure there would be no further skirmishes in the southern theatre. As a further precaution, the French left the *Romulus* and two frigates at the mouth of the Chesapeake to guard against British activity by water in or out of the James and York Rivers.[60]

Washington had moved most of the American regulars back to New York to protect West Point and to await the signing of the final treaty officially terminating the war. General Wayne and most of his men headed south. For the most part, the militia returned home. The French escorted the British and Hessian prisoners west to prison camps in Winchester and Frederick, while Cornwallis and his officers were given safe passage to New York. The seriously wounded French and Americans were hospitalized in Williamsburg, the former at the College of William and Mary and the latter at the Governor's Palace.[61]

Rochambeau knew that the American general still contemplated the possibility of marching on Quebec. However, for the time being, the allies held everything at status quo. During the ensuing year in Virginia, Rochambeau, his staff, and part of his army, consisting of seven companies of the Royal Deux-Ponts and the Bourbonnais regiments, were quartered in Williamsburg. Although there were certainly times when the military suffered boredom from the monotony of garrison duty, the Williamsburg fall social season managed to resume in full swing with its primary goal to entertain the French visitors.[62]

With Williamsburg no longer the center of Virginia since the capital had been moved to Richmond in 1780, the town welcomed the French victors into their hearts and homes. Closen described the town as having been damaged by the British occupation. He saw "very few horses since all the wealthy citizens had sent them to the interior" to keep them from Cornwallis.[63] As seen through Closen's eyes, the college, the capitol, and the Governor's Palace were in very bad condition.[64] In spite of the disarray, the French were treated to hunts, balls, banquets, and plays. They enjoyed all manner of gaming, and were taken fishing, crabbing, and boating. The dinners often featured a main course of Virginia smoked ham, which was much appreciated by the French palate. Rochambeau and his men enjoyed Virginian hospitality to the fullest.

On November 23 the festivities were dampened when a fire broke out in the college president's house. The French officers escaped unhurt. Rochambeau very graciously asked King Louis to send funds to cover repairs.[65] On a happier note, December 15 was declared a day of celebration for the Victory at Yorktown. Rochambeau arranged for a *Te Deum* mass to be sung in Williamsburg.[66]

Unfortunately, on December 23, another fire, this time probably set deliberately, destroyed the Governor's Palace. Over one hundred sick and wounded soldiers escaped unhurt. One died in the flames. Rochambeau wrote to Washington, "We saved all the sick, most of the effects, and prevented the fire from spreading to the neighboring houses, notably my [headquarters] which is the first of those occupied by your Excellency and which was covered all night with a rain of fire. We have fathered [sheltered] all our sick in the Capitol and this day I have given them all the help in my power."[67]

That winter Rochambeau took advantage of the peace and quiet to make a tour of the state of Virginia. In fact, in February Rochambeau visited former Governor Nelson who offered the French general an evening's entertainment in the form of a cockfight. Afterward he went on to visit Senator Jefferson's well-appointed home. Rochambeau continued on his tour through what he called the *"Jardin de la Virginie,"* stopping at Richmond, the capital, and then moving on to Cape Henry, which overlooks the opposite side of Chesapeake Bay from Yorktown.[68]

Later that winter of 1782, Rochambeau, ever mindful of his fatherly duties towards his men, took some measures to counteract the winter doldrums. To brighten their dull evenings during that particularly harsh winter, he arranged for some soirées and invited some of the ladies of the local area. One of these ladies was the charming descendant of the Indian princess, Pocahontas, whose allure was her Indian heritage.[69] These social evenings were reminiscent of the ones that Papa Rochambeau presided over at Newport the year before.

In spite of the decisive battle at Yorktown, the winter and spring of 1782 were fraught with the winds of war. Unsettling news fluttered back and forth from the West Indies to Versailles to Rochambeau and Washington with fear that the British would launch another attack rather than come to the peace table. British troops strengthened in America and still numbered close to thirty thousand, a significant cause for concern for the allied commanders.

After capturing St. Kitts and Montserrat, the French fleet did not fare well in the Caribbean, and the British fleet was gaining strength once more. De Grasse was defeated and taken as prisoner back to England. Not good news for the allies. The remainder of De Grasse's fleet sailed to Boston in case the British retaliated with an attack in the north.

Funds were low for the French during this period of supposed recuperation. To make matters worse, the summer of 1782 brought oppressive heat, and the French suffered throughout the ranks, from high-ranking generals down to the foot soldiers. Washington and Rochambeau did their best to anticipate British movements.[70] According to Robert D. Harris's *French Finances,* "French expenditures for the war for the years 1776–1782 were set at 928.9 million livres (as opposed to 2,270.5 million livres for the British), with another 125.2 million to be added for the year 1783."[71] De Grasse had brought 1.2 million just before the battle at Yorktown. This amounted to "over 1% of the total cost of the war as well as outright subsidies about 9 million."[72] About 48 million livres were doled out to aid the American rebels.[73] King Louis XVI calculated that this was far more cost effective than invading England as he had originally planned, and it led to a re-balancing of world powers and world trade, which proved to be advantageous to the French. Freedom isn't free after all.

BRITISH QUIT NEW YORK—
ROCHAMBEAU QUITS WILLIAMSBURG

By June 9, 1782, Rochambeau received news that the British were quitting New York. From Williamsburg he wrote in his diary, "The moment I received this news I decided to march the Army North, to unite my forces with General Washington and menace the place [New York]."[74] By July 11 the French had packed up and moved out of Williamsburg to retrace their steps northward.

When departing Williamsburg on June 23, 1782, Rochambeau said, "I cannot, gentlemen, but be pleased with the circumstances which have enabled me to form with you an intimate connection, a connection wholly independent of the Great Objects of the war and of public affairs. During the time I have spent with you I have enjoyed those social qualities by which the inhabitants of this great and flourishing country are so eminently distinguished."[75]

Baron von Closen and the Comte de Custine spent a few days on the march north at Mount Vernon. They enjoyed the gracious hospitality of Mrs. Washington, the beauty of the grand house, and the fruits of the abundant gardens. A certain Captain de Bellegarde presented Mrs. Washington with a fine set of porcelain on behalf of Custine, from his own factory near Phalsbourg, France. A large bowl was donated to the National Gallery in Washington.[76] Apparently the captain found Martha Washington's recently widowed daughter-in-law quite fetching and stayed on an extra day to enjoy her company. In remembrance of the visit he cut a silhouette of the charming Mrs. Custis and pressed it in his journal.[77]

The French army moved north through the scorching summer heat. In Philadelphia, they made a memorable stopover. There, Rochambeau represented himself before Congress as "the first soldier in the army of General Washington."[78] He continued by declaring that he and his troops could be "counted upon in life and death as brothers and best friends."[79] A huge victory ball on July 15, 1782, punctuated their visit. It was given to celebrate two events of historic importance: first, the winning of the War of Independence, and second, the birth of the Dauphin of France, the first-born son of King Louis XVI and Marie Antoinette. His birth had been awaited for a decade. The war against the British had lasted almost that long as well. Both were excellent in outcome and therefore more than adequate reasons to trip the light fantastic on the dance floor of the pavilion built for the occasion in the garden of the French legation of Chevalier de La Luzerne.[80]

La Luzerne distributed one thousand tickets to the ball, giving "forty each to the governors of the states for officials, and forty to Washington for his ranking officers, and the members of his staff and 'family.'"[81] "Quaker ladies whose conservatism prevented them from being comfortable enough to join the assembly were indulged with a sight of the company through a gauze curtain."[82] This was an example of how the French minister did his utmost to make everyone comfortable at the celebration. The evening began with dancing at eight-thirty followed by fireworks galore to regale the invitees.[83] At midnight, a luxurious candlelight dinner was offered under three huge tents joined together as one. Despite the levity of the evening, the French and American generals found time to talk over their next military move.[84] The many toasts included those addressed to our "Generous Ally, His Most Christian Majesty, the King of France...the King of Spain...the States General of The Netherlands," all for their assistance in the war. The last of the jubilant guests retired by three in the morning.[85]

Rochambeau remembered that all along the army's route from Virginia to Boston, he and his men received the grateful thanks of the American people whose rights he helped to preserve. At length, General Rochambeau united his troops with those of Washington once again near New York. "The general [Washington], as a mark of respect to France, and of gratitude for the services she had rendered America, made us march through a double row of his troops, and, for the first time since the Revolution, equipped and armed and clad with arms and clothes, brought partly from France, and partially acquired from the British storehouses taken from Cornwallis and which the French generously gave up to the American army."[86] The military review was accompanied by a French tune and looks of mutual satisfaction throughout the ranks.

Just prior to leaving for Boston, Rochambeau related in his memoirs that a sheriff's officer approached, thanking him for the services he rendered "but that it was his duty to take me prisoner." Rochambeau answered in jest, "Very well...but take me if you can."[87] It is not clear why the officer proclaimed it his duty to arrest Rochambeau, but of course that was an impossibility, as Rochambeau was surrounded by his four thousand armed men.

Upon departure of the French, on December 14, 1782, General George Washington wrote this fond farewell to his French allied commander with whom he had worked for two and a half years: "I cannot permit you, my dear General, to leave this country without again expressing to you the high appreciation I feel for the services you have rendered America—by the close attention you have always shown in her interests, by the order and discipline you have invariably maintained in the army corps under your command, and by your promptness on every occasion to facilitate the joint operations of the combined armies. In addition [to] this testimony I give to your public character and conduct, I would not be true to the sentiments of my heart did I not express to you the happiness which has come to me through our personal friendship, the memory of which will always remain one of the most agreeable of my life."[88]

The French army, led by General Vioménil, reached Boston, their final destination in America. By November 1782 four thousand officers and men began loading onto ships under the command of Admiral Vaudreuil to depart for the West Indies and eventually sail home to France. On December 24 Vaudreuil put to sea, taking with him the only foreign army to set foot on American soil that ever "campaigned in their country on their behalf."[89] According to Rochambeau's memoirs, "The army embarked at length... carrying with it the universal blessings of our allies of the thirteen states without exception."[90] General Rochambeau then returned to Maryland to prepare for his own departure from American shores.

Rochambeau took his leave after a job well done and sailed from Annapolis, Maryland, on January 29, 1783, on the *Emeraude*.[91] The bare minimum of administrative services and Lauzun's Legion remained in Maryland to protect the heavy siege artillery and stores until all danger of attack was past.[92] Lauzun had returned from Paris to resume leadership of his legion in America. His surveillance completed, Lauzun left America on May 11, 1783, with the remainder of his legion—about 530 loyal soldiers and officers. They set sail for the French port of Brest, which they reached on June 11, 1783.

Thus concluded the remarkable campaign of a capable and compassionate French general sent by a generous French monarch to save America from the rule of a tyrannical English monarch. The final peace treaty between the British and the Americans was signed in Paris and Versailles on September 3, 1783, officially ending the American War of Independence. By November that year the remaining British troops sailed from America.[93]

The French *éxpédition particulière* crossed approximately three thousand miles of Atlantic Ocean, marched over two hundred miles from Newport to New York, then resumed their overland trek to Yorktown covering another four hundred miles. They traversed nine of the thirteen colonies, established two winter camps, the first in the winter of 1780–81 in Connecticut and Rhode Island, and the other, the following winter, in Virginia. Then they re-traced their steps a year later to embark on ships once again, this time to quit American shores with mission accomplished. Along the route, they touched virtually all Americans in the colonies in one way or another. The French hard currency was a boost to the local economy from Newport to Yorktown. Many preconceived prejudices against Catholics and French were eclipsed by the generosity, fine discipline, and good manners of the visiting French army. Prior to their arrival in America in July 1780 France had been considered more of an enemy than a friend because of the French and Indian War. A Virginia militia colonel wrote on October 26, 1781, "The French are very different from the ideas formerly inculcated in us of a people living on frogs and coarse vegetables. Finer troops I never saw."[94]

Following the Battle of Yorktown, Rochambeau, the Frenchman on whom the Americans relied for victory, was honored everywhere he went. He appeared in their darkest hour, and "he came to the rescue like a hero in an old-fashioned melodrama."[95] Because of his sound military strategy, America was released from the British to live in freedom.

A poem by John Greenleaf Whittier aptly describes the victory:

> From Yorktown ruins, ranked and still,
> Two lines stretch far o'er vale and hill;
> Who curbs his steed at the head of one?
> Hark! the low murmur: Washington!
> Who bends his keen approving glance
> Where down the gorgeous line of France
> Shine knightly star and plume of snow?
> Thou too art victor Rochambeau![96]

The special delivery of French soldiers and specie from France to America, led by General Rochambeau, arrived at the moment of George Washington's greatest need in the midst of America's Revolution and returned to France having completed its mission to aid in the freeing of the American rebels from the British yoke of domination. No, Rochambeau was not a lieutenant per se, but a lieutenant general. Nonetheless, following orders from King Louis XVI,

Rochambeau rendered himself subservient to Washington who was his commander in chief while serving in America.

Rochambeau, older and more experienced as a military leader than his commander, served as Washington's lieutenant in the truest sense of the word. This fact was further established in the account of Rochambeau's aides-de-camp who complimented their leader's facility in interfacing with their chief by referring to him as Washington's ideal lieutenant. Although Rochambeau's suggestion to take the fight to the lesser force in Virginia was not readily accepted, he waited patiently for events to evolve in the allies' favor, tendered advice when expedient, followed orders when issued, and prudently suppressed the take-charge attitude of most generals in deference to Washington. Rochambeau proved himself to be a successful lieutenant, serving his general well, so well in fact that he and Washington were able to beat the odds and scuttle Cornwallis, Clinton, Graves, Hood, Tarleton, and King George III. Although Rochambeau held the title of general, he deftly served as Washington's faithful, obedient, and effective lieutenant until the close of the American Revolution.

CHAPTER TWELVE

Honors, Revolution, and Memorials

"He is no more, this Nestor of the worries of our age;
He was in life an emulator once of Washington
By all that he has done; And by his virtues, Sage."

—LARDIER, FRIEND OF ROCHAMBEAU

ROCHAMBEAU ARRIVED IN FRANCE on February 20, 1783. He went directly to Versailles. King Louis XVI received him with accolades for his victory over Cornwallis and the British at Yorktown. The king soon rewarded Rochambeau with the *Cordon Bleu* of the Order of the Saint Esprit.[1] For this the aging general was greatly pleased. Rochambeau was not hailed in the streets of Paris as Lafayette had been upon his arrival in the capital city. But he was not the kind of man to complain or to feel slighted. On the contrary, he was a man who felt comfortable in his own skin. Knowing he had the respect of his officers and men mattered most to him. Lauzun and some of Rochambeau's officers who had participated in the *expédition particulière* were given promotions and bonuses.[2]

For exemplary service in America the king also gave Rochambeau a bonus and assigned him a prestigious military posting in Calais, impressive for any general. Rochambeau would hold sway over three provinces in the northwest of France: Flanders, Picardy, and Artois—names that would take on great significance in World War I. The king granted him a year's grace before taking up his post.

Rochambeau, like Washington, returned to his family and his farm for a welcome period of rest.[3]

In the following year Rochambeau spent time with his family, recuperated his health, and took care of business at his homes in Paris and in Vendôme. He took time to travel abroad to London and to Portsmouth, England, where he visited the port and the fortifications. He was received by Admiral Hood as an old friend. Two men who had fought on opposing sides of the American Revolution could afford to let down their defenses.[4] Rochambeau served four years in Calais during which time he maintained constant contact with George Washington through the many letters they sent each other. Rochambeau wrote these missives in his best English.

THE SOCIETY OF THE CINCINNATI

In early 1784 Rochambeau traveled to Paris for his installation as a member of the Société des Cincinnati de France. The American society had been formed on May 10, 1783; membership was offered to officers who had fought in the Continental army and the French army and navy in the War of Independence in America. Many details had to be worked out before the induction ceremonies could be held in both countries. Regarding the induction, it was the first time in France's history that a foreign order was to be bestowed on her soil. In this case King Louis XVI had made a quick decision on December 18, 1783, to allow his subjects to become members of the society in order to strengthen ties between France and America. "His Most Christian Majesty," wrote Minister of War Ségur to Rochambeau, "directs me to inform you that he consents to your acceptance of this honorable invitation. He wishes you also, on his behalf, to assure His Excellency, George Washington, that he will always regard with extreme satisfaction everything which may tend to maintain and strengthen ties formed between France and the United States. The successes which have resulted from this union and the glory which has been the fruit of it has shown its advantages. You may therefore inform the general officers and colonels who served in the Army which you commanded, that the King permits them to join the Association of the Cincinnati."[5]

Membership was to be carried on by primogeniture, the right of inheritance passed from father to eldest son, a practice that some of the original invitees and others, not invited, found objectionable. They felt that the rules were too close to the former standards practiced under the ancien régime, which, after the Revolution, were outmoded in America and seemed to resemble the hierarchical traditions of the feudal system still practiced in England and France. These two obstacles were overcome.

In the beginning, French army and naval officers along with American army officers were invited to join the society. Of that number, 2,150 accepted the offer, about two hundred of which were French. Today there are thirteen individual societies in the United States and one in France that are active. The group as a whole is referred to as the Cincinnati Fourteen, taken from the thirteen original American colonies with the fourteenth being France. Their headquarters in America is the Anderson House in Washington, D. C. Its library and museum are open to the public, and a concert series is offered. Society members and their families may reserve rooms in a private area of (what was) the large former home of the Andersons.[6]

Major General Henry Knox is credited with having had the first idea for the creation of the Society in 1776. He longed for a symbol, a medal he could wear on his hat or on his lapel that would remind him and future generations of their having fought for the cause of liberty in the American Revolution. The founders chose the Roman senator Lucius Quintius Cincinnatus as the inspiration for the new society and its medal. Cincinnatus, who lived 2,200 years before, reminded them of George Washington who, like Cincinnatus, left his plow to pick up the sword and serve his country. And then, after throwing off a dictator, Cincinnatus returned to his plow in peace.

Pierre-Charles L'Enfant drew the design of the eagle medal made of gold, precious metals, and painted enamel. Depicted on both sides of the enamel are scenes of Cincinnatus giving up his plow for the sword and vice versa. An eagle surrounds the images. The medal hangs from a blue and white ribbon with a pin to be mounted on a lapel or hung around the neck. The blue represents America, while the white stands for the royalty of the king of France. Together they symbolize the friendship between America and France. A unique diamond eagle pin was made for George Washington who would be the first president general of the Society. This pin is stunning, studded with diamonds, rubies, and emeralds set in gold around the eagle and with a replica of the enamel painting of Cincinnatus on both sides like the unadorned eagle medal given to the full membership. Washington's diamond eagle is passed from president general to president general in perpetuity. At the beginning of the twenty-first century the American society counts about three thousand members.[7]

On the day of the first investiture, January 7, 1784, Rochambeau opened his house in Paris on Rue du Cherche-Midi to the French officers who had marched with him in the *expédition particulière* in America. These included Lauzun and Chastellux. On the same day, Lafayette hosted the French officers who had marched with Washington, including L'Enfant and Duportail. Admiral d'Estaing also hosted the naval officers prior to the formalities. Afterward they convened at the Rochambeau residence for the formal ceremony of the pinning on of the medals.[8] Two hundred sixteen years later, the French Society has four hundred members. Rochambeau was honored to be asked by the king to distribute the gold medals to the original members in France. The American Society of the Cincinnati would meet for their initial gathering in Philadelphia on May 11, 1784.

It was not long before the Société des Cincinnati de France, whose membership consisted of aristocrats (military officers of the eighteenth century were normally a part of the aristocracy), was dispersed by the revolutionaries during the French Revolution that erupted in 1789. As a result, the once prestigious Société des Cincinnati de France, which had espoused the cause of liberty, ceased to exist. The members of the society went into hiding or were imprisoned. The Order of the Society of the Cincinnati was discontinued in France due to the danger facing anyone who admitted to membership. It was not re-instituted until 1923.[9]

THE FRENCH REVOLUTION INTERFERES

Unfortunately France came under hard times as the French Revolution fomented and broke out into chaos. But in 1789 Rochambeau was sent by the king to a place of relative safety to be governor of Alsace. There he quelled the roiling situation with a heavy military hand.[10] In early 1791 Rochambeau was offered the position of minister of war, which he refused.[11] However, on December 28, 1791, King Louis XVI, in his final months of power, conferred on Rochambeau, age sixty-seven, the coveted title of Maréchal de France, the highest nonmilitary honor awarded in the kingdom. It is granted to generals for their exceptional achievements on the battlefield. The maréchal wears seven gold fleurs-de-lis on a midnight-blue ground; he also carries a baton decorated in the same manner. Thereafter, according to Michel de Rochambeau, his ancestor was no longer called general, but maréchal.

His son Donatien, still active in the army, was made lieutenant general. The younger Rochambeau became known thereafter as General Rochambeau. He was twice made governor-general of Saint-Domingue. Later he was forced to leave the West Indies when the blacks there took over and gained their independence. On his way out of Cap Français he was captured by the British and taken to England where he remained for seven years. While he was waiting to be exchanged, his wife eventually was allowed to join him, as was often the case in those days. That left their three children, Augustine, Thérèse-Constance, and Philippe de Vimeur, in the care of their grandparents, the maréchal and Jeanne-Thérèse. Apparently it was an agreeable arrangement. While their father remained incarcerated in England, the children were raised by doting grandparents. In time

Jeanne-Thérèse found suitable husbands for the girls, and provided their dowries. Philippe entered artillery school in Strasbourg.[12] Donatien had spent precious little time, if any, at home after his return from the America. Although he was finally exchanged in 1811, he had been unable to be at his father's side when he died in 1807. Nonetheless, Donatien continued in the Rochambeau family tradition of warriors. He served in the French army under Napoleon from January 7, 1813, and died October 20 that year following a mortal wound at the Battle of Leipzig, Germany, at the age of sixty-three.

As the French Revolution grew more violent, Maréchal de Rochambeau could have emigrated with his family to Switzerland or another friendly country in Europe, but he chose not to do so. In 1792 the king assigned him to the command of the 60,000-man army of the north. At sixty-seven his health was simply not up to the strain. He returned home to Vendôme.[13] By 1794, after managing to stay below the radar of the post-Revolution French authorities, he was called up to defend himself before Robespierre. Rochambeau, in spite of the fact that he had served under the revolutionaries and had remained loyal, was singled out for questioning. There was no denying it: he was, after all, an aristocrat.

During the Reign of Terror, Robespierre, compelled by his own revolutionary standards of eliminating the aristocracy and anyone who had served under King Louis XVI, sent four commissioners of the Committee of Public Safety to the Château de Rochambeau to arrest Rochambeau. Robespierre named him "the last marshal of France to be chosen by the last tyrant of France."[14] These were the words that described Rochambeau in the record books of the Paris Conciergerie prison. Robespierre's emissaries arrived at the Château de Rochambeau on the morning of April 4, 1794. The general was deemed to be an enemy of the state, although his captors found nothing incriminating in his personal papers. He quickly prepared his defense, but, like so many others falsely accused, was not given time to prepare a proper defense, nor was he given a fair trial. And, even though he carried a certificate verifying that he had several wounds from previous battles and that one in particular had to be left open to drain because of his recurring blood vomiting, they did not give him the special medical treatment he required. Further, the officials denied him the respect he deserved, knowing that his son Donatien had served the new republic in the West Indies.

ROCHAMBEAU IMPRISONED IN THE CONCIERGERIE

On April 21, 1794, Rochambeau was taken to the Conciergerie prison in Paris. At length Rochambeau, who was quite ill, finally received care for his wounds in the Archbishop's hospital, which undoubtedly gave him courage to face whatever lay ahead. There were a few occasions during his two-week hospital stay when, surprisingly, Rochambeau and twelve fellow prisoners shared precious moments of camaraderie. Despite the cramped quarters of two rooms, they were heartened to spend time together. It was a pleasant respite for them until the fifteenth day when the court bailiffs entered to make an announcement. They were bearing twelve writs of accusation, which Rochambeau saw as burial certificates. He heard the names called out one by one to the scaffold.[15]

When he did not hear his name, the aging Rochambeau, then somewhat hard of hearing and leaning on his walking stick, must have had a quizzical look on his face, not sure if his name had been called. The bailiff in charge said to Rochambeau, "You did not hear what I said when I came in, Marshal? There's nothing for you."[16] Two days later all twelve were executed with Madame Elisabeth, sister of Louis XVI, but Rochambeau was spared for the time being. He languished in prison for three months longer, ever in fear of being called to the guillotine. Daily he watched as friends and army comrades lost their lives to the lethal diagonal blade.

Ultimately he was brought before the Revolutionary Tribunal at which time judge De Liège could find no evidence against the aged marshal. Then followed a period during which Rochambeau hoped for his release. But, again, months passed and no word came. During this period, known as the Reign of Terror, Robespierre was increasingly cruel and swift in meting out punishment.

For some distraction from the distressing events happening around him, Rochambeau managed to focus on the writing of his memoirs. It is certain that prison conditions had improved under King Louis XVI. However, when Rochambeau was incarcerated, prisons had worsened considerably with the influx of thousands of poor souls during the French Revolution and the Terror that followed.

On July 28, 1794, there was a swift reversal of power as Robespierre was overthrown and immediately guillotined with his henchmen. Perceiving an opportunity to be released, Rochambeau sent many written appeals pleading that the judges would finally set him free. In his last appeal he wrote, "I cannot believe that in this era of equality a former aristocrat has no rights except to march to the scaffold before anybody else, and be the last man to be allowed to prove his innocence. Those are not the principles I learned from Washington my colleague and my friend when we were fighting side by side for American independence."[17] Some say that with these words he was set free.

However, the story the Rochambeau family tells of the maréchal's last days in the Conciergerie is slightly different. Michel de Rochambeau recounted that Rochambeau was still under the death sentence when his name came up for execution. He was summoned and stood waiting his turn to climb into the *charrette* (wooden cart), which carried the condemned to the Place de la Révolution where the guillotine stood (today's Place de la Concorde). Apparently he was standing in line beside a lady as the ill-fated ones waited their turn to step into the wagon. The gallant Rochambeau said to her: "After you, Madame," and he helped her into the cart. Just as Rochambeau began to step into the conveyance, the guard put his arm out in front of the general and said, "That is all for today; the *charrette* is full. You will have to come back tomorrow." The next day, October 24, 1794, the prisons were opened and the prisoners were released. The Reign of Terror was ended. Rochambeau had survived six months of incarceration, avoiding his death sentence by one step! On the day Rochambeau was freed he returned for the first time to his Paris home on Rue du Cherche-Midi. His house had been sealed and boarded up by Robespierre's Committee of Public Safety since the day of his arrest.[18]

LAST PEACEFUL DAYS ON HIS ESTATE

Later Rochambeau and Jeanne-Thérèse returned to Vendôme with his longtime army friend, Foulon D'Ecotais, who had been imprisoned with him. Both were freed by the same decree. For the maréchal, there would be no reunion with his son Donatien, who remained imprisoned in England until 1811. The aging marshal returned to Paris one last time in 1805 when Napoleon invited him to make the trip in order to receive the newly created Légion d'Honneur.

After his release from prison the last marshal of France and his wife spent thirteen more years together. Although he continued to suffer from his old wounds, respiratory problems, and increasing deafness, he found the strength to finish his memoirs at his desk surrounded by mementos of the American campaign. Because of his experience, his unfailing sense of duty, and his enduring patience, he had proven himself the ideal lieutenant to his commander, General Washington. Together they had led their combined land and sea forces to victory at Yorktown. Rochambeau, the French gentleman and general who did so much to bring freedom to Americans, slipped quietly away, succumbing to an early spring cold on May 12, 1807. He had been reading in his favorite armchair, where he watched the swans swimming peacefully in the Loir River.

Rochambeau's greatest contribution was the precise and capable way in which he carried out his orders from King Louis XVI and his ministers without flaw. He saw that the British were conquered and ousted from America. He worked very well under his new commander, George Washington, from July 1780 to January 1783 when peace was assured and America was free. He proved himself to be Washington's "ideal lieutenant" in every way, always deferring to his commander in chief, even though he may not have agreed with him all the time, even though he had more experience than Washington and had led more sieges than his younger commander. He kept strict discipline in his army for which he was well known and through diplomacy and patience the Americans welcomed him with open arms everywhere he went.

He should also be remembered for what he did not do. Rochambeau and his French army did not come to American shores to take over the country for the French crown, or to occupy it for their own purposes. Instead, King Louis XVI, America's first publicly declared friend since the signing of the French-American Alliance in 1778, sent one of his best generals to America to set her free and to assure her liberty.

The wide-ranging result of Rochambeau's American *expédition particulière* paved the way for a working model on which to build the kind of government suggested by the Magna Carta in England in 1215. This theory of government, born from the individual rights of man, would be by consent of the governed, with the power of government guaranteed by a written constitution. Although a powerful legacy, reaching back over five hundred years, it was not fully realized until the American Constitution was written and implemented. Rochambeau played a role in making it possible for this style of government to prevail.

In effect, Rochambeau and De Grasse, with their land and sea forces, did much to resolve a conflict spanning the Atlantic. Moreover, the outcome was long-lasting for the cause of freedom that is born in every man's soul. It is, therefore, fair to assume that because of France's assistance and Rochambeau's fruitful cooperation with his commander, George Washington, a wider world war was averted.

Many Americans who met or observed Rochambeau and his men commented that the French left a civilizing effect everywhere they went. This was evidenced in the responsible comportment of the French troops, the pride shown in maintaining an appropriate dress code, respect for American property, and their good manners, from officers to foot soldiers. In fact, Rochambeau's inspiring legacy to America is typified in the attributes of the general himself, as a devoted, steadfast leader who demonstrated the courage of his convictions, a strong sense of diplomacy and decorum, superb military prowess, and a deeply ingrained respect for authority.

Not to be overlooked, Rochambeau also bequeathed to Americans an appreciation of the sonorous French language. French was reinforced as the language of diplomacy for well over two hundred years following the American Revolution. Many Americans began their love affair with all things French at this time.

America owes a debt of gratitude to General Rochambeau for a reason not heretofore mentioned. In implementing the plan that steered the final battle of the American Revolution away from New York to the lesser force in Virginia, countless lives were saved while the desired outcome was achieved.

The overall result equaled that of two other great battles, which shifted the balance of world power, yet the Yorktown victory was won at much lower cost in human lives. First, during the American Civil War at the Battle of Gettysburg, Pennsylvania, July 1–3, 1863, some 51,000 men from both sides died. The Union won, and the country was united, thus restoring the pre-war balance of power around the northern Atlantic. Second, at the Battle of Waterloo in Belgium fought on June 18, 1815, French Emperor Napoleon was defeated by the English Duke of Wellington, with the total lost numbering about 52,000. Napoleon was halted in his effort to expand his empire. The British thwarted French dominance.

As for the Battle of Yorktown, Virginia, which ended on October 19, 1781, there were under 1,000 killed. America was no longer a British colony. The balance of power was redistributed among France, America, England, and Spain. The numbers speak for themselves. The results of all three battles were earthshaking in that the balance of power around the Atlantic was greatly affected. From a humanitarian point of view, the direct benefit of losing fewer soldiers on both sides at Yorktown than would have been the case in either a frontal attack on England or on the British seat of command in New York is one of Rochambeau's most stunning contributions.

MEMORIALS

In the 1990s, a movement began as an example of Franco-American cooperation, in memory of Rochambeau's role in America's War of Independence, to commemorate his "March to Victory" as the "Washington-Rochambeau Revolutionary Route" (W3R). This national historic trail, signed into law on March 30, 2009, serves as a reminder of how two great generals and two great countries marched side by side to establish America as a free and independent country. All the historic sites along the W3R have been documented to include the army campsites en route to Yorktown in 1781 and back to Boston in 1782. Many towns along the route are offering special plaques to houses that were standing when Rochambeau and his entourage passed. The plaques denote homes of historic interest in American's heritage. Each state is installing its own historic markers along the entire route from Rhode Island to Virginia to educate history buffs, tourists, and students of all ages about the role of France in helping America become free.

There are ongoing annual celebrations in Yorktown on October 19 to commemorate the importance of the battle won there. Daily tours of the battlefield are conducted year round. Statues, streets, theatres, hotels, plaques, bridges, ships, and schools all carry the name of Rochambeau. For example, in Southbury, Connecticut, the Rochambeau Middle School not only carries the name, but also proudly sports an impressive permanent mural depicting scenes of Rochambeau's march through the area. It is an acrylic painting fifty-one inches tall and forty-four feet long in the school's all-purpose room. The mural's central theme is Rochambeau and his troops crossing the Housatonic River to the west of Southbury. It includes a camp scene with soldiers, their tents and campfires. Also featured in the mural are local farmers and blacksmiths. This project was planned and carried out during the 1994–1995 and 1995–1996 school years by students in grades seven and eight along with their teachers.[19]

As a part of the Paris International Exposition, which opened in April 1900, three magnificent statues symbolizing Franco-American friendship were unveiled. One of these statues commemorated General Rochambeau and was erected in Vendôme, his birthplace. It was dedicated on June 4, 1900. The other two were an equestrian statue of George Washington, dedicated July 3 that summer in Paris, and that of the Marquis de Lafayette, dedicated the next day, July 4, also in Paris, in the courtyard of the Louvre Museum.[20]

The Rochambeau statue was designed and sculpted by Vendôme artist Jean-Jacques-Fernand Hamar. Trained at the École des Beaux-Arts in Paris, he was working out of his studio when approached to enter a competition for this piece. Hamar's representation of Rochambeau shows the general on the eve of the siege of Yorktown. In his hand he carries a map of the intended battle the next day. At his feet are a captured cannon and a branch of laurel.[21] It may be inferred that the cannon symbolizes the two cannon that General Washington sent to the maréchal after his return to France. The American chief sent them in thanks and remembrance for Rochambeau's help in capturing America's independence from the British.

The following is inscribed on the statue: "Commander-in-chief of the French army in America, took Yorktown in 1781 and assured the Independence of the United States."[22] The existence of the statue and the apt inscription bear witness to all future generations that General Rochambeau will be forever remembered for this successful campaign at Yorktown, his most significant achievement. Prior to the unveiling, the statue was covered with the French and American flags denoting friendship and cooperation between the two republics as well as the fact that Rochambeau bridged the two countries, on two continents, serving them both with utmost patriotism and honor.

Unfortunately, during World War I, in 1942 when the Germans occupied France, the original statue of Rochambeau was melted down for their war machine. With great forethought, the mayor of Vendôme had a mold made and preserved it in hiding. When France was liberated by the Americans on August 14, 1944, a plaster bust of the general, which had been sculpted in secret, was placed on the empty pedestal. The bust held sway until another thirty years had passed. Then, in 1974, an identical bronze replacement statue was donated by American members of the Society of the Cincinnati of which Generals Washington and Rochambeau were original members.[23]

One more Rochambeau statue was erected in Paris on Avenue Pierre-1er-de-Serbie, not far from the Arc de Triomphe. This replica of the Hamar work of art stands in the Place Rochambeau and was dedicated on November 6, 1933. A photograph was taken that day which appeared later in the *New York Herald Tribune* showing General John J. Pershing, Marshal Philippe Pétain, and members of the Rochambeau and Lafayette families among the many honored guests.[24]

President Franklin D. Roosevelt sent a message lauding Rochambeau from an American perspective: "…but we of the United States also claim our part of him. A smaller-minded man could never have adapted himself to the ungainly command of Newport and Yorktown. But Comte de Rochambeau possessed, above all force, wisdom, and tact, the simplicity of greatness."[25]

The inscription on the base of the statue is a quote from a letter written by Washington to Rochambeau. It reads, "To the generous support of your nation and to the bravery of its troops must be attributed to a great degree, that independence for which we have fought and which, after a severe conflict of more than seven years, we have obtained."[26] The funds for the Paris statue of Rochambeau were raised by the Friends of Loir-et-Cher, the French department of the Vendôme region, and the City of Paris.[27]

These unveilings in France represented an affirmation of France's continued high esteem for America. They also encouraged a continuum of mutual good feelings between France and America, evidenced by still another outpouring of good faith, the gift of the Lady Liberty to America in 1886. The Statue of Liberty was created by the well-known French sculptor Frédéric Auguste Bartholdi.

America was also busy creating her own permanent remembrance to honor Rochambeau's victory at Yorktown. In 1781 the United States Congress provided for the construction of a monument recognizing the alliance and victory in Yorktown, but failed to begin the project until one hundred years later.[28] The promise was kept, however, and the cornerstone was laid on October 18, 1881, by "the order of the Ancient Free and Accepted Masons as the appropriate opening for the Yorktown Centennial celebration," and finally completed in 1884.[29] It consists of a base, a podium, and a slender shaft of Hallowell Maine granite. At the top of this tall, imposing monument stands the figure of Liberty herself, a symbol of freedom from tyranny and oppression.[30]

On the south side is the following inscription: "At York on October 19, 1781, after a siege of nineteen days by 5,500 American and 7,000 French troops of the line, 3,500 Virginia Militia under the Command of General Thomas Nelson, and 36 French Ships of War, Earl Cornwallis, Commander of the British forces at York and Gloucester, surrendered his army of 7,251 officers and men, 840 seamen, 244 canon and 24 standards to His Excellency George Washington, Commander-in-Chief of the combined forces of America and France, to his Excellency the Comte de Rochambeau, Commanding the Auxiliary Troops of His Most Christian Majesty in America, and to His Excellency, The Comte de Grasse, Commander in Chief of the Naval Army of France in Chesapeake."[31]

Another important statue of Rochambeau, a near replica of the first one in Vendôme, France, stands on the southwest corner of Lafayette Park opposite the White House in Washington, D. C. We have a persistent French diplomat to thank for this beautiful rendering of the general. In 1900 Jules Boeufvé, French chancellor to the United States and attaché of the French embassy, approached the U. S. Congress to commission a copy of Hamar's Rochambeau in Vendôme. The first attempt failed in committee but was taken up a short time later and passed with little debate on March 3, 1901. This was extremely rapid passage of the bill since there were other statues also under request that session. Only four were funded, including the Rochambeau.[32]

An impressive statue of Lafayette by sculptors Jean Falguière and Marius Mercie had already graced the square opposite the White House since 1891. The form of this earlier work was similar to that of Rochambeau in France, but a bit larger. To keep in balance with the Lafayette statue, Hamar had to make some adjustments in scale. When completed, the Rochambeau bronze figure was almost eleven feet tall (the Rochambeau in Vendôme is nine feet), the pedestal nineteen feet, and the base one foot, while the Lafayette figure was eleven feet, the pedestal seventeen feet, and the base three feet.

Enhancing the base of the Lafayette statue was the bare-breasted female figure representing Liberty, handing Lafayette a sword. Hamar added to his base a dramatic allegorical bronze grouping entitled "Victory and the American Eagle" in which the goddess Minerva (or Athena) symbolizes the protector of the state who is holding up two flags, French and American, with a sword in one hand that protects the bald eagle, a symbol of the United States. He added breaking waves beneath her feet as she and the eagle stand on the prow of a huge ship. The latter represents the arrival of the French army in Newport. The symbolism is striking and unmistakable and also includes the early American flag of thirteen stars and stripes and the sprigs of laurel for peace. Rochambeau is dressed in his uniform as Maréchal de France, the highest honor bestowed on him by King Louis XVI. He wears his tricorn hat with cockade, and his coat is festooned with the medal of the Order of St. Esprit. Like the first statue in Vendôme, he holds the map of Yorktown in his left hand.[33]

On the east side of the pedestal is the crest of the Family Rochambeau with their motto, and on the west is the French coat of arms featuring the fleur-de-lis, symbol of the Royal House of Bourbon kings including King Louis XVI, under whom the general served while on his *expédition particulière*. With the many customized changes to the Washington statue, Hamar indeed created a new one, not simply a copy.[34]

The inscription, a quote from a letter that George Washington wrote to Rochambeau on February 1, 1784, reads as follows: "We have been contemporaries and fellow laborers in the cause of liberty, and we have lived together as brothers should do in harmonious friendship."[35] Jean-Jacques Hamar, deaf since birth, traveled to Washington for the unveiling on May 24, 1902. Present at the dedication were President Theodore Roosevelt, the Count and Countess de Rochambeau, the French ambassador James Cambon, Hamar, and a host of dignitaries.[36]

An amusingly unexpected event took place at the reverent unveiling ceremony in Washington. As the huge American flag was to be pulled off the statue to reveal its beauty to the world, there was a hitch. The flag got stuck on Rochambeau's outstretched arm and would not come free. President Roosevelt, with his uncanny sense of humor and impeccable timing, was quick to fill the void by shouting out, "Leave it where it is...it clings to the hero as he did to us."[37]

Since many people seemed to have assumed that this likeness of Rochambeau was sent as a gift to the United States, in September 1902 the following was inscribed on the granite ledge: "By the Congress May XXIV MDCCCCII,"[38] so there would be no mistaking who paid for the monument.

Still another reminder of the Frenchman who saved America, a fourth replica of the statue faces the harbor at Newport, Rhode Island, where Rochambeau landed with his gallant soldiers in July 1780. Near the water's edge overlooking Newport Harbor and Narragansett Bay, Rochambeau points to the sea and ultimately to France from whence he came with his ships full of French fighting men ready to meet the British in battle. Today he faces the grand Newport Bridge from his pedestal in King Park.

The Newport statue has a history worth mentioning. It has not always stood by the water's edge. It was originally placed at Vanderbilt Circle (opposite Equality Park) on Broadway, donated by A. Kingsley Macomber, who had been present at the Paris unveiling in 1933. It stood at Vanderbilt Circle from the day of its extravagant military and naval dedication on July 13, 1934, for six years, until the group who had originally preferred that it be installed by the harbor renewed its proposal and won approval.[39]

Accordingly, the statue of Rochambeau was moved to its current spot in King Park near the Admiral de Ternay cairn and was rededicated on July 4, 1940. The move was shouldered financially by a private citizen, Mr. Perry Belmont. Due to rainy weather, the ceremony was held in the Colony House, with the actual unveiling later in the day as the weather cleared, by Mrs. John Nicolas Brown (Anne S. K. Brown), a collector of military history and subsequent editor of *The American Campaigns of Rochambeau's Army (1972)*.[40]

There may be a plan, although unconfirmed by the Newport Historical Society, to move the Rochambeau statue once more, according to a descendant of the general, Eric de Rochambeau. There is considerable evidence that the sea wall is being eroded by the weather, and thus it would seem prudent, in order protect the statue, to move the entire monument farther inland.[41] So, America's hero may again be on the move in Newport.

Lauzun and his famous Legion of Foreign Volunteers are immortalized on The Green in New Stratford, now Monroe, Connecticut. A granite monument, referred to as the upright sign-post, stands about five feet tall. It is the only monument in the United States dedicated uniquely to the Duc de Lauzun. The monument was dedicated on July 1, 2003. This is the day of Rochambeau's birthday, not Lauzun's, as far as we know. But it is the date on which the famous Lauzun made his encampment there.

The dedication celebration covered three days, beginning with the arrival of re-enactors who were marching from Newport, Rhode Island, along the entire route of the W3R to Yorktown, Virginia. They and the Boy Scouts camped on The Green as Lauzun's Legion had done 222 years before. Participating were the Monroe townspeople, the Sons of the American Revolution, the Scouts, and the American Legion. Officiating were Richard A. Orr, Master of Ceremonies and Chairman of the Duc de Lauzun Celebration, Congressman Chris Shays, State Representative DebraLee Hovey, First Selectman Andrew Nunn, and the Governor's Horse Guard. Following the flag raising and singing of the "Star Spangled Banner," Reverend Kurt Huber gave the invocation. Monsignor John Sabia was also in attendance in honor of Lauzun's chaplain who probably said mass on The Green before setting out to join Rochambeau and Washington in New York State.[42]

In America's schools and beyond, eager history buffs of all ages continue to study the great legacy of General Rochambeau, Washington's "ideal lieutenant." Rochambeau's contribution to America's freedom, still being celebrated and enjoyed 229 years after the Yorktown victory, is immeasurable.

Long may we remember those who came to the aid of a fledging United States, which sought to throw off British tyranny. Let us not forget them, from the lowliest foot soldiers and sailors, to the highest-ranking generals and admirals, even a king and his counselors. Yes, there were those who only wanted revenge and others who were self-seeking adventurers and took advantage of America's need, but there were thousands more who gave their all to our cause for independence. "Their throbbing hearts have long been still, but ours now beat the stronger for their bravery."[43]

ACKNOWLEDGMENTS

*"May the words of my mouth and the meditation of my heart
be pleasing in your sight, O Lord."*
—PSALM 19:14

I GIVE HUMBLE THANKS and praise to God who has been my greatest inspiration for my writing from the beginning of this book. Next, my deepest thanks to my loving husband, John, without whose constant support and assistance in all things I could not have found the courage or the strength to complete this enormous work. As I became more and more involved with the research and writing, John took over the running of the household and gardens. He helped me find the sources for lost quotes on countless occasions and drove me to historical societies and out-of-the-way places as I traced the footsteps of Rochambeau and his army from the Château de Rochambeau in France to the battlefield at Yorktown.

Next I give my heartfelt gratitude to my dear daughter, Heather Woodring, who devoted three years of her time to help edit the book; I cannot thank her enough for her attention to the endless details. She worked through computer issues, checked facts, inserted and tracked endless sources, and even worked on proposals as I searched for a publisher who would best fit my needs. When I was stressed and discouraged, she would say to me, "Mom, just enjoy the process." And we did, together. Heather, through her gift of discernment, also really put me to the test by posing many difficult questions about the details of the manuscript and without doubt, helped me make countless improvements. God, John, and Heather are indeed my co-authors.

My son, Rusty Dyer, was an essential link in the events that led to the writing of this book. It was he who joined me in France in 1993 and accompanied me on my first visit to the Château de Rochambeau at the invitation of Count Michel and Countess Madeleine de Rochambeau, both now deceased. It was an inspirational visit that brought to mind the pivotal role of their ancestor, General Rochambeau, in the founding of our country and the lack of public awareness of his contribution. As a film producer, Rusty documented our tour of the château, and as a graphic artist he created the initial book cover and helped format the illustrations.

Here I wish to express a special merci to my son-in-law, Stuart Woodring, who supplied me with invaluable information on the Society of the Cincinnati, of which he is a member, and for his helpful suggestions after reading a late draft of the book. My grandson, Sam Woodring, deserves my gratitude as well since it was he who made up the first glossary, as well as compiled a list of names and places for the index. Likewise, my granddaughter, Jessie Woodring, accustomed to writing French papers, helped me find the French accents on a new computer.

I will always remain grateful to Michel and Madeleine, Count and Countess de Rochambeau, for their hospitality over the years. I learned much from them on my visits and always found them to be gracious in receiving Americans into their lovely home. I especially enjoyed meeting Virginie, granddaughter of Michel and Madeleine, on our first visit in 1993, as I discovered that we are both named for the state of Virginia, where the name of Rochambeau will always be revered in the annals of American and French history.

I owe much to my friend and mentor, Jacques Bossière, Ph.D., founder and first chair of the Washington–Rochambeau Revolutionary Route, who read and annotated my manuscript, enabling me to assess the book from a broader point of view than my own. I value his experience and his devotion to the cause of educating readers of all ages, tourists as well as devotees of history.

Just like Rochambeau's timing in the Revolution was perfect, so was the help I received from Jacques de Trentinian, researcher on the "War for America," Vice-President-General of the National Society of the SAR (Sons of the American Revolution), and member of the Société des Cincinnati de France as descendent of Captain Jean-Jacques de Trentinian of Lauzun's Legion. Jacques helped Heather and me by providing information he collected through primary sources such as military, naval, and diplomatic archives, enriched by cross checking with journals of combatants. He was tireless in his attempt to help me improve my manuscript. I only wish I could have included the vast details that Jacques provided.

I asked friends and experts for advice and humbly accepted offers of help on a range of technical needs, namely, Andrew Barnett, Kevin Kallsen, and Heather Woodring. Thanks to my morale boosters, Kim Burdick, Nicole Yancy, Ed Ayres, Genie Rigopulos, and my faithful bridge group. I especially want to remember my dear departed friend, Lea Winslow, who waited for me to finish the book. Sadly, she did not live to see it in print.

My grateful thanks go to my many friends who prayed for me, especially my dear ones, Jackie and Bill Stempfle, who prayed unceasingly for the successful completion of my tome to the glory of God. I found it providential that my faithful writing companion, Leonore Templeton, invited me to join her in taking a writing class in the winter of 2006 from Bill Gregware, who advised me to write an entire book on Rochambeau rather than the short version for young readers that I had already completed in draft form. I am glad I did.

Rachel LePine painted the Rochambeau château used in the book cover design and assisted me in the final edit process. She and Victoria Kallsen ably typed for me and did admirable work deciphering my handwriting while also checking on the accuracy of sources and endnotes. Merci beaucoup to my Sweet Briar College roommates, Sandy Sylvia and Mary Davis, who drove me around Newport and took photos of all the Rochambeau sites for me when I forgot my camera. *Merci infiniment* to Lily and Claude Ressouches for sending me material on La Pérouse and on Lafayette's ship, the *Hermione*, which is being restored in France; to Kathy Sierakowski, who provided information on the funding of the American Revolution and planned various research trips in Connecticut, Massachusetts, Virginia, and Washington, D.C.; to Richard Orr, who reminded me of Lauzun's significant role in Monroe, Connecticut; and to David Wagner, painter for the W3R, for his patience as I finished the book and chose some of his paintings to illustrate Rochambeau's role in the American Revolution.

And warm thanks also are due to all who read my manuscript in part or in its entirety and provided feedback: Sallie Tullis de Barcza, Chairman, Board of Directors, W3R-US; Carol Bauby, Regent, Trumbull-Porter Chapter, National Society, Daughters of the American Revolution; Bill Cox, Assistant Director, Rochester Public Library (retired); Professor Roberta Marggraff; Professor Cindy Eastman; Helene Agnew, Honorary Chapter Regent, Trumbull-Porter Chapter, National Society, Daughters of the American Revolution; Bill Stempfle; Sarah Jane Moore; Ariana Rosa; and my daughter Amy Dyer. Amy helped to expedite the completion of the index, for which I am very grateful. I am grateful to Judy Anderson, former curator of the Jeremiah Lee Mansion in Marblehead, Massachusetts, who shared with me remarkable information on the early covert French funding of the American Revolution by way of Jeremiah Lee and his international trading company.

Thanks, too, are in order to individuals, bookstore owners, librarians, historical societies, museums, and universities, all of whom enabled me to collect material from Vendôme, France, to Newport and Yorktown: Michel de Rochambeau, Eric de Rochambeau, Bob Selig, Peter Harrington, Ron Potvin, Shelley Goldstein, Maria Allen, Kathy Dowling, Maryse Labbé, Nancy Richardson, Lise Rinaldi, Cat Styvel, Alicia Wayland, Frank Jazzo, and Robert Stackpole. Let me not forget the contribution of the Silly Sisters of Fredericksburg, Virginia, who hand-stitched for me a perfect reproduction, eighteenth-century gown that allows me to shed my baggy writer's garb so I can reenact the part of a fine lady of Rochambeau's era.

Last, but certainly not least, thank you to Tom Costello of Word Association Publishers for his encouragement and help in the final steps of publishing this book, to Nan Newell for her careful attention to the final editing details, and to Julie Csizmadia for her role in the design and formatting of the book and in making a multitude of final changes.

André, John, Major (1750–1780). Adjutant general with the rank of major who served under General Henry Clinton. After meeting with traitor Benedict Arnold, André missed the British ship that was to carry him back to Clinton. André was discovered in the Continental camp in disguise and apprehended outside New York on September 23, 1780. Upon the discovery of plans for the surrender of West Point in his boot, André was tried and hanged as a British spy on the orders of George Washington.

Aranda, Pedro Pablo Abarca de Bolea, Conde de (1719–1798). Spanish ambassador to France (1773–1787). He believed that an independent United States was less of a threat to Spain than a united British Empire. He was a proponent of American independence and of France entering the war on the side of the insurgents.

Arnold, Benedict, General (1741–1801). Arnold, the hero of the Battle of Saratoga, New York, was the American general who gave the plans for West Point to a British officer, John André, thus betraying America and his former friend, George Washington. Arnold joined the British army and was sent to Virginia where he commanded the destruction and pillage of that state, taking Richmond and later Fort Griswold near New London, Connecticut, in September 1781. In December 1781, he and his family sailed to England where he stayed until his death. He escaped capture and was never tried for his treason.

Barras, Jacques-Melchior Saint-Laurent, Comte de (1752–1839). After the death of Admiral de Ternay and the interim command of Destouches, Barras arrived at Newport in May 1781 to take over the command of the French fleet. During the second sea Battle off the Virginia Capes in which De Grasse defeated British Admirals Hood and Graves, Barras and his squadron successfully entered Lynnhaven Bay undetected by the British. Barras's entrance into the mouth of the Chesapeake signaled the safe arrival of the essential heavy siege artillery that Rochambeau had brought from France.

Beaumarchais, Pierre-Augustin Caron de (1732–1799). French dramatist who wrote *The Barber of Seville* and *The Marriage of Figaro.* He encouraged King Louis XVI to become involved in the American Revolution on the side of the colonists. On April 26, 1776, he learned of the king's decision to aid the insurgents. He sent volunteers, munitions, and supplies covertly to America through the Rodrigue Hortalez Company.

Berthier, Louis-Alexandre (1753–1815). A captain in the French army, Berthier, along with his brother, joined Rochambeau in Newport, Rhode Island, on September 30, 1780, having missed the original departure from Brest, France. He was appointed to the Soissonnais regiment as assistant quartermaster general. His greatest contribution were the maps he drew (111 are housed at the Princeton University Library) and the itineraries which documented the march of Rochambeau's French army from Newport to Yorktown and the return trip to Boston. Equally important was his journal of the historic overland march.

Berthier, Charles-Louis-Jean, Chevalier (1759–1783). Traveled with his brother, Louis-Alexandre, to America. They worked together as cartographers for General Rochambeau. The two brothers left a detailed heritage of the *expédition particulière* in their carefully drawn and beautifully painted maps of the route and campsites.

Blanchard, Claude (1742–1803). As commissary in chief of the French Auxiliary Army in America, he was in charge of gathering supplies and establishing hospitals for the French army. His surviving journal gives almost daily accounts of military, social, and political events as he interpreted them.

Bonvouloir, Julien-Alexandre Achard, Chevalier de (1749–1783). Sent by Vergennes as secret emissary to the Continental Congress at Philadelphia where he met with the Committee of Secret Correspondence in December 1775. He sent a message to Vergennes in January 1776 that America was interested in receiving aid from France. This news encouraged Vergennes to persuade King Louis XVI to begin sending covert aid to the American rebels.

Bougainville, Louis-Antoine, Comte de (1729–1811). He was the first Frenchman to circumnavigate the world (1766–1769). In August 1781 he was given command of the 80-gun warship, *Auguste*. He served in the Caribbean as navy captain under Admiral de Grasse when the fleet sailed to the Chesapeake to aid Rochambeau in his upcoming fight against General Cornwallis. On September 5, after having landed troops, Bougainville put out to sea again to join in the second Battle off the Virginia Capes between the French fleet under De Grasse and the British fleet commanded by Admirals Graves and Hood. Bougainville led the attack on Graves's flagship, the *Terrible*.

Carlos III, King (1716–1788). Former king of Naples and Sicily and former duke of Parma and Piacenza; born Catholic into the House of Bourbon, the same family as King Louis XVI of France. He married Maria Amalia of Saxony, ascended to the throne of Spain in 1759, and reigned until his death in 1788. King Carlos did not fully support American independence since he thought it might ignite an uprising in his own country, but he tolerated and supported covert aid beginning in 1776. After declaring war on Britain in 1779 he continued to aid the American cause in indirect ways while at the same time meeting Spain's goals. At the request of Rochambeau and La Luzerne, De Grasse assembled the funds needed for the siege of Yorktown from Carlos's subjects in Havana, Cuba.

Castries, Charles-Eugène-Gabriel de La Croix, Marquis de (1727–1801). Fought in the Seven Years' War, seasoned diplomat, made commandant général of the cavalry in 1748, and sent to St. Lucia in 1756 and the Battle of Clostercamp in 1760 where he distinguished himself. He was named governor of Flanders. In 1780 he became minister of the French Royal Navy until 1787. He was honored to become a marshal of France in 1783. As minister of the navy he worked with Vergennes to bring Rochambeau and De Grasse to America.

Chastellux, François-Jean de Beauvoir, Chevalier (later Marquis), Maréchal de Camp, Major General (1734–1788). He achieved military glory in the Seven Years' War and literary acclaim for his book of philosophy. He was chosen to be a member of the French Academy in 1772. Chastellux sailed to America with Rochambeau and traveled extensively in the colonies. His journal, *Travels in North America in the years 1780, 1781 and 1782,* is filled with firsthand observations and experiences.

Choisy, Claude-Gabriel, Marquis de (1723–unknown). Brigadier General Choisy was the hero of the siege of Cracow and arrived in America with the Berthier brothers on September 30, 1780, after having been left at the dock with the second division in Brest, France, in May 1780. When the French army marched west to meet Washington, Choisy was chosen to remain in Rhode Island with the remainder of Rochambeau's troops to protect French/American interests there. He later sailed with Barras to the Chesapeake and commanded allied forces including the Virginia militia on the Gloucester Peninsula in order to block Cornwallis's escape.

Clermont-Crèvecoeur, Jean-François Louis, Comte de (1752 – c. 1824). Lieutenant Crèvecoeur of the Auxonne regiment, Royal Corps of Artillery, who traveled with Rochambeau, kept a detailed journal covering the French expedition in America.

Clinton, Sir Henry, General (1738–1795). Clinton was named supreme commander of the British army in the American colonies in 1778 on the retirement of General Howe. General Clinton made his headquarters in New York. He left Lord Cornwallis as his second-in-command in charge of his army in the South.

Closen-Haydenbourg, Hans Christoph Frederich Ignatz Ludwig, Baron von (1752–1830). Beyond his duties as second captain in the Royal Deux-Ponts regiment, he wrote a voluminous, descriptive journal covering the expedition in America. Aide-de-camp of Rochambeau, he served as interpreter and messenger between Rochambeau and important high-ranking officers in the allied armies. He began the overland march with two servants and four horses.

Cornwallis, Charles, 2nd Earl, Lord, General (1738–1805). Cornwallis, a veteran of the Seven Years' War, originally opposed British policies in the colonies. In 1776 he aided the Howe brothers in driving Washington out of Long Island and New York into New Jersey. In 1780, in support of the British cause, he was victorious over American General Horatio Gates at the Battle of Camden, South Carolina. Cornwallis commanded the British Army of the South. He moved north into Virginia where the Marquis de Lafayette finally cornered him at Yorktown. Cornwallis was defeated by the combined American and French Armies of Generals Washington and Rochambeau and the French fleet under Admiral de Grasse at the Battle of Yorktown, Virginia. He absented himself from the official surrender on October 19, 1781.

Custine-Sarreck, Adam-Philippe, Comte de (1740–1793). He was a colonel in the Saintonge regiment, Second Brigade, who shipped over to America with General Rochambeau in 1780. During the winter doldrums in Newport an argument arose, resulting in a suicide that was blamed on Custine.

Deane, Silas (1737–1789). Deane was born in Groton, Connecticut, and graduated from Yale in 1758. He was sent as a secret American emissary by Congress to Paris in March 1776 to obtain financial and military assistance. It was in Deane's Paris apartment that the French-American Alliance was signed on February 6, 1778, negotiated by himself, Benjamin Franklin, and Arthur Lee.

The Alliance made France the first nation to recognize the United States as an independent country. Deane was later charged by Arthur Lee with embezzlement and disloyalty, but the charges were never proved.

Desandrouins, Jean-Nicolas, Vicomte de, Colonel (1729–1792). He fought in the War of Austrian Succession, was trained as an engineer, and served in Canada and America from 1756–1760, distinguishing himself on many occasions for which he was awarded the Cross of Saint Louis. He returned to France to continue his career in the engineer corps but later came back to America with Rochambeau as chief of the Royal Corps of Engineers. Due to illness he did not participate in the siege of Yorktown.

Destouches, Charles-René-Dominique Gochet, Chevalier (1727–1794). He was a naval captain who served as interim commander of the French fleet in Newport after the unexpected death of Admiral de Ternay in December 1780. He commanded the French fleet in the first Battle Off the Virginia Capes in an attempt to curtail re-supplying of Benedict Arnold in Virginia. Destouches held that post of commander of the French fleet in Newport until the arrival of his replacement, Admiral de Barras, in May 1781.

Deux-Ponts, Christian, Marquis de Forbach de (1752–1817). The elder brother of the Deux-Ponts family served as colonel of the German-speaking Royal Deux-Ponts regiment under Rochambeau in America.

Deux-Ponts, Guillaume de Forbach, Comte de (1754–1807). Guillaume served as lieutenant colonel of the Royal Deux-Ponts regiment in the French *expédition particulière* in America. He distinguished himself as a hero at the storming of Cornwallis's redoubt 9 at the Battle of Yorktown in October 1781.

Dillon, Robert-Guillaume, Comte (1754–1831). Lauzun's *colonel en second* who spent the winter of 1780-1781 in the home of William Williams in Lebanon, Connecticut.

Dumas, Guillaume-Mathieu, Comte (1753–1837). He joined the French army in 1773 and sailed with Rochambeau to

America in 1780. He served as assistant quartermaster general and as Rochambeau's aide-de-camp. He attended the general at high-level meetings with George Washington and fought at the siege of Yorktown.

Duportail, Louis Le Bègue de Presle, Chevalier, Brigadier General (1743–1802). Benjamin Franklin arranged secretly for Duportail and three other French engineers to come to America, arriving in Philadelphia in July 1777. Duportail worked as commander of the engineers of the Continental army under General George Washington from 1777 to 1783. He was taken prisoner in April 1780 at the Battle of Charleston and exchanged in November 1780. In the summer of 1781 he provided figures that dissuaded Washington from attacking the British at New York.

Estaing, Jean-Baptiste-Charles-Henri-Hector, Comte d' and Marquis de Saillans (1729–1794). French Admiral D'Estaing led two unsuccessful expeditions to aid the colonists, one in Newport, Rhode Island, in 1778 and the other in Savanna, Georgia, in 1779.

Fersen, Hans Axel Count von (1755–1810). Fersen was a Swedish officer from a prominent, wealthy Swedish family who served in the French army. He was also a confidant of Marie Antoinette both before and after his service on the French expedition in America. He was a senior aide-de-camp to Rochambeau.

Flohr, Georg Daniel (1756–unknown). German-speaking Flohr served with Rochambeau's *expédition particulière* in America. An enlisted man, he was one of the few of his rank to be known through his eloquent, beautifully illustrated *Account of the travels in America which were made by the Honorable Regiment of the Zweibrücken* ["Deux-Ponts" in French]*on water and on land from 1780 to 1784*. He filled 251 pages of text and thirty pages of illustrations.

Franklin, Benjamin (1706–1790). American printer, inventor, publisher, author, scientist, and diplomat, Franklin was chosen as emissary to Paris in 1776. He was a founding father of America, helping to draft and then sign the Declaration of Independence. He was instrumental in convincing King Louis XVI and his ministers to recognize the United States as an independent nation.

George William Frederick III, King of England (1738–1820). He became king in 1760 at the age of twenty-two. After the Treaty of Paris of 1763, Britain was supreme on land and on sea. King George, along with Parliament, became oppressive toward the American colonists in an attempt to make up for war expenditures. During the ensuing American Revolution, surrounded by corruption and indecision, the British king lost his claim to America by the Treaty of Paris, 1783.

Grasse, François-Joseph-Paul, Comte de (1722–1788). Admiral de Grasse was the French naval commander who sailed his large convoy from the West Indies to the mouth of the Chesapeake Bay to come to the aid of Generals Rochambeau and Washington at Yorktown. He engaged the British fleet under Admirals Graves and Hood, handily defeating them at the little-known second Battle off the Capes of Virginia. This ocean battle was fought out of sight of land with no Americans involved, yet it sealed the fate of General Lord Cornwallis by preventing his rescue by the British. Admirals de Grasse and Barras, along with Generals Rochambeau, Lafayette, and Washington succeeded in surrounding Cornwallis and the British army, thus winning the Battle of Yorktown, the final decisive battle of the American Revolution.

Hamilton, Alexander (1755–1804). Born in Nevis, West Indies, he entered the American Revolution as a captain in 1776 and became one of Washington's aides-de-camp in 1777. He traveled with Washington to meet with General Rochambeau, and because of his facility with French and his fine penmanship, he took part in their negotiations and penned most of Washington's dictated letters. Hamilton, who had wanted a battalion of his own, finally convinced his commander in chief of his capability. So, at the Battle of Yorktown in October 1781, he led the attack on British redoubt 10 which led to the defeat of Cornwallis.

Heath, William (1737–1814). Major General Heath commanded the Rhode Island and Massachusetts militia. He made preparations for Rochambeau and his expedition's arrival in Rhode Island. He greeted them with 5,000 militiamen to aid their settlement. When the allied forces marched to Virginia, General Heath stayed behind at New York to guard West Point and the Hudson Highlands and to prevent General Clinton from rescuing Cornwallis.

Howe, Richard Carl, Lord (later Viscount) (1726–1790). Admiral Howe and his brother, William, cooperated on the 1776 attack of Long Island and Manhattan leading to the defeat of Washington.

Howe, William, General (1729–1814). Howe succeeded General Thomas Gage as commander in chief of the British army. He defeated George Washington in the Battle of New York in 1776. It was well known that he did not have his heart in the fight against the colonists. He enjoyed his creature comforts more than he should have and ultimately was sent back to England and replaced by General Henry Clinton in 1778.

Kalb, Johann, Baron de (1721–1780). De Kalb was born in Bavaria of peasant stock, was fluent in many languages, and joined the German-speaking Löwendal regiment of the Royal French Army. His extensive European military experience included the War of Austrian Succession and the Seven Years' War. In 1768 the Duc de Choiseul, predecessor of Vergennes, sent him to America to determine the attitude of the colonists toward Britain. Later he was dispatched by Silas Deane to Philadelphia as a major general in the American army, arriving in September 1777. He commanded Maryland and Delaware divisions and served alongside General Horatio Gates in Camden, North Carolina, where he was wounded several times in a fierce battle in August 1780. He was taken prisoner by the British and died there of his wounds.

Knox, Henry, General (1750–1806). In March 1776 Knox was the hero of the Battle of Dorchester Heights, Massachusetts, having brought 120,000 pounds of captured British artillery from Fort

Ticonderoga to Boston through snow and ice to defeat the British. He was an aide-de-camp and chief of artillery to General Washington and accompanied him to meetings with Rochambeau and Admiral De Grasse on the *Ville de Paris* near Yorktown. He had the first idea for the Society of the Cincinnati and become its second president after Washington.

Lafayette, Marie-Joseph-Paul-Yves Roch-Gilbert du Motier, Marquis de (1757–1834). He was a wealthy French nobleman who wished to help the American cause for liberty. He sailed to America on his own in 1777 and was commissioned as a major general in the American Continental army. He fought with distinction at Brandywine in September 1777. After befriending General Washington he returned to France to entreat King Louis XVI to send aid the colonists. He played an important role in cornering Cornwallis in Virginia before the Battle of Yorktown and was instrumental in the founding of the Society of the Cincinnati. Lafayette and George Washington forged a father-son relationship, which lasted until the death of the latter in 1799.

La Luzerne, Anne-César, Chevalier de (1741–1791). Major General La Luzerne was a skilled diplomat, the French minister plenipotentiary to the United States, stationed at Philadelphia from 1779–1784 while Rochambeau was in America. He and Rochambeau corresponded by letter on matters of strategy with a few face-to-face meetings. Luzerne County, Pennsylvania, is named for him.

La Pérouse, Jean-François de Galaup, Comte de (1741–1788). A French navy captain, he was the first to circumnavigate the world for his country. La Perouse was chosen by General Rochambeau to take the Vicomte de Rochambeau back to France to request the second division promised by King Louis XVI and his minister, Vergennes. After the fastest crossing in decades, La Pérouse returned with hard currency to continue to finance the French and colonists' cause against the British in America.

Lauberdière, Louis-François-Bertrand du Pont d'Aubevoye, Comte de (1759–1837). The 350-page journal of Lauberdière, written during the American campaign with Rochambeau, was lost to the public for two hundred years, but once found, it revealed many fascinating details surrounding their expedition. As Rochambeau's twenty-one-year-old nephew, he was his youngest aide-de-camp. He held the rank of captain in the Saintonge regiment.

Laurens, John, Colonel (1754–1782). He served as an aide-de-camp to George Washington. His father, Henry Laurens, was a founding father of the republic and was captured and held in a British prison. John was sent to France in late March 1781 to request the second division that had been left behind as well as further monetary aid from the king of France. Laurens led the third column to storm redoubt 10. After the Battle of Yorktown he negotiated the terms of surrender.

Lauzun, Armand-Louis Gontaut, Duc de (later Duc de Biron) (1747–1793). Lauzun raised colonial troops and took Sénégal in 1779 for France. His legion, *les Volontaires Etrangers de Lauzun,* (Lauzun's Legion of Foreign Volunteers), created by King Louis XVI in March of 1780, sailed with Rochambeau to Newport. He and about one-third of his legion wintered in Lebanon, Connecticut, re-joining the main French army in June 1781 for the march to meet Washington at New York. Lauzun's Legion marched on the left flank of Rochambeau to protect the French from an attack by the British who held the Connecticut shoreline. The Duc de Lauzun and his mounted hussars fought valiantly at Yorktown, defending the Gloucester Peninsula.

L'Enfant, Pierre-Charles (1754–1825). L'Enfant was trained as an artist under his father at the Royal Academy in Paris. In 1776 he volunteered to join the American Continental army and sailed with the Marquis de Lafayette in 1777 to work under General Washington as an engineer. He was wounded at the Siege of Savannah and captured by the British in Charleston, but later, after being exchanged, he continued to work with the Continental army as captain of engineers. He created the design for the medal of the Society of the Cincinnati.

Lincoln, Benjamin, Major General (1733–1810). As regiment commander of the southern forces of the Continental army, he was forced to surrender his army of 7,000 troops to the British at the Battle of Charleston on May 12, 1780. He was a leading player at the surrender of the same British army after the Battle of Yorktown, October 19, 1781, only this time he was on the winning side.

Louis XVI, King of France (1754–1793). King Louis XVI was the last reigning Bourbon king of the ancien régime. He followed his grandfather to the throne of France and reigned with his wife, Queen Marie Antoinette, from 1774–1793 when he was sent to the guillotine during the French Revolution. In 1778 he signed the French-American Alliance as the first sovereign nation to recognize America as an independent country. He sent General Rochambeau and 5,500 French soldiers to America in 1780 to aid the American colonists in throwing off the British yoke. The king continued to send troops, ships, and hard currency until the end of the American Revolution, assuring that the rebels would win over their British oppressors led by his archenemy, King George III.

Marie Antoinette (1755–1793). The wife of King Louis XVI, she was the last queen of France in the ancien régime. She was born in Austria as the eleventh daughter of Emperor Francis the First of the Holy Roman Empire and Empress Marie Theresa. In order to cement the French-Austrian alliance she came to France in 1770 to marry Louis, the French dauphin. Through a series of unfortunate incidents and political smearing in pamphlets of the period she acquired a bad name, and the country that had loved her in the beginning began to hate her. She died at the guillotine on October 16, 1793.

Martin, Joseph Plumb (1760–1850). Born in Becket, Massachusetts, well educated and living with his grandparents in Milford, Connecticut, the young Martin entered the army at the age of fifteen. He returned home for several months and re-enlisted in the Continental army in 1777. He took part in many important battles up and down the east coast. He spent a winter at Morristown. He witnessed John André going to his execution, and took part in the siege of Yorktown. He was assigned to the Corps of Sappers and Miners in the 8th Connecticut regiment and rose in the ranks to the rank of sergeant. He and his vanguard cleared the field ahead of the storming of redoubt 10. The narrative that he wrote in 1830, titled *A Narrative of a Revolutionary Soldier: Some of the Adventures, Dangers, and Sufferings of Joseph Plumb Martin,* is used as a primary resource by historians and researchers.

Montbarrey, Alexandre Marie-Léonore de Saint Mauris, Prince de (1732–1796). French Minister of War (1778–1780) who, along with Vergennes and King Louis XVI, chose General Rochambeau to lead the *expédition particulière* to America. He was replaced by the Marquis de Ségur.

Morris, Robert (1734–1806). He was born in Liverpool and moved to Philadelphia where he set up a worldwide import-export business. As one of the wealthiest merchants in America, he signed the Declaration of Independence and was the "Financier of the American Revolution." In 1781 he became superintendent of finance and proposed the first national bank, the Bank of North America. After six years of war against England, his finances dwindled and he borrowed funds from Rochambeau to be used by Washington and the Continental army. This loan allowed the American army to outfit themselves and march to Yorktown.

Necker, Jacques (1732–1804). A Swiss-born Protestant, he became the minister of finance in France under Louis XVI in 1777. Necker wrote a letter to Rochambeau in late 1780, saying that he would send him the money he needed but that he (Rochambeau) must be very frugal with it. Flattering him into being wise with the funds, Necker wrote, "It is in looking after everything at once that you outstrip the ordinary man." In 1781 Necker's *"compte rendu au roi"* or financial account presented to Louis XVI painted all too rosy a picture of the French finances leading up to the French Revolution. Necker overstated the funds available and failed to set up a plan of taxation to provide for these funds.

Noailles, Louis-Marie-Antoine, Vicomte de (1756–1804). Like Lafayette, Noailles was born into a prestigious French family. He and the Marquis de Lafayette married cousins in the Noailles family. Noailles came to America with Rochambeau as a lieutenant colonel in the Soissonnais regiment. He resided at the Robinson home overlooking the water in Newport. Noailles distinguished himself at the Battle of Yorktown. He and Laurens represented the French and Americans respectively at the surrender negotiations.

O'Hara, Charles, General (1740–1802). O'Hara was a British brigadier general who served with Cornwallis at the Battle of Guilford Courthouse, North Carolina, in March 1781. It was he who surrendered the sword of Cornwallis to American General Lincoln after the Battle of Yorktown, Virginia, on October 19, 1781. He had meant to give it up to General Rochambeau, who directed him instead to Lincoln.

Rochambeau, Jean-Baptiste-Donatien de Vimeur, Comte de, General (1725–1807). He was chosen by King Louis XVI as the best general to fulfill the desire of the French to conquer the British and to restore a more favorable balance of power. Rochambeau was made a lieutenant general to lead the *expédition particulière* in 1780 to aid George Washington and the American colonists in their fight for independence from England. He brought with him a force of 5,500 French troops, yet yielded to the orders of George Washington while in America. He led a combined French and American assault on General Cornwallis at Yorktown, winning with George Washington and the Continental army the last great battle of the American Revolution.

Rochambeau, Donatien-Marie-Joseph, de Vimeur, Vicomte de (1750–1813). Donatien, the son of General Rochambeau, accompanied his father on the American expedition. He served as a second colonel in the Bourbonnais regiment and as his father's aide-de-camp. In the fall of 1780 Donatien was sent back to Versailles to request the remaining second division promised by the king and the hard currency needed to resupply the expedition. After his return to

America with the funds, but without the long-awaited second division, Donatien traveled with the expedition to Yorktown to take part in the battle.

Rochambeau, Jeanne-Thérèse Telles d'Acosta, Comtesse de (1730–1824). She was the daughter of a wealthy Portuguese merchant in foodstuffs. The list of her dowry suggests that her parents held an elevated station in life probably due to the success of her father's business. Beyond a goodly sum of money, she was also endowed with fine linens, laces, and jewelry. Her marriage to Rochambeau on December 22, 1749, was arranged through family connections and lasted until his death in 1807. Not much is known of her interests, but we know she was beautiful as evidenced in the portrait of her by Maurice-Quentin de La Tour.

Saint-Simon-Montbléru, Claude-Anne du Rouvroy, Marquis de (1743–1819). Major-General Saint-Simon commanded an army in the French West Indies. He brought 3,200 troops with him on De Grasse's ships to the Chesapeake to prevent Cornwallis's escape. Saint-Simon's army was offloaded prior to the second Battle off the Virginia Capes against the British in September 1781. He and his troops fought at the Battle of Yorktown.

Steuben, Frederick William Augustus, Baron von (1730–1794). Von Steuben was a Prussian-born career military man. In 1777 he left Germany following unsavory conduct. He was given a recommendation from Benjamin Franklin and Silas Deane as a lieutenant general in the king of Prussia's service and arrived in America in December that year. Despite von Steuben's fake credentials, Washington made him inspector general with the rank of major general. He drafted "Regulations for the Order and Discipline of the Troops of the United States" (1779). He helped to train American soldiers under George Washington during the Revolutionary War and took part in the siege of Yorktown. Prior to participating in the American Revolution von Steuben began to call himself "de Steuben" and did so until his death.

Ternay, Charles-Louis d'Arsac, Chevalier de (1723–1780). French Admiral de Ternay skillfully transported Rochambeau and his *expédition particulière* from Brest, France, to Newport, Rhode Island. He accompanied Rochambeau and his entourage to the first meeting with George Washington in Hartford, Connecticut, in September 1780. Ternay suffered from a lingering illness during most of his time away from France and finally succumbed to malignant fever on December 15, 1780. He was buried in Newport with great pomp and ceremony.

Trumbull, Jonathan (1710–1785). He was governor of Connecticut from 1769–1784. His home and war office, which he maintained during the war, were on the mile-long green in Lebanon, Connecticut. Lebanon was the winter quarters of Lauzun and his mounted legion during the winter months of 1780–1781. Under Trumbull's leadership Connecticut became known as the "provision state," supplying desperately needed food and ammunition to the Continental army winter quarters at Valley Forge and Morristown and later to the French army as well.

Vergennes, Charles Gravier, Comte de (1719–1787). Vergennes was the foreign minister under King Louis XVI of France. After sending Bonvouloir to America he was convinced to persuade the king to begin secretly sending financial aid to America in 1776. He, along with Prince de Montbarrey and King Louis XVI, chose Rochambeau to lead the *expédition particulière* to America. Their goal was to find a more favorable balance of power following the Treaty of Paris of 1763, which favored England.

Verger, Jean-Baptiste-Antoine de (1762–1851). Born in the French-speaking Bishoporic of Bâle, now a part of Switzerland, he was a diarist who traveled with the French expedition to America. Verger was a sublieutenant in the Royal Deux-Ponts regiment. His diary is illustrated with a colorful self-portrait and drawings of soldiers, Indians, and places he saw on his journey in America.

Vioménil, Antoine-Charles du Houx, Baron de (1725–1793). A lieutenant general, Antoine-Charles was Rochambeau's second-in-command in the French expedition. He was promoted to major general as he led the successful French assault on Cornwallis's British redoubt 9 at the Battle of Yorktown.

Vioménil, Charles-Joseph-Hyacinthe, Comte de (later Marquis) (1734–1827). Charles-Joseph was the younger brother of Antoine. He ranked third under General Rochambeau as a major general in the French expeditionary force.

Wadsworth, Jeremiah, Colonel (1743–1804). Born in Hartford, Connecticut, he was a champion of colonial rights, and in April 1778 Wadsworth was appointed commissary general of the American Continental army, retiring in December 1779; nonetheless, he continued to keep the allied armies amply supplied under difficult conditions. It was at his home in Hartford that Washington and Rochambeau met for the first time in September 1780.

Washington, George (1732–1799). He was born the son of Augustine and Mary Ball Washington in Westmoreland County, Virginia. By 1752 he inherited Mount Vernon, the family estate that he dearly loved for the rest of his life. By 1780 the American Revolution had been underway for six years and General Washington was fighting desperately to oust the British from American shores. The American cause was at a low ebb when he welcomed General Rochambeau and his 5,500-man army as well as his even larger navy. Washington and Rochambeau met and corresponded for a year before deciding to meld their armies at New York and take the fight for independence to Cornwallis at Yorktown, Virginia.

TIME LINE

Events listed here are not intended to be a comprehensive list of events leading to the American Revolution or the Battle of Yorktown, but they do constitute a record of key events mentioned in this book.

1725

July 1. Jean-Baptiste-Donatien de Vimeur, Comte de Rochambeau, born.

1740-1748

War of Austrian Succession.

1763

February 10. Treaty of Paris officially ending the French and Indian War in America and the Seven Years' War in Europe.

1773

December 16. Boston Tea Party.

1775

February 15. Letter written to wealthy Massachusetts ship owner Colonel Jeremiah Lee regarding munitions he ordered through a French agent to be shipped out of Bilbao, Spain, to the colonists.

April 19. Battles of Lexington and Concord, the shot heard 'round the world.

June 15. George Washington made commander in chief of the Continental army.

December 18. Bonvouloir attends first meeting with the Committee on Secret Correspondence at Carpenters' Hall in Philadelphia.

1776

April 26. Beaumarchais learns of King Louis's decision to covertly aid the American insurgents.

May 2. King Louis XVI releases one million livres earmarked for arms to be sent to America under the guise of Hortalez.

July 4. Congress ratifies Declaration of Independence.

August 27. British defeat George Washington at Long Island.

September 15. British occupy New York.

December 20. Benjamin Franklin, head of the American delegation, arrives in Paris hoping to secure economic and military assistance.

1777

July 5. Louis Duportail, French military engineer, arrives in Philadelphia to aid Washington.

July 31. Congress appoints Marquis de Lafayette as major general of the Continental army. Many others arrive from France to fight with the rebels.

October 17. British forces surrender at Saratoga, signaling to other European countries the viability of the rebel cause.

1778

February 6. American diplomats in Paris sign three-part Treaty of Alliance between France and America. France is the first country to recognize America as an independent nation and, therefore, her first friend.

March 7. British General William Howe replaced by General Clinton.

July 10. France and England at war.

July 29. French Admiral D'Estaing arrives at Newport, Rhode Island, to aid the Americans. The French fail to follow through after being deterred by a storm and the incoming British fleet.

1779

April 12. France signs alliance with Spain, and together they formulate a plan to attack England. The attack does not materialize.

June 16. Spain at war with England.

October 9. French Admiral Jean-Baptiste D'Estaing and American General Benjamin Lincoln defeated by British forces at Savannah, Georgia.

1780

February 3. French Admiral de Guichen's fleet on its way to the Caribbean.

May 2. Rochambeau and his 5,500 troops of the *expédition particulière* depart Brest, France, with Admiral de Ternay commanding the 42-ship convoy.

May 12. Charleston, South Carolina, surrenders to the British; American General Lincoln suffers the loss.

July 11. Rochambeau and the *expédition particulière* land in Newport, Rhode Island.

August 16. American General Horatio Gates loses the Battle at Camden, SC, to Lord Cornwallis and Lieutenant Colonel Tarleton.

September 21. General Rochambeau meets for the first time with General Washington at Hartford.

September 25. Washington writes to Colonel Wade at West Point telling him that Benedict Arnold's treasonous plan to hand over West Point to the British has been foiled. Arnold flees on the ship *Vulture*.

October 28. The Vicomte de Rochambeau leaves for France to request the second division of French troops and continued funding.

November 20. Lauzun and about 225 hussars move to winter quarters in Lebanon, Connecticut. His four hundred infantry remain in Rhode Island for the winter.

December 15. Admiral de Ternay dies unexpectedly of natural causes at Newport.

1781

March 6. Generals Washington and Rochambeau meet for a second conference in Newport. Washington and the Americans are formally received aboard the *Duc de Bourgogne*.

March 16. First Battle off the Virginia Capes: Captain Sochet Destouches, who after Ternay's death temporarily replaced the admiral as commander of the squadron that brought Rochambeau to America, sets sail for the Chesapeake on a second mission to supply and strengthen Lafayette and prevent Benedict Arnold from being re-supplied in Virginia. Destouches fails to land the regiments. This battle is deemed an indecisive engagement against British Admiral Marriott Arbuthnot.

March 22. Admiral de Grasse sails his three-decker *Ville de Paris* to the West Indies.

March 26. Admiral Barras leaves for Rhode Island to take command of Ternay's and Destouches's squadron.

May 21. Generals Washington and Rochambeau meet for a third conference in Wethersfield, Connecticut, to continue strategy talks.

June 10. French army begins march from Newport, Rhode Island, to join forces with General George Washington on the highlands above the Hudson River, New York.

June 19. Rochambeau and the army cross into Connecticut en route to New York.

June 21. Lauzun's Legion departs Lebanon for the march to New York.

July–August. Lord Cornwallis moves his army toward Yorktown, Virginia.

July 1. Rochambeau's 56th birthday is celebrated in Ridgebury (Ridgefield), Connecticut.

July 2. Rochambeau's first brigade meets with Lauzun at Bedford, New York, for a joint, two-pronged campaign against the British planned by Washington. The campaign fails.

July 6. Rochambeau's army arrives at the place of encampment in Philipsburg, New York.

July 21–23. Joint expeditions of French and Americans carry out the Grande Reconnaissance, or reconnoitering forays, into British-held territory in the New York region to assess the strength of the enemy.

August 14. Rochambeau and Washington receive letter from Admiral de Grasse saying that he will meet them at the Chesapeake at the end of August. Washington makes final decision to move to Virginia and instructs Rochambeau and the Continental army to prepare for the march to Virginia to engage General Cornwallis.

August 19. The Franco-American armies begin their march from Philipsburg to Virginia. They set up a ruse to suggest to General Clinton that they are ready to attack New York but instead march directly into New Jersey and on to Philadelphia.

September 5. In the second Battle off the Virginia Capes French Admiral de Grasse defeats British Admirals Graves and Hood, thus preventing them from rescuing General Cornwallis at Yorktown, Virginia. At the same time De Grasse manages to draw attention away from Barras who sails unnoticed into Lynnhaven Bay, transporting the heavy siege guns that Rochambeau carried from France.

September 14. Rochambeau, Washington, and Lafayette meet in Williamsburg.

September 28. The siege of Yorktown, Virginia, begins.

October 14. The storming of Cornwallis's redoubts 9 and 10 by the French and Americans, respectively.

October 17. Cornwallis asks for a ceasefire.

October 18. The writing of the Articles of Capitulation at the Moore House in Yorktown.

October 19. The Articles of Capitulation, having been approved by General Washington, are sent to Cornwallis for his approval in the morning. By afternoon the official surrender ceremony of the British to Generals Washington and Rochambeau takes place at Yorktown. The British fleet leaves New York to rescue Cornwallis.

Winter 1781–1782. Washington leaves for Philadelphia, and his troops march back to Newburgh, New York, leaving the French in Williamsburg.

1782

July 11. French troops begin to retrace their march back to Boston.

December 24. French Admiral Vaudreuil sails from Boston with the French troops. They head for the West Indies.

1783

January 29. Rochambeau embarks from Annapolis, Maryland, to return to France.

May 11. The remainder of Lauzun's Legion, about 530 soldiers and officers, embarks from Wilmington, Delaware, for Brest, France. The crossing takes exactly one month, bringing to a close the *expédition particulière.*

September 3. The Peace of Paris (a set of treaties commonly known as the Treaty of Paris) is signed at Paris by representatives of the United States and Britain, concluding the American Revolution. The Treaties of Versailles are signed by representatives of King Louis XVI of France and King Charles III of Spain.

1789

July 14. French Revolution breaks out in Paris with the storming of the Bastille.

1793

January 21. King Louis XVI put to death at the guillotine.

July. Reign of Terror begins in France after the death of King Louis XVI.

October 16. Queen Marie Antoinette put to death at the guillotine.

1794

April 21. Rochambeau imprisoned in the Conciergerie in Paris.

July 27–28. Reign of Terror under Robespierre ends with his arrest and execution at the guillotine.

October 24. Rochambeau and all prisoners freed.

1807

May 12. Rochambeau dies peacefully at the Château de Rochambeau.

GLOSSARY

Abatis. A defensive barricade made up of closely spaced, felled trees, their pointed tops and branches facing the enemy.

Ague. An illness involving fever and shivering.

Aide-de-camp. A subordinate military or naval officer acting as a confidential assistant to a superior, usually to a general officer or admiral.

Ancien régime. The political and social system of France before the French Revolution.

Anglo-Saxon. Relating to or denoting the Germanic inhabitants of England from their arrival in the fifth century up to the Norman Conquest; of English descent.

Artillery. Large-caliber guns used in warfare on land; a military detachment or branch of the armed forces that uses such guns.

Astern. In a position behind a specified vessel.

Battalion. A body of foot soldiers, subdivided into companies; sometimes identical with regiments.

Beam. The extreme width of a vessel.

Bear away. Also, bear off. Change course away from the wind or steer away from something, typically the land.

Bloody flux. An abnormal or morbid discharge of liquid matter from the bowel (an early name for dysentery).

Bowline. A rope attached to the edge of a square sail and leading forward, thus helping the ship sail nearer the wind.

Brigade. A military force consisting of two or more regiments.

Busby. A tall fur hat with a colored cloth flap hanging down on the right-hand side and often a plume on the top, worn by soldiers or certain regiments of hussars and artillerymen.

Cable. 608 feet.

Caparison. To outfit a horse with ornamental covering.

Capstan. A windlass, rotating in a horizontal plane for winding rope or cable by hand.

Catafalque. A raised platform used to support a casket or coffin during a funeral.

Cavalry. The part of a military force composed of troops that serve on horseback.

Chasseur. One of a body of cavalry or infantry troops equipped and trained for rapid movement; light infantry.

Chevaux-de-frise. Timber fence arranged like vertical X's tipped with iron spikes, calculated to stop infantry and, if submerged in water, to stop ships. First developed in the province of Friesland, Spanish Netherlands; literally translated as Frisian horses; an adaptation of the traditional abatis traditionally used to prevent land forces from breaching an enemy's earthworks.

Circumvallation. The surrounding of a structure by a rampart or wall.

Cockades. Rosettes of ribbon worn on the hat of a uniform.

Convoy. A group of military vehicles (in this case, ships) traveling together for protection.

Coppering. Metal used to protect the underwater hull of a ship. The process of affixing copper to the outside of the hull was pioneered by the British Royal Navy in 1708 by Charles Perry. The advantage of the copper-sheathed ships was that they could stay at sea longer. The copper cost seven times as much as wood, but these protected ships were much faster. By July 1779 all ships up to the size of forty-four guns were coppered.

Cordage. Cords or ropes, especially in a ship's rigging. Rigging: the system of ropes, cables, or chains employed to support a ship's masts and to control or set the yards and sails.

Covered. Wearing a hat. Uncovered: hatless.

Corvette. A small eighteenth century warship with a flush deck and one tier of guns.

Division. A group of army brigades or regiments.

Doubling. Getting caught between two firing ships.

Dragoons. Heavily armed cavalry; America's first mounted men who served as bodyguards to Washington and also as special couriers between him and Rochambeau.

Dropsy. An old-fashioned or less technical term for edema, an abnormal accumulation of fluid beneath the skin or in one or more cavities of the body.

Dray. A cart, especially one with low sides, for delivering heavy loads.

Earthworks. An earthen embankment, especially when used as a fortification.

Écus. Ancient silver French coins; one écu equals three livres.

Edema. See dropsy.

En flute. Empty gun ports, resembling the holes in a flute.

Epaulette. An ornamental shoulder piece worn on military uniforms.

Fascines. Bundles of sticks and twigs quickly constructed and tightly bound together, used for erecting gun platforms, especially on soggy ground or for filling ditches to permit infantry, cavalry, and artillery to pass.

Field artillery. Artillery pieces mounted on wheeled carriages for use in combat.

Field-batteries. Fortifications equipped with artillery.

Firebrands. Pieces of burning wood or other material.

Fireships. Vessels filled with combustibles and explosives, ignited and set adrift to destroy an enemy's ships.

First rate ship. A ship carrying at least one hundred guns and a minimum of eight hundred men to work the guns.

Flagship. A ship carrying the flag officer or the commander of a fleet, squadron, or the like, and displaying the officer's flag.

Flotilla. A group of small naval vessels, especially a naval unit containing two or more squadrons.

Foretop. A platform around the head of the lower section of a sailing ship's foremast.

Fusil. A light flintock musket.

Frigate. A fast naval vessel of the late eighteenth and early nineteenth centuries, generally having a lofty ship rig and heavily armed on one or two decks. Square-rigged.

Gabion. A cylindrical wicker basket filled with earth and stones, formerly used in building fortifications.

Grenadier. A soldier who was specially trained and equipped to throw grenades. Later when grenade usage declined, these were the strongest elite assault troops.

Ground weapons. The laying down of weapons at a surrender ceremony.

Guillotine. A device for beheading a person by means of a heavy blade that is dropped between two posts serving as guides; widely used during the French Revolution.

Hogshead. A large cask.

Hornwork. An additional layer of defense surrounding a fortification.

Knot. A unit of speed equivalent to one nautical mile per hour, used especially in relation to ships and winds.

Legion. A military or semi-military unit; an infantry brigade numbering from 3,000 to 6,000 men and usually combined with 300-600 cavalry.

Linchpin. An essential element.

Line ahead. To form a line abreast.

Livres. French currency until the late eighteenth century.

Loyalist. An American colonist who signed an oath of loyalty to the British crown in 1776; sometimes referred to as a tory.

Malignant fever. A fever likely to cause death.

Manual of arms. An instruction book for handling and using weapons in formation, whether in the field or on parade.

Marshal. A military officer of the highest honor; available only to generals of the highest rank, as in the French and other armies. (French: *Maréchal;* not to be confused with maréchal de camp.)

Materiel. Military materials and equipment.

Matross. One of the solders in a train of artillery who assisted the gunners in loading, firing, and sponging the guns.

Oakum. Hemp fiber.

Palisade. A high fence around a defensive enclosure made of tall poles anchored in the ground; stockade.

Parapet. A protective wall over which defenders fired their weapons.

Parley. A conference between opposing sides in a dispute, especially a discussion of terms for an armistice.

Parterre. A formal garden on a level surface.

Picket. A soldier or detachment of soldiers placed on a line forward of a position to warn against an enemy advance. Likely to be composed of light infantry.

Platine. A metal plate covering the lower throat and suspended from a chain around the neck.

Plenipotentiary. Official invested with complete authority to act independently; having full power.

Pungies. Schooners built on Chesapeake Bay for oyster fishing or trading.

Quarterdeck. The part of a ship's upper deck near the stern, traditionally reserved for officers.

Rapier. A sword used for thrusting that has a long narrow blade with an elaborate guard.

Redan. V-shaped earthwork, sometimes called an arrow, usually projecting from a fortified line.

Redoubt. Earthwork enclosed on all sides except for a narrow passageway built to protect soldiers. A temporary or supplementary fortification; an entrenched stronghold or refuge.

Regiment. A permanent unit of an army typically commanded by a colonel and divided into several companies, squadrons, or batteries; often comprised of two battalions.

Ruche. Pleated ribbon.

Sappers and miners. Soldiers in a military unit of engineers employed in the construction of trenches and fortifications.

Saucissons. Extra-long fascines.

Scurvy. A disease caused by a deficiency of vitamin C, characterized by swollen bleeding gums and the re-opening of wounds, which particularly affected poorly nourished sailors until the end of the eighteenth century.

Sea-lane. A route designated for shipping.

Second. In a duel, a mediator who tries to reconcile the parties involved.

Sentry. A soldier stationed to keep guard or to control access to a place.

Sortie. A rapid movement of troops from a besieged place to attack the besiegers.

Spike. To temporarily put a cannon out of action by hammering a spiked implement into the touchhole.

Squadron. A portion of a naval fleet or a detachment of warships; a subdivision of a fleet.

Tender. A boat used to ferry people and supplies to and from a ship.

Tertian fever. A fever characterized by pathol (a severe attack) that recurs every third day.

Three-deckers. Warships outfitted with three levels of guns and gun ports.

Toise. Archaic French word for a unit of length called a fathom (6.395 feet).

Tory. An American colonist who supported the British side during the American Revolution.

Touchhole. A small hole in early firearms, especially cannon, through which the charge is ignited.

Tours livres. A monetary unit used during the early modern period. Also known as livre tournois.

Tow. A coarse linen shirt.

Troglodyte. A cave-dweller.

Van. The vanguard or leading ship.

Wear together. Nautical maneuver to direct a sailing vessel or line of vessels onto another tack by bringing the wind around to the stern, by pivoting.

Weather gage. When a ship or fleet is to windward of another or has the advantage, she is said to have the weather gage of her.

Whaleboat. A beamy, broad rowboat.

Whig. A member of the patriotic party during the Revolutionary period: supporter of the Revolution.

NOTES

CHAPTER ONE
From Seminarian to King's General

1. Here Rochambeau is referred to as General "de" Rochambeau which is the correct form of his name from the French perspective. However, he will primarily be referred to as "Rochambeau" or "General Rochambeau" for the purposes of this book.

2. Weelen, Rochambeau, *Father and Son,* 1.

3. Ibid.

4. According to the late Count Michel de Rochambeau.

5. Six years later he was granted three payments by Charles de Lorraine, the Duc de Guise, to compensate in part for the three horses shot out from under him while under his command.

6. Forbes and Cadman, *France and New England,* Vol. I, 117.

7. Ibid.

8. Ibid., 118.

9. Ibid.

10. General Rochambeau's maternal uncle, Michel Bégon, was appointed by Jean-Baptiste Colbert, finance minister to King Louis XIV, as intendant commissioner of the French Islands of the Caribbean. His interest in botany and the native flora of the islands led to his name being given to the begonia plant. These flowers now adorn gardens, private and public, around the world.

11. Forbes and Cadman, *France and New England,* Vol. I, 118.

12. Ibid.,120.

13. Birth date was not given, just date of baptism.

14. Weelen, *Rochambeau, Father and Son,* 7.

15. Whitridge, *Rochambeau, America's Neglected Founding Father,* 6.

16. Ibid., 9.

17. Ibid.

18. Forbes and Cadman, *France and New England,* Vol. I, 120.

19. Whitridge, *Rochambeau, America's Neglected Founding Father,* 10.

20. Ibid.

21. Ibid., 7.

22. Ibid.,17-19.

23. Ibid.,19-20.

24. Ibid., 22.

25. Ibid., 23.

26. Ibid.

27. Ibid., 24.

28. Ibid.

29. Ibid., 25.

30. Weelen, *Rochambeau*, 16.

31. Whitridge, *Rochambeau, America's Neglected Founding Father*, 25.

32. Ibid.

33. Weelen, *Rochambeau*, 32.

34. Whitridge, *Rochambeau, America's Neglected Founding Father*, 28.

35. Ibid., 25.

36. Forbes and Cadman, *France and New England*, Vol. I, 121.

37. Weelen, *Rochambeau, Father and Son*, 33-34.

38. Ibid., 34.

39. Ibid., 34; *Whitridge, Rochambeau, America's Neglected Founding Father*, 27-28.

40. Weelen, *Rochambeau, Father and Son*, 35.

41. Ibid.

42. Whitridge, *Rochambeau, America's Neglected Founding Father*, 28.

43. Hermann-Maurice, comte de Saxe (1747), *maréchal de France*.

44. Whitridge, *Rochambeau, America's Neglected Founding Father*, 31.

45. Ibid., 32.

46. Ibid., 33-34.

47. Ibid., 38.

48. The British had severely handicapped France by seizing three hundred merchant ships and their six thousand crewmen even before the declaration of war, so depriving the French Royal Navy of her usual main source of recruitment. These men were kept in unhealthy British jails for the entire duration of the war. Less than half survived. This was one of the reasons the French thought a preventive war was necessary and helped the patriots as early as 1776. (Background information provided by Jacques de Trentinian, researcher on the "War for America.")

49. Weelen, *Rochambeau, Father and Son*, 43.

50. Ibid., 43-44.

51.Weelen, *Rochambeau, Father and Son, 44*; *Whitridge, Rochambeau, America's Neglected Founding Father*, 34-35.

52. Whitridge, *Rochambeau, America's Neglected Founding Father*, 35.

53. Weelen, *Rochambeau, Father and Son,* 45.

54. Whitridge, *Rochambeau, America's Neglected Founding Father,* 36.

55. Weelen, *Rochambeau, Father and Son,* 47.

56. Ibid., 48.

57. Whitridge, *Rochambeau, America's Neglected Founding Father,* 38.

58. Ibid., 41.

59. Ibid., 45.

60. By the Royal Ordinance of 1757 the chasseurs companies were introduced to balance the action of the grenadiers on the wings of each battalion. At the time of the Seven Years' War (1763), Rochambeau was but one of the infantry inspectors in charge of local groups of regiments working under minister Choiseul. (Susane, Louis, *Histoire de l'Ancienne Infanterie Français,* 299; Saujon, Campet de, *Service Historique;* Jacques de Trentinian, e-mail message September 9, 2010.)

61. Whitridge, *Rochambeau, America's Neglected Founding Father,* 46.

62. Ibid., 47.

63. Weelen, *Rochambeau, Father and Son,* 54.

64. Ibid., 52.

65. Ibid., 54.

66. Ibid.

67. Ibid., 54-55.

68. Ibid., 55.

69. Ibid.

70. Whitridge, *Rochambeau, America's Neglected Founding Father,* 48.

71. Weelen, *Rochambeau, Father and Son,* 56.

72. Whitridge, *Rochambeau, America's Neglected Founding Father,* 47.

73. Weelen, *Rochambeau, Father and Son,* 56, 65-67.

74. Forbes and Cadman, *France and New England,* Vol. I, 121.

75. Whitridge, *Rochambeau, America's Neglected Founding Father,* 49.

76. Ibid.

77. Weelen, *Rochambeau, Father and Son,* ix.

78. Renard, *Rochambeau: Liberateur de l'Amerique,* 76-77.

79. Ibid., 78-79.

80. Ibid., 79.

81. Ibid.

82. Lillback, *Sacred Fire,* 19.

83. Ibid., 18-19.

84. McJoynt, "Rochambeau," 3.

85. Weelen, *Rochambeau, Father and Son,* ix.

86. The caption under the photo says that Rochambeau was using this residence at 40 Rue du Cherche-Midi in Paris when he was called to Versailles by King Louis XVI to the *expédition particulière.* The photo clearly depicts the façade

of the house showing all four floors, chimney, and types of windows; Cadman and Forbes, Vol. 1.,118.

87. Whitridge, *Rochambeau, America's Neglected Founding Father,* 48-49.

88. Ibid., 57.

CHAPTER TWO
France to the Rescue

1. Roads, *History and Traditions of Marblehead,* 117-18.

2. Vessels owned by Colonel Lee are listed in the probate inventory of 1775-6, docket 166611.

3. Marblehead Museum & Historical Society, *Who was Jeremiah Lee?;* A summary of Colonel Lee's wealth, based on 1768-1771 Massachusetts tax valuation, is noted on page 81 of Volume 1 of 5.

4. Clark, *Naval Documents,* 401, 818.

5. Roads, *History and Traditions of Marblehead, 126-7;* Gramage, *Spirit of '76 Lives,* 104; Austin, Life of Elbridge Gerry, Vol. 1, p 69.

6. Dull, *Diplomatic History of the American Revolution,* 49.

7. Ibid.

8. Karsh, *The Unlikely Spy.*

9. Ibid., 50.

10. Karsh, *The Unlikely Spy.*

11. Ibid., 57.

12. Rawson, *1776 A Day-by-Day Story,* 278.

13. *Spain's Contribution to the American War for Independence,* Xenophon Group: Military History Database; Dull, *The French Navy and American Independence,* 48.

14. Rawson, *1776 A Day-by-Day Story,* 278. "While European statesmen were thus playing with the fate of America, France was aiding America all she could without risking discovery. Beaumarchais, backed by the royal treasury, but acting under a false name and company reported to the Americans that he procured for them." Please note there are different reports of the munitions sent by Beaumarchais.

15. Kite, *Beaumarchais and the War of American Independence.* (e-mail correspondence with Jacques de Trentinian, September 2010).

16. Latané, *Our Debt to France,* (e-mail correspondence with Jacques de Trentinian, September 2010).

17. Dull, *Diplomatic History of the American Revolution,* 95.

18. Ibid.

19. Library of Congress, *Treaty of Alliance;* Avalon Project, *Treaty of Amity and Commerce.*

20. Library of Congress, *Treaty of Alliance.*

21. U.S. Department of State, *French Alliance.*

22. The day of the signing of the French-American treaty is still remembered and re-enacted annually in Hartford, Connecticut's Old State House where Rochambeau and Washington met for their first conference.

23. Whitlock, *La Fayette,* Vol. I, 133.

24. Ibid., 134.

25. Dull, *Diplomatic History of the American Revolution,* 108.

26. Bemis, *Diplomacy of the American Revolution,* 42.

27. Dull, *Diplomatic History of the American Revolution,* 107-108.

28. Ibid., 110.

29. Ibid.

30. Selig, *Hussars in Lebanon,* 16.

31. King Louis XV began seriously depleting France's treasuries in the War of Austrian Succession (1741-1748), followed by the Seven Years' War (1756-1763); King Louis XVI continued the same practice to a tipping point in the American Revolution (1777-1783). All this money was spent for two reasons: First, to conquer the British in America, France's greatest enemy since French Queen *Alienor d'Aquitaine* married the man who was to become Henry II, king of England. As her dowry, she took French Aquitaine with her. Aquitaine became a part of England during her reign. Second, to regain France's world status after the Treaty of Paris, 1763. It is said that the overall cost of the War in America to the Royal French budget was 1,500 million livres or about 5 billion euros or as of 2006 in the US$, about $5.130 billion. (sar.org) (sarfrance.net)

32. According to Chartrand's book, *The French Army in the American War of Independence,* the 1776 regulation uniforms were altered when the Prince de Montbarrey became minister of war in September 1777. In 1779 his new regulations were put into effect. The 1779 uniforms were more of the French style than the previous ones, which had a Prussian air about them. However, by 1780, when departing on the American campaign, a soldier could take any one of at least three different uniforms with him. All four of the regiments on the *expédition particulière* wore basically white breeches with white waistcoat and white coat. Only the Deux-Ponts wore a dark sky blue coat. The *Bourbonnais* wore white lapels and black cuffs. The *Royal Deux-Ponts* wore crimson lapels and cuffs, long tails with white turnbacks, and tricorn hat with plumes. The *Soissonnais* wore crimson lapels and cuffs and tricorn hat with plume. The *Saintonge* wore white lapels and green cuffs (some seen at Yorktown with aurore cuffs and lapels). Each left France with two battalions. Lauzun's Legion uniforms are described in Chapter 5.

33. Forbes and Cadman, *France and New England,* Vol. I, 102.

34. Ibid.

35. Rice and Brown, *American Campaigns,* Vol. I, 225.

36. Ibid., 221.

37. Keim, *Rochambeau: A Commemoration,* 296-98.

38. NPS, *Statement of National Significance,* 4-8.

39. Ibid.

40. Ibid.

41. Acomb, *Journal of von Closen,* xxv.

42. Selig, *Rochambeau in Connecticut,* 45.

43 Ships of the line: These warships took their places in a line of like vessels standing opposite the ships of the line of the enemy. These large ships had guns on as many as four decks. In the case of the *expédition particulière* the largest ships of the line carried as many as 80 guns and as few as 64 guns; however, the *Ville de Paris* had 104 at the time.

44. Rice and Brown, *American Campaigns,* Vol. I, 117-18; Whitridge, *Rochambeau, America's Neglected Founding Father,* 85.

45. Rice and Brown, *American Campaigns,* Vol. I, 118.

46. Ibid.

47. Bonsal, *When the French Were Here,* 9.

48. Rice and Brown, *American Campaigns,* Vol. I, 119.

49. Whitridge, *Rochambeau, America's Neglected Founding Father,* 83-84.

50. Bonsal, *When the French Were Here,* 11.

51. Rice and Brown, *American Campaigns,* Vol. I, 16.

52. Ibid., 119-20.

53. Weelen, *Rochambeau, Father and Son,* 198-202.

54. Keim, *Rochambeau: A Commemoration,* 283.

55. Whitridge, *Rochambeau, America's Neglected Founding Father,* 84.

56. Ibid.

57. Selig, *Rochambeau in Connecticut,* 46.

58. Ibid., 44.

59. Selig, *Rochambeau in Connecticut,* 46; Selig, *Deux-Ponts Germans.*

60. Ibid.

61. Ibid.

62. Selig, *Deux-Ponts Germans.*

63. Bonsal, *When the French Were Here,* 11.

64. Ibid.

65. Kiem, *Rochambeau: A Commemoration,* 285.

CHAPTER THREE
Hope Arrives in Newport

1. Martin, *Narrative of a Revolutionary Soldier,* 148.

2. Blanchard, *Journal,* 37.

3. Selig, "German Soldier," 49.

4. Terry, "Coming of the French Fleet," 69.

5. Powel, "A Few French Officers," 17.
6. National Park Service, *Statement of National Significance*, 4-3.
7. Terry, "Coming of the French Fleet," 70.
8. Keim, *Rochambeau: A Commemoration*, 300.
9. Powel, "A Few French Officers," 17.
10. Rice and Brown, *American Campaigns* Vol. I, 17.
11. Keim, *Rochambeau: A Commemoration*, 313.
12. Forbes and Cadman, France and New England, Vol. I, 106.
13. *Les Régiments Français,* Xenophon Group: Military History Database.
14. Forbes and Cadman, *France and New England*, Vol. I, 112.
15. Rice and Brown, *American Campaigns* Vol. I, 18-19.
16. Blanchard, *Journal*, 45-47.
17. Ibid.
18. Woodbridge, "Rochambeau," 81.
19. Ibid., 82.
20. Rice and Brown, *American Campaigns* Vol. I, 18.
21. Ibid., 19.
22. Ibid., 18-19.
23. Ibid., 18.
24. Keim, *Rochambeau: A Commemoration*, 317.
25. Whitridge, *Rochambeau, America's Neglected Founding Father*, 88.
26. Ibid.
27. Rochambeau, *Memoirs*, 13.
28. Bonsal, *When the French Were Here*, 31.
29. Ibid.
30. Rice and Brown, *American Campaigns* Vol. I, 121-22.
31. Ibid., 122.
32. Rochambeau, *Memoirs*, 24.
33. Woodbridge, "Rochambeau," 83.
34. Selig, *Rochambeau in Connecticut*, 54.
35. National Park Service, *Statement of National Significance*, 4-1.
36. Ibid.
37. Ibid.
38. Selig, *Rochambeau in Connecticut*, 58.
39. Blanchard, *Journal*, 122.
40. Bonsal, *When the French Were Here*, 70-71.
41. Ibid., 70.
42. Forbes and Cadman, *France and New England*. Vol. I, 110.
43. Simpson, "A New Look at How Rochambeau Quartered His Army," 91-92.
44. Ibid., 102-103.
45. Ibid., 98.

46. Ibid., 95.

47. Ibid., 97.

48. Bonsal, *When the French Were Here*, 57.

49. Simpson, "A New Look at How Rochambeau Quartered His Army," 119.

50. Ibid., 116.

51. Ibid.

52. Ibid.

53. Bonsal, *When the French Were Here*, 58.

CHAPTER FOUR
Rochambeau Meets Washington

1. Claremont Institute, "Rediscovering George Washington."

2. Ellis, *Founding Brothers*, 130-31.

3. Woodbridge, "Rochambeau," 77.

4. Ibid.

5. Rossiter, *Washington's Journey Through Litchfield*, 18.

6. Ibid.

7. Ibid., 19.

8. Forbes and Cadman. *France and New England*. Vol. II, 110.

9. Weelen, *Rochambeau, Father and Son*, 212.

10. Forbes and Cadman, *France and New England*, Vol. I, 110.

11. Rochambeau, *Memoirs*, 19.

12. Ibid., 18-19.

13. Ibid., 18.

14. Brass, *History of Andover*, 56; Selig, *Rochambeau's Cavalry*, 16.

15. Donohue, Mary, Survey and Grants Director and Architectural Historian for the Connecticut Commission on Culture and Tourism, Historic Preservation and Museum Division, telephone call; site of the present Charter Oak Bridge.

16. Rossiter, *Washington's Journey Through Litchfield*, 18.

17. Ibid., 20; the name of the fifth aide was not mentioned.

18. Cronin, *Diary of Elihu Hubbard Smith*, 28.

19. Ibid.

20. Forbes and Cadman, *France and New England*, Vol. II, 111.

21. Ibid.

22. Ibid.

23. Selig and Donohue, *En Avant*, 110; Harrison and Donahue, "The Conference State," 20; "The original house, built around 1730, yielded its site to the Atheneum in 1842 and was moved to the south side of Buckingham Street west of John Street, where it remained until demolished in 1887."

24. Forbes and Cadman, *France and New England*, Vol. II, 110.

25. Wayland, *Around the Lebanon Green*, 16-17.

26. Harrison and Donahue, "The Conference State," 2; "The Bunch of Grapes" was on the west side of Main Street near the corner of Asylum Street at 777 Main Street where the Bank of America Building replaced it—see the plaque on the bank.

27. Selig and Donohue, *En Avant*, 110.

28. Rossiter, *Washington's Journey Through Litchfield*, 18.

29. Selig, *Rochambeau's Cavalry*, 18.

30. Woodbridge, "Rochambeau," 85.

31. Kennett, *French Forces in America*, 59-60.

32. Ford, *Writings of George Washington: 1779-1780*, 448-49.

33. Rochambeau, *Memoirs*, 20.

34. Selig and Donohue, *En Avant*, 112.

35. Ibid.

36. Ibid., 113.

37. Ibid.

38. Cronin, *Diary of Elihu Hubbard Smith*, 28.

39. Ford, *Writings of George Washington: 1779-1780*, 449.

40. Martin, *Narrative of a Revolutionary Soldier*, 171.

41. Ibid., 176.

42. Ibid.

43. Historic Valley Forge, "Who Served Here?"

44. Ibid.

45. Ellis, *His Excellency George Washington*, 129.

46. Ibid.

47. Rochambeau, *Memoirs*, 22.

48. Ibid., 25-26.

49. Selig, *Rochambeau's Cavalry: Lauzun's Legion in Connecticut*, 20. The eighteenth-century frigate *Hermione* had brought the Marquis de Lafayette back to Boston on March 10, 1780, on his second trip to America. The *Hermione* is now being rebuilt in Rochefort, France, where it was originally constructed in five months from late 1778 to early 1779. With the return of Lafayette, the ship heralded the good news that King Louis XVI was sending General Rochambeau with 5,500 soldiers to aid George Washington and the American insurgents. She returned to France on February 25, 1782. The reconstruction of the *Hermione* was begun in 1997 and may miss its second or third projected completion date in 2012 due to lack of funds. Early on, there were problems finding the supplies of oak and other hard-to-duplicate materials that were needed, whereas, nearing the end of the project, there is dwindling monetary support. When she is ready to sail, the city of Boston will be waiting to celebrate her arrival. (Ballu, *L'Hermione*, 128.)

50. Weelen, *Rochambeau, Father and Son*, 91.

51. Whitridge, *Rochambeau, America's Neglected Founding Father*, 127.

52. Decré, *Rochambeau and America's Independence*, 68-69.

53. Selig and Donohue, *En Avant*, 113.

54. Ibid.

55. Rochambeau, *Memoirs*, 32.

56. Ibid., 30.

57. Blanchard, *Journal*, 82-83.

58. Ibid.

59. Bonsal, *When the French Were Here*, 61.

60. Powel, "A Few French Officers," 21.

61. Ibid.

62. Bonsal, *When the French Were Here*, 62.

63. Ibid.

64. Ibid.

65. Brass, *History of Andover*, 56.

66. Bonsal, *When the French Were Here*, 62.

67. Ibid., 63.

68. Ibid.

69. Ibid.

70. Ibid.

71. Ibid.

72. Ibid., 64.

73. Ibid.

74. Ibid.

75. Jusserand, "Washington and the French."

76. Decré, *Rochambeau and America's Independence*, 69.

77. Kennett, *French Forces in America*, 99.

78. Ibid., 99-100.

79. Lewis, *Admiral de Grasse*, 128.

80. *The First Naval Battle of the Virginia Capes*.

81. Rochambeau, *Memoirs*, 36.

82. Ramsay, "Life of George Washington."

83. Ibid.

84. Selig, *Hussars in Lebanon*, 33.

85. Rice and Brown, *American Campaigns*, Vol. I, 26; Selig, *Rochambeau in CT*, 57.

86. Weelen, *Rochambeau, Father and Son*, 101.

87. Ibid.

88. Selig, "Conference at Hartford."

89. Weelen, *Rochambeau, Father and Son*, 101.

90. Ibid., 100.

91. Ibid., 102.

92. Rochambeau, *Memoirs*, 38-39.

93. Cronin, *Diary of Elihu Hubbard Smith,* 28.

94. Ibid.

95. Harrison and Donahue, "The Conference State," 3; Selig, *Rochambeau's Cavalry.*

96. Selig, *Rochambeau's Cavalry,* 23; some sources state May 23.

97. Ibid.

98. Ellis, *His Excellency George Washington,* 131.

99. Woodward, "What Happened in Wethersfield?", 39-43.

CHAPTER FIVE
The March to Victory Begins

1. Whitridge, *Rochambeau, America's Neglected Founding Father,* 80.

2. Simpson, "A New Look at How Rochambeau Quartered His Army," 92.

3. Forbes and Cadman, *France and New England,* Vol. I, 137.

4. Ibid.

5. Ibid.

6. Ibid.

7. Ibid., 137-38.

8. *Lauzun's Légion,* http://www.lauzunslegion.com; Jacques de Trentinian.

9. Lauzun, *Memoirs,* 272; 364.

10. Ibid., 298.

11. Selig, *Hussars in Lebanon,* 19-20.

12. Ibid., 17, 27.

13. Ibid., 19.

14. Ibid., 43.

15. Wayland, *Around the Lebanon Green,* 35.

16. Ibid., 34.

17. Ibid., 18-19.

18. Selig, *Hussars in Lebanon,* 71

19. Wayland, *Around the Lebanon Green,* 12-13.

20. Selig, *Hussars in Lebanon,* 58, 71, & 97; Wayland, *Around the Lebanon Green,* 10-11.

21. Selig, *Rochambeau's Cavalry,* 32.

22. Selig, *Hussars in Lebanon,* 57.

23. Wayland, *Around the Lebanon Green,* 23.

24. Ibid., 34.

25. Selig, *Hussars in Lebanon,* 66.

26. Ibid.

27. Ibid., 63.

28. Ibid., 68.

29. Selig, *Rochambeau's Cavalry,* 32.

30. Selig, *Hussars in Lebanon,* 69.

31. Rochambeau, *Memoirs,* 28-29.

32. Selig, *Hussars in Lebanon,* 83.

33. Second Continental Light Dragoons, *Sheldon's Horse.*

34. Ibid.

35. Ibid.

36. Connecticut Commission, "Revolutionary Route in Connecticut."

37. Rochambeau, *Memoirs,* 54.

38. Rice and Brown, *American Campaigns,* Vol. II, 9.

39. Acomb, *Journal of von Closen,* 87.

40. Rice and Brown, *American Campaigns,* Vol. I, 247.

41. Richard Orr, telephone interview; see also, 301.

42. *Rochambeau's Cavalry,* 37.

43. Ibid.

44. Forbes and Cadman, *France and New England,* Vol. I, 151.

45. *Rochambeau's Cavalry,* 38.

46. Forbes and Cadman, *France and New England,* Vol. I, 152.

47. *Rochambeau's Cavalry,* 35-38.

48. Ibid., 39.

49. Ibid., 30.

50. Shelton, *The Salt-Box House,* 162-63.

51. Richard Orr, telephone interview; see also, 301.

52. Forbes and Cadman, *France and New England,* Vol. I, 153.

53. Richard Orr, telephone interview; see also, 301.

54. Ibid.

55. Shelton, *The Salt-Box House,* 163.

56. Selig, "Lauberdière's Journal," 34.

57. Ibid., 33.

58. Rice and Brown, *American Campaigns,* Vol. I, 27-28.

59. Whitridge, Rochambeau, *America's Neglected Founding Father,* 147.

60. Ibid., 147.

61. Rochambeau, *Memoirs,* 51.

62. Ibid., 51.

63. Selig, *Rochambeau in Connecticut,* 60-61; King's stock could be cash, liquor, or beef.

64. Ibid., 59.

65. List taken from: *Rochambeau papers,* Paul Mellon Library, printed in Whitridge's *Rochambeau, America's Neglected Founding Father,* 164 (original spellings retained).

66. National Park Service, *Statement of National Significance,* 4-8.

67. Selig, *Rochambeau in Connecticut,* 70.

68. Ibid.

69. Ibid., 71.

70. Ibid.

71. Ibid.

72. Ibid.

73. Washington, Original letter, date June 30, 1781; Beinecke Rare Book and Manuscript Library, Yale University. 1780-1794. Collection: GEN MSS 146 Box 2 folder 84.

74. Selig, *Rochambeau in Connecticut,* 72.

75. Rice and Brown, *American Campaigns,* Vol. I, 31.

76. Washington, Original letter, dated June 30, 1781; Beinecke Rare Book and Manuscript Library, Yale University. 1780-1794.

77. Rice and Brown, *American Campaigns,* Vol. I, 31.

78. Ibid., 32.

79. Ibid.

80. Selig, *Rochambeau in Connecticut,* 73.

81. Ibid.

82. Rice and Brown, *American Campaigns,* Vol. I, 31-32.

CHAPTER SIX
Layover at New York

1. Rice and Brown, *American Campaigns,* Vol. I, 32.

2. Ibid.

3. Ibid.

4. Ibid., 249.

5. Ibid., 32.

6. Ibid., 248-49.

7. Ibid., 33.

8. Ibid., 32.

9. Acomb, *Journal of von Closen,* 90-91.

10. New Castle Tribune, "French Troops Advanced."

11. Rice and Brown, *American Campaigns,* Vol. I, 249.

12. Ibid., 33.

13. Selig, *Route in the State of New York,* 92; Lauberdiere, *Journal,* fol. 74v.

14. Acomb, *Journal of von Closen,* 90-92.

15. *America Meets France Outside New York,* 111.

16. Selig, *Route in the State of New York,* 111.

17. Blanchard, *Journal,* 118.

18. Ibid., 120.

19. Ibid., 122.

20. Ibid., 123.

21. Rice and Brown, *American Campaigns*, Vol. I, 249.

22. Ibid.

23. Ibid., 33.

24. Ibid.

25. Rochambeau, *Memoirs*, 56-57.

26. Ibid., 48.

27. Ibid., 48-49.

28. Westchester County Historical Society, "Rochambeau Headquarters."

29. Selig, *Route in the State of New York*, 90; McDonald Papers Vol. 1, p. 138; The McDonald papers consist of personal interviews of over 200 people ages 70 and up who lived in Westchester County during the Revolutionary War. According to the Westchester County Historical Society, the interviews are known as the McDonald Papers even though his name was spelled MacDonald.

30. Selig, *Route in the State of New York*, 90.

31. Ibid., 90-91.

32. Ibid.; The McDonald Papers: Jackson Odell, September 12, 1845, 2.

33. Behind the current WFAS radio station.

34. Selig, *Route in the State of New York*, 91; The house of John Tomkins still stands on Healy Avenue South (Scarsdale) near the eastern border of the Sunningdale Country Club.

35. Selig, *Route in the State of New York*, 91.

36. Ibid.

37. Ibid., 90; The McDonald Papers: William Griffen, November 5, 1846, 61.

38. Rice and Brown, American Campaigns, Vol. I, 250.

39. Ibid.

40. Ibid.

41. Ibid.

42. Ibid., 33.

43. Ibid.

44. Selig, "Lauberdière's Journal," 33.

45. Selig, *Route in the State of New York*, 95.

46. Ibid.

47. Ibid.

48. Ibid., 95-96.

49. Ibid., 96.

50. Selig, *Rochambeau in Connecticut*, 110.

51. Selig, *Route in the State of New York*, 97.

52. Scott, *From Yorktown to Valmy*, 57.

53. Rice and Brown, *American Campaigns*, Vol. I, 34.

54. Blanchard, *Journal*, 121.

55. Selig, *Route in the State of New York*, 97.

56. Kennett, *French Forces in America,* 65-66.

57. Selig, *Route in the State of New York,* 98.

58. Ibid.; McDonald Papers Vol. 5, p. 722.

59. Selig, *Route in the State of New York,* 98.

60. Ibid.

61. Kennett, *French Forces in America,* 65-66.

62. Ibid., 66.

63. Ibid., 67.

64. Rice and Brown, *American Campaigns,* Vol. I, 35.

65. Selig, *Route in the State of New York,* 106; Rice and Brown, *American Campaigns,* Vol. I, 251-53.

66. Selig, *Route in the State of New York,* 107.

67. Rice and Brown, *American Campaigns,* Vol. I, 36.

68. Ibid.

69. Ibid., 37.

70. Ibid.

71. Ibid., 252-53.

72. Ibid., 253.

73. Rochambeau, *Memoirs,* 58-59.

74. Rice and Brown, *American Campaigns,* Vol. I, 252.

75. Kennett, *French Forces in America,* 124.

76. Ibid.

77. Bonsal, *When the French Were Here,* 114.

78. Lewis, *Admiral De Grasse,* 138.

79. Ibid.

80. Whitridge, *Rochambeau, America's Neglected Founding Father,* 182; Saint-Domingue now Santo Domingo.

81. Mitchell, "Bankrolling the American Revolution," 25.

82. Ibid., 24-25.

83. Whitridge, *Rochambeau, America's Neglected Founding Father,* 182.

84. Rice and Brown, *American Campaigns,* Vol. I, 326.

85. Bonsal, *When the French Were Here,* 116; Lewis, *Admiral De Grasse,* 140.

86. Lewis, *Admiral De Grasse,* 140.

87. Rochambeau, *Memoirs,* 61.

88. Bonsal, *When the French Were Here,* 116.

89. Ibid.

90. Ibid., 115.

CHAPTER SEVEN
Rochambeau vis-à-vis Washington

1. Ellis, *His Excellency George Washington*, 70.

2. Whitridge, *Rochambeau, America's Neglected Founding Father*, 29-30.

3. *Washington Papers*, Washington to Jonathan Trumbull, January 7, 1776, 130-31.

4. Ibid.

5. Unger, *The Unexpected George Washington*, 116.

6. Ibid., 117.

7. Bonsal, *When the French Were Here*, 34.

8. Whitridge, *Rochambeau, America's Neglected Founding Father*, 116.

9. Unger, *The Unexpected George Washington*, 125.

10. Ibid.

11. Ellis, *His Excellency George Washington*, 120.

12. Kennett, *French Forces in America*, 59.

13. Whitridge, *Rochambeau, America's Neglected Founding Father*, 104.

14. Rochambeau, *Memoirs*, 18.

15. Ellis, *Founding Brothers*, 133.

16. Rev. Jacques Bossière, Ph.D., personal interview March 18 & 31, 2008.

17. Jusserand, "Washington and the French."

18. Ibid.

19. Heitmann, "Rochambeau in Westchester," 81.

20. Morris, *Images of America*, 69.

21. Rev. Jacques Bossière, Ph.D., personal interview March 18 & 31, 2008.

22. Ibid.

23. Kennett, *French Forces in America*, 126.

24. Rev. Jacques Bossière, Ph.D., personal interview March 26, 2008.

25. Woodward, "What Happened in Wethersfield?", 40-43.

26. Bonsal, *When the French Were Here*, 83.

27. Ibid., 104.

28. Kennett, *French Forces in America*, 128.

29. Ibid.

30. Ibid.

31. Ibid.

32. Ibid.

33. Kennett, *French Forces in America*, 129.

34. Kennett, *French Forces in America*, 128.

35. Ibid.

36. Rochambeau, *Memoirs*, 60.

37. W3R-US, *Actions near New York City*.

38. Rochambeau, *Memoirs*, 56.

39. Kennett, *French Forces in America*, 122.

40. Selig, "Francois Joseph Paul Compte de Grasse," 29.

41. Ibid, 27.

42. Heitmann, "Rochambeau in Westchester," 81.

43. Rochambeau, *Memoirs*, 51.

44. Ellis, *His Excellency George Washington*, 14-15.

45. Unger, *The Unexpected George Washington*, 26-28.

46. Ibid., 28.

47. Ellis, *His Excellency George Washington*, 22.

48. Ibid.

49. Lillback, *Sacred Fire*, 43-45.

50. Ibid.

51. Larrabee, 181.

52. Whitridge, *Rochambeau, America's Neglected Founding Father*, 138.

53. Ibid., 137-138.

54. Ibid.

55. Heitmann, "Rochambeau in Westchester," 81.

56. Bonsal, *When the French Were Here*, 115.

57. Weelen, *Rochambeau*, 45.

58. Whitridge, *Rochambeau, America's Neglected Founding Father*, 184.

CHAPTER EIGHT
The Secret March to Virginia

1. Keim, *Rochambeau: A Commemoration*, 413.

2. Ibid., 413-14.

3. Rice and Brown, *American Campaigns*, Vol. I, 40.

4. Ibid.

5. Ibid.

6. Ibid.

7. Rochambeau, *Memoirs*, 62.

8. Ibid.

9. Bonsal, *When the French Were Here*, 120.

10. Rochambeau, *Memoirs*, 62.

11. W3R-US, *Focus Shifts to Yorktown*.

12. Ibid.

13. Ibid.

14. Ibid.

15. *White Plains Press*, "Westchester Saw Epic March."

16. Whitridge, *Rochambeau, America's Neglected Founding Father*, 163.

17. Diamant, *Chaining the Hudson*, 38-39.

18. Ibid., 44.

19. Ibid., 40.
20. Ibid.
21. Ibid., 156.
22. Ibid.
23. Ibid., 6, 183.
24. Ibid., 156-57.
25. Blanchard, *Journal,* 115.
26. Bonsal, *When the French Were Here,* 123.
27. Lewis, *Admiral De Grasse and American Independence,* 154.
28. Keim, *Rochambeau: A Commemoration,* 419.
29. Blanchard, *Journal,* 128.
30. Martin, *Narrative of a Revolutionary Soldier,* 191.
31. Ibid., 192.
32. Ibid., 193.
33. Ibid.
34. Ibid., 192-93.
35. Ibid., 193.
36. Ibid.
37. Blanchard, *Journal,* 135.
38. Bonsal, *When the French Were Here,* 126.
39. *Encyclopedia Britannica,* 859.
40. Keim, *Rochambeau: A Commemoration,* 414.
41. Stember, "En Avant with our French Allies," 68.
42. Bonsal, *When the French Were Here,* 127.
43. Rice and Brown, *American Campaigns,* Vol. I, 45-46.
44. Ibid., 46.
45. Bonsal, *When the French Were Here,* 122.
46. Rice and Brown, *American Campaigns,* Vol. I, 46.
47. Ibid.
48. Ibid.
49. Ibid.
50. Ibid.
51. Bonsal, *When the French Were Here,* 127.
52. Ibid., 128.
53. Ibid.
54. Blanchard, *Journal,* 137.
55. Ibid.
56. Rice and Brown, *American Campaigns,* Vol. I, 46-47.
57. Ibid., 47.
58. Ibid., 48.
59. Ibid.

60. Ibid.

61. Ibid.

62. Bonsal, *When the French Were Here,* 128.

63. Blanchard, *Journal,* 136.

64. Bonsal, *When the French Were Here,* 128; The number of ships that sailed with De Grasse was often exaggerated as in this case.

65. Ibid.,129.

66. Ibid.

67. Ibid.

68. Hallahan, *Day the Revolution Ended,* 151.

69. Ibid.

70. Ibid.

71. Bonsal, *When the French Were Here,* 130.

72. Rochambeau, *Memoirs,* 63.

73. Ibid., 61.

74. Bonsal, *When the French Were Here,* 130-131.

75. Ibid., 130.

76. Whitridge, *Rochambeau, America's Neglected Founding Father,* 195.

77. Bonsal, *When the French Were Here,* 130.

78. Ibid., 129.

79. W3R-US, *March Through Delaware.*

80. Ibid.

81. Ibid.

82. Selig, *Revolutionary Route in the State of Delaware,* 84.

83. Ibid., 74.

84. Ibid.

85. Ibid.

86. Ibid., 75.

87. Lewis, *Admiral De Grasse,* 141.

88. Ibid., 142.

89. Bonsal, *When the French Were Here,* 131.

90. Rochambeau, *Memoirs,* 63

91. Ibid.

92. Ibid.

93. Rice and Brown, *American Campaigns,* Vol. II, 83; Jacques de Trentinian.

94. Bonsal, *When the French Were Here,* 131.

95. Ibid., 132.

96. Ibid.

97. Rice and Brown, *American Campaigns,* Vol. I, 52.

98. Ibid., 53.

99. Ibid.

100. Bonsal, *When the French Were Here*, 132.
101. Ibid., 133.
102. W3R-US, *March and Ship Transport Through Maryland and DC.*
103. Bonsal, *When the French Were Here*, 133-34.
104. Maxson, *Rochambeau's March to Yorktown-1781.*
105. Bonsal, *When the French Were Here*, 133.
106. W3R-US, *March and Ship Transport Through Maryland and DC.*
107. Bonsal, *When the French Were Here*, 132.
108. Ibid.
109. Ibid.
110. Blanchard, Journal, 143.
111. Martin, *Narrative of a Revolutionary Soldier*, 194.
112. Ibid., 195.
113. Rice and Brown, *American Campaigns*, Vol. II, 83.
114. Lewis, *Admiral de Grasse*, 173.
115. Rice and Brown, *American Campaigns*, Vol. II, 83.
116. W3R-US, *March and Ship Transport Through Maryland and DC.*
117. George Washington Foundation, *Kenmore History.*
118. George Washington Foundation, *George Washington's Ferry Farm.*
119. Preservation Virginia, *Mary Washington House.*
120. Weelen, *Rochambeau*, 46.
121. Whitridge, *Rochambeau, America's Neglected Founding Father*, 200-201.
122. W3R-US, *March and Ship Transport Through Maryland and DC.*
123. Stember, "En Avant with our French Allies," 69.
124. Ibid., 65.
125. Lauzun, *Memoirs*, 322.
126. Ibid.
127. Ibid.
128. Ibid., 323.
129. Kennett, *French Forces in America*, 138.
130. Whitridge, *Rochambeau, America's Neglected Founding Father*, 213.
131. Kennett, *French Forces in America*, 137.
132. W3R-US, *March and Ship Transport Through Maryland and DC.*
133. Rice and Brown, *American Campaigns*, Vol. II, 83-84.
134. Ibid.
135. Rice and Brown, *The American Campaigns*, Vol. 1, 52-53.
136. Ibid.
137. W3R-US, *March and Ship Transport Through Maryland and DC.*

CHAPTER NINE
Admiral de Grasse Fights Pivotal Sea Battle

1. Lewis, *Admiral De Grasse,* 141.
2. Ibid., 95-97.
3. Larrabee, *Decision at the Chesapeake,* 6.
4. Selig, "Francois Joseph Paul Comte de Grasse," 27.
5. Lewis, *Admiral De Grasse,* 120-21.
6. Ibid., 122.
7. Selig, "Francois Joseph Paul Comte de Grasse," 28.
8. Larrabee, *Decision at the Chesapeake,* 136.
9. Ibid., 150.
10. Ibid., 140.
11. Ibid., 140-41.
12. Ibid., 142; Rev. Jacques Bossière's letter, March 24, 2008.
13. Larrabee, *Decision at the Chesapeake,* 156.
14. Ibid.
15. Ibid., 159.
16. Ibid., 147.
17. Ibid., 142-43.
18. Ibid., 142.
19. Ibid., 162.
20. Ibid., 166-69; Lewis, *Admiral De Grasse,* 204-205.
21. Ibid., 179.
22. Ibid., 177.
23. Ibid., 179.
24. Ibid.
25. Ibid.
26. Ibid.
27. Ibid., 180.
28. Ibid.
29. Ibid., 181.
30. Ibid., 183.
31. Ibid., 184-85.
32. Ibid., 186.
33. Ibid.
34. Ibid., 188.
35. Dull, *The French Navy and American Independence,* 239.
36. Larrabee, *Decision at the Chesapeake,* 189.
37. Ibid., 188-89.
38. Ibid., 188.
39. Ibid.

40. Ibid., 190.

41. Lewis, *Admiral De Grasse*, 156.

42. Ibid.

43. Ibid., 157.

44. Morgan, *The Pivot Upon Which Everything Turned*; Lewis, *Admiral De Grasse*, 157.

45. Cable length (608 feet in the British navy): Morgan, *The Pivot Upon Which Everything Turned*; Lewis, *Admiral De Grasse*, 157-58.

46. Lewis, *Admiral De Grasse*, 158.

47. Ibid.

48. Larrabee, *Decision at the Chesapeake*, 193.

49. Casson, *Ships and Seamanship*, 280.

50. Lewis, *Admiral De Grasse*, 158.

51. Ibid.; Selig, "Francois Joseph Paul Comte de Grasse," 31.

52. Lewis, *Admiral De Grasse*, 158.

53. Selig, "Francois Joseph Paul Comte de Grasse," 31.

54. Lewis, *Admiral De Grasse*, 158.

55. Ibid.

56. Larrabee, *Decision at the Chesapeake*, 201-02.

57. Ibid., 203.

58. Lewis, *Admiral De Grasse*, 159.

59. Larrabee, *Decision at the Chesapeake*, 203.

60. Lewis, *Admiral De Grasse*, 160-61.

61. Ibid., 161.

62. Ibid., 161-62.

63. Larrabee, *Decision at the Chesapeake*, 204.

64. Rochambeau, *Memoirs*, 64.

65. Lewis, *Admiral De Grasse*, 167.

66. Whitridge, *Rochambeau, America's Neglected Founding Father*, 189-91.

67. Lewis, *Admiral De Grasse*, 163.

68. Ibid.

69. Ibid.

70. Larrabee, *Decision at the Chesapeake*, 203.

71. Lewis, *Admiral De Grasse*, 164.

72. Hallahan, *Day the Revolution Ended*, 163-64.

73. Ibid.

74. Ibid.; Lewis, *Admiral De Grasse*, 174.

75. Ibid.

76. Lewis, *Admiral De Grasse*, 174.

77. Ibid.

78. Ibid., 175.

79. Kennett, *French Forces in America,* 144.

80. Whitridge, *Rochambeau, America's Neglected Founding Father,* 203.

81. Bonsal, *When the French Were Here,* 140.

CHAPTER TEN
The Battle of Yorktown

1. Kennett, *French Forces in America,* 145.

2. Davis, *Campaign That Won America,* 185-86.

3. Rice and Brown, *American Campaigns,* Vol. I, 57.

4. Ibid.

5. Ibid.

6. Kennett, *French Forces in America,* 145-46.

7. Davis, *Campaign That Won America,* 138.

8. Ibid., 139.

9. Ibid., 142.

10. Colonial Williamsburg Foundation, *Peyton Randolph House.*

11. Walklet, Jr., *Window on Williamsburg,* 30.

12. Colonial Williamsburg Foundation. *Biography of George Wythe.*

13. Stevens, *Old Williamsburg,* 267-68.

14. Colonial Williamsburg Foundation, *George Wythe House.*

15. Kennett, French Forces in America, 146.

16. Johnston, *Yorktown Campaign,* 105.

17. Ibid.

18. Davis, *Campaign That Won America,* 183.

19. Rice and Brown, *American Campaigns,* Vol. I, 57.

20. Davis, *Campaign That Won America,* 197.

21. Hallahan, *Day the Revolution Ended,* 175.

22. Ibid.

23. Thompson, *Historic Resource Study,* 62.

24. Morrissey, *Yorktown 1781,* 74.

25. Rice and Brown, *American Campaigns,* Vol. I, 57.

26. Thompson, *Historic Resource Study,* 62.

27. Hallahan, *Day the Revolution Ended,* 174.

28. Ibid.

29. Morrissey, *Yorktown 1781,* 74.

30. Rice and Brown, *American Campaigns,* Vol. I, 57.

31. Ibid.

32. Ellis, *His Excellency George Washington,* 135.

33. Davis, *Campaign That Won America,* 192.

34. Kennett, *French Forces in America,* 142.

35. Ibid.

36. Davis, *Campaign That Won America,* 193.

37. Ivy, *Yorktown Our Ancestral Home;* National Park Service, *Yorktown National Battlefield: The Town of York.*

38. National Park Service, *Yorktown National Battlefield:* The Town of York.

39. Ibid.

40. Whitridge, *Rochambeau, America's Neglected Founding Father,* 209.

41. National Park Service, *Yorktown National Battlefield, Seige.*

42. National Park Service, *Historic Yorktown*

43. Whitridge, *Rochambeau, America's Neglected Founding Father,* 187.

44. Ibid., 190.

45. Ibid., 191.

46. Davis, *Campaign That Won America,* 183.

47. Rochambeau, *Memoirs,* 67.

48. Larrabee, *Decision at the Chesapeake,* 270.

49. Whitridge, *Rochambeau, America's Neglected Founding Father,* 210; Closen, 133.

50. Whitridge, *Rochambeau, America's Neglected Founding Father,* 211.

51. Ibid.

52. Ibid.

53. Johnston, *Yorktown Campaign,* 106.

54. Hallahan, *Day the Revolution Ended,* 167.

55. Ibid.

56. Ibid., 168.

57. The National Park Service (NPS) did a complete survey of the Washington–Rochambeau Revolutionary Route (W3R) and all events related to it. They issued a statement on January 30, 2003 in preparation for the United States Congress's vote on the establishment of the W3R as a national historic route, from Newport to Yorktown and back to Boston.

58. National Park Service, *Statement of National Significance,* 4-18.

59. Rice and Brown, *American Campaigns,* Vol. I, 56.

60. Ibid.

61. Morrissey, *Yorktown 1781,* 60.

62. Selig, "Duc de Lauzun and his Legion," 60.

63. Ibid.

64. Ibid.

65. Ibid.

66. Rochambeau, *Memoirs,* 68; Rice and Brown, *American Campaigns,* Vol. I, 56.

67. Rice and Brown, *American Campaigns,* Vol. I, 57.

68. Ibid.

69. Scott, *From Yorktown to Valmy,* 70.

70. Ibid.

71. Selig, "Duc de Lauzun and his Legion," 60.

72. Rice and Brown, *American Campaigns,* Vol. I, 57-58.

73. Ibid., 58.

74. Ibid.

75. Whitridge, *Rochambeau, America's Neglected Founding Father,* 217; Lauzun, *Memoirs,* 326-27.

76. Whitridge, *Rochambeau, America's Neglected Founding Father,* 217.

77. Ibid.

78. Scott, *From Yorktown to Valmy,* 70.

79. Ibid.

80. Hallahan, *Day the Revolution Ended,* 176.

81. Rice and Brown, *American Campaigns,* Vol. I, 58.

82. Scott, *From Yorktown to Valmy,* 70.

83. Ibid.; Jacques de Trentinian.

84. Selig, "Duc de Lauzun and his Legion," 61.

85. Martin, *Narrative of a Revolutionary Soldier,* 198-99.

86. Ibid., 199.

87. Rochambeau, *Memoirs,* 69.

88. *The First Foot Guards, Dictionary of Terms.*

89. Kennett, *French Forces in America,* 145.

90. Hallahan, *Day the Revolution Ended,* 178.

91. Martin, *Narrative of a Revolutionary Soldier,* 200.

92. Weelen, *Rochambeau,* 46.

93. Scott, *From Yorktown to Valmy,* 70.

94. Rochambeau, *Memoirs,* 68-69.

95. Hallahan, *Day the Revolution Ended,* 179.

96. Martin, *Narrative of a Revolutionary Soldier,* 201.

97. Hallahan, *Day the Revolution Ended,* 179.

98. Ibid.

99. Ibid.

100. Martin, *Narrative of a Revolutionary Soldier,* 201.

101. Ibid.

102. Scott, *From Yorktown to Valmy,* 70.

103. Kennett, *French Forces in America,* 146.

104. Hallahan, *Day the Revolution Ended,* 171.

105. Ibid., 180-81.

106. Shepard, *Marching to Victory,* 24.

107. Rice and Brown, *American Campaigns,* Vol. I, 59.

108. Selig, "Georg Daniel Flohr's Journal."

109. Ibid.

110. Whitridge, *Rochambeau, America's Neglected Founding Father*, 220.
111. Weelen, *Rochambeau*, 47; author's translation.
112. Hallahan, *Day the Revolution Ended*, 185.
113. Martin, *Narrative of a Revolutionary Soldier*, 201.
114. Ibid., 202.
115. Ibid., 201.
116. Rice and Brown, *American Campaigns*, Vol. I, 60.
117. Rochambeau, *Memoirs*, 70; Rice and Brown, *American Campaigns*, Vol. I, 60.
118. Selig, "Georg Daniel Flohr's Journal."
119. Whitridge, *Rochambeau, America's Neglected Founding Father*, 221.
120. Ibid.
121. Ibid.; It is unclear exactly how many Rochambeau meant when he wrote of the loss of one-third of their effectives.
122. Selig, "Georg Daniel Flohr's Journal."
123. Rice and Brown, *American Campaigns*, Vol. I, 60.
124. Ibid., 59-60.
125. Scott, *From Yorktown to Valmy*, 70.
126. Whitridge, *Rochambeau, America's Neglected Founding Father*, 220.
127. Ibid.; Bonsal, *When the French Were Here*, 161.
128. Morrissey, *Yorktown 1781*, 64; Whitridge, *Rochambeau, America's Neglected Founding Father*, 220.
129. Bonsal, *When the French Were Here*, 161.
130. Ibid., 161.
131. Ibid., 162.
132. Morrissey, *Yorktown 1781*, 75.
133. W3R-US, *Siege and Victory at Yorktown*.
134. Scott, *From Yorktown to Valmy*, 70.
135. Hallahan, *Day the Revolution Ended*, 186.
136. Blanchard, *Journal*, 150.
137. Hallahan, *Day the Revolution Ended*, 186.
138. Ibid.
139. Scott, *From Yorktown to Valmy*, 70
140. *The First Foot Guards, Dictionary of Terms*.
141. Rice and Brown, *American Campaigns*, Vol. I, 60.
142. Rochambeau, *Memoirs*, 72.
143. Rice and Brown, *American Campaigns*, Vol. I, 60.
144. Rochambeau, *Memoirs*, 71.
145. Rice and Brown, *American Campaigns*, Vol. I, 60.
146. Ibid.
147. Blanchard, *Journal*, 151.

CHAPTER ELEVEN
British Surrender and Aftermath

1. Hallahan, *Day the Revolution Ended,* 191.
2. Ibid., 192.
3. Ibid.
4. Ibid.
5. Davis, *Campaign That Won America,* 258.
6. Morrissey, *Yorktown 1781,* 73; Hallahan, *Day the Revolution Ended,* 194.
7. Davis, *Campaign That Won America,* 260.
8. National Park Service, *Yorktown Battlefield Moore House.*
9. Ibid.
10. Ibid.
11. Hallahan, *Day the Revolution Ended,* 195.
12. Ibid.
13. National Park Service, *Yorktown Battlefield Moore House*
14. Ibid.
15. Hallahan, *Day the Revolution Ended,* 195.
16. Ibid.
17. Ibid., 196.
18. Ibid., 193.
19. Ibid.
20. Ibid.
21. Comments on famous painting of the *Siege of Yorktown (1781).*
22. National Park Service, *Yorktown Battlefield Moore House.*
23. Hallahan, *Day the Revolution Ended,* 201.
24. Richard Ferrie, "The World Turned Upside Down," 131.
25. Hallahan, *Day the Revolution Ended,* 201.
26. Whitridge, *Rochambeau, America's Neglected Founding Father,* 226.
27. Weelen, *Rochambeau,* 47.
28. Ibid.
29. Weelen, *Rochambeau,* 47; Weelen, *Rochambeau, Father and Son,* 116.
30. Hallahan, *Day the Revolution Ended,* 200.
31. Ibid.
32. Martin, *Narrative of a Revolutionary Soldier,* 206-07.
33. Blanchard, *Journal,* 151-52.
34. Ibid.
35. Selig, "Duc de Lauzun and his Legion," 61.
36. Whitridge, *Rochambeau, America's Neglected Founding Father,* 223-24.
37. Crèvecour dictated in his journal: "Our [the French] losses during the siege amounted to 4 officers killed, including 2 from the artillery, and 20 wounded of whom 3 died of their wounds. M. de Choisy had 15 men killed and 21 wounded;

and we [Crèvecour's French regiment], 70 killed and 169 wounded, making a total of 299. The Americans lost 10 officers and 260 men in killed and wounded. The English lost 30 officers and 600 men in killed and wounded. The garrison taken prisoners of war numbered 6,918 soldiers and 1,500 sailors. There were 68 captured during siege, making a grand total of 8,486, not counting 100 deserters, or the Tories and sutlers who were not reckoned as prisoners of war. The guns captured included 140 iron and 74 bronze pieces totaling 214; in addition, there were 7,320 muskets and 22 flags. Vessels captured in the port numbered 63. Some that were sunk can easily be raised, such as the frigate *Guadeloupe* of 26 guns (which is now in Brest). The 22 flags captured from the enemy have been sent to Court of France as a gift from Congress, delivered by the Marquis de La Fayette." (Rice and Brown, *American Campaigns,* Vol. I, 61.)

Verger wrote in his journal that fifty-nine French soldiers were killed and one hundred and eighty-two were wounded; one French officer was killed while 17 were wounded. This all occurred between October 1 and 17, 1781. (Rice and Brown, *American Campaigns,* Vol. I, 144.)

38. Whitridge, Rochambeau, *America's Neglected Founding Father,* 224.
39. Mitchell, "Bankrolling the American Revolution," 18.
40. Blanchard, *Journal,* 152-53
41. Morrissey, *Yorktown* 1781, 78.
42. Kennett, *French Forces in America,* 155.
43. Rev. Jacques Bossière, Ph.D.
44. Blanchard, *Journal,*152.
45. Rice and Brown, *American Campaigns,* Vol. I, 62.
46. Selig, "Duc de Lauzun and his Legion," 62.
47. Rice and Brown, *American Campaigns,* Vol. I, 62, 65.
48. National Center, *George III's Letter.*
49. Chanset, "La Double Victoire," 55-74.
50. Chanset, "La Double Victoire," from *Introduction* written by Howard C. Rice Jr.
51. Author's translation.
52. Rice and Brown, *American Campaigns,* Vol. I, 62-63.
53. Ibid., 64.
54. Ibid., 63.
55. Ibid., 64.
56. Ibid.
57. Ibid.
58. Weelen, *Rochambeau, Father and Son,* 116.
59. Weelen, *Rochambeau,* 47.
60. Rice and Brown, *American Campaigns,* Vol. I, 65.
61. Geist, "Colonial Williamsburg," 36-38.

62. Weelen, *Rochambeau*, 47.

63. Geist, "Colonial Williamsburg," 38.

64. Ibid.

65. Ibid., 40.

66. Ibid., 39.

67. Ibid., 40.

68. Weelen, *Rochambeau*, 48.

69. Ibid., 47.

70. Bonsal, *When the French Were Here*, 214.

71. Selig, *Rochambeau in Connecticut*, 79; Harris, *French Finances*.

72. Ibid.

73. Ibid.

74. Bonsal, *When the French Were Here*, 215.

75. Geist, "Colonial Williamsburg," 40-41.

76. Bonsal, *When the French Were Here*, 217.

77. Ibid., 218.

78. Weelen, *Father and Son*, x.

79. Ibid.

80. Bonsal, *When the French Were Here*, 218-19.

81. Ibid., 219.

82. Ibid., 221.

83. Ibid.

84. Ibid., 222

85. Ibid., 222-23.

86. Rochambeau, *Memoirs*, 89-90.

87. Ibid., 94.

88. Bonsal, *When the French Were Here*, 229-30.

89. Kennett, *French Forces in America*, 162.

90. Rochambeau, *Memoirs*, 96.

91. Ibid., 98.

92. Kennett, *French Forces in America*, 162.

93. Morrissey, *The World Turned Upside Down*, 79.

94. National Park Service, *Statement of National Significance*, 4-4.

95. Stevens, *Old Williamsburg*, 168.

96. Weelen, *Rochambeau, Father and Son*, xi.

CHAPTER TWELVE
Honors, Revolution, and Memorials

1. *Jean-Baptiste Donatien de Vimeur, comte de Rochambeau*, Xenophon Group: Military History Database.

2. Whitridge, *Rochambeau, America's Neglected Founding Father*, 255.

3. Ibid.

4. Ibid., 257.

5. Ibid., 259.

6. Society of Cincinnati, Anderson House brochure.

7. Ibid.

8. Whitridge, *Rochambeau, America's Neglected Founding Father,* 259.

9. Ibid., 260.

10. Forbes and Cadman, *France and New England,* Vol. I, 123.

11. Whitridge, Rochambeau, *America's Neglected Founding Father,* 276.

12. Ibid., 315.

13. Forbes and Cadman, *France and New England,* Vol. I, 123.

14. Whitridge, *Rochambeau, America's Neglected Founding Father,* 305.

15. Ibid., 304.

16. Ibid.

17. Ibid., 308.

18. Decré, *Rochambeau and America's Independence,* 124.

19. Selig and Donohue, *En Avant,* 77.

20. National Park Service, *Rochambeau Statue.*

21. Forbes and Cadman, *France and New England,* Vol. I, 127.

22. National Park Service, *Rochambeau Statue.*

23. LaFrance, "History of the Rochambeau Statue," 165.

24. Ibid., 167.

25. Ibid.

26. Ibid., 170.

27. Ibid., 167.

28. National Park Service, *Yorktown Victory Monument.*

29. Ibid.

30. Ibid.

31. National Park Service, *The Yorktown Victory Monument Inscriptions.*

32. National Park Service, *Rochambeau Statue.*

33. Ibid.

34. Ibid.

35. Ibid.

36. LaFrance, "History of the Rochambeau Statue," 167.

37. Ibid.

38. National Park Service, *Rochambeau Statue.*

39. LaFrance, "History of the Rochambeau Statue," 170.

40. Ibid., 171.

41. Eric Comte de Rochambeau, telephone March 21, 2007.

42. Richard Orr, telephone interview; see also, 301.

43. Powel, "A Few French Officers," 14.

BIBLIOGRAPHY

PRIMARY SOURCES

Blanchard, Claude. *The Journal of Claude Blanchard, Commissary of the French Auxiliary Army Sent to the United States During the American Revolution 1780-1783*. Translated from original French manuscript by W. Duane and T. Balch. J. Munsell. Albany, 1876.

Kean, Thomas M. "Original letters." Compiled by Beinecke Rare Book and Manuscript Library. Yale University. 1780-1794.

Lafayette, Marquis de. "Original letters." Beinecke Rare Book and Manuscript Library. Yale University, 1780-1794.

Lauzun, Duc de, (Armand Louis de Gontaut duc de Biron) *Memoires of the Duc de Lauzun 1747-1783*. Translated from French by Jules Méras. (The Court Series of French Memoirs.) Sturgis & Walton Company, 1912.

Martin, Joseph Plumb. *A Narrative of a Revolutionary Soldier*. New York: Signet Classic, 2001.

McDonald, John M. *McDonald Papers* (1844-1850). Westchester County Historical Society.

Rice, Jr., Howard C. and Brown, Ann S. K., eds. *The American Campaigns of Rochambeau's Army 1780, 1781, 1782, 1783: Itineraries, Maps and Views and Journals of Crèvecoeur, Verger and Berthier*. Vols. I-II. Princeton: Princeton University Press, 1972.

Rochambeau, Eric, Comte de. Interview by Jini Vail. Kingstown, R.I., 2007. (Descendant of Jean-Baptiste-Donatien de Vimeur, Comte de Rochambeau.)

Rochambeau, Michel, Comte de. Interview by Jini Vail. Château de Rochambeau, Thore La Rochette, France, 1993-2007. (Descendant of Jean-Baptiste-Donatien de Vimeur, Comte de Rochambeau.)

———. Letters addressed to Jini Vail, 1993-2007. (Descendant of Jean-Baptiste-Donatien de Vimeur, Comte de Rochambeau.)

Rochambeau, Jean-Baptiste-Donatien de Vimeur, Comte de. *Memoirs of the Marshal, Count de Rochambeau.* Eyewitness Accounts of the American Revolution Series III. New York: Arno Press, 1971.

———. Original handwritten letters from Rochambeau to George Washington, Lafayette, invitation from Society of Cincinnati to Rochambeau. New Haven: Beinecke Rare Book and Manuscript Library, Yale University, 1780-1794.

Saujon, Campet de. *Collections des Ordonnances.* Service Historique de la Défense: 1757.

Washington, George. *George Washington Papers* at the Library of Congress, 1741-1779, Series 3c Varick Transcripts. George Washington to Jonathan Trumbull, January 7, 1776; 130-31.

———. *Original letters.* Beinecke Rare Book and Manuscript Library, Yale University. 1780-1794. Collection: GEN MSS 146 Box 2 folder 84.

SECONDARY SOURCES

BOOKS

Acomb, Evelyn M., ed. *The Revolutionary Journal of Baron Ludwig von Closen.* Translated by Evelyn M. Acomb. Chapel Hill: The University of North Carolina Press, 1958.

Anderson, Dale. *The Battle of Yorktown.* Milwaukee: World Almanac Library, 2005.

Anderson D. D., Joseph, ed. *The Town and City of Waterbury: Connecticut from the Aboriginal Period to the Year Eighteen Hundred and Ninety-Five.* New Haven: The Price and Lee Company, 1896.

Austin, James T. *The Life of Elbridge Gerry,* Vol. 1. Boston: Wells and Lilly, 1828.

Ballu, Jean-Marie. *L'Hermine, l'aventure de sa reconstruction.* Lyon: Pictoris Publishing, 2007.

Barbée, Maurice Linÿer de la. *Le Chevalier De Ternay.* 2 vols. Grenoble, France: Editions de Quatre Seigneurs, 1972.

Bemis, Samuel Flagg. *The Diplomacy of the American Revolution.* Indiana University Press, 1957.

Bernier, Olivier. *Lafayette Hero of Two Worlds.* New York: E.P. Dutton, Inc., 1983.

Bliven, Jr., Bruce. *Battle for Manhattan.* New York: Henry Holt and Company, 1955.

Bonsal, Stephen. *When the French Were Here: A Narrative of the Sojourn of the French Forces in America and Their Contribution to the Yorktown Campaign, Drawn from Unpublished Reports and Letters of Participants in the National Archives of France and the MS Division of the Library of Congress.* Garden City: Doubleday, Doran and Company, Inc., 1945.

Brass, Philip D. *The History of Andover, Connecticut.* Andover: The Andover Historical Society, 1849.

Casson, Lionell. *Ships and Seamanship in the Ancient World.* Baltimore: Johns Hopkins University Press, 1995.

Chanset, Caron du. "La Double Victoire." Poèm Dédié à Madame la Comtesse de Rochambeau 1781: with an introduction by Howard C. Rice Jr. Washington: Institut Francais, 1954.

Chartrand, Rene. *The French Army in the American War of Independence.* Oxford: Osprey Publishing, 1991.

Châteaux de la Loire. *Guide Verte. Paris: Michelin et Cie.* Proprietaires- Editeurs Pneu Michelin, 1985.

Clark, W.B., ed. *Naval Documents of the American Revolution.* Vol. I. Washington, D.C., 1964.

Collier, Christopher, with Bonnie B. Collier. *The Connecticut Scholar: The Literature of Connecticut History.* Occasional Papers of the Connecticut Humanities Council. Number 6. New Haven: The Connecticut Humanities Council, 1979.

Cronin, James F., ed. *The Diary of Elihu Hubbard Smith.* Philadelphia: The American Philosophical Society, 1973.

Davis, Burke. *The Campaign That Won America; The Story of Yorktown.* United States: Eastern Acorn Press, 1970.

Decre, Antoine. *Rochambeau and America's Independence.* Bloomington: Author House, 2005.

Diamant, Lincoln. *Chaining the Hudson: The Fight for the River in the American Revolution.* New York: Carol Publishing Group, 1994.

Dull, Jonathan R. *A Diplomatic History of the American Revolution,* New Haven: Yale University Press, 1985.

——. *The French Navy and American Independence: A Study of Arms and Diplomacy 1774-1787.* Princeton: Princeton University Press, 1975.

Ellis, Joseph J. *His Excellency George Washington.* New York: Alfred A. Knopf, 2004.

——. *Founding Brothers: The Revolutionary Generation.* New York: Vintage Books, 2000.

Fischer. David Hackett. *Washington's Crossing.* New York: Oxford University Press, 2004.

Forbes, Allen and Paul F. Cadman. *France and New England.* Vol. I, II, III. Boston: State Street Trust Company, 1925.

Ford, Worthington Chauncey, ed. *The Writings of George Washington: 1779-1780.* Vol. VIII. New York: G.P. Putnam's Sons, 1890.

France, The Green Guide. Proprietaires-Editeurs. Watford: Michelin Tyre Public Limited Company, 2001.

Fraser, Bruce. *The Land Of Steady Habits: A Brief History Of Connecticut*. Connecticut Historical Commission: Hartford, 1988.

Friddell, Guy. *Miracle at Yorktown*. Virginia Independence Bicentennial Corporation: Richmond, 1981.

Gamage, Virginia C. and Lord, Priscilla S. *The Spirit of '76 Lives: Marblehead*. Radnor, Pennsylvania: Chilton Book Company, 1972.

Greater Hartford Coordinating Counsel for the Arts. *Guidebook to Greater Hartford: Tours and Tales*. Hartford: Connecticut Printers, Inc., 1966.

Hallahan, William H. *The Day the Revolution Ended: 19 October 1781*. Hoboken: Castle Books, 2006.

Johnston, Henry P. *The Yorktown Campaign and The Surrender of Cornwallis: 1781*. New York: Harper & Brothers, Franklin Square, 1881.

Jusserand, Jules J. *With Americans Past and Present*. New York: Charles Scribner's Sons, 1916.

Keim, DeB. Randolph. *Rochambeau: A Commemoration by the Congress of the United States of America of the Services of the French Auxiliary Forces in the War of Independence*. Washington: Government Printing Office, 1907.

Kennett, Lee. *The French Forces in America, 1780-1783*. Westport, CT: Greenwood Press, 1977.

Ketchum, Richard M. *Victory at Yorktown: The Campaign that Won the Revolution*. New York: Henry Holt and Company, A John Macrae Book, 2004.

Kite, Elizabeth S. *Beaumarchais and the War of American Independence*. 1917.

Lagarde, Andre et Michard, Laurent. *Les Grands Auteurs Francais Textes et Litterature du Moyen Age au XXe Siecle*. Paris/Bruxelles/Montreal: Bordas, 1971.

Larrabee, Harold A. *Decision at the Chesapeake*. New York: Clarkson N. Potter, Inc., 1964.

Latané, John H. *Our Debt to France*. Washington, D.C., 1936.

Lewis, Charles Lee. *Admiral De Grasse and American Independence*. Annapolis: United States Naval Institute, 1945.

Lillback, Peter A. *Sacred Fire*. Bryn Mawr, PA: Providence Forum Press, 2006.

McCullough, David. *1776*. New York: Simon & Schuster, 2005.

——. *John Adams*. New York: Simon & Schuster, 2001.

Michelin Tourist Guide to Brittany, France. Seventh Edition. Proprietaires-Editeurs. London: Michelin Tyre Public Limited Company, 1983.

Mitford, Nancy. *Madame de Pompadour*. New York: The New York Review of Books, 1953.

Morris, Michèle R. *Images of America in Revolutionary France*. Georgetown: Georgetown University Press. 1990.

Morrissey, Brendan. *Yorktown 1781: The World Turned Upside Down*. Oxford: Osprey Publishing, 1997.

Peterson, Charles E. *The Moore House: The Site of the Surrender – Yorktown*. A National Park Service Historic Services Report. Washington, D. C.: National Park and Conservation Association, 2001.

Rawson, Jonathan. *1776 A Day-by-Day Story*. New York: Frederick A. Stokes Company, 1927.

Renard, Marceau-Ch. *Rochambeau: Liberateur de l'Amerique*. Paris: Fasquelle Editeurs, 1951.

Rivoire, Mario. *The Life and Times of Washington*. Philadelphia/New York: Curtis Books, 1967.

Roads, Samuel. *History and Traditions of Marblehead*. Marblehead: Press of N. Allen Lindsey & Company, 1897.

Rossiter, Ehrick K. *Washington's Journey Through Litchfield County En Route from Tappan, N.Y. to Hartford, Connecticut September 18, 1780 - September 25, 1780*. Siena: 1930.

Scott, Samuel F. *From Yorktown to Valmy: The Transformation of the French Army in an Age of Revolution*. Niwot, CO: University Press of Colorado, 1998.

Selig, Ph.D., Robert A. and Mary Donohue. *En Avant with our French Allies*. Hartford: Connecticut Commission on Culture and Tourism, 2001.

Selig, Ph.D., Robert A. *Hussars in Lebanon, A Connecticut Town and Lauzun's Legion During the American Revolution*. Lebanon: The Lebanon Historical Society, 2004.

———. *Rochambeau in Connecticut: Tracing His Journey, Historical and Architectural Survey*. Hartford: Connecticut Historical Commission State of Connecticut, 1999.

———. *Rochambeau's Cavalry: Lauzun's Legion in Connecticut 1780 -1781; The Winter Headquarters of Lauzun's Legion and the March Through the State in 1781; Rochambeau's Conferences in Hartford and Wethersfield*. Hartford: Connecticut Historical Commission, State of Connecticut, 2000.

Shelton, Jane de Forest. *The Salt-Box House: 18th Century Life in a New England Hill Town*. New York: The Baker and Taylor Co., 1900.

Shepard, E. Lee. *Marching to Victory: Capt. Benjamin Bartholomew's Diary of the Yorktown Campaign May 1781 to March 1782*. Richmond: Virginia Historical Society, 2002.

Shepherd, Henry L. *Litchfield: Portrait of a Beautiful Town*. Litchfield: Litchfield Historical Society, 1969.

Stevens, William Oliver. *Old Williamsburg and Her Neighbors*. New York: Dodd, Mead & Company, 1938.

Towle Mfg Company, Silversmiths. *An Account of the Life of Marie Joseph Paul Yves Roch Gilbert du Motier, Marquis de La Fayette: Major-General in the Service of America, and Noblest Patriot of the French Revolution*. Newburyport: Towle Mfg Company, 1907.

Unger, Harlow Giles. *Lafayette*. New York: John Wiley & Sons, Inc., 2002.

———. *The Unexpected George Washington: His Private Life*. Hoboken: John Wiley & Sons, Inc., 2006.

Walklet, Jr., John J. *Colonial Williamsburg, Incorporated*. A Window on Williamsburg. New York: Holt, Rinehart and Winston, Inc., 1966.

Wayland, Alicia. *Around the Lebanon Green: An Architectural and Historical Review of Lebanon, Connecticut*. Lebanon: Town of Lebanon, 1999.

Weelen, Jean-Edmond. *Rochambeau*. Paris: Société Archeologique du Vendome, Editeur: Plon, 1934.

———. *Rochambeau, Father and Son*. New York: Holt and Co., 1936.

Weinberg, Bernard, ed. *French Poetry of the Renaissance*. Carbondale and Edwardsville: Southern Illinois University Press, 1979.

Wheeler, Richard. *Voices of 1776*. New York: Meriden Penguin, 1991.

Whitlock, Brand. *La Fayette*. Vol. I & II. New York: D. Appleton and Company, 1929.

Whitridge, Arnold. *Rochambeau, America's Neglected Founding Father*. New York: The Macmillan Co., 1965.

ARTICLES, REPORTS, AND BROCHURES

Connecticut Commission on Culture & Tourism Brochure. "Washington-Rochambeau Revolutionary Route in Connecticut." Hartford. (c. 2005).

Dawson, Warrington. "The 2112 Frenchmen Who Died in the United States from 1777 to 1783 While Fighting for American Independence." New York: *Journal de la Societe des Americanistes*. New Series, XXVIII (1936).

DePold, Hans. "The Revolutionary Road in Connecticut Newsletter." Issues #1-#55 Bolton Town Historian. Bolton. (1996-2006).

Ferrie, Richard. "The World Turned Upside Down."

"French Troops Advanced through Bedford 150 Years Ago." *New Castle Tribune*, Chappaqua. (August 27, 1931).

Gall, Lawrence. "Washington–Rochambeau Revolutionary Route News, Project Overview." National Park Service, U.S. Department of the Interior. Washington. (Fall 2003; Summer 2004).

Geist. Christopher. "Colonial Williamsburg." *The Journal of Colonial Williamsburg Foundation*. (Autumn 2008): 39-41.

Harris, Robert D. "French Finances and the American War, 1777-1783." Journal of Modern History 48, no. 2 (1976) 233-48.

Harrison, Ann and Mary Donahue. "The Conference State." *Hog River Journal*. (Fall 2005).

Heitmann, Thaddeus F. "Rochambeau in Westchester." *The Westchester Historian Quarterly of the Westchester County Historical Society.* Volume 57, Number 4 (Fall 1981).

Hume, Edgar Erskin, Lieutenant Colonel. "Rochambeau: Marshal of France, Friend of America." Address at the dedication of the Rochambeau Monument, Newport, RI. (July 4, 1940).

LaFrance, A. Curtis. "Newport History: History of the Rochambeau Statue." *Journal of the Newport Historical Society.* Vol. 68, Part 4, no. 237 (Newport: 1998): 165-71.

McJoynt, Albert Durfee. "Rochambeau." *Journal of Early Modern Warfare.* Gorget & Sash. (1990).

Mitchell, Barbara A. "Bankrolling the American Revolution: Gold and silver from Havana allowed American troops to trap Lord Cornwallis and his army." *The Quarterly Journal of Military History.* (Spring 2007): 16-25.

Morgan, William James. "The Point Upon Which Everything Turned: French Naval Superiority That Ensured Victory at Yorktown." Naval Historical Foundation. Washington, DC. (1981).

National Park Service, U.S. Department of the Interior, Northeast and Capital Regions. *Statement of National Significance, Washington-Rochambeau Revolutionary Route Study. Revised Draft Report.* Goody Planning and Associates, Planning and Architecture and Selig, Robert A. Ph.D., Project Historian. (January 30, 2003).

Powel, Miss Mary Edith. "A Few French Officers to Whom We Owe Much (1921)." *Journal of the Newport Historical Society.* Vols. 72-73 (Fall 2003 – Spring 2004).

Ramsay, David. "The Life of George Washington – Chapter Eight: The Campaign of 1781."

Scofield, Carlton B. "When the French Came to Peekskill." Peekskill Historical Society, Peekskill, NY. (October 4, 1956).

Selig, Ph.D., Robert A. "America the Ungrateful." *American Heritage Magazine.* (February/March 1997).

———. "The Duc de Lauzun and his Legion: Rochambeau's most troublesome, colorful soldiers." *Colonial Williamsburg.* (December 1999/January 2000): 56-63.

———. "Francois Joseph Paul Comte de Grasse, the Battle off the Virginia Capes, and the American Victory at Yorktown." *Colonial Williamsburg.* (October/November 1999): 26-32.

———. "A German Soldier in New England During the Revolutionary War: The Account of Georg Daniel Flohr." *Newport History.* Vol. 65, Part 2, No. 223 (Fall 1993): 48-65.

———. "Lauberdière's Journal." *Colonial Williamsburg.* (Autumn 1995): 33-37.

———. "Private Flohr's America. From Newport to Yorktown and the Battle that won the War. A German Foot Soldier who fought for American Independence and tells all about it in a newly discovered Memoir." *American Heritage*. Vol. 43, No. 8 (December 1992): 64-71.

———. Project Historian. *The Washington-Rochambeau-Revolutionary Route in the State of Delaware, 1781-1783, A Historical and Architectural Survey.* (Delaware: 2003).

———. *The Washington-Rochambeau Revolutionary Route in the State of New York: An Historical and Architectural Survey, America Meets France Outside New York City.* (2001).

Simpson, Alan and Mary M. "A New Look at How Rochambeau Quartered His Army in Newport (1780-1781)." *Journal of the Newport Historical Society.* Vols. 72-73 (Fall 2003 – Spring 2004).

The Society of the Cincinnati and its Headquarters. Anderson House brochure. (1995).

Stember, Sol. "En Avant with our French Allies to Yorktown Victory." Washington: *Smithsonian Magazine*. (May 1977).

Thompson, Erwin N. *Historic Resource Study The British Defenses of Yorktown, 1781 Colonial National Historical Park Virginia,* Denver: Denver Service Center Historic Preservation Division, National Park Service, United States Department of the Interior. (September 1976).

Terry, Reverend Dr. Roderick. "The Coming of the French Fleet (1928)." *Journal of The Newport Historical Society.* Vols. 72-73 (Fall 2003 – Spring 2004).

Vail, Jini Jones. "France to the Rescue" original paper presented to Sexta Feira, Watertown, CT, 120 year old literary group. December 3, 1999.

Vail, Jini Jones, script and voice-overs, with Rusty Dyer, filming and editing. *At Home with Rochambeau – A Virtual Tour of the Château de Rochambeau* (DVD) with live introduction. Watertown/Northfield: DigiDyer Productions, 2006.

Washington, George. "George Washington's Vision of our Future" Washington: Library of Congress. (1777).

Westchester County Historical Society. "Rochambeau Headquarters (Odell House) Ridge Road, Hartsdale." Collection of Robert Stackpole.

White Plains Press. "Westchester Saw Epic March in Revolution 150 Years Ago Today as French Army Passed." (August 21, 1931).

Wood, Anna Wharton Smith. "The Robinson Family and Their Correspondence with the Vicomte and the Vicomtesse de Noailles (1922)." *Journal of The Newport Historical Society.* Vols. 72-73 (Fall 2003 – Spring 2004).

Woodbridge, George. "Rochambeau: Two Hundred Years Later (1980)." *Journal of The Newport Historical Society.* Vols. 72-73 (Fall 2003 – Spring 2004).

Woodward, Walter W. "What Happened in Wethersfield?" *Cincinnati Fourteen Journal of the Society of the Cincinnati.* Volume 43, No.1 (Fall 2006).

Websites

Avalon Project, The. *The Treaty of Amity and Commerce Between the United States and France.* http://avalon.law.yale.edu/18th_century/fr1788-2.asp.

Claremont Institute, The. *PBS: Rediscovering George Washington. Timeline: Revolutionary War.* 2002. http://www.pbs.org/georgewashington/timeline/revolutionary_war.html.

The Colonial Williamsburg Foundation. *Biography of George Wythe.* http://www.colonialwilliamsburg.com/Almanack/people/bios/biowythe.cfm.

———. *George Wythe House at Colonial Williamsburg.* http://www.colonialwilliamsburg.com/Almanack/places/hb/hbwythe.cfm.

———. *Peyton Randolph House.* http://www.colonialwilliamsburg.com/Almanack/places/hb/hbran.cfm.

The Fort Edwards Foundation. *The Conflict Begins-Washington Begins French & Indian War; surrenders Fort Necessity.* http://www.fortedwards.org/1754.htm.

The George Washington Foundation. *George Washington's Ferry Farm.* http://www.kenmore.org/ff_home/html.

———. *Kenmore History.* http://www.kenmore.org/kenmore/history.html.

Hermann-Maurice, Comte de Saxe (1747), *maréchal de France.* http://www.axonais.comsaintquentin/musee_lecuyer/saxe.html.

Historic Valley Forge, *Who Served Here?* Benedict Arnold. Courtesy National Center for the American Revolution/Valley Forge Historical Society. http://www.ushistory.org/ValleyForge/served/arnold.html.

Hudson River Valley Institute. *The Conference at Hartford, September 18-24, 1780.* http://www.hudsonrivervalley.net/luuzunionconference/The%20Conference%20at%20Hartford.pdf.

Hudson River Valley Institute. http://www.hudsonrivervalley.org/themes/pdfs/rochambeau_revolutionary_route.pdf.

Ivy, Dick. "Yorktown Our Ancestral Home." http://www.nicolasmartiau.org/yorktown.

Jusserand, Jules J, *With Americans of Past and Present Days, Washington and the French,* section III, part IV. (New York: 1916) http://www.bartleby.com/238/34.html.

Karsh, Carl G. *The Unlikely Spy.* http://www.carpentershall.org/history/french.htm.

Lauzun's Légion. http://www.lauzunslegion.com.

Library of Congress. *Primary Documents in American History: The Treaty of Alliance with France.* http://www.loc.gov/rr/program/bib/ourdocs/alliance. html.

Marblehead Museum & Historical Society. *Who was Jeremiah Lee?* http:/www. marblehead museum.org/Whois _Lee/htm.

Maxson, Ray. *Rochambeau's March to Yorktown: 1781.* http://www.ncssar. com/articles/rochmarch.htm.

Morgan, William James. Mecklenburg Chapter of the National Chapter Society of the Sons of the American Revolution. *The Pivot Upon Which Everything Turned: French Naval Superiority That Ensured Victory at Yorktown.* Navy Department Library, Washington, DC (1981). http://www.history.navy.mil/library/online/pivot.htm.

Murry, Dr. Mildred and Lampman, Chuck. *Spain's Role in the American Revolution From the Atlantic to the Pacific Ocean.* http://americanrevolution. org/hispanic.html.

The National Center for Public Policy Research. *George III's Letter on the Loss of America.* http://www.nationalcenter.org/GeorgeIIILossofAmericas.html.

National Park Service. *Historic Yorktown: The Town of York, General History.* http://www.nps.gov/york/historyculture/historic-yorktown.htm.

——. *President's Park (White House): Rochambeau Statue.* http://www.nps.gov/whho/historyculture/rochambeau.htm.

——. *Rochambeau Statue.* http://www.nps.gov/whho/historyculture/rochambeau.htm.

——. *Yorktown Battlefield: Moore House.* http://www.nps.gov/york/historyculture/moore-house.htm.

——. *Yorktown National Battlefield: Seige of Yorktown, Investment of Yorktown.* http://www.nps.gov/history/history/online_books/hh/14/hh14b3.htm#top.

——. *Yorktown National Battlefield: The Town of York.* http://www.nps.gov/history/history/online_books/hh/14/hh14c.htm#top.

——. *Yorktown Victory Monument. Colonial National Historic Park.* http://www.nps.gov/york/historyculture/vicmon02.htm.

——. *The Yorktown Victory Monument Inscriptions-Victory Monument Yorktown, Virginia.* Colonial National Historic Park. http://www.nps.gov/york/historyculture/vicmon.htm.

Preservation Virginia. *Mary Washington House.* http://www.apva.org/marywashingtonhouse.

Selig, Ph.D., Robert A. *Deux-Ponts Germans: Unsung Heroes of the American Revolution.* http://www.americanrevolution.org/flohr2.html.

——. *The Duc de Lauzun and his Legion: Rochambeau's most colorful, troublesome soldiers.* http://www.americanrevolution.org/lauzun.html.

———. "George Daniel Flohr's Journal: A New Perspective." http://www.american-revolution.org/flohr/flohr1.html.

Second Continental Light Dragoons. *Sheldon's Horse.* http://dragoons.info/Past/French_Connection.html.

U.S. Department of State. *French Alliance, French Assistance, and European Diplomacy during the American Revolution, 1778-1782.* http://www.state.gov/r/pa/ho/time/ar/14312.htm.

W3R-US. *The Focus Shifts to Yorktown: March from New York through New Jersey.* http://www.w3r-us.org/history/hist-04.htm.

———. *March through Delaware.* http://www.w3r-us.org/history/hist-05a.htm.

———. *March and Ship Transport Through Maryland.* http://www.w3r-us.org/history/hist-md.htm.

Xenophen Group. *Comments on famous painting of the Siege of Yorktown* (1781). http://www.xenophonegroup.com/mcjoynt/yrkt-z.htm.

———. *First Naval Battle of the Virginia Capes.* http://xenophongroup.com/mcjoynt/capes_1.htm.

———. *Jean-Baptist Donatien de Vimeur, comte de Rochambeau (1725-1807).* http://xenophongroup.com/mcjoynt/rochamb1.htm.

———. *Les Régiments Français.* http://xenophongroup.com/mcjoynt/regmts.htm.

———. *The Second Naval Battle of the Virginia Capes (1781).* http://xenophongroup.com/mcjoynt/capes_2.htm.

———. *Spain's Contribution to the American War for Independence.* http://xenophongroup.com/mcjoynt/spain01.htm.

Reference Works

Atkins, Beryl T. et al, ed. *Robert & Collins Dictionnaire FRANCAIS-ANGLAIS ANGLAIS-FRANCAIS,* Nouvelle Edition. Paris: Dictionnaires Le Robert, 1988.

Auge, Claude et Paul. *Nouveau Petit Larousse Illustre.* Paris: Librairie Larousse, 1958.

Encyclopedia Britannica, Inc. Chicago: William Benton, 1971.

First Foot Guards. *Dictionary of terms in common use in the 18th century.* http://footguards.tripod.com/01ABOUT/01_dictionary.htm.

Random House Dictionary of the English Language (The Unabridged Edition). New York: Random House, 1969.

INDEX

André, John, Major, 83-85, 183, 307
Annapolis, 195-96, 200, 204
   departure of Rochambeau, 280
Aranda, Pedro Pablo Abarca de Bolea,
   Conde d', 39, 118, 154, 157, 307
Arnold, Benedict, 92-93, 274, 307
   attempt to hand over West Point 83-
   85, 181, 183, 249
artillery (in American campaign):
   Barras's convoy and, 149, 180, 200,
   217
   Cornwallis faces threat of, 233, 245,
   249, 270
   De Grasse's convoy and, 148, 195
   Rochambeau's army and, 43, 45, 47,
   60, 63, 117, 119, 122, 128-29, 132-
   33, 149, 178, 188, 193, 195-96, 203,
   249-51, 256
   Lauzun's legion and, 104-105, 113,
   280
   Washington's army and, 78, 99, 179,
   182-83, 241

Baltimore, 197
Barras, Jacques-Melchior Saint-Laurent,
   Comte de, 97, 132, 144, 148, 213,
   238, 308
   commands French fleet at Newport,
   89, 96
   transports heavy siege artillery to
   Yorktown, 149, 180, 184, 200, 215-17,
   225
Beaumarchais, Pierre-Augustin
   Caron de, 36-37, 154, 308
Berthier, Charles-Louis-Jean, Chevalier,
   44, 202, 308
Berthier, Louis-Alexandre, 44, 113, 128-
   29, 134, 142-44, 177, 178, 202, 205,
   263, 308
Blanchard, Claude, 56, 61, 68, 130-31, 183,
   185-86, 199, 257, 267, 269-70, 309

Bonvouloir, Julien-Alexandre Achard,
   Chevalier de, 309
   Committee of Secret
   Correspondence, 35, 37
Boston, 33, 49, 52-53, 61-62, 87, 96, 117,
   121, 154, 185, 276, 294
   departure of French army, 279
Bougainville, Louis-Antoine, Comte de,
   Second Battle off the Capes, 219-20,
   222, 224, 309
Brest, France, 42-43, 66, 161, 174, 194,
   280
   French army departs, 32

camps list, Newport to Yorktown, 119-20
Carlos III, King of Spain, 36, 147, 309
Castries, Charles-Eugène-Gabriel de La
   Croix, Marquis de, 24, 94, 97, 207,
   310
Chastellux, François-Jean de Beauvoir,
   Chevalier, 72, 109, 110, 134, 142, 190,
   227, 286, 310
   Mount Vernon, 198
   Philadelphia, 187
   route through CT to NY, 102-103,
   117
Chester, PA, news from De Grasse,
   191-97
Choisy, Claude-Gabriel, Marquis de, 310
   Chesapeake, 241-45
   Newport, 112, 132-33
Clermont-Crèvecoeur, Jean-François
   Louis, Comte de, 63, 74, 134-35, 140,
   178, 183, 195-95, 253, 256, 265-66,
   273, 310
   Bedford, 125-26
   Breakneck Hill, 122
   Hudson Highlands, 128-29
   march to Yorktown, 231, 235, 243, 250
   Newport, 58-60
   Philadelphia, 189-90

Clinton, Sir Henry, 49, 55, 65-66, 74, 214-15, 310
  arrives in America, 154
  command at New York, 76, 89, 98, 138, 158, 173
  Cornwallis, 187, 203, 209, 231, 233-34, 242, 250, 260, 282
  fooled by Chatham bake-ovens, 178-81, 184
  Grande Reconnaissance,141-42, 144-45, 167, 176, 177
Closen-Haydenbourg, Baron von, 45, 89, 113, 129-30, 142, 235, 239, 275, 311
Clostercamp, Battle of, 24-25, 102, 117, 253
clothing and supplies. See uniforms
convoy list, expédition particulière, 47
Cornwallis, Charles, 2nd Earl, Lord, 107, 270, 311
  Clinton, 144-45, 177, 188, 209, 233
  gift to Rochambeau, 269
  Lafayette, 160-61, 165, 210-12
  New York, 155
  Rochambeau, 76, 118, 168, 203, 239-40, 269, 282
  surrender, 259-62, 264-68, 274-75, 279, 297
  Virginia, 92, 117-18, 138, 205-206, 210
  Yorktown, 149-150, 160, 169, 190, 225, 227, 229, 231, 233-34, 236-38, 242, 249-50, 252, 255-58
Custine-Sarreck, Adam-Philippe, Comte de, 117, 196, 203,
  visits Mount Vernon, 277

Deane, Silas, 82, 99, 311
  Franco-American Treaty of Alliance, 38, 155-56
De Grasse. See Grasse
Desandrouins, Jean-Nicolas, Vicomte de, 77, 141, 150, 312
Destouches, Charles-René-Dominique Gochet, Chevalier, 312
  First Battle off the Capes, 94
  commands French fleet, 89, 92-93
Deux-Ponts, Christian, Marquis de Forbach de, 57, 312
Deux-Ponts, Guillaume de Forbach, Comte de, 180, 256-57, 270, 312
  redoubt 9 (Yorktown), 252

Dillon, Robert-Guillaume, Comte, 115, 312
Lebanon, 108
Divine Providence (providential), 152, 169, 171-72, 181, 257
Dumas, Guillaume-Mathieu, Comte, 59, 114, 134, 142-43, 173, 251, 265-66, 312
  conferences with Washington and Rochambeau, 77, 82
Duportail, Louis Le Bègue de Presle, Chevalier, 37, 141, 167-68, 193, 227, 313

Estaing, Jean-Baptiste-Charles-Henri-Hector, Comte d', 58, 89, 286, 313
expédition particulière, 3, 32, 42, 54, 69, 113, 121, 163, 211, 274, 280, 283, 286, 292, 299

Fersen, Hans Axel Count von, 77, 80, 83, 180, 313
Flohr, Georg Daniel, 52-53, 56-57, 251-53, 313
Franklin, Benjamin, 32, 102, 182, 313
  Franco-American Treaty of Alliance, 38, 155
  meets Bonvouloir at Philadephia, 35
funding, 31, 33-38, 41-43, 54, 75, 86-87, 96-
  98, 138-40, 145-47, 177-78, 184-85, 187, 192, 208, 272, 276-77
  Continentals pay with IOUs, 193
  French pay their way, 69, 137
  French vs. American soldiers' pay, 246
  King Louis XVI's motives, 95
  undermined, 57

George William Frederick III, King of England, 31, 33, 41, 160, 212, 259, 271, 282, 314
glossary of terms, 329
Gloucester, VA, 145, 203, 257, 274, 297
  Battle of, 241-45, 270, 272-73
  surrender of, 259-60, 263, 267-68
God, 7, 9, 21, 25, 27, 67, 92, 169, 172, 192, 199, 270-71
  Providence (Divine), 169, 172, 199
  Rochambeau encouraged in devotion to, 9
  Rochambeau's father's Christianity,

7, 25
Rochambeau's reverence for 27, 67,
    92, 192
Te Deum, 21, 25, 270-71, 275
Washington's reverence for, 171
Grasse, François-Joseph-Paul, Comte de,
    Admiral, 239, 272, 276, 314
    Chesapeake, 149, 168, 190-92, 194-
        95, 199-200, 204, 241, 269
    convoy, 148, 190
    Cuban funds, 146-47, 192, 276-77
    meets with Rochambeau and
        Washington, 227-29
    news at Chester, 191-97
    prepares to join forces with
        Rochambeau, 97, 138, 144-45
    Rochambeau commands, 174
    Rochambeau suggests Chesapeake,
        117-18, 144-147, 168, 177
    Second Battle off the Capes, 207-29,
        272
    strategy and timing of, 168-69, 192,
        226-27
    Washington accepts naval strategy,
        176, 177-78

Hamilton, Alexander, 78, 80, 150, 227,
    253-55, 314
Hartford, 125, 160-61
    conference at, 76-83, 97, 163
Hartsdale, 128
    Rochambeau's New York
        headquarters, 133, *149*
Head of Elk, 176, 186, 191, 195-98,
    203-205
Heath, William, 59, 61-62, 179-80, 233,
    315
historic homes:
    Connecticut
        Hartford:
            Wadsworth Atheneum, 79
        Lebanon:
            Redwood House (David
                Trumbull), 107, *110*
            Trumbull House (Governor
                Jonathan, Sr.), 79, 90
            Trumbull House (Jonathan, Jr.), 107
            Wadsworth Stable, 79
            War Office, 107
        Middlebury:
            Breakneck Hill Monument, 122
            Josiah Bronson, 122-123

Wethersfield:
    Webb-Deane, 99
New York
    Hartsdale:
        Odell, 131, 133, *149*
Rhode Island
    Newport:
        Cowley, 72
        Hunter, Thames St., 69, 72, 106
        Hunter, Washington St., 87
        Maudsley, 72
        Robinson, 72
        Vernon, 70-71
        Wanton, Thames St., 72
        Wanton, Washington St., 72, 88
Virginia
    Fredericksburg:
        Ferry Farm, 201
        Kenmore, 201
        Mary Ball Washington House, 201
        Mount Vernon Estate, 91, 153, 197-
            201, 277
    Williamsburg:
        Governor's Palace, 274-75
        Peyton Randolph House, 231-32
        Wythe House, 232
    Yorktown:
        Moore House, 252, 259-61
        Nelson House, 237, 240, 261
    Washington, D.C.
        Anderson House, 285
Howe, Richard Carl, Lord, 58, 154-55,
    157-58, 315
Howe, William, 154-55, 157-58, 315

Indians (Native Americans), 66-68, *67*,
    322

Kalb, Johann, Baron de, 37, 315
Key Participants (biographical sketches),
    307-23
Knox, Henry, 78, 167, 187, 227-28, 241,
    248, 315
    and Society of the Cincinnati, 285

Lafayette, Marie-Joseph-Paul-Yves Roch-
    Gilbert du Motier, Marquis de, 37-
    39, 154, 164, 295-98, 316
    Hartford, 78, 80
    Newport, 53, 61, 64-65
    Rochambeau correspondence with,
        64-65

Lafayette *(cont.)*:
  Society of the Cincinnati, 286
  Virginia, 92-93, 117, 160-61, 165,
  178,
    190, 195, 201-202, 209-12, 227, 232
  Washington, correspondence with,
  156, 167, 209
  Yorktown, 145, 150, 240, 253-54, 264
La Luzerne, Anne-César, Chevalier de,
  83, 118, 145-46, 154, 157, 160,
  165,
    209, 316
  first fête, 90, 190-91
  meets Rochambeau at New York,
  128
  second fête, 278
La Pérouse, Jean-François de Galaup,
  Comte de, 86, 316
Lauberdière, Louis-François-Bertrand
  du Pont d'Aubevoye, Comte de, 41,
  123, 130, 135, 137, 143, 316
  horse incident, 116
  Wethersfield, 100
Laufeldt, Battle of, 13-16, 20
Laurens, John, 86-87, 184-85, 254, 317
  Articles of Capitulation, 261-62
Lauzun, Armand-Louis Gontaut, Duc
  de,
    43, 60, 103-105, 286, 300-301, 317
  march to New York and Gloucester,
  113-16, 119, 123-25, 127-29, 134,
  142, 188, 191, 193, 196, 203, 241-
  45, 267-68
  Newport, 63, 72
  reports victory, 270-71
  return from France and final
  departure of, 274, 280
  winter in Lebanon, 90, 105-10
Lebanon, CT, 79-80, 90, 103, 112, 119
  Lauzun's winter camp, 105-11, 113-
  16, 126
Lee, Jeremiah, 33-35, 318
L'Enfant, Pierre-Charles, 14, 37, 317
  and the Society of the Cincinnati,
  285-86
Lincoln, Benjamin, 49, 127-28, 142, 178-
  79, 196, 204, 240, 318
  Yorktown surrender, 264-67
Louis XV, King of France, 11-12, 14, 17,
  22, 29
Louis XVI, King of France, 27, 29, 36,
  42,

  66, 86, 88, 94-95, 96, 104-105, 161,
  187, 199, 212, 263, 270-72, 278, 281-
  82, 283-84, 287, 291-92, 298, 318
  chooses Rochambeau, 30, 163
  decision to aid America, 31, 41-42,
  74, 94-95, 154
  Te Deum, 270, 275

Marblehead, 33-34
Marie Antoinette, 42, 77, 207, 278, 318
Martin, Joseph Plumb, 55-56, 84, 185,
  318-19
  Chesapeake Bay, 185-86, 199-200,
  Yorktown, 241, 245-46, 252, 267
Minorca, Battle of, 20-22, 184
Montbarrey, Alexandre Marie-Léonore
  de Saint Mauris, Prince de, 31, 45,
  94-95, 161, 165-66, 319
  chooses Rochambeau, 163
Morris, Robert, 177-78, 186-87, 319
Mount Vernon. *See* historic homes

Necker, Jacques, 41-42, 94-95, 97, 319
Newport, 86-88, 98, 112-13, 129, 131-33,
  137, 141, 144, 148, 184, 200, 249
  arrival of French fleet, 3, 49-54,
  55-73
  billeting, 69-73
  conference at, 89-92
  French departure from, 116-19
  Rochambeau statue, 299-300
  Washington meets with
  Rochambeau, 89-92
New York, 51, 62-65, 74, 80-81, 93, 98,
  100, 113, 116-18, 124-26, 131-33
  Benedict Arnold, 83-84
  British response, 209, 213-16, 225,
  227, 233-34, 250, 260, 277
  chaining Hudson, 182-83
  Hudson Highlands, 128-29
  layover at, 127-51
  provisions, 112
  Rochambeau's march from Newport
  to, 113, 116-26, 133, 142, 178,
  279-80
  strategy, 81, 129, 138, 144-45, 150,
  152, 154-58, 160-69, 173, 178-81,
  209, 229, 293
  Washington and, 141, 173, 179
  West Point, 181, 274
Noailles, Louis-Marie-Antoine,
  Vicomte de, 72, 95, 256, 320

O'Hara, Charles, 320
    surrender at Yorktown, 264-67

Philadelphia, 144, 147, 182, 185, 204
    Committee of Secret
        Correspondence, 35
    La Luzerne in, 118, 128, 165, 190
    Rochambeau in, 186-91, 278
    Society of the Cincinnati, 286
Philipsburg, NY:
    Rochambeau in, 128-34, 139, 141,
        178-79
    Washington headquarters in, 98,
        102, 123, 133-34, 176, 177-78
Providence. *See* Divine Providence
Providence, RI, 61, 63, 68-69, 77, 103,
    112, 117, 119

Ridgefield, 119, 123
Rochambeau, Donatien-Marie-Joseph
    de Vimeur, Vicomte de, 17, 41, 65,
        70, 77, 86-87, 95-98, 112, 119, 208,
        251, 287, 320
Rochambeau, Jean-Baptiste-Donatien
    de Vimeur Comte de, 320
    Annapolis, departure from, 280
    awards:
        Légion d'Honneur, 291
        Maréchal de France, *iv,* 287, 298
        Order of the Saint Esprit, *vi,* 283,
            298
        Society of the Cincinnati, 284
    Château de Rochambeau, 4-9, 17-18,
        272, 288
    conferences with Washington,
        74-101
        Hartford, 76-83
        Newport, 89-92
        Wethersfield, 98-101, 117, 158,
            156, 165-66
    death, 291
    early life, 4-5
    family, immediate, 6-8
    family motto, 3, 5, 299
    French army in America:
        departure of, (Rochambeau), 280;
            (army), 277-82
        convoy to, 47
        first allied assault 126-28
        Gloucester, siege of, 241-45
        Grande Reconnaissance, 140-44
        New York, march to, 116-26

Newport, 55-112
    surrender of, 267-68
    Yorktown, siege of, 230-58
        ideal lieutenant, 163, 173, 282,
    291,
        292, 301
    imprisoned in Conciergerie, 288-91
    Indians, interactions with, 66-68, 67
    Lafayette and, 64-65, 80, 145, 156,
        160-61, 164, 174, 231-32, 296-98
    Louis XVI (king) summons, 30
    marriage, 15-19, 291
    meets with De Grasse, 227-29, 269
    military career in Europe, 10-30
        Austrian Succession, War of,
        10-15
            Laufeldt, 13-15
        French army, reorganization of,
        26-28, 75-76
        Seven Years' War, 19-28
            Auvergne regiment,
                commander of, 23
            Clostercamp, 23-25, 117, 253
            Minorca, 20-22, 117, 184
    military heritage, 5-6, 8-9
    news at Chester, 191-97
    Odell House, 131, 149
    Society of the Cincinnati, 284-87
    statues of, 295-300
    strategy finalized for Franco-
        American allies, 152-76
    Virginia, march to 177-206
        Mount Vernon visit, 197-201
        with Lafayette in Williamsburg,
            201-202
    voyage to America, 44-54
    Washington and, 152-76
        See conferences
        farewell to, 279
    Williamsburg, 230-232
        departure from, 277
        winters in, 247-77
    Yorktown, siege of, 230-58
        See also Yorktown
        battle joined, 247-58
        surrender (white flag), 259-67
        sword debacle, 264-67
Rochambeau, Jeanne-Thérèse Telles
    d'Acosta, Comtesse de, 15-19,
        287-88, 291, 321

Saint-Domingue (Santo Domingo;
    Haiti), 118, 147-48, 287

Saint-Simon-Montbléru, Claude-Anne du Rouvroy, Marquis de, 23, 118, 190, 201-202, 211-12, 240-41, 247, 321
ships. *See* convoy list
Society of the Cincinnati, 284-87, 296
  Anderson House, 285
Steuben, Frederick William Augustus, Baron von, 209, 240, 255, 321

Ternay, Charles-Louis d'Arsac, Chevalier de, 59, 61-65, 72, 77-82, 87-89, 92, 96, 161, 300, 322
  French fleet, 41-53
time line, 324-28
Trumbull, David, 107-10
Trumbull, Jonathan, Sr., 79-82, 90, 99-100, 106-108, 154, 166, 322
Trumbull, Jonathan, Jr., 107

uniforms, 56, 60, 122, 135-36, 159, 263

Vendôme, 25, 30, 284, 288, 291, 295-98
  Château de Rochambeau, 4-10, 17-18, 272, 288
  statue of Rochambeau, 295-96
Vergennes, Charles Gravier, Comte de, 31, 35-36, 40-41, 87, 95-96, 146, 153-54, 157, 161, 163, 322
Verger, Jean-Baptiste-Antoine de, 46, 48, 66, 268, 322
Vioménil brothers, 72, 91, 195, 200, 240-41
  Antoine-Charles du Houx, Baron de, 93-94, 117, 197, 204, 250-52, 322
  storms redoubt 9, 252-53, 255
  Charles-Joseph-Hyacinthe, Comte de, 117, 180, 323
Virginia Capes, 205-206, 216
  First Battle off, 93-94
  Second Battle off, 216-29

W3R, *xx, xxii,* 269, 294, 301
Wadsworth, Jeremiah, 68, 77, 79, 81-82, 99, 106-109, 112, 323
Washington, George, 323
  conferences with Rochambeau, 74-101
    Hartford, 76-83
    Newport, 89-92
    Wethersfield, 98-101, 117, 158, 165-66
  early military career 152-56

farewell to Rochambeau, 279
final strategy, 152-76
joins with French army in New York, 127-40
  first allied assault, 127-28
  Grande Reconnaissance, 140-44
Lafayette and, 38-39, 64-65, 80, 156, 160-61, 164, 167, 201-202, 209-12, 227, 253-54
meets with De Grasse, 227-29
news at Chester, 191-93
Odell House, *149*
prayer, 171
receives Rochambeau at Mount Vernon, 197-201
siege of Yorktown, 230-58
  battle joined, 247-58
  night under mulberry tree, 235
  stay at Wythe House, 232
  surrender (white flag), 259-67
  sword debacle, 264-67
Society of the Cincinnati, 284-87
Williamsburg, 230-32
Washington, D.C.:
  statues of Lafayette and Rochambeau, 297-99
Wethersfield, conference at, 98-101, 117, 158, 165-66, 209
Williamsburg, 119-20, 191, 195, 198-205, 209, 216, 224-25, 229, 230-32, 238, 249, 257, 268, 270, 273, 274-77
  allied forces meet, 201-206
  French winter camp, 274-277
  march into Yorktown, 230
women on French march, 45, 121-22

Yorktown:
  allied forces march in, 230-31
  Rochambeau's plan, 174, 176, 217, 227, 293
  siege of, 230-258
    Articles of Capitulation, 261
    casualties, 268
    surrender, 259-67
  Victory Monument, 297-98

Jini Jones Vail

Jini Jones Vail, wife, mother of three, and grandmother of six, was raised in Hornell, NY. She is a retired French teacher who graduated from Sweet Briar College with a degree in French literature and who did graduate work at the Universities of Touraine and Bourgogne. She has done extensive studies in French language and history, as well as travelled considerably in France. A passionate writer of poetry, children's stories, essays, and a play, *Conversations with Aliénor,* featuring her ancestor Aliénor D'Aquitaine, she combines her love of French and American history in the writing of this book. Jini is the former commissioner, Connecticut Governor's Advisory Commision on American and Francophone Cultural Affairs, a member of Alliance Française, Daughters of the American Revolution Trumbull-Porter Chapter, and a 125-year-old literary group, Sexta Feira. She is a presenter on French history, Rochambeau, and the Washington-Rochambeau Revolutionary Route, with special interests in church, friends, cooking, gardening, and music.

WA